DATE DUE

JUL 1999	MAR 0 1 2000
	MAR 2 3 2000
JUL 2 7 1999	JUN 2 0 2000
AUG 0 5 1999	SEP 2 8 '00
AUG 3 1 1999	3-2-03
SEP 2 2 1999	10-10-05
SEP 2 7 1999	
NOV 1 1 1999	
DEC 1 4 1999	
JAN 1 1 2000	
FEB 0 3 2000	

DEMCO, INC. 38-2931

Yankee Doodle Dead

Carolyn Hart

Yankee Doodle Dead

A DEATH ON DEMAND MYSTERY

WHEELER
PUBLISHING, INC.
ROCKLAND, MA

★ AN AMERICAN COMPANY ★

Published in Large Print by arrangement with Avon Books, Inc. in the United States and Canada

Wheeler Large Print Book Series.

Interior maps by Bruce R. Winchester

Set in 16 pt Plantin.

Library of Congress Cataloging-in-Publication Data

Hart, Carolyn G.
  Yankee Doodle dead / Carolyn Hart.
    p. (large print) cm.(Wheeler large print book series)
  ISBN 1-56895-718-1 (softcover)
  1. Darling, Annie Laurance (Fictitious character)—Fiction. 2. Darling, Max (Fictitious character)—Fiction. 3. Women detectives—South Carolina —Fiction. 4. Private investigators—South Carolina—Fiction. 5. South Carolina—Fiction. 6. Large type books. I. Title. II. Series
[PS3558.A676Y36 1999]
813'.54—dc21   99-19338
                                                            CIP

To my cherished sister-in-law,
Linda Hart Wood

Author's Note

Miss Dora Brevard's vivid charcoal sketches of women important to the history of South Carolina are based upon essays in *South Carolina Women* by Idella Bodie, Sandlapper Publishing Inc., an enchanting tribute to the accomplishments and graces of women who made a difference for the Palmetto State.

Prologue

Gail Oldham drove too fast. Dust plumed behind the black Jeep as it bucketed along the rutted gray road. She almost missed the turn. She wrenched the wheel sharply and the car crunched onto the oyster-shell drive, past the mailbox topped by wooden replicas of books spine-out: Max on the larger book, Annie on the smaller.

Tears blurred Gail's vision, smearing the lime-green fronds of the weeping willows and the crimson bougainvillea and the orange and yellow and pink hibiscus blooms into splotches of impressionist color. She jolted to a stop in front of the multilevel sand-toned wooden house that shimmered with glass expanses. Gail flung herself out of the car, ran up the wooden steps to push the bell beside the spectacular front door, its red and green and purple art-glass insets sparkling in the bright July sun.

She was sobbing now and knew it would be hard to speak. But she had to tell someone, had to ask for help. Surely someone would help her.

Damn Bud. Damn him.

The sun burned against her. Finally, hiccuping in despair, her hand dropped. Annie wasn't home.

Gail stood at a loss. Oh God, what was she going to do?

"Hello. May I help?" The throaty voice was kind and gentle.

Gail looked around. Could anyone help her? Would anyone help her?

The ax head glittered in the hot July sun. Samuel Kinnon swung the shaft high, his smooth dusky skin glistening with sweat. The ax split the log cleanly and he smelled the aromatic sweetness of the cedar. There was always work to be done on an acreage in the summer—old trees to fell, fences to mend, oyster shells to burn to make tabby. He'd always loved making tabby, burning the shells, then adding sand and more oyster shells to create a compound as good as cement. Dad wanted him to fix up a batch to mend some rain damage to the house.

Samuel's face was set in a stiff mask. His eyes burned. Sweat dripping down, that was all. Men don't cry. And he didn't mind helping out his dad. He would have been glad to make the tabby, slap it into place neat as a plasterer; to chop wood, weed, whatever, on weekends or after work on the long summer days when the sun sank slowly westward and the days stretched out like saltwater taffy. But he should have had his job. He was good with the kids. Why did they take his job away?

Not they. The general. Damn his sneering white face.

Samuel lifted the ax, swung it with all the force of misery, and saw the general's face disintegrate into pieces instead of chips of cedar.

Jonathan Wentworth sat for a moment after

turning off the motor. Emily was already home. Sometimes her bridge group played into the dinner hour. He was accustomed to fixing a snack, settling in front of the television. Sad that he now preferred that. He grabbed his flight helmet, wished he could recapture the exhilaration of the afternoon. But it was gone, the ineffable sense of peace he always had when flying. He slammed the car door, strode briskly up the wooden steps, donned his practiced smile.

In the front hall, he called out. "Emily? You home?" The mirror reflected short white hair, a lean face with farseeing eyes and firm mouth, a wrinkled tan flight suit. And the wooden smile.

"Jonathan, what a day!" Emily moved briskly out of the kitchen, the martini shaker in her hand, the rolled-up afternoon newspaper in the other. "Did you have a good flight? I'll come with you next time. That will be fun. When we live in Scottsdale, you can fly all the time. Oh, some good news about the house. The real estate agent brought two couples by today. She left a note, said they're both interested." She didn't wait for his response, chattered on. "All part of an A-one, first-class, lucky day! Jonathan, you won't believe it! I had a grand slam, doubled and redoubled, vulnerable!" She talked fast, recounting the afternoon's battles, how she'd trumped this ace, finessed that jack. She was pouring the drinks, her green eyes glittering with triumph. Her once golden hair was now a shining white in smooth waves and her beautifully made-up face was smooth, as if time had never touched her.

Emily always moved at top speed, her mind intent upon victory: on the golf course, investing in the stock market, playing bridge. She crammed movement and effort into every waking moment. He'd been afraid she might resist selling the house, moving. But she loved paying golf in Scottsdale. She'd not resisted at all.

Jonathan understood why her mind and body moved at such a frenetic pace. His heart still ached for Emily. And for himself. But her answer to pain was to immerse herself so completely in life that there was never a moment for thought or reflection—or suffering. Golf and bridge consumed her.

As she turned at the end of the room, a shaft of sunlight touched her and he saw the Emily of long ago. It was a trick of the light and his memory that, just for a moment, he saw his golden girl, before she donned an armor of nonstop chatter and movement.

Then she strode to the sofa and the illusion fled. She was still talking, of course. She had to keep going. It was habit now, a habit she would never break. He'd stopped trying to pierce the shell she'd created. They were still Jonathan and Emily, they could talk and dance and fly, make love, but there was no real connection. Something had died in Emily, the softness and willingness to give, to be open to love. Because then you could be hurt, hurt so terribly.

He sat beside her on the sofa. The newspaper

rustled as she skimmed through it. He drank his martini and didn't listen. The time was close now. She would become ever more frenetic. It was always the time that worried him. But Sharon would help. And soon, they'd be moving.

Emily gasped, surged to her feet. Her martini spilled and the drink was cold and sticky as it splashed over him. She lowered the paper, pointed to a page, her hand shaking.

"Why didn't you tell me?" Her voice was deep and hoarse and frightening. The veneer was gone. Her face twisted with unutterable pain.

Bud Hatch swiped the towel across his flat abdomen. He stood in the at-ease stance, shoulders back, feet apart. It was his habitual posture. He was as trim and muscular at sixty-three as he'd been at sixteen. A man then, a man now. By God, he could still wear his first Dress Blue uniform.

Slack, that's what most people were. He had no use for them, cowardly second-raters without any guts. Nobody could ever say Bud Hatch was a second-rater. Or cowardly. He saw his duty and he did it. He wasn't going to put up with any of this political-correctness bullshit from anybody, including the director of the library—the present director—and his supporters.

As for the festival, it was a good thing he'd realized the mess it was in and taken steps. Women were all right in their place but, by God, they'd forgotten what that place was.

Women.... Necessary, but a damn lot of trouble.

He dressed quickly, navy polo shirt, chino slacks, tasseled loafers. He had a lot to take care of today.

He'd start at the library.

Chapter 1

Annie Laurance Darling moved swiftly. Or as swiftly as she could propel her body through air thicker than congealing Jell-O. Her hair curled in tendrils. Her skin felt as moist as pond scum. If it got any more humid, Calcutta would be a resort in comparison. She thought longingly of cool air. Maybe she would read *The Yellow Room* by Mary Roberts Rinehart. It was always cool in Maine. Rinehart's heroine shivered. And lit fires.

Why had she ever come to this island where the summer air was heavier than mercury? She had a sudden, unsettling, cold sensation. She knew why she'd come to the land of no-see-ums, swamps and fragrant magnolias. She'd come to Broward's Rock a few years earlier because she was running away from a close encounter with one Maxwell Darling. How weird! What if Max hadn't, in his own imperturbable, incredibly determined way, followed her? What if now she wasn't Annie Laurance Darling, but just Annie Laurance? It would be a cold world indeed. She felt like flinging out her arms and embracing the humid, spongy air. What did a little heat matter?

Annie stopped at the door of her store and grinned. What could be better than a nice hot day in her own very happy corner of the world? Dear Max. And her wonderful store. She studied the name with pleasure—DEATH

ON DEMAND—in tasteful gold letters. Without doubt it was the finest name for the finest mystery bookstore east of Atlanta. Smaller letters, also in gold, announced: "Annie Laurance Darling, Prop." She felt warm all over, a nice, comfortable, happy inner warmth that had nothing to do with humidity. Max. Her store. Her books. Hers to enjoy. It would, in fact, be an utterly lovely day—except for the library board. She had tried to ignore a niggling sense of uneasiness all day. But her nerves quivered like snapping flags heralding a coming storm. The solution was obvious. Easy. *No.* She knew how to say no. That was all that was required to stay free of the controversy swirling around the library.

Determinedly, she stared at the Death on Demand window. She didn't really need to look at the window. After all, she'd put in the new display only last week. But it was clever, if she said so herself: a cherry-and-green-striped parasol open behind a mound of golden sand, a tipped-over beach bucket with a shower of brightly colored paperbacks spilling out— *Miss Zukas and the Library Murders* by Jo Dereske, *Something's Cooking* by Joanne Pence, *Murder on a Girls' Night Out* by Anne George, *Memory Can Be Murder* by Elizabeth Daniels Squire, and *Blooming Murder* by Jean Hager.

Good mysteries. Fun mysteries. And that's what summer was all about: snow cones and walking fast on hot sand to plunge into cool water and mounds of mysteries; buckets of clams and kissing in the moonlight and piles of paperbacks with smoking guns or blood-dripping daggers on front covers, yellow, red and blue crime scenes on back covers.

Of course, those colorful covers were déclassé today. But paperback mysteries published in the forties and fifties, oh, what great back covers they had—drawings of the manor house, sketches of the library where X marked the spot, maps of the village showing the rectory and the church, the graveyard and the shops along the high street. And, even more fun, the reader often found inside an equally colorful description of the book's contents, such as:

WHAT THIS MYSTERY'S ABOUT—

A bloodstained handkerchief.
The reason the cat meowed at midnight.
A dog named Petunia.
The contents of the rosewood box.
A woman with one husband, two lovers,
  and an angry sister.
A gun, a dagger, and a missing rhinoceros.

Golly, those were the great days of the mystery. And she always remembered Uncle Ambrose when she thought about old, great mysteries. Death on Demand had been his store originally, a smaller, much more masculine retreat. He'd welcomed his sister's daughter there every summer through her childhood and carefully chosen books for her: *The Ivory Dagger* by Patricia Wentworth, *The Franchise Affair* by Josephine Tey, *The Secret Vanguard* by Michael Innes, offering them with a gruff "Think you'll like these." Like them! She'd loved every sentence, every paragraph, every page. And especially the wonderful mysteries with maps on the back cover.... For a moment, Annie forgot all about the heat and the boxes of books to be unpacked and the mouse heads that Dorothy L. kept depositing on the kitchen steps at home and the increasing bitterness of the schism on the library board. She stood with a finger to her lip, wondering if anyone had a complete collection of all the Dell mysteries with crime maps on the back. Now that would be—

"Annie."

Annie didn't turn at the swift, sharp clatter of shoes on the boardwalk. She recognized the voice despite its unaccustomed ferocity. Annie knew the fury wasn't directed at her. Nonetheless, she thought plaintively, this wasn't what summer was all about. But, as she took a deep breath and practiced saying no in her mind, this is what mysteries were all about—anger, power, and fractured relationships. Annie wanted to contain misery between the bright covers of books where everything came out right in the end.

Henny Brawley, Annie's best customer, a retired teacher, and a mainstay of the Broward's Rock library board, didn't bother with a salutation. Her angular face sharp-edged as a red-tailed hawk diving for a rat, Henny yanked open the door to Death on Demand and stalked inside.

Annie followed, welcoming the initially

icy waft of air-conditioning that almost instantly seemed tepid, proof indeed of the summer heat, into the nineties and climbing.

"Henny, your blood pressure," she warned. She waved hello to Ingrid at the cash desk and blinked at her own reflection in a wavery antique mirror. The humidity had frizzed her blond hair. Her face was flushed with the heat. Only her gray eyes looked cool. And worried. She felt trouble coming on like a fortune-teller with a broken crystal ball. She followed Henny's clattering footsteps to the back of the store and the coffee bar.

Agatha, resident bookstore cat and imperial mistress of Annie, lifted her head languidly, her golden eyes flicking from Annie to Henny, then into the distance, quite as if she observed some infinitely fascinating, obscurely subtle scene, nirvana beyond earthly comprehension.

Annie reached out, petted the sleek black head, through long practice adroitly avoided the whip of shiny white fangs, and resisted the impulse to say vulgarly, "Come off it, Agatha." She'd found Agatha as a stray in the alley behind the bookstore a few months after she'd inherited the store from her Uncle Ambrose. But Agatha had no memory of abandonment and instead obviously considered herself to the manor born and Annie a quite fortunate serf.

Annie slipped behind the coffee bar. "Iced mocha, Henny?" Agatha watched intently.

"Iced caffè latte. Please." Henny slid on a barstool, pointed to the tall silver-rimmed glasses. "I'll take that one."

11

White mugs with the names of famous mysteries in red script sat on shelves behind the coffee bar. Recently, Annie had added glasses for cool drinks. The glasses carried book names in silver script. Without comment, Annie lifted down *If the Coffin Fits* by Day Keene. In a moment, she handed the cool, foam-topped drink to Henny.

"I could kill that man." Henny's voice was as thin-edged as a razor.

Annie didn't have to ask the name of the intended victim. "Henny, I just got in Wendy Hornsby's latest Maggie MacGowen and it's absolutely fab—"

"Maybe with a hunting knife." Delight lifted Henny's voice.

"Not terribly original," Annie mused.

"At a skating rink?" Henny arched an eyebrow.

"*Killed on Ice*. William L. DeAndrea," Annie said automatically.

Henny nodded in appreciation. "Let's be more subtle. Caffeine poisoning." Her eyes glinting, she watched Annie as intently as Agatha.

Annie murmured, "Caffeine poisoning...."

"*The Corpse at the Quill Club*. Amelia Reynolds." Henny's voice was mellowing. "Or death by whirlpool." She shot a condescending glance at Annie, waited long enough to make Annie's lack of response painfully apparent, then said casually, "*Strike Three, You're Dead*. R. D. Rosen."

Annie was accustomed to thumb-wrestling Henny for supremacy when it came to mystery knowledge. "Very obscure," she said stiffly.

"Actually, I think *The Murder of Bud Hatch* calls for something scintillatingly creative." Henny stirred her iced caffè latte and ice cubes rattled. "Piranhas in his swimming pool. Now that's a thought." Her momentary good humor evaporated faster than a sardine in Agatha's bowl. "Do you know what our most odious new resident is doing now?" Henny didn't wait for an answer. "He's gone behind my back. Contacted all the veterans' groups and called a meeting to enlist volunteers for what he's calling Points of Patriotism."

Annie pushed back a sprig of damp hair. Was the air-conditioning even working? She took a deep swallow of the iced mocha-laden coffee. It jolted her system like the Anne McLean Matthews suspense novel *The Cave,* which was guaranteed to put a permanent shiver down the reader's back.

Henny popped down from the stool, began to pace. "...war scenes! That's all he has in mind, war scenes!" She faced Annie, lifted her hands in outrage.

"Testosterone tells. After all, he's a retired general. Look, Henny, why don't you compromise and—"

Henny slapped her hands on her hips. "I'd rather do a slow waltz with a boa constrictor." A bright look. "Or wrap a boa around Bud's neck. How's that for a murder weapon?" Henny squared her shoulders. "Look, Annie, I need help."

"No." It came out firm, declarative, crisp. So might Joan Hess's Claire Malloy have rejected a plea from Caron and Inez. Any plea.

"Solidarity." Henny's dark eyes bored into Annie's.

"Henny, I've got loads of books to unpack—"

"Ingrid. And she can get Duane to help her." Henny had her not-going-to-take-no-for-an-answer gleam in her eyes.

"I've promised Ingrid some time off. She and Duane are going to New Orleans to celebrate their anniversary." Momentarily diverted, Annie asked, "Have you read *Voodoo River* by Robert Crais? Did you know he grew up in Baton Rouge?"

"Everybody knows that. Of course I've read it. I never miss an Elvis Cole book. Now look, Annie." Henny marched to the coffee bar, planted her hands firmly on the mahogany top. "I want you to come to the board meeting tomorrow morning. I need every vote I can get."

Henny didn't wait for an answer. She whirled and darted up the central aisle.

Annie heard the slap of Henny's shoes across the heart-pine floor, Ingrid's farewell, the silvery ring of the bell as the front door closed.

Dammit, she'd said no. But she was a member of the library board. Henny needed her. Henny was counting on her.

NO.

Instead of a booming echo in her mind, the little negative shriveled to a faint gasp. Maybe it was time to root around in her car for that assertiveness tape she'd bought a few years

14

ago, listen while she drove. But actually, the island was so small, she'd never gotten past the stern opening injunction: "Speak Your Mind." It was certainly an appealing motto, but putting it into action might alienate customers, not to say friends, at an awesome rate.

Annie carried her glass—*A Toast to Tomorrow* by Manning Coles—to a table in front of the dusty fireplace. She'd already planned tomorrow, an early swim with Max—which could lead to other morning pleasures—books to unpack, then books to pack for the booth allotted to her for the festival, a busy, happy, cheerful day.

She didn't want to get caught up in the explosive dissension threatening to wreck the first-ever Broward's Rock festival. It had sounded like so much fun in the beginning and such a terrific way to celebrate the Fourth of July and raise money for the library. The island was teeming with tourists and the festival was sure to attract even more. It was all Henny's idea, really; a celebration of South Carolina history from the earliest days to the present. But this was history with a twist, history from a woman's perspective. The various women's groups from the churches were thrilled. Henny, as president of the library board, was directing the overall program.

Everyone loved the idea.

Everyone except Brigadier General (retired) Charlton (Bud) Hatch. Hatch was a newcomer to the island, but he had plunged into island society—the golf club, the church,

15

the Chamber of Commerce and the library board—with all the gusto he'd exhibited in his military career.

And now, soon—tomorrow, to be exact—two opposing forces were going to clash with a bang that would resound all over the island.

Agatha jumped up on the table, sniffed at Annie's glass, gave her a disdainful glance.

"So you don't like coffee."

Agatha bared her fangs.

"Don't be so touchy." Annie sipped the heavenly mocha, then stroked Agatha's sleek satiny fur, black as a raven's wing. "Agatha, why are humans so impossible?"

But even Agatha had no answer for that question, though she looked thoughtful.

"It was all going to be so much fun." Annie had truly gotten into the spirit of the Fourth of July plans. She looked up at the five paintings hanging on the back wall. They were a perfect addition to the festivities. Every month a local artist did watercolors of five superb (in Annie's estimation) mysteries. The first person to identify the books and authors correctly received a free book, excluding, of course, pricey collectibles, such as a signed first edition of *Bitter Medicine* by Sara Paretsky for $150 or a first English edition of *In the Teeth of the Evidence* by Dorothy L. Sayers for $240. One did have to have limits.

Once she'd tried to retire Henny from the competition, hoping to give ordinary readers a sporting chance. Henny threatened a boycott and since she was by far the store's best customer, Annie retreated.

Annie smiled as she admired this month's offerings. Henny was so absorbed in producing the festival, she'd yet to look them over. But Annie knew she would be pleased. They were so appropriate for America's favorite holiday.

In the first painting, moonlight shed its radiance over the river bank and the dark flowing water. A heavy-shouldered man with short-cropped hair knelt beside a dying man. Blood bubbled from the victim's mouth and from the stab wound in his chest. The dying man was small. He wore the fancy blue, red, and gold satin clothes of a seventeenth-century continental gentleman, white lace at his wrists and collar and ribbon bows at his knees and on his shoes. On the ground lay a red velvet hat with a blue feather. The man kneeling by the body was plainly dressed in brown duffel breeches and clogs and wore no shirt, his skin pale in the moonlight.

In the second painting, a workroom held many necessary implements: a loom, a great walking wheel for spinning wool, a small flax wheel, and a quilting frame. There were rods for candle dipping and great iron pots to boil soap. Softly colored crewel yarns in several shades of rose, indigo, green, and gold hung from a pole suspended in front of the fireplace. A man with a wide face and hooded eyes the color of brandy stood with a child by the quilting frame. His reddish-brown hair curled over his collar. His beard and mustache were reddish brown, too. The little girl, with a pale face and reddish-brown hair, watched him intently as he pointed to the yellow tom cat on the hearth. The man and child were closely observed by a woman in a bright red cloak of felted wool who stood quietly by the door. Her slender face held restless brown eyes behind square-cut wire spectacles. Her curly brown hair was cut short.

In the third painting, a shaggy white terrier jumped in a frenzy near the young woman on the towpath. She stared in horror at the body bobbing in the dark water of the canal. The shocked observer was an attractive young woman with red hair. She wore a long dress, the skirt over a bustle, and high-laced white shoes, damp now from her walk through the long grass.

In the fourth painting, the young typist's straight reddish-brown hair was pulled back and tied with a black ribbon at the nape of her neck. Her green eyes glittered in concentration as her fingers flew over the silver-rimmed round keys of the tall black, shiny typewriter. A copy of *Pride and Prejudice* lay open beside her. She was the epitome of the well-dressed businesswoman in her pleated white shirtwaist.

In the fifth painting, both men were redheads. But the man with the upturned nose and deeply cleft bulldog jaw had stopped suddenly on the marble stairway landing, a spittle of blood on his mouth, his arms reaching out. A quarter-sized black powder burn around a small bullet hole marred the front of his tan linen suit jacket. The second man was bigger, taller. His face creased in concern, he appeared to be running up the marble steps, a nine-millimeter gun in one hand.

Between perusing the paintings and drinking the utterly delicious chocolate-laced coffee, Annie felt her spirits rise.

"Dear Annie."

The call of an oh-so-familiar husky voice didn't exactly dampen Annie's mood. But she looked warily toward the open door to the storeroom and her mother-in-law, Laurel Darling Roethke. Actually, there were several more names before you got to Roethke, Laurel being no stranger to wedding vows. But, presently, Laurel was a widow and quite friendly with a local widower. Annie smiled determinedly. Well, everybody had a mother, including Max, of course. And really, truly, honestly, she liked Laurel, though perhaps she might have enjoyed Laurel a bit more had she stayed in Connecticut and not moved to Broward's Rock. And Annie might be even more appreciative of her mother-in-law if Laurel didn't possess a disconcerting habit of arriving unexpectedly. And often. Though perhaps it wasn't Laurel's arrival that disconcerted, but the absolute unpredictability of her enthusiasms. Since Annie had known her, they'd ranged from wedding customs (in re Annie and Max's ceremony) to Southern ghosts.

Laurel beamed.

Annie felt her smile soften. Laurel had this effect on everyone, especially men, though Annie didn't stress that fact with Max. Laurel never seemed to age. Her golden hair shone like spun moonlight, her finely chiseled features were smooth and perfect, her

Mediterranean-blue eyes sparkled with delight, and something more, a vivid and vital liveliness that fascinated and charmed.

However, Annie knew better than to succumb to Laurel's charm. She managed to keep her voice even, but perhaps an edge of concern was evident. "What's up, Laurel?"

"Up," Laurel repeated, as if first encountering the word. "Dear me. Yes. Of course. Parbleu, as dear Hercule would say. Up! Annie. It's simply providential that I've come to you. Up, indeed."

Annie took a deep breath. Perhaps if she closed her eyes and counted to five hundred, this apparition would be gone when she looked again.

But Laurel was across the room and Annie smelled the sweet scent of lilac and felt the light touch of Laurel's lips on her cheek.

Laurel whirled away and looked up at the watercolors over the fireplace.

Annie stiffened.

"There." Laurel swept a beautifully manicured hand with fire-truck-red nails. "Up." A tinkling laugh. "Those paintings can come down."

"No." Maybe she didn't need that assertiveness tape. So might Truman have told MacArthur.

Laurel's graceful hand gave a magnanimous wave, yielding the point.

Annie wasn't fooled. She hadn't studied classical warfare, but she'd read enough Phoebe Atwood Taylor mysteries featuring Leonidas Witherall to know that when a frontal assault was repelled, watch your flank. Or as Witherall (aka Bill Shakespeare) was wont to intone: "Remember Cannae." Annie concentrated on Cannae.

"Dear Annie." Laurel's husky voice was full of concern. "Are you not feeling well?"

"I'm fine. Fine. Absolutely fine." But her eyes never left Laurel's lovely face.

"You look strained." Laurel wafted near, touched Annie's brow with a light hand.

Annie backpedaled. She wondered if this was how a fly caught in a web felt. "Laurel," she said desperately, determined to frame a rational discourse, "what do you want?"

Laurel smiled a sweet, kindly, forgiving smile, clearly willing to ignore her daughter-in-law's gaucherie. "It is not what I want, my dear child. It's simply that I've been struck with a realization." Her dark blue eyes were dreamy.

And deranged? Annie squashed the disloyal thought. But if Annie's nerves had earlier snapped like wind-tossed pennants, now they twanged like power lines in a hurricane.

Laurel delved into her mesh bag, pulled out a handful of old-fashioned hand fans, the kind with scalloped edges. "These," she said simply, "are the answer. I can envision them arranged above the fireplace in lieu of the paintings, perhaps as many as fifty of them. Oh, what a glorious sight that would be."

"Not my fireplace." The words were clipped. Maybe just thinking about that tape was helping her hold her own. But she kept trying to make some sense of Laurel's arrival.

21

"Laurel, back up. Explain. What was the question?"

Laurel proclaimed, "It's the Fourth of July."

Annie reached out, gripped the beveled edge of the coffee bar. It was hard, real, and solid. And it wasn't the Fourth of July. "Laurel, it's not the Fourth yet."

"My dear child, of course not." Laurel's tone was kind and gentle and forbearing.

If Laurel called her dear child one more time, Annie was going to put her hair up in pigtails and wear red sneakers and if Max asked why, she'd tell him.

"But," Laurel swept on, "our dear island—"

Dear child.

Dear Hercule.

Dear island.

Well, at least Annie was in good company.

"—is poised for a grand celebration of America's most glorious, soul-stirring holiday." Those dark blue eyes glowed with excitement. "And I've realized that the focus is wrong, utterly wrong. Think for a moment, Annie. What happens when you hear a Sousa march and you see the flag rippling in the breeze and watch the fireworks sparkle against the night sky?" She looked encouragingly at Annie.

Annie looked back.

Laurel's graceful hand—the one unencumbered by fans—beckoned hopefully, inviting a response.

"Uh." Annie realized this was not adequate. She cleared her throat. "Well," she temporized.

Laurel's fingers fluttered like the wings of a monarch in a hurry to get to Mexico.

Annie hadn't felt this much social pressure since she went to her senior prom. "Uh, you feel—I feel—I guess it's exciting." She continued with more confidence, "That's it. Exciting. Thrilling." She watched those mesmerizing blue eyes and knew she didn't have it right. Not yet. "Exhilarating?" she ventured.

Laurel's fingers stopped fluttering. Her smile was kindly. "Love," she said simply.

"Love?" If Laurel had suddenly begun to speak in Turkish, Annie couldn't have been more lost. "Love?"

"Annie, it's so clear. The Fourth has always been a celebration of love of country. But what is love of country?" This time Laurel didn't wait for Annie to answer, no doubt having concluded that the dear child wasn't quite bright. "Why, it's so obvious. Love of country is a love of fellow citizens. And how can we best celebrate the Fourth? Oh, it has come as a revelation to me. We can celebrate by focusing on love and there is no greater way— well, perhaps there is but one can't do that universally—" this aside was in a reflective undertone. "In any event, we can best celebrate the Fourth by calling forth Shakespeare."

Annie wondered how she was going to break it to Max. Laurel had lost it. This was surely proof. The Fourth of July and Shakespeare?

"Dear William." Laurel might have given him a hug just moments ago, her tone indicated such familiarity. "No one has ever captured the depth and breadth of love better than he. We must share the joy and vigor of his verse with all the citizenry. So," she concluded briskly, "I know you'll come to the library board meeting in the morning."

Annie stood absolutely still as Laurel darted back toward the storeroom door.

Laurel paused, gave a fleeting glance back, once again lifted the fans. "We must share love."

Annie was seized by an almost overpowering desire to follow that first precept of assertiveness training, Speak Your Mind. The Speak Your Mind that begged to be said: Laurel, sweetheart, sharing love can get you in a whole lot of trouble.

Annie managed to remain silent as her mother-in-law wafted a kiss with crimson-tipped fingers.

Annie's thoughts swirled chaotically between fireworks, love, Shakespeare, and the library.

"Why the library?" she asked aloud.

But there was no answer. A gentle click marked the closing of the storeroom door that opened into the alley behind the shops.

Agatha looked at Annie curiously.

Annie knew her expression was odd, one of amusement struggling with uneasiness. Amusement won out. Annie grinned. "Agatha, I have a feeling the library board meeting tomorrow will have more fireworks than the Fourth. I think I'll go."

The bell over the front door tinkled. Perhaps it signaled the arrival of a customer. Surely one out of three wasn't too much to hope for.

A hollow thump sounded on the heart-pine floor.

Annie's smile fled. Not a customer.

"Hello, Miss Dora. How are you today?" Ingrid sounded genuinely pleased.

Easy for Ingrid, Annie thought. Ingrid only worked here. But whatever Miss Dora Brevard wanted, Annie knew it would be made clear. Unlike Laurel. In fact, a refreshing contrast to Laurel. Annie started eagerly up the center aisle, pleased to free her mind of Shakespeare, love, the library, and the Fourth. Miss Dora Brevard was the doyenne of Chastain, South Carolina, a charming antebellum town not far from the ferry stop to Broward's Rock. Annie had first met the wily and wise elderly resident when Annie became involved in creating a mystery program for the House-and-Garden Week in Chastain. On another occasion, Annie and Max had helped Miss Dora solve a long-ago crime involving the Tarrant family.

The thump of Miss Dora's cane mingled with a hoarse commentary. "There's adequate space. Some of the books can be put away until the festival's over."

Annie's eagerness abruptly flagged, but she managed to keep her smile squarely on her face. "Miss Dora, how lovely that you could come over today." Living on the mainland seemed no deterrent to frequent island visits by Miss Dora. Annie wondered if the old lady traveled to the ferry in a horse-drawn carriage. It would be fitting.

Miss Dora was arrayed in her usual voluminous folds of black drapery that would have been perfectly appropriate at Queen Victoria's funeral. Annie always pictured a frayed leather chest in a dusky corner of an attic, chock-full of diminutive dresses in black bombazine.

Her shaggy silvery hair unfazed by the soggy summer air, Miss Dora lifted her ebony cane to point toward the back of the room. She swept past Annie, her shoes pattering against the shining floor, making a soft flutter like bat wings lifting from a cave at sunset.

Annie followed. It seemed to be a day for following. Diverted, she again vowed to find that old assertiveness tape. For an instant, tantalizing possibilities danced in Annie's thought, examples of Speak Your Mind:

To Henny, It was such a pleasure to visit with Miss Pettigrew, the new curator of the museum. She reads more than a hundred mysteries a month and she knows more mystery trivia than you do. So there! Nyah, nyah, nyah.

To Laurel, Max absolutely, positively, beyond a shadow of a doubt, does NOT get more like you every day. Oh, God, what subterranean fear prompted that?

To Miss Dora, social arbiter for all the society that counted in Chastain, South Carolina, Whatever it is, the answer's no. I will not be bullied by you today or at any time in the future.

But tantalizing possibilities they remained.

Instead, Annie said meekly, "What can I do for you, Miss Dora?"

Miss Dora carefully eased a large cardboard portfolio onto a table, flipped it open, and peered up at Annie, her wrinkled parchment face expectant.

Annie stepped around her and looked down at a charcoal drawing: Two young women dressed in men's clothing sprang from the deep shadows beneath a live oak tree, muskets in hand, to accost a messenger escorted by two British officers.

"Nighttime. Heard the horses coming, jumped out with their guns." Miss Dora's hoarse voice was triumphant. "They got the papers, sent them to Nathanael Greene. A great help to the Colonials."

"That's very nice," Annie began.

Miss Dora's eyes slitted. "South Carolina women always prevail."

"I'm sure they do." Annie didn't doubt it for a minute. Not even a New York minute.

Miss Dora's thin lips spread in an approximation of a smile. It reminded Annie irresistibly of the alligator that lived in the lagoon behind her house. Not a creature that she ever intended to rile.

"Miss Dora," she said heartily, "this is quite fascinating—"

"Grace and Rachel Martin."

Annie looked around in bewilderment. She hadn't heard the door.

Miss Dora cleared her throat.

The front of the shop lay quiet. Annie looked back at her guest, met a disdainful gaze.

Shaggy hair bristling, Miss Dora inclined her head toward the drawing.

Annie quickly nodded. "Oh, certainly. Of course. Grace and Rachel Martin."

Miss Dora began to shake.

Annie stared at her in concern, then realized the crinkled parchment face was quivering with laughter.

Miss Dora clapped her hands together gleefully. It made no sound because she wore half-gloves. "When the girls got away with the courier's papers, they raced home. The officers and the messenger turned back. They stopped at the Martin household, demanded to be put up for the night, said they'd been waylaid by some lads and lost their papers. And they never knew the women who housed them were those very same 'lads.' Grace and Rachel."

Annie stared at the softly brushed charcoal, which gave a sense of movement to the scene. She could almost hear the ghostly hoofbeats, imagine two young women, their hearts pounding, their hands tight on the guns, willing to risk their lives for the land they loved.

Miss Dora spread other drawings on the tabletop:

A stalwart woman moved among rows of injured Confederate soldiers.

A pretty girl bent over her diary, pen in hand, to write that Confederate money was losing value, with ordinary shoes costing from sixty to one hundred dollars and butter going for seven dollars a pound.

An elegant artist smoothed clay to create Joan of Arc astride a horse, her sword aloft.

"Louise Cheves McCord, Floride Clemson Lee, Anna Hyatt Huntington. Among South Carolina's finest." There was reverence in Miss Dora's raspy voice.

Miss Dora peered up at the paintings on the back wall, then at Annie. "A good half dozen will fit—"

"No." Finally, a stern, strong, unyielding declaration. Perhaps she didn't really need that assertiveness tape.

Miss Dora pursed her tiny mouth.

"Although they certainly are lovely." Annie truly was impressed. "Did you draw them, Miss Dora?" Each sketch was done with a minimum of strokes, but they radiated energy, the figures looking as if at any moment they would move.

A benign nod. "Southern women always have an understanding of the arts."

"Yes. Of course." This was a facet of Miss Dora Annie had never known. It did not, however, come as a surprise. Nothing Miss Dora did would surprise Annie.

"The front window—"

"No." A ringing declaration.

Miss Dora's eyes slitted. "Where then?"

Annie's mouth opened. Closed.

"That Yankee refuses to permit them in the library." The dark eyes glittered with disgust.

Annie didn't have to inquire which Yankee.

Miss Dora stroked the musket held by either Grace or Rachel. "When he first came to town, he volunteered to be in charge of library displays. Henny welcomed him. Then." The single word crackled with import. "She's come to rue the day. I could have told her. Never put a Yankee in charge. He's been doing the display for several months and he says my drawings are too restricted in content." An affronted sniff. "Just another way of a man saying women's work and women's lives don't count."

Annie's eyes widened. To hear Miss Dora make the equivalent of a feminist pronouncement was so mind-boggling that Annie volunteered immediately, "I'll put up some of the drawings, Miss Dora. I think they're wonderful."

Miss Dora's nodded in satisfaction, her shaggy hair swinging. She filled Annie's arms with rolled-up drawings.

"But if I were you, I'd keep after them at the library," Annie said desperately. Certainly the library had more space than she did. It was always a crush to find room for new books and posters and her used-book section was expanding at an awesome rate. She now had a complete collection of E. Phillips Oppenheim.

"Good. You'll be at the meeting tomorrow. I knew I could count on you." Miss Dora pattered up the aisle, paused long enough to look back and say with a smile—it was a smile and not a grimace, wasn't it?—"After all, you are now a South Carolina woman."

Feeling rather as though she'd been knighted, Annie clutched the rolls and listened to the brisk thump of Miss Dora's cane.

It wasn't that she was a pushover. But she couldn't be rude to the doyenne of the Low Country. Could she?

Not, apparently, in this lifetime.

She counted. Five drawings to display. And, in addition, now she definitely had to go to that board meeting. But the meeting wasn't until tomorrow morning.

Like another famous Southern heroine, she'd think about that tomorrow. And she would under no circumstances spend one more minute worrying about Brig. Gen. (ret.) Charlton (Bud) Hatch.

In a far reach of the universe, the gods of malice hooted in delight.

Annie rolled the grocery cart down the candy aisle. After all, it was the quickest way to get to produce. She needed to bring some snacks for tonight's meeting of the festival program committee. Being named chair of that committee still rankled. Just because she'd missed the library board meeting in April didn't mean Henny had the right simply to name Annie as chair of the program committee and to announce the appointment publicly at the next board meeting just after designating Annie's store as the provider of books for the festival. Annie felt a quiver of panic. She must, absolutely must, get the books packed that she intended to display in her booth Friday.

Annie picked up two sacks of candy. And she'd snag a pre-packaged mixture of carrots, cauliflower and broccoli and some kind of light dip. Something for everybody. If some people wanted to pretend they were rabbits, it was a free country.

She was debating whether to open one of the candy sacks, so she took her attention away from the cart just for an instant.

Whang!

Annie felt jolted to her toes.

"Annie, I'm so sorry." Sharon Gibson owned the gift shop three doors down from Death on Demand. "Are you okay? Did I break anything?"

"No harm done. How are you, Sharon?" The Speak Your Mind was tempting: Training for the Roller Derby?

"Oh, I'm fine." She pulled her cart back, began to go around Annie. Sharon didn't look fine. A tall, slender blonde with alabaster skin, she was pale and drawn, and her eyes had the dull, blank look of someone whose thoughts are far away and not pleasant.

"Are you ready for the holiday?" Annie asked.

Sharon's cart stopped. "The holiday. Oh, yes, the holiday. Yes, we're all stocked." For an instant, her eyes lighted. "We've got the cutest wooden cutouts of the Statue of Liberty. Your mother-in-law made them." Momentarily, she looked puzzled. "Each one has a different quotation on it. From Shakespeare. They're just darling." Sharon laughed. "That's good, isn't it? Although I know her name isn't Darling now."

And hadn't been, Annie thought to herself, for at least two or three husbands. No, four, to be accurate.

Sharon's smile fled. "Actually, Annie, I was going to call you. I can't make that meeting tonight." Her face drew down in a tight frown. "In fact, I won't be taking part in the festival." Her voice was weary.

"Sharon, what's wrong?"

"Too much to do. That's all." She swung her cart out to pass Annie, then came to a sudden halt, staring up the aisle, her face taut. For an instant, Sharon stood as if frozen, then she jerked her cart around and rushed off in the opposite direction.

Annie looked up the aisle.

The well-built man striding toward her lifted his arm. So might a trainer gesture to a dog. Was it his arrival that sent Sharon scurrying away? He lifted his arm again imperiously. Stand, Spot.

Annie looked to see if he could be gesturing toward someone else, but they were now alone in the aisle. Nope. She had to be the lucky one. But she wasn't a dog. Quite deliberately, Annie ignored him and grabbed the handle of her basket.

"Annie. Yo, Annie."

Another tantalizing Speak Your Mind phrase came unbidden:

To Brig. Gen. (ret.) Charlton (Bud) Hatch, Yo, Butthead.

Instead, she waited with a polite smile. Miss Manners would have been proud of such a triumph of civility.

"So here you are, little lady. Your clerk said you would be shopping. Always a pleasure for ladies, I know." Bud Hatch's navy polo fit him snugly, revealing a muscular chest with no vagrant fat cells. The crease in his chinos would have pleased a master tailor. He stared down at Annie, his rough-hewn features in command mold.

Annie stared back icily. Little lady indeed! "Is it more a pleasure for women than for men?"

"Beg pardon?" He looked puzzled.

"To shop!" Annie snapped.

He gave a perfunctory laugh.

Once again, Annie was tantalized with a possible Speak Your Mind:

To Brig. Gen. (ret.) Charlton (Bud) Hatch: You are welcome to take laugh lessons from my cat. When she coughs up fur balls, it sounds just like Santa's ho-ho-ho. When you laugh, you sound like a cat coughing up fur balls.

That it remained only a possibility was either a tribute to her upbringing, a result of acculturation as a female, or several years spent as a shopkeeper.

"Well, little lady, I won't keep you from your shopping. I know you have a husband to take care of. But I'm expecting your support at the board meeting tomorrow. I've gotten the word out to the merchants' association about the importance of having an all-American Fourth and how we need to focus on what made America great." He clapped Annie's shoulder. "I'll see you then."

His stride was still equal to the parade ground. He was ten feet away before Annie managed to call out, "Bud." She choked a little at using his first name, but she'd be damned if she'd call him General or Mr.

Hatch looked back impatiently. He'd told the little lady. What more was needed?

"All the board members I've spoken to"—

and he didn't have to know that number was comprised of herself and Henny—"are thrilled that the festival is featuring South Carolina women. At the board meeting, we plan to pass a motion commending Henny Brawley for her terrific job as festival director." Annie felt sheer joy as she shed restraining influences: to heck with upbringing, she was a new-century woman, and good old Bud wasn't a customer.

Hatch looked at her sharply. His eyes were cold.

But Annie wasn't finished. "And what did you do to Sharon Gibson?" The words were out before she thought and she regretted them mightily. Sharon obviously was greatly distressed. It wouldn't help matters for Annie to reveal that to old slab face.

But Hatch merely frowned impatiently. "Sharon Gibson? Who's she?"

Now Annie was caught by surprise. She couldn't be wrong. The only person in the entire length of the grocery aisle when Sharon turned and ran, her face twisted with anger, was Brig. Gen. (ret.) Charlton (Bud) Hatch.

And Hatch didn't even know Sharon? Or was he pretending?

Whatever the truth, Annie was puzzled.

"I'll see you tomorrow, little lady." Hatch gave her a grim smile. "You'd better count your votes."

Chapter 2

"Above and beyond the call of duty." Max sprawled on the floor, the phone and a list of numbers beside him.

Annie looked down at her husband and wished abruptly that she didn't have to go to the meeting of the festival publicity committee. Maxwell Darling was Joe Hardy all grown up and sexy as hell: a thick brush of blond hair, a merry face with eminently kissable lips, and a wonderful muscular body. He was almost perfect, though Annie wished he had a bit more—well, it wasn't fair to say he had no ambition. But, actually, "ambition" was not a word in Max's job description. Fun, fun, fun came closer to describing his interests. She was always a little surprised at how well suited they were. Because she was, face it, a worker to her fingertips. And Max—well, Max put a good face on it. He had an office. But did he ever do anything besides practice his putting on that little green rug she'd bought him for an anniversary present?

He eyed her quizzically. "Has my hair turned purple?"

"No, I was just thinking...." But her assay of his character was lost in his nearness. She leaned down and kissed him.

Max's blue eyes gleamed. With unmistakable sexual interest. He reached for her. With alacrity and enthusiasm.

"No. I mean, not now." Annie slipped away.

He came after her, and suddenly she was in his arms.

"Max." Her voice was muffled against his chest. "That's scary."

"Scary?" He tilted his head, looked down with a puzzled but still eager face.

"You were reading my mind. That's like an old married couple."

"We"—and his lips brushed her cheek—"are not an old married couple." In a minute, he continued, "But I understand that sex just gets better and better and—"

It was her turn to look puzzled. "How could it be any better?"

Annie was twenty minutes late in leaving for her meeting, and Max was very cheerful as he began calling the members of the library board.

The Lucy Kinkaid Memorial Library, forty thousand volumes in the main building and a computer center in a recently constructed adjunct building, was in a rather obscure part of the island, thanks to the fact that empty pockets don't dictate location. The original library had been in a shabby strip shopping center near the ferry stop. Ten years previously, Lucy Banister Kinkaid had died, bequeathing her ancestral home to the library with the proviso that the library be housed in the home and that the adjoining grounds be used for community purposes. The town fathers were delighted to accept and the small library moved, hired a director, began building an especially fine collection of

Southern history, and was renamed in honor of its benefactress.

The three-story Greek-revival building sat in solitary majesty at the end of a winding dusty gray road that twisted around dense pockets of wax myrtle, curved by a cattail-rimmed lagoon, and plunged darkly up an avenue of live oaks. Made of tabby, that indigenous island building material, the big house was painted a jaunty coral pink. The four majestic columns were, of course, white as a ghost's nightdress. Four huge cobalt-blue vases sat atop the roofed portico. Annie wondered where the vases came from. They looked vaguely Chinese. Had some sailing ship anchored in the sound long ago with crates from far away for the plantation owner?

The roofed portico featured rocking chairs and was a shady retreat in deep summer. Double stairways led down to the ground. The library had enclosed some of the storage space beneath the elevated house for closed research areas. The first floor, reached from the portico, contained the public reading rooms, periodicals, the computerized catalogs, and staff offices. The second floor held meeting rooms, rest rooms, and the director's office. The open-stack collection was housed in what had been a third-floor ballroom which still flaunted its original stuccowork cornice and a white marble Adam mantel. The coved ceiling was a soft cream with magnificent plaster medallions, the walls pale blue.

Annie loved all of it. She delighted in the dusty, gray winding road and could imagine a Southern belle sidesaddle on a horse pausing to pick a magnolia blossom for her hair. This was the kind of road that beckoned, promising adventure around every curve. An old family cemetery could be glimpsed just before the avenue of live oaks. Tradition held that a daughter of the house, grieving for her sweetheart lost at the Battle of Secessionville, had hurried up the road at the sound of hoofbeats in the moonlight and was said to have seen him. Realists insisted, however, that her glimpse of movement in the late-night shadows had been nothing more than a cougar in search of prey.

The tunnel beneath the live oaks was dim and shadowy. Annie drove too fast, knowing she was late. She scarcely spared a glance at the magnificent facade of the library and the paved turnaround with reserved parking slots for board members. Instead, she curved to the west and the public and staff parking area screened by saw palmettos. Gray dust billowed as she swung into the lot, then jammed on her brakes, stopping just short of a stocky young man leaning against the fender of a very old blue-black sedan that brought to mind a motorcade during FDR's first term.

He scrambled out of the way.

Annie rolled down her window. "Samuel, I'm sorry. I didn't mean to scare you."

The young black man gingerly rotated his right foot. "That's all right, Mrs. Darling." But his face was grim. And he didn't return her apologetic smile.

Annie maneuvered the car around him,

parked, grabbed her book bag and purse, and raced across the dusty ground. She burst out of the lot into the garden.

"Guilty conscience?" came a call from above. It wasn't quite a snarl, but the voice was as shrill as a blue jay buzzing a cat.

Annie looked up.

Edith Cummings, reference librarian, hung out of a second-floor window. She took a deep drag on her cigarette. "Come on up. I believe you're in charge of the meeting."

"Sorry I'm late, Edith," Annie called.

She clattered up the back steps, crossed the porch and thudded in a service entrance. When she reached the second-floor meeting room, Edith was still draped over the sill.

"Come in. Be my guest. All stragglers welcome." Smoke drifted over Edith's head. If body language could talk, hers was a snarl.

"Don't throw the stub out the window," Annie warned. "It's so dry, you could burn the island down."

Edith's feet wiggled in response. Slowly, the librarian dropped down to the floor, clutching a pop bottle that contained an ounce of cola and a soggy cigarette stub. "You're late," she said accusingly. "And they don't even have a smoking lounge anymore. We have to go outside." She held up the bottle. "A smoker's best friend. Thank God for an old-fashioned building with windows that actually open. Of course I don't throw stubs out of windows. Would I want Smokey the Bear sobbing in his beer?" Curly black hair framed a mobile face.

Bright dark eyes glinted with amusement, intelligence, and a touch of defiance.

"Bears don't drink beer." The voice was placid, serious, and prim.

Annie and Edith both looked at the speaker, a demure young woman with wide-spaced eyes.

Someone less charitable, Annie thought, might deem them empty eyes. In any event, chalk up another clear hit by Pamela Potts, who worked as a temp and volunteered all over the island with unwavering determination to do good.

Annie had taken a deep breath, wondering, Why me, oh Lord? when Pamela arrived at the first meeting of the committee. But volunteer committee heads do not turn away willing hands, not even when threatened with terminal boredom. And, as a matter of fact, this was only a four-person committee: Annie the chair, Pamela the willing worker, Edith, a library employee coerced into attendance by her boss, Director Ned Fisher, and the absent Sharon Gibson.

Annie smiled genially. "Hi, Pamela." And did not utter the Speak Your Mind that begged to be said:

To Pamela Potts, "And bears don't talk either."

Annie rushed into speech. "I really appreciate your coming—"

"Thirty minutes late. Three-zero." Edith wasn't amused. She darted to a blackboard and drew foot-high numbers and underlined them three times. "Of course, I work here and what is my free time but to be proffered on the altar of total subservience to my paymaster. I was supposed to get off at six-thirty. Does it matter to me that I am trapped here for a committee meeting when my life is just one long round of similar engagements? Why should I want to go home? Could it be to see my loved ones? But what matter they when the Great Library calls?"

"I'm sure dear Annie had an excellent reason." Pamela looked at her earnestly.

Annie felt her cheeks burn, tried to ignore Edith's suddenly lascivious grin, and fumbled with her book bag, pulling out a covered dish of M&Ms and a tray of rabbit fodder. Plus a covered bowl of yogurt-based dip. She peeled back the foil. Sure, she knew her way around the politically correct snack world. She put the peace offerings in the middle of the table, then grabbed her folders. "Let's see where we are. Edith, you're going to print the programs here on one of the computers." She slid into a chair at the long oak table, hoping to lead by example.

Pamela obediently plumped into the opposite chair and fixed Annie with that serious gaze.

Edith skipped toward the table, softly whistling the tune to a supremely vulgar ditty beloved of children on school-bus excursions. She pulled out an end chair with armrests and sprawled in it. "If Pamela gets the ads to me in time, the programs will be ready. If, that is, Herr General Hatch stops screwing things up."

Bud Hatch again. Annie sighed. "What now?"

"Oh, nothing much." Edith waved her hands airily. "Nothing except doubling my workload. I had the copy all ready to go about the Gallant Women of South Carolina and now, this afternoon, I get an urgent memo, Attn: Program Editor, and a bunch of scrawled notes about Points of Patriotism. Twice as much program as I'd expected. All this, of course, is on top of my regular job. And believe it or not, I have duties here which fill my day quite adequately." She grabbed a handful of candies and munched morosely.

Annie turned to Pamela. "How are the ads coming?"

"Oh, yes." Pamela opened a notebook. "The general has made *all* the difference."

Edith stopped munching. Her dark eyes glittered with inquiry.

"He did?" Annie's question was brusque.

Pamela preened a little at their attentiveness. "Yes, he talked to a bunch of businessmen, persuaded them to sponsor ads in honor of famous moments in South Carolina history."

"Such as?" Edith prompted, her voice silky.

"The assault of the breastworks at Savannah when Count Pulaski and Sergeant Jasper gave their lives. The upcountry resistance led by Sumter, Pickens and Francis Marion. And, of course"—she gazed at them proudly— "Generals John Barnwell, Stephen Bull and Thomas Heyward, Jr., who distinguished themselves at the Battle of Port Royal. And this is just a sampling from the Revolutionary War."

"Just an itty-bitty sampling," Edith murmured. "Any ads about colonial women, like Judith Giton Manigault, who felled trees to help create a farm? She was here in 1685 when it was a wilderness. She went hungry a lot of the time. After her first husband died, she married Pierre Manigault and kept boarders in addition to caring for her family. Their descendants made Manigault a great merchant name in Charleston. Or how about Henrietta Deering Johnson of Charleston? She was America's first pastelist. After her husband's death, she supported her family by painting local dignitaries. She'd make a terrific ad."

Pamela's eyelashes fluttered. She glanced down at her notes. "No. I don't believe there are any women." She brightened. "But, after all, the general spoke to his golfing friends at the Whalebranch Club."

Annie and Edith looked at each other, then at Pamela. Whalebranch had a men's course and a family course. It was a fairly new club on the island. When it opened, Max had spoken admiringly of the men's course, designed by one of the great golf architects. Annie's reply: "Don't even think about it."

Pamela's gaze remained placid. And, of course, serious.

"Do you play golf?" Annie inquired.

"Golf?" Pamela's tone put it on a par with bungee jumping. "Oh, no."

Edith wasn't deflected. "What," the librarian

asked patiently, "is the theme of the festival, Pamela?"

"The Gallant Women of South Carolina." Pamela beamed, awaiting her gold star.

"Think about it," Edith urged.

Annie and Edith watched as Pamela drew her brows down, pressed her lips together. Finally, she said triumphantly, "Why, we need some ads about women!"

"Brava." Edith leaned over and thumped Pamela on the shoulder. Almost gently.

Pamela smiled happily. Slowly, the smile ebbed. "But the ads I've gotten almost fill the program."

Annie believed in the art of compromise, though she wasn't sure Henny would approve. "It will work out beautifully, Pamela. We'll have a double program and facing ads, one celebrating women, the next men, all the way through and raise even more money for the library. And Edith, it will work perfectly with that extra copy."

Pamela clapped her hands together. "So I need to find an equal number of ads for women. Oh, Annie, you are just an inspiration. I'll go home and map out my campaign right this minute. There isn't a minute to lose. I have to get the material to Edith tomorrow. But I can do it." The last was spoken like the little Dutch boy at the dike.

Annie waited until the door closed. "Map out her campaign," she repeated. "I wonder if the general gave her a battlefield commission?"

"She'll be cashiered in a bleeping heartbeat

when the general finds out what's going on."
Edith grabbed another handful of candies. "But
to get along, you gotta go along. So I'll do the
copy for the Points of Patriotism as well as the
Gallant Women of South Carolina. And maybe
Pamela will get some ads celebrating women.
As the downtrodden well know, half a loaf is
better than none even if it clogs in your
throat. And in the next lifetime, it's my turn
to be a raja. Or a pasha. Or whoever the hell
it is who runs the show."

"Hey, Edith, this is going to be great."
Annie pushed aside the dip, found the candy
dish. "Imagine the general's surprise when he
sees the program. And he can't complain
because every ad brings in money."

"Trust me, he'll cause trouble about it,
one way or another," Edith cautioned indis-
tinctly, her mouth full of candies. "The general is a very determined man. He hit the library
this morning—"

Even through the closed door, they heard
Bud Hatch's booming voice. "Little Miss
Pamela, what a pleasure to see you. And
how's..."

Edith popped up, crossed to the door faster
than Superman after Lois Lane, and eased it
open a fraction.

"...your ad campaign coming?"

"Splendidly, General, splendidly. I've just
had—"

Annie and Edith simultaneously scrunched
their faces in dismay.

"—the most helpful—"

"That's fine, little lady, that's fine. You

keep right on, just like I told you, and we'll have a program that will honor the distinguished heroes of South Carolina. Now, if you'll excuse me, I'm making an unannounced swing through the building. That's the way to keep the troops on their toes." Brisk footsteps clipped down the hall.

Edith shut the door, leaned against it. She flicked off the light. "The officious bastard will probably check this room anyway, but I can do without another run-in with God's gift to white male supremacy." There was a dark, angry edge to the librarian's voice, unlike her customary wry, sardonic tone.

Annie closed her folders. "What happened?"

Edith glanced at her watch. "Damn. I'm late and I don't have anything for dinner and Ken's always ravenous after baseball practice. Oh, hell, I'll pick up hamburgers. I've got to tell somebody or bust—and I can't lay it on Ned. God knows it's not much fun to be director of the library with the general horsing everyone around. No, Ned's got his own problems." Edith paced across the room, pushed the window open and stood by it as she lit a cigarette, took a hungry drag. "Shit, I've got to stop this one of these days. Ken gives me a health lecture every night. Isn't it something, a twelve-year-old who sounds like the surgeon general? But do you have any idea how hard it is to quit smoking?" She spewed a lungful of smoke toward the open window, coughed. "If you want a blow-by-blow account of how it feels to be a pariah, just ask any smoker. And, of course, our dear general smelled cigarette smoke here the other day and rampaged around like somebody'd gassed him with cyanide." A vivid smile lifted her frown. "Not a bad idea. You got any loose cyanide pellets at your store, Annie?"

"Sorry. Fresh out," Annie said lightly.

"Everybody covered for me, said they had no idea who'd smoke in the building. Now, I ask you Annie"—smoke wreathed her face— "this building's been here since 1910. It's made out of tabby. It's not a fire hazard."

Annie thought about people with allergies and asthma. There were more hazards to cigarette smoke than fires. And that didn't even address what the smoke was doing—had done—to Edith's lungs. But one look at the librarian's glum face kept Annie silent.

"That doesn't matter. Ned won't fire me." She took a final drag, stuffed the stub into the pop bottle. "But that jerk general's a loose cannon. Do you know what he's trying to do to the Haven?"

The Haven was a community recreation center. Soccer and baseball, Ping-Pong and swimming, arts and crafts for kids who didn't come from the posh part of the island.

In a little corner of her mind, Annie considered the word "posh." It originated from "port out, starboard home" for well-to-do Brits traveling from England to the Empire outposts and back, preferring the shady side of the ship. Its usage spread to mean any upper-crust milieu. Of course, upper crust was an interesting term—

"Dammit, he's going to ruin it." Edith

plowed her hands through her unruly hair, until she looked like a cat who'd explored a light socket. "He got on the board—"

What board wasn't Hatch on? Annie wondered.

"—and he's persuaded a couple of the other men that what the kids need is to be drilled."

At Annie's blank look, Edith stood at attention, saluted. "Marching. Like recruits. Merits. Demerits. Scaling walls. Map exercises. Annie"—it was a wail—"the military's all right, but we don't need drill instructors marching the kids around. You know what could happen. Bullies. Hazing. Most of all, it just won't be the Haven. They can do that kind of stuff in scouting. Or set up a junior ROTC in high school. But the Haven's always been such a down-home, easygoing place. I always felt Ken was safe there. He's such a gentle kid and he loves the crafts, and he's too big for day care and—" She broke off, took a deep breath, coughed. "God, I don't know how I got off on all that. Sorry. You don't even have kids." Her dark eyes flickered over Annie, and Annie got the message only too clearly. She not only didn't have kids, she had money— actually, Max had pots of it—and if Annie had kids she could stay home and look after them or have a nanny or put a nursery at the back of her bookstore. Annie didn't have to worry about a twelve-year-old kid with time on his hands and a single mom who had to work.

Edith charged for the door. "Forget all that. Not your problem. I've got to get my stuff and go home. God, I used to like it around here!"

The door closed behind her.

Annie took her time gathering up her papers. She felt even more troubled about the upcoming library board meeting tomorrow. And certainly her small gathering this evening hadn't been exactly cheery, although Pamela would probably do a super job of expanding the program. But Annie couldn't forget the seething anger in Edith's voice—or the fear in her eyes. The feisty librarian might well be worried about more than the fate of the Haven. How secure was Edith's job, if she'd offended the general? And what did she mean about Ned, the director, having his own problems? Annie liked Ned Fisher, who was soft-spoken and kind, and passionate about increasing the library's collection plus high-gearing the library into the information age. He ran classes on Saturday mornings about the Internet for kids from the Haven. Donated his time and the library computers.

But Annie knew that Ned Fisher with his shoulder-length curly hair and his wispy handlebar mustache and weedy physique and primary-color trousers, held up by bright, season-oriented suspenders (stars and bars for the upcoming Fourth, dancing jackhammers for Labor Day, whirling pumpkin pies for Thanksgiving, et cetera) definitely was not the kind of man the general admired.

Okay. Her path was clear now. She had to attend the board meeting in the morning. And if Max's phone calls had gone well,

Henny would have a strong cadre of supporters.

Annie rewrapped the rabbit food and dip. She popped some candies in her mouth, then her head jerked up as an odd thud sounded. Almost immediately, there was a hoarse shout, then running footsteps. The sounds—whatever they were—had a muffled quality. But they definitely were out of the ordinary.

Annie was across the room in flash. She yanked open the door. For a moment, she stood uncertainly in the hallway. More shouts. She ran to the end of the hall and a wide window that looked out over the front porch and the drive and lawn. Pushing up the window, she clung to the sill and leaned out.

Forty feet below, great shards of blue pottery and clumps of dirt and masses of vari-colored petunias dotted the crushed oyster-shell drive.

A teenager on a bike pointed toward the portico, his sun-burned face upturned. "Cool," he shouted. "Bam. Splat. Any more coming down?"

"What happened?" Annie called.

He flipped back a thick mane of blond hair tied in a frizzy ponytail. "Special effects. Big time."

Annie wanted to stamp her feet in frustration. "What happened?" she screamed.

"A big blue pot fell down from the roof. Almost hit an old geezer." He put his bike on its stand. His hands on his hips, he looked up expectantly. "Hey, there's three more of 'em."

Annie twisted her head, looked up, but

the portico blocked her view. She knew what was atop the portico, or what should be atop the portico: four pedestals with four big vases.

How could a vase have fallen? And who had shouted?

Annie rushed back down the hallway, calling, "Edith! Edith!"

"What's going on out here?" Ned Fisher, the director of the library, was running, too. They met near the main stairway. "Annie, what's happened?" His head swiveled as he looked up and down the hall.

Annie had always thought of Fisher as young and eager, but now he looked strained and middle-aged and distinctly worried.

"One of the vases fell off the roof." She pointed toward the open window where she'd leaned out.

"Fallen? That's impossible! Oh, God. Anybody hurt?" He darted around her, started down the stairs.

"I don't know," she called after him.

Fisher stopped midway down the stairs, as if he'd run into a wall.

Bud Hatch, his face dangerously red, jolted to a stop in front of Fisher. The general shouted, "See anybody?"

It clicked like a roulette ball landing on black. The geezer.

Annie stared at him. "The vase? Did it fall?"

Hatch looked past Fisher, glared at her. "Pennies fall from heaven, little lady. Not vases. Somebody pushed it and it damn near got me. Seen anybody?" His eyes glistened. He looked from Annie to the director.

Hatch was, Annie realized abruptly, having a hell of a time. Probably the most fun since he'd commanded troops.

He jerked his head impatiently when neither replied. "Check out this floor," he barked. "Fisher, you take the front rooms. Annie, you take the back." And Hatch was running up the stairs to the third floor.

Annie was halfway down the hall, banging back doors and poking her head into empty rooms when she realized she'd responded automatically to the note of authority.

Hey, wait a minute! She wasn't in Bud Hatch's army. Then she moved on down the hall. Okay, no matter how much she didn't like the general, she didn't approve of people shoving vases off the library portico. It could be dangerous to people's health.

What if Edith had been leaving at the same time? But Edith would leave by the back door. It was closest to the staff lot. Where was Edith?

Annie ran to the end of the hall, peered down toward the staff lot. Edith was opening the door to a shabby VW and ignoring the occasional burst of sound from the library. The general, of course, issuing more orders. He'd probably enrolled everyone he saw in his posse of searchers, right along with Annie and Ned. Edith gunned her car backward, then took off in a flurry of gray dust.

Annie turned around. She caught sight of a door closing. And realized Ned Fisher was nowhere to be seen.

Slowly, cautiously, she eased up the hallway, stepping lightly on the polished wooden floor.

LADIES.

Someone was in the women's rest room. Not Edith Cummings. Surely not Ned Fisher. Why didn't the occupant come out to see what all the fuss was about? Unless there was a reason to hide. On the other hand, the person who'd pushed the vase certainly wasn't waiting around to be discovered. Anyone who knew how to get to the roof would also be familiar with both the front and back stairways.

Annie looked up and down the hall. Ned Fisher had to be nearby. She could shout for help if necessary. Annie grabbed the heavy, old-fashioned knob and opened the door.

There were a single washstand and doors to two stalls. One door was ajar, the other closed. Annie peered. No feet. Why was the door closed? "Well, nobody here," she said loudly. She scuffed to the door, opened it, walked in place, shut it firmly, all the while watching the closed stall. And waited.

Navy tennis shoes dropped lightly to the floor of the stall. The door opened.

Annie stared into startled, vividly blue eyes.

A blue ball cap perched atop Laurel's spun-gold hair. She looked jaunty in a navy T-shirt and slacks. In quick order, surprise, chagrin, and a soupçon of irritation flickered across her lovely face, followed by profound, unmistakable disappointment, the kindly but sad condemnation of one reluctantly discovering unexpected perfidy.

"Annie, dear Annie, don't you think subterfuge is perhaps a quality one should abhor?" A soft tsk, then Laurel, soft-footed as a cat burglar in the sneakers, sped toward the door.

Annie was so shocked, she couldn't reply. After all, she wasn't the one who'd perched on a toilet seat.

Laurel pulled the door open.

Annie caught up with her in the hallway. "Laurel," she hissed, "what are you—"

Laurel slipped her arm through that of her daughter-in-law. "The library has an absolutely wonderful collection of South Carolina poets. Had I but known that, I would have been tempted to include some local scribes on the fans. But dear William came to me first. And he did write so much." A sweet laugh. "But perhaps next—"

Far down the hall, Bud Hatch burst out of an office. "We've had a burglary, too. I'm going to call the police." He dashed down the main stairs.

"A burglary!" Annie exclaimed.

"A burglary," Laurel echoed brightly.

Annie swung toward her mother-in-law.

Laurel gave her a sweet smile. "So many exciting events at the local library."

"Laurel—" Annie's tone was intense.

"I must be off, my dear. So many miles to travel. That sort of thing. But remember: 'What is love? 'Tis not hereafter; Present mirth hath present laughter.'"

"Laurel—"

Her mother-in-law was nimbly skipping down the hallway, intent on reaching the central stairs.

Annie stood irresolute. But she couldn't lasso Laurel, insist that she remain. And certainly she couldn't tell Bud Hatch that Laurel was hidden in the ladies' room after the vase fell. After—face it—the vase was pushed.

Not Laurel. Laurel was spacey, Laurel was...well, different...yes, that was undeniable. At least no one denied it but Max. Annie was willing to accept that everyone had a few illusions that had to be indulged. But Laurel wouldn't push a huge vase off a roof and endanger anyone's life. And, as far as Annie knew, Laurel wasn't even acquainted with Bud Hatch. Though Bud had managed to make himself known the length and breadth of the island in his short time here.

But why had Laurel been hiding? And what had been stolen?

Annie darted up the hall. Yes, this was the office Bud Hatch had departed, announcing a burglary. She stepped inside. Oh, of course. This was the room with small private cabinets for all members of the library board. She'd never used hers. She glanced at the bronze nameplates. The top plate read: "Henny Brawley." Annie scanned the other names, including her own. All of the panels were closed except one. Its wooden door hung askew, revealing a messy heap of papers.

Annie stepped closer and stumbled. She looked down at the chisel she'd tripped on, then back at the open storage space. Gouge marks showed at the edge of the panel.

She reached up, tugged on Henny's panel. It didn't budge. Annie used her elbow—she hadn't read crime fiction her entire life to go around planting her fingerprints on a burglary site—and wasn't surprised to find Brig. Gen. (ret.) Charlton Hatch's name on the prized-open panel.

Only Hatch's space had been invaded.

Annie heard the faraway rumble of Hatch's deep voice. She scooted back into the hall.

A prized-open locker. A tumbling vase. Laurel in the ladies' room. There couldn't be a connection. But Annie was already halfway up the stairs to the third floor. It wasn't that she harbored any idea that Laurel had been responsible for the launch of the vase. No, not a single shred of reasoning would lead her to that conclusion. But, she thought grimly, she'd better take a look.

The door to the roof was open. It was a small opening, perhaps four feet tall, three feet wide, intended obviously for the access of repairmen, not for general traffic.

Heat radiated from the tarred roof, even though the sun was beginning to slide low on the horizon. It had been a long, hot day. Annie felt as if she were dancing across a sizzling skillet. She ducked around a huge chimney.

The second vase from the south was gone. Even in the dim light, Annie could see bright, fresh scars amid crumbly pieces of stone on the pedestal. Something had been jammed beneath the vase.

She thought of the chisel in the office with the cabinets for board members. But surely a chisel wasn't long enough to use to lever the urn free. She came close, looked at the streaks. Maybe an inch wide.

Careful not to touch the parapet, she looked over. A long way down. It would be easy to look over the parapet and see anyone coming out of the library. Once again she saw the broken shards of pottery scattered on the oyster shells.

If the vase had connected squarely, it would surely have killed a passerby. But Annie, whose mind was filled with ingenious means of murder, shook her head. Whoever pushed the vase intended to scare Hatch. But not to kill him. It would take enormous luck—if that was the right word—for the container to hit a target.

A siren rose and fell. Dust boiled up on the curving gray road.

Annie dashed to the other end of the roof.

The police car wheeled into the lot. Out climbed the gentle, good-humored giant Billy Cameron, who'd been promoted to sergeant when the Broward's Rock force was expanded to include two more officers in addition to the chief.

Hatch pounded down the back steps two at a time. Ned Fisher was right behind him.

Hatch waited for Billy. "Took you long enough." Hatch glanced at his watch. "Nine minutes thirty-two seconds."

"Yes, sir," Billy said smoothly. "What's the problem here?"

"Attempted murder. Burglary." Hatch was looking sharply around the lot. "Where's Samuel?"

"Sir?" Billy looked at him inquiringly.

"Samuel Kinnon," Hatch snapped. "Smart-mouth kid. Send out an APB."

"Samuel Kinnon?" Billy was a good, serious cop and he knew every man, woman, and child who lived on Broward's Rock. "What did Samuel do?"

Hatch slammed a fist into a palm. "Some craven fool shoved over a vase from the roof. Damn near killed me. It would be the kind of thing Samuel'd do."

"Oh, I doubt that, General." Ned Fisher's tone was conciliatory. "Samuel's a fine young man. Did you see him on the roof?"

Billy held up a big hand. "If we could start at the beginning." He looked at Hatch. "All right, mister."

"General. General Hatch." It was a stand-up-and-salute voice.

"Yes, sir." Billy nodded. "First, I need to know what's happened."

"I'll show you." Hatch headed for the front of the library.

Billy followed. Ned Fisher took a deep breath and trotted after them.

Annie decided it might be as well if she quitted the roof. No law said she couldn't be up here, but even good-humored Billy Cameron might wonder why she was there. Annie wanted to avoid any mention of Laurel's presence. And quick departure.

Annie hurried down to the second floor and

ducked into the room where she'd held her committee meeting, tucked the foods and her papers into her book bag. As she came out, she heard the general's crisp voice down the hall in the office with the prized-open panel.

Annie stepped out into the hall. She walked very quietly. If anyone happened to look out and wonder, she was on her way to the main stairs. But she could hear every word being said.

"...these are compartments for the use of our library board members." Ned Fisher spoke briskly.

"Are they kept locked?" Billy Cameron asked.

Annie edged close enough to peer into the office.

"Yes. This affords the board members a place to keep confidential material." Fisher stood with his arms folded, staring at the cabinet.

"What would that be?" Billy sounded puzzled.

"Oh, personnel matters. Library minutes. That kind of thing." The director stepped to the cabinet, tugged on several of the lockers. "The rest of them seem to be all right."

Billy bent to look at the broken panel. "So this one belongs to you, General?" Billy asked.

"That's right. And someone's broken in." Hatch was impatient.

"Can you tell me if anything is missing, sir?" Billy wasn't going to be rushed.

Hatch pawed through the heap of papers. "Doesn't appear to be." But his face was dangerously red, his eyes abstracted.

"Nothing taken?" Billy repeated, watching Hatch closely.

Hatch shook his head. "It doesn't matter whether anything's missing. No one has the right to break into my private files."

"It doesn't make sense," Fisher exclaimed. "There's nothing that sensitive in library matters."

Annie left them wrangling. The general was furious. Why should he care, if nothing had been disturbed? That was easy to answer. He had an idea why someone would nose around in his private compartment and he didn't like it at all. Something was gone, all right, but it wasn't anything he was willing to describe. Annie quirked an eyebrow. So what did the old martinet keep there? Girly mags? Smutty videos? Locations of cockfights? Hmm.

When she reached the main stairwell, Annie stopped and frowned. A faint memory teased her mind. She hesitated, then, turning, ran quickly back to the women's rest room. She opened the door, stepped inside, closed the door, and looked at it fully, looked directly as she had not when she closed it earlier and waited to see if someone hid in one of the stalls.

The charcoal drawing wasn't quite straight, as if it had been placed there hurriedly. Again the strokes of charcoal gave life and movement. A young woman with dark curls and a pale face ducked inside a military tent. Her dress was travel-crumpled. A patriot general looked at her keenly. Beneath the drawing, thick black spidery handwriting proclaimed: Emily Geiger brings word to General Sumter from General Greene after a death-daring ride across Tory country.

Hatch had forbidden Miss Dora to post her drawings of South Carolina heroines in the library. But this was one place in the library off limits to the general. Annie grinned. Then her smile faded. When had Miss Dora been here? But even if she'd been at the library when the vase fell, certainly tiny Miss Dora wasn't strong enough to have leveraged it loose.

Annie shook her head impatiently. The vase wasn't her responsibility. Nor was Miss Dora. As for Laurel, Annie intended to have a heart-to-heart talk with her mother-in-law as soon as possible. They had many things to discuss and Shakespeare wasn't even on the list. She was undecided whether to start with breaking and entering, absconding with private property, or pilferage.

"Now, Annie." Max shoved a hand through his thick blond hair. "That's absurd."

Annie poured chocolate syrup over the vanilla ice cream. Dear chocolate syrup. Zero grams of fat. She looked at Max. "Zero grams of fat. Do you want some?"

"No, thanks." He shook his head impatiently. "It doesn't mean a thing that Mother was in the rest room."

"Hiding in the rest room." Annie said it pleasantly but firmly.

"Well, I'm sure she'll have a good reason." Max's face was getting its bulldog look.

"Why don't you call and ask her?" Annie plopped on a wicker couch beneath the ceiling fan. Of course their house was air-conditioned, but for the summer in the Low Country one could not have too many methods of cooling. She spooned a smooth dark dollop of chocolate syrup. She'd get to the ice cream in a minute.

Max paced in front of the couch. "Of course she had a good reason."

Annie wondered if he heard the plaintive tone in his voice.

"I'll call her." He strode to the telephone.

Annie edged a smidgeon of ice cream on the tip of the spoon, dipped the whole into the syrup. She closed her eyes and swallowed. And listened.

"Hi, Mother." Max's tone was hearty.

Annie knew he was worried. Otherwise, he would have called her Laurel.

"...did you realize there was a robbery at the library this evening?"

The spoon moved rhythmically.

"Annie said the general was really angry even though he said nothing was missing." Max held the phone away from his ear.

Annie heard a silver peal of amusement.

"What's so funny, Mother?" he demanded crisply. He nodded quickly. "That's right. Annie heard the general talking to the police." A pause. "Yes, he called the police. What? No, I don't suppose they can do anything about it if the general doesn't say what was taken.

But whoever did it could still be arrested for vandalism. Or breaking and entering. Now if you have any idea what—"

Max listened, frowning. Slowly, he hung up the phone. He looked at Annie, his dark blue eyes full of concern. "Do you know what she said?" He rubbed his cheek. "She said, 'If wishes were horses, beggars would ride.' Annie, what in the world does that mean?"

It meant, Annie felt certain, that General Hatch could whistle for his lost property. Whatever it was.

A Speak Your Mind tempted: At the best of times, your mother has the criminal instincts of a cat burglar. Instead, she smiled sweetly. "Laurel is very poetic." She spooned a tiny sliver of ice cream floating in syrup. Be interesting to know what had been taken. But it probably didn't really matter. Be interesting to see how the old geezer behaved at the board meeting in the morning. Annie was sure of one thing only. As soon as the meeting was past, she intended to dismiss Brig. Gen. (ret.) Charlton (Bud) Hatch from her thoughts. Absolutely. Completely.

She concentrated on her last spoonful of chocolate.

Chapter 3

Max waggled his new putter. Hmm. A nice weight. He took the proper stance, sighted from the ball to the hole to the ball. Click. The ball headed straight for the cup. At the last instant, the pebbled white sphere curved left.

"I can't believe it!" He stared at the artificial putting green. But actually, as with all golfers, he could believe it. The perennial question tantalized him: Why did anyone play a game where one day your shots flew straight and true down the fairway and the next they hooked or sliced or simply died? Why endure the torture, frustration and misery called golf?

Max's secretary stuck her head in the doorway. "Did you call me?" A statuesque blonde, she favored multifloral shifts dominated by bright red hibiscus. Thick hair puffed in what Annie assured him was called a beehive hairdo.

Max glared at the putter. "No. I'm thinking about taking up dominoes." He turned and grinned at Barb's cheerful, inquiring face. "Do you think dominoes are as unpredictable as golf balls?"

Barb said consolingly, "Did you read your horoscope this morning? It said, 'Adventure and success are yours for the taking.'" Her brown eyes were earnest.

"No kidding?" Max poked the putter in his golf bag, which he often brought to the office. Just in case. He might be called upon to solve the Mystery of the Disappearing Golf Balls, though everybody on the island knew better than to fish around in the lagoons for errant shots. Water hazards lived up to their name on the South Carolina barrier islands, which harbored many alligators as well as buckets of balls.

"I'd settle for a case." He strolled toward his desk. There might be a copy of the most recent *Ellery Queen's Mystery Magazine*. When Annie asked how his day had gone, as she would, he could truthfully report that he was keeping up with news in the field. And maybe there would be a new Robert Barnard story.

"Something will turn up." Barb gave him a sunny smile.

Barb's cheerful demeanor was one reason Max liked having her as his secretary. Besides, she was always able to occupy herself, even when there wasn't really any work to be done. Recently, she'd created a snazzy web page for the office: a huge magnifying glass, a jaunty deerstalker hat, and "Confidential Commissions" in art deco typeface. It included the ad that appeared daily in the personals column of the *Island Gazette:* "Troubled, puzzled, curious? Whatever your problem, contact Confidential Commissions."

In addition to the phone number, the web page offered an E-mail address. Whenever a prospective client called, Max was always quick to point out that although he was a lawyer, he was not practicing law since he'd never been admitted to the bar of South Carolina, and he wasn't, as he stressed to local law-enforcement officials, a private detective. He was simply in the business of helping people with unusual problems. A counselor, so to speak.

Barb pushed her glasses higher on her nose, which gave her a scholarly appearance.

She would have been the first to admit that appearances definitely can be deceiving. "My horoscope said, 'Be alert. A surprise call requires extra effort.' So don't worry. My horoscope's never wrong."

She gave him another cheerful grin as she closed the door.

Max settled behind his Italian Renaissance desk. Yes, there was the magazine, resting next to an absolutely untouched legal pad. He picked up the magazine, leaned back in his well-padded chair. But instead of reading, he studied the photograph in the silver frame that sat on his desk.

Short blond hair with streaks of gold framed a face always lovely to him. Serious gray eyes looked at him steadily. Wonderful, fun, happy Annie, despite her incredible propensity for work. Dear Annie. Always striving. He was no expert on genealogy but he was sure Annie's forebears must have been Puritans. In fact, this very morning Annie had suggested, not too gently, that perhaps Max might like to close down Confidential Commissions since his last client had been several months ago. Max didn't see why she was concerned. As Barb said, something always turned up. Actually, he wasn't averse to periods of quiet. Perhaps Annie had never truly recognized his capacity for reflection. Max grinned at the photograph. That was the ticket. This evening, he'd tell Annie he was simply in a reflective phase—

His door opened. Barb poked her head in. "A client." It was practically a warble. A muscular middle-aged man hurried in.

Max came around the Italian Renaissance desk, hand outstretched. "Hi, Luther. How are you?"

The stocky black man's big-cheeked face was deeply creased with laugh lines. He attempted a smile. It hung for a moment like forgotten laundry on a wash line, then he looked somberly at Max. "Poorly, Max. Poorly. I've come to see if you can help me."

Luther Kinnon had his own business, Island Landscapes. He'd kept Max and Annie's garden and lawn in excellent shape for several years. Luther's wife, May, worked at a day-care center. They had four children, the oldest a partner with Luther, the second a local chef, the third a teacher in Savannah. The fourth, Samuel, had graduated from high school in May.

They shook hands, and Max gestured to the chair that faced his desk, a chair not too often in use. Max was sorry if Luther had problems but eager to prove the viability of his enterprise. That morning, when Annie had proposed that he close Confidential Commissions, Max had replied that he could not in good conscience do that. Why? she'd inquired. Because, he replied, there was no other office on the island or in all of the state that provided its customers with his original and particular talents. He was, he announced grandly, a facilitator. What, Annie had inquired darkly, was a facilitator? One, Max replied firmly, who facilitates. He had then observed in the spirit of a man making a purely philosophical comment that Annie's expression, though of course well-meant, reminded him irresistibly of Agatha when she contemplated a fanged attack. On that note, he'd kissed his wife cheerily and strode down the boardwalk to Confidential Commissions, leaving Annie at the door to Death on Demand.

Now he settled behind his desk and looked at a weary and worried man. "What's wrong, Luther?"

Luther's strong hands gripped the chair arms. "Max, I want you to find Samuel. He didn't come home last night." The older man's eyes were milky with fatigue and fear. "And"—his voice was low, almost inaudible—"the police are looking for him."

"For Samuel?" Max remembered Samuel Kinnon clearly. He'd been in his early teens when Max first hired Luther to keep the lawn and gardens. Max had watched Samuel grow from a slim kid to a big young man topping six feet, a young man with a ready grin and a cheerful disposition, who worked hard for his dad and older brother and who'd made a name for himself on the local sports page as a promising young golfer in the pro-gram run by the Haven. But even good kids could get in a lot of trouble. Max hoped Samuel wasn't in big trouble. "What's the problem, Luther?"

Luther hunched forward. "Somebody pushed a big vase off the library roof yesterday and it almost hit General Hatch. The general says Samuel did it. The general and Samuel—they had words outside the library just before the vase came down." He pulled a handkerchief from a back pocket, wiped it over his face. "It's a damn lie. But the police are looking for Samuel. I'm afraid they'll arrest him."

"Did you talk to Samuel?" Max picked up a pen and pulled a clean legal pad closer.

Luther's eyes fell. "He didn't come home last night." His voice was anguished. "But I know Samuel didn't do it. I want you to find him, tell him to come home. Tell him we'll fight it. We'll get a lawyer."

Max tapped the pen on his desk. "I know the general's managed to irritate a lot of people. Why was Samuel mad at him?"

Luther leaned back in the chair, stared blankly at a life-size bronze sculpture of a golfer teeing off, his three-wood at the top of its back swing. Visitors to Max's office had been known to stop short and exclaim, "Won't the ball break the window?" before they realized they were addressing a statue. Annie had given the sculpture to Max for their third wedding anniversary. Max smiled every time he looked at it.

Luther balled the handkerchief tight in one hand and stared down at it. "Last week, the general got the director of the Haven to fire Samuel. Samuel was teaching wood-working to the middle-school kids."

Max balanced the pen between his fore-fingers and waited.

The older man's gaze slid back to Max. "The general's got himself on the board and he has lots of ideas of how to improve the Haven. He came into Samuel's class one day and the kids were having a paper airplane fight and they were running and giggling and one of them ran right into the general. He told Samuel he needed to make his kids shape up, learn to stand at attention when an adult came in the room, speak respectfully. Anyway, Samuel told him this was a place for kids to have fun and they didn't have to sit still and be quiet." Luther rubbed his face with the wadded-up handkerchief. "Next thing Samuel knew, the director—Mrs. Kerry—told him she was sorry but the general was threatening to get some of the funding cut off and she was going to have to let Samuel go. She paid him up-to-date. Samuel asked for a reference and she was embarrassed, she wouldn't look him in the eye, but she said she couldn't do that. Samuel said he needed the reference from his summer job to be able to get a student job at the college next fall. She told him she'd had her instructions from the board. Samuel has to work to be able to go to school. He's real worried about it."

"So Samuel was pretty mad?" On the legal pad, Max sketched the front of the library, minus one vase.

Luther's voice deepened. "He had a right to be mad. The general had no call to treat Samuel like that. The general wants black people to say 'Yes, sir, no, sir' to him and to clean up his yard. But he doesn't want us to have a job a white boy could have."

Max rubbed the side of his nose with the cap of his pen. "Luther, what makes you—"

"I don't think. I know. A white boy got Samuel's job, the son of a friend of the gen-

71

eral's. And he's a no-account kid who's never been able to keep a job." Luther folded his arms across his chest, looked grimly at Max. "I got a friend who does the maintenance there. He told me all about it."

Racism still reared its ugly head, racism and sexism and all the other -isms. Max knew that. He didn't doubt Luther's word. That might infuriate a kid who'd played the game straight and done his best and now might see his chance to go to college shot down for no good reason.

Luther planted two big hands on his knees. "Yeah, it's a rotten deal. But even so, I know my son. He wouldn't sneak around and shove something off a roof at a man, no matter how bad a man he might be. Samuel wouldn't do it. But the general's blaming him. We've got to find Samuel. I know he's scared. I'm afraid something bad may happen to him."

A black teenager with the police after him—yes, something bad could happen. Max nodded. "Okay. I'll do my best. First, who are Samuel's friends? Let's start there. Somebody has to know where Samuel is."

It was bumper-to-bumper on the dusty library road. The traffic moved at a crawl, so Annie had plenty of time to check out the front of the library. Three vases. Not that she would have expected a replacement the very next day, but the empty pedestal was incredibly notice-able. The drive in front of the library was clear, however. The broken pieces of pottery and the clumps of dirt and the masses of flowers were gone.

Annie finally found a place to park in a spillover lot past the regular parking area. Women streamed toward the rear of the library. Women's voices, rising and falling like the chirp of Carolina wrens, made a light counterpoint to the bang of hammers and call of men setting up a series of low stages in a semicircle. A temporary band shell was also under construction across a grassy expanse. The lagoon behind the band shell shimmered in the summer sun. Friday night, the fireworks would be set off from a boat in the middle of the lagoon. Admission to the festival grounds cost five dollars for adults, one dollar for children.

Annie got out of her Volvo, waving hello to several friends. The entire scene was summery and cheerful. She felt a thrill of anticipation. This Fourth was going to go down in Broward's Rock history as the best ever despite Bud Hatch. Feeling magnanimous, she thought it would be fine to have Hatch's Points of Patriotism along with the celebration of South Carolina women. After all, there were great South Carolinians of both sexes. Annie understood Henny's wish to concentrate on the contributions of women since they rarely received the focus of attention. On a beautiful day like this, however, who needed controversy?

Annie wondered if Hatch was already in the meeting room. If he'd parked in front he might not be aware of the turnout for the board meeting.

The second-floor hallway was crowded.

"Hi, Annie." "Hello, Annie." "Is Mary Higgins Clark's latest novel in?" "How's Max?" "Do you have an autographed copy of Sparkle Hayter's new book?"

Annie smiled, nodded, and replied as she moved slowly with the crowd of women in summery frocks. Inside the meeting room, all the chairs were taken. Women were standing at the back. Henny sat behind a table at the front, looking over the capacity audience. She was much too savvy to look openly satisfied, but Annie was certain Henny was glowing inside.

So there, Bud Hatch.

Annie's sense of triumph was short-lived.

Hatch strolled up the center aisle, shaking hands, smiling, as self-possessed as if all the chattering women were there for his benefit.

Annie slowly worked her way toward the front. Everybody who was anybody was in attendance. She spotted blunt-faced Emma Clyde, the island's claim to literary fame, creator of Marigold Rembrandt, America's most famous fictional sleuth. Emma nodded genially.

"Annie!" The hoarse tone was urgent.

Annie looked down.

Miss Dora thrust a charcoal drawing into Annie's hands. "You can hang it from the board table. Everyone will see it."

Including the general? Annie wondered.

The old lady didn't wait for an answer, thumping past with an armload of drawings.

When Annie reached the table, she unrolled the drawing and saw a portrait of a striking black woman with a broad, strong face, a brush of white hair and a joyous smile. In Miss Dora's spidery script, Annie read at the bottom of the sheet: "Mary McLeod Bethune, who rose from sharecropper's daughter to walk the halls of the mighty always in search of support for the education of black youth. Patterned after the portrait which hangs in the South Carolina State House." She grabbed a couple of empty water glasses and used them to anchor the drawing in front of the end seat.

"I'm so glad it's warm in here," Laurel confided, her husky voice brimming with cheer. She handed Annie an old-fashioned paper fan, bright red with scalloped edges.

Now that Laurel mentioned it, Annie realized the library's always inadequate cooling system was overborne by the throng of visitors. She had that old familiar Jell-O feeling, as if she were submerging in moist, warm air. She looked around and realized there was another sound in addition to women's voices, the swish-swish of paper fans vigorously waved.

Laurel waggled a fan at Annie and moved on, leaving behind a faint scent of lilac. Laurel should have looked absurd in a red-white-and-blue cotton blouse and skirt but instead was probably going to set a new style on the island as women turned their heads in envy and admiration. How, Annie wondered, did Laurel do it? Of course, it helped to be captivatingly lovely, slim with golden hair and exuding a mystique compounded of great wealth, utter confidence, and dazzling charm.

Annie glanced down. She wondered what Shakespeare would think could he see his words blazoned on fans: "They do not love that do not show their love." Certainly the verse was easily read, white against red. Annie's eyes crinkled in concern. But, simply because Laurel quoted from a poet, surely it did not mean she was taking the poem personally. Did it? It was certainly the route to madness to try and divine order and meaning in Laurel's enthusiasms.

Annie slipped around the table and took the end chair at the left. She waved the fan, welcoming the tiny breeze, and scanned the room for Laurel's golden head and slim form. Why had Laurel hidden in the library ladies' room yesterday? There had to be a reason. Annie spotted her mother-in-law near the windows, smiling and offering fans. Shakespeare, the library.... Annie nodded firmly. All right, if it took the dogged persistence of Georges Simenon's Jules Maigret combined with the unsquashable good humor of Jill Churchill's Jane Jeffry, Annie would fathom this puzzle. Without, of course, smoking a pipe or managing a car pool.

At the stroke of ten, Henny rose from behind the conference table.

"Good morning." Her well-modulated voice carried to the far reaches of the room over the central microphone. "I'm delighted we have such an enthusiastic turnout for the final meeting before the festival begins. Many of you are here representing other organizations. With the leave of the board"—Henny looked up and down the table—"I will begin our meeting today with the visitors' reports."

Annie looked at her fellow board members, and her pleasure at the superb turnout began to fade. Everyone looked grim and strained, with the notable exception of Henny and Bud Hatch. Hatch was at Henny's right, his rough-hewn face genial and interested. He was natty in a crisp navy blazer. He sat squarely in his chair, every inch a warrior. There was just a hint of well-done-Little-Lady in his demeanor.

Jonathan Wentworth was at the far right end of the table, his face remote and still. He was probably in his mid-seventies, with short white hair and a sun-burned face. His crisp tan summer suit was vaguely reminiscent of a uniform. He sometimes came to the store to buy mysteries for his wife. Her favorite authors were Elizabeth Peters and Anne Perry. Annie often saw Emily Wentworth at church, a swift-moving, beautifully dressed woman with metallic eyes and a bright smile. Jonathan was kindly and courtly, another retired military man. But what a contrast to Bud Hatch! Annie wouldn't even have known that Wentworth had been a Navy captain, except for the biographical information about board members included in the annual library report. And of course the *Gazette* had done extensive coverage about the upcoming festival and several stories had described the board members. Hatch always managed to mention his Army service in every conversation.

Annie glanced swiftly around the room. She didn't see Sharon Gibson, the Wentworths' daughter and the owner of the Gifts for Everyone shop three doors down from Death on Demand. It was Sharon Gibson who'd looked angrily down the aisle toward the general in the grocery store yesterday afternoon. The general had professed not to know Sharon. He certainly knew Jonathan Wentworth. Sharon had decided not to take part in the festival, yet her father was on the library board. Wasn't that odd?

Gail Oldham, a high school English teacher, slumped next to Annie. Annie had met Gail several years ago in a tennis league. Gail was a perky redhead with a spatter of freckles on a gamine face. There was no saucy smile this morning. In fact, she looked ill, her face pale, dark circles beneath her eyes. She was making an effort to appear pleasant and engaged, but she sat stiffly, her hands tightly clasped on the table.

Ned Fisher sat between Gail and Henny. The library director's angular face sported a determinedly pleasant expression, but one thin hand nervously fingered his drooping mustache. He kept glancing uneasily toward the back of the room.

Annie looked, too. She immediately spotted Toby Maguire, Ned's significant other. Toby's lumpy face and oddly sleek red beard made him readily visible, even in the back row. Toby glowered, his powerful arms crossed across his burly chest. Toby was a reclusive but increasingly acclaimed artist, becoming well known for his Low Country landscapes. Annie occasionally saw Ned and Toby on the beach or out at dinner, but Toby wasn't active in island circles, not even the artistic ones.

Librarian Edith Cummings sat in a chair just to the side of the table, holding a notepad. She served as the secretary of the board, but not as a voting member. Her face was composed, attentive, noncommittal, but her dark eyes regarded Hatch with the cool detachment of a biologist studying slime.

The president of the Community Council concluded her enthusiastic presentation, "...happy to announce that nine women's groups, from the Ladies of the Leaf Book Club to the Saint Xavier Altar Society, have contributed volunteers to staff the various historical displays. We have enough participants to truly share with all islanders the achievements of South Carolina women through our long and glorious history."

Applause boomed like storm surf.

Bud Hatch surged to his feet. He held up his hand.

Henny nodded pleasantly. In a jonquil-yellow linen dress, Henny looked cool, elegant, and completely unflappable. She spoke quickly enough to precede Hatch, but in a measured, confident voice. "General Hatch wishes to contribute."

Hatch gazed at Henny for a long moment, then smiled.

That look revealed his anger. For an instant,

his sharp features were wolflike and predatory.

"Uh-oh," Annie murmured. Henny definitely better watch her flank.

"Thank you, ma'am." The general graced Henny with another glittering smile, then faced the audience. "I know I speak for my fellow board members when I say we are fortunate indeed—"

"A point of order." The call came in a rasping voice that carried like a crow's caw. Thump. Thump. Thump.

Hatch looked down at the petite old lady moving up the central aisle, her cane loud on the wooden floor. "Ah, Miss Dora."

No flies on the general. He knew the local aristocracy even though Miss Dora lived on the mainland.

"Young man." She stood directly in front of Hatch, one hand clasping her cane. In her other hand, she waggled a portfolio. "I have long been a supporter of this library as well as the library in Chastain. My cousin often prevailed upon me to make contributions."

"Your cousin?" Hatch shook his head, like a man surrounded by buzzing gnats.

A murmur rose from the audience. "Lucy. Kinkaid. Lucy. Kinkaid." The syllables hummed like a drumbeat.

Miss Dora didn't deign to explain. She fixed Hatch with a malevolent gaze. "It is not to be expected that a latecomer to the island should be cognizant of how intertwined has been the history of this island and my town. Therefore, when I learned that the director

80

of your library board proposed a Fourth of July Celebration in honor of the Gallant Women of South Carolina, I felt, of course, that it was my duty to offer what aid and assistance I could."

She poked her cane toward Ned Fisher. "Young man, if you will be kind enough to provide an easel—"

"Madam," the general began.

"Why, of course we wish to hear you out, Miss Dora," Henny said quickly.

The general folded his arms across his chest, his face tinged with copper.

Ned popped to his feet. "Yes, ma'am. Of course." In a moment, he was pulling an easel from a nearby cupboard. He brought it around the table and set it up in the central aisle.

"Thank you, young man." Miss Dora's smile was almost coquettish. "I know everyone here today is excited about our grand program which will honor the women of our state. It is my pleasure to share with you my drawings of outstanding South Carolina women."

Annie was too far away to see the drawings distinctly, but she—and everyone in the room—heard the roll call of famous names with brief snippets of history:

Sarah Moore Grimké and Angelina Emily Grimké, courageous fighters against slavery and for women's rights....

Mary Boykin Chesnut, who kept a diary that became the greatest record of a Southern woman's war years....

Matilda Arabella Evans, the first native

South Carolina black woman doctor in the state, opening her practice in Columbia in 1897....

"And these are simply a few of our gallant women." Miss Dora paused. Every eye was on her as she looked regally about the room. "Will you salute them?" Miss Dora held her cane high.

Huzzahs and frenzied applause rocked the room.

The president of the Community Council bounded to her feet. "Miss Dora, this is a wonderful contribution to our efforts. I suggest the library mount these superb drawings and exhibit them at the perimeter of the Fourth of July Celebration, then provide space in the library for the rest of the month." She looked at Ned Fisher.

Fisher glanced at the general.

The audience was on its feet, cheering, clapping.

Henny bent close to the microphone. Her voice sounded even above the tumult. "Our community has spoken. Ned, we have a mandate." Henny nodded to Bud Hatch. "General, I know you are delighted to see this enthusiastic welcome for the work of a long-time supporter of the Lucy Banister Kinkaid Library."

Hatch was nobody's fool. "I'm sure Miss Dora's drawings will be a wonderful addition to our celebration."

The look of relief on Ned Fisher's face was almost embarrassing.

Hatch glanced from the director to the

other board members. "It is, of course, wonderful to see these great tributes to the women of South Carolina. I know all of you will be equally pleased that our veterans' groups will provide superb tributes to the men who have fought and died for this great state."

More cheers.

Henny's smile was fixed, but she, too, understood reality. "That's quite wonderful, General. We will have the greatest possible celebration of South Carolina history at our Fourth of July festival." Henny looked out toward the audience. "Thank you for coming today. Working together, we're going to have a great celebration tomorrow. Thank you." She smiled graciously, picked up her papers.

As she stepped toward the aisle, Hatch blocked her way. He spoke clearly, his voice resonating over the still live microphone, "I suggest we meet next week to tally up the proceeds from the Fourth celebration."

"I've already called a meeting," Henny replied briskly.

"Good. I'll take the opportunity to address some personnel matters." His face was still red.

People were moving unhurriedly up the aisles, women's voices once again light and cheerful. Hatch's voice was almost submerged, but not quite.

"I don't have that on the agenda." Henny tried to step past him.

Hatch moved at the same time, and they were face-to-face only inches apart. "It's new business," Hatch said smoothly. "The board members have been properly notified. They'll find the addition to the agenda in their boxes. The discussion will focus on medical coverage for library employees and how dependents can be defined." The general flicked a glance toward the director, who stood stock-still, his young face suddenly looking old. "There is also the matter of library employees who flaunt health and safety standards. And the further question of whether a board member can be dismissed for trifling in another member's private papers."

Annie looked toward the members of the board, still standing behind the table.

Jonathan Wentworth gazed somberly at Hatch. Wentworth's face was still remote, but his eyes were icy with disdain.

Ned Fisher jammed his hands in the pockets of his slacks. He stared at the wooden floor, his cheekbones gaunt.

Gail Oldham shivered and turned away. She hurried up the aisle, her heels clicking loudly on the floor. As an English teacher, she usually had much to offer at board meetings. Today she'd been silent and subdued.

Edith Cummings pushed back her chair, stuffed her notebook into her purse.

Henny's face hardened. She lifted her chin. Before she could speak, Jonathan Wentworth was at her elbow. "Henny"—and he firmly turned her away from Hatch—"I need to speak...." His voice fell away, out of range of the microphone.

Hatch watched them go. In a moment, he was alone by the table, the board members moving quickly away. Hatch didn't seem to mind. He smiled. It wasn't a nice smile.

Max ducked out of the way of the two-by-four.

"Mister"—the young black man's voice was polite but determined—"the boss doesn't pay us to talk to people."

Max followed Harry Wileman. "Do you get a break?"

"In a while. They blow a whistle." He didn't slacken his pace as he talked.

"I'll wait." Max threaded his way past wheelbarrows and laborers. He reached the shade of a huge magnolia and leaned against the gnarled trunk, welcoming the respite from the July sun and the sweet scent of the blooms. The construction scene was organized chaos, but it had a steady, pulsing rhythm. Max felt profoundly grateful he didn't have to work that hard, although there had to be a gut-deep sense of satisfaction in seeing a structure evolve from the effort of muscle and bone.

He was placing his hope of finding Samuel Kinnon squarely on the shoulders of the wiry young man diligently moving two-by-fours. This was Max's last stop. He'd talked to Samuel's girlfriend, Krissa, who was miffed. "That Samuel better not stand me up or I'll give him what-for! He hasn't called me in two days. I don't have to sit around and wait for him, I'll tell you that!" And to a co-worker at the Haven, Raoul: "Man, Samuel was pissed!" And to Samuel's brother, Jack: "I don't have any idea where he is. Dumb to run away. But Samuel has his own ideas about things."

Max waited. Occasionally, Harry Wileman glanced toward the magnolia, then bent back to work.

A whistle shrilled. The constant swarm of choreographed activity suddenly ceased. Men ambled toward the water bucket, shook cigarettes free from sweaty shirt pockets.

Carrying a bottle of sport drink, Max's quarry ducked under a low branch. Sweat stained Harry's shirt, patched his jeans. He used the tail of a kerchief to wipe his gleaming face. He was sinewy and lean, muscles moving smoothly in his arm. He had the angular, swift grace of a young panther.

"You want to see me about Samuel? Why?" He watched Max coolly, reserving judgment.

"Samuel's dad asked me to find him." Quickly Max explained.

Harry squatted on his heels, tipped the bottle and drank thirstily. He finished, took a deep breath. His face creased in thought. "Samuel didn't like the general."

"I know." Max fished out his handkerchief, wiped the sweat from his face.

Harry studied Max, his dark eyes taking in every detail, from Max's short thick blond hair clinging damply to his head to his pale-blue polo shirt, once crisp, now limp, to his white slacks, smudged from leaning against the tree trunk, to his Italian loafers, coated with gray dust.

"I'm on Samuel's side," Max said quietly.

Slowly Harry stood. He tucked the empty

plastic bottle under one arm, wiped his face and neck again. "Samuel said the general's a bastard."

"I know. He got Samuel fired—"

Harry shook his head impatiently. "Yeah, that made Samuel mad. But Samuel's not the kind of guy to knock a vase off a roof. What if somebody else walked out? Samuel's not stupid. But Samuel was really upset because of a kid named Ken Cummings."

The whistle shrilled. Harry looked around.

"What about Ken?" Max knew he was out of time and he still didn't know where Samuel was.

"The general wanted to make everybody at the Haven march, big time. Samuel said Ken's mom was really hacked. She said the general ought to be shot." Harry tossed the bottle into the trash.

The whistle sounded again. Harry turned.

Max called after him. "Harry, if you know where Samuel is—"

Harry looked back, his dark face unreadable. "No way for me to know." And he was hurrying across the dusty ground.

Men worked. Dust rose. Max walked slowly toward his car.

Annie was midway down the stairs from the second floor of the library when a hand gripped her arm. A weary voice announced, "Annie, I'm here to deliver the ads to Edith. Mission accomplished."

Annie looked into bleary, but sincere eyes. "That's wonderful, Pamela," she said heartily.

87

"Would you like to see the mock-up?" Pamela wavered on her feet. "I've been up all night." A wrinkled pink-striped blouse was messily tucked into a skirt with red and blue patches. Worn backward.

Annie knew she was seeing selfless dedication gallantly (and blatantly) evinced. But to refuse would have been like dashing a child's Easter-egg basket to the ground.

"Of course." Annie pointed down the steps. "Let's find an empty room."

Pamela led the way. Annie noticed, not too charitably, that she moved with alacrity. Feeling somewhat akin to the spoils of war, Annie followed. She glanced down the hall, catching a glimpse of Henny and Jonathan stepping into the board members' room.

Annie caught up with Pamela, urged her into the first empty room.

Pamela spread open the program mock-up and went page by numbing page. Annie danced impatiently from one foot to the other.

Pamela paused. "Uh, Annie, do you—"

"No," Annie said sharply, "I'm fine." She reached out, attempted to flip the pages closed.

Pamela was extraordinarily strong.

Annie retreated. "Pamela, this is truly marvelous. This program is a brilliant coup."

Pamela leaned forward, like a flower to raindrops.

"Truly extraordinary." Annie gripped the edge of the table.

Pamela glowed.

Annie was from Texas. She took a deep breath. "Bastante," she hissed.

Pamela's eyes widened. "I beg your pardon?"

Annie coughed. "But tantalizing."

Pamela looked puzzled.

Annie spoke rapidly. "Simply tantalizingly lyrical in its evocation of the great men and women of South Carolina." Annie came around the table, clasped Pamela by the shoulders. "Now you must, like a good soldier"—she felt Pamela's muscles stiffen, her posture straighten—"prepare yourself for tomorrow. Go home, seek your rest and be assured that what you have achieved for the library shall be celebrated"—Annie forbore saying, "...in song and verse..." though mightily tempted—"throughout the annals of recorded time."

Even Pamela found this laudatory commendation sufficient.

Annie smiled, almost saluted, then whirled and was through the door and down the hall. She pushed open the door to the boardroom.

It was empty.

Damn. Annie dreaded talking to Henny. But she must. Bud Hatch clearly intended to wreak revenge by attacking Ned Fisher and Edith Cummings and an unnamed board member Hatch thought guilty of trifling with his private papers. Private papers! The rifled cabinet was here in the library boardroom!

A warm breath tickled Annie's ear. She jerked around and looked into familiar serious eyes.

"I heard about that!" Pamela pointed at the

wooden panel hanging ajar. "Do you know," she said, her voice deep and portentous, "someone must think the general has secret papers!"

Annie wondered if Pamela's most recent adventure reading had featured the Happy Hollisters. "I don't think," Annie said gently, "that we have an E. Phillips Oppenheim situation here."

Pamela looked at her blankly.

Annie tried again. "Secret papers are passé." A pause. "Pamela, no one would break into the general's cubicle here expecting to find secret formulas or anything like that."

"Then why did they break in?" Pamela asked reasonably.

Annie opened her mouth, shut it. Why, indeed? She turned, looked at the broken panel.

"...and someone used a wire cutter to snip off the lock."

Annie realized she'd missed something. "What lock, Pamela?"

"The general's locker at Whalebranch," Pamela explained. Her voice dropped, she nodded sagely. "Now why would anyone break into the general's locker at a golf club unless there was something valuable hidden there?"

Not hidden, Annie thought, simply stashed at the club for safekeeping. Something, obviously, he couldn't keep at home. The general was retired. He had no office. Perhaps the only places he could safely keep something he didn't want anyone (his wife?) to see would be at his golf club or at the library.

"It's quite odd," Pamela said darkly. "There is a clue. The general missed it, but I have it safe for him."

Annie blinked.

"My brother plays at Whalebranch," Pamela explained smugly, "and he was there yesterday afternoon right after the general discovered his locker had been broken into. The general's," Pamela explained carefully, "not my brother's. My brother's locker—"

Annie balled her hands into fists to keep from throttling Pamela. "Pamela, I get it. What happened to the general's locker?"

"It was broken into."

Annie took a deep breath, a very deep breath.

"Annie, are you hyperventilating?" Pamela asked with concern. "I've got some—"

"The general's locker!" Annie bellowed.

"But I've been telling you." Pamela's tone was aggrieved. "It was broken into—"

"When?" Annie was trying to juggle times in her mind. Laurel had hidden in the ladies' room at the library about seven-thirty.

Pamela's voice was patient. "Well, obviously nobody knows when it happened. I mean, then they'd know who did it. And they don't—"

Annie managed not to shout. "Pamela, tell me! When did they discover the locker was broken into?"

"Oh." Pamela tilted her head. "Well, I talked to Archibald—that's my brother—last night and he finished playing golf about four and that's when he was at his locker and the general came in from his round and he immediately wanted to know who'd broken into his locker. Archibald said the general was furious. He asked who'd been in the locker room and all that sort of thing. No one saw anyone besides the usual players, but"— she scrabbled in her carryall—"look what my brother found later, kicked under a bench. You know, those low benches—"

Annie nodded impatiently.

Pamela fished out a gallon-size plastic Baggie. Clearly visible beneath the clear plastic covering was an old-fashioned fan, bright red with a verse in white: "Speak low, if you speak love."

Annie managed not to hyperventilate. In fact, she would later recount to Max with pride her immediate response, which she attributed to a lifetime of reading detective fiction. With only a millisecond of hesitation, she reached out and grabbed the fan. "Oh, someone found it! I'm so pleased! Max told me he'd lost it at the club and I was simply heartbroken. Pamela, I'm so sorry. It has nothing to do with the mystery of the general's locker. Terribly sorry. I know how exciting it is to think one has found a clue." The brilliance of her smile was simply a reflection of her desperation. "But I will be forever and always in your debt. This fan"—Annie touched it to her cheek—"has the most tender memories for me. Dear Max gave it to me on our first wedding anniversary. To commemorate—oh, well, that is simply too personal, too intimate. But you have saved my heart from a grievous wound. God bless you." Annie bussed the bewildered Pamela soundly on both cheeks. And fled.

As she ran down the hall, the fan tight in her hand, she had a goal.

Laurel.

Chapter 4

Annie's cell phone rang.

"De—Hello." Some habits were hard to break.

"Annie." There was a hiss, then a crackle.

Annie smiled. "Hi, Max. Where are you?" She braked quickly for a mother duck marching across the dusty road, followed by—Annie counted—eight, nine, ten downy baby ducks, their light blond feathers glistening in the sun. "Be careful, Mom," she called as the car scooted past.

"What did you say?" There was the slightest edge of wariness in Max's voice.

"Your mother!" Annie exclaimed. "Max, we've got to do something. Lord knows what she's up to. But I can tell you that the general is not a man to cross." Annie turned onto the main island road, Gull Circle.

"What does Mother have to do with the general?" He sounded confused.

Quickly Annie related Pamela Potts's tale from the Whalebranch Club. And how she, quick-witted Annie, had divested Pamela of the fan. "And if that isn't a damning piece of evidence, what is?"

"Evidence of what?" Max had the familiar

defensive tone he often assumed when they discussed Laurel.

"Breaking and entering. Just like at the library." She made each word distinct, then jammed on her brakes. How had she managed not to see the cement truck lumbering along ahead of her? Maybe cell phones weren't such a good idea. She vowed to be extra vigilant. But she didn't punch the power button. "Look, Max, yesterday she was hiding in the ladies' room at the library—"

"Laurel would have absolutely no reason to push that vase off." Max sounded utterly confident. Almost. "I've never heard her mention the general. Besides, she isn't mechanical. She's—"

The rest of his sentence was lost in a roar of men's voices.

"Max, where are you?"

"Umm." Another shout went up.

"Max?"

"The Men's Grill at the Whalebranch Club. I'm not a member," he said quickly.

"Neither is Laurel," Annie said darkly. "The Men's Grill?"

"Well, actually there's a big-screen TV and Tiger Woods just hit a birdie on the fourth green at—"

Shouts. Yells.

"I thought you were looking for Samuel." Annie slowed to edge onto a traffic circle, which the island had created to emulate its upscale neighbor Hilton Head as traffic increased, and switched lanes to veer off onto Night Heron Drive.

"No luck. I came out here because he has a friend who caddies, but he hasn't seen him either. That's why I called. At the library yesterday, did you talk to Samuel?"

Annie had a quick memory of Samuel diving out of the way of her car and his grim expression. She'd thought then it was because of her driving skills. In light of the plummeting vase, she wasn't certain. But the memory included the dark, old-fashioned coupé—

Annie jammed her brakes again. The car slewed a little sideways.

"Annie. Annie?"

"Miss Dora," Annie said loudly.

"Not Miss Dora. Samuel!" Max sounded as frustrated as she'd felt earlier with Pamela Potts. Was there a message here? Annie devoutly hoped not.

"Miss Dora's car. Samuel was leaning up against it." Annie put the Volvo in reverse. "I just spotted the car. At the Painted Bunting. I'll check it out. Then I'm going to talk to Laurel. Max, get busy out there at Whalebranch. Talk to people about the general. See if you can pick up on any gossip about him. Bye." She clicked the "off" button. Of course, asking Max to pick up on gossip was rather like asking a nun to go to an R-rated movie. Max had the odd—to Annie—masculine disinclination to discuss people's private affairs. Of whatever sort.

Annie turned into the circular drive of the Painted Bunting Bed and Breakfast. The two-story white wooden house stood on brick pillars, affording a dusky, easily accessed basement. A wide piazza with slender Doric columns ran along the front and both sides. A curving staircase led up to the main entrance. A recently painted sign proclaimed: "Painted Bunting Inn, 1832." If unwary tourists assumed it had been an inn since then, that was fine with the proprietor, a plump, jovial widow from Ohio, Olivia Barclay.

Parked in the shade of a spreading live oak was the shiny blue-black coupé Annie remembered from the library yesterday. It had to be that coupé or its twin and surely there weren't two such old cars on the island. Annie stopped beside it. As she got out of her car, a young black man rose from a bench in the shade of a willow near a pond. He put a glass of lemonade on a rickety wooden table.

"Sam—" she began.

"No, ma'am. I'm Samuel's cousin, Reggie." There was no family resemblance. Reggie was tall, skinny, and wore thick-lensed glasses.

"Oh." Annie was standing in the sun. She joined Reggie in the shade of the willow. It didn't help much, but it helped a little. "Hi, I'm Annie Darling. I'm looking for Samuel," she said brightly. "Have you seen him?" No-see-ums swarmed around her. She swatted her hands futilely at the tiny little gnats with a blood lust on a par with Jack the Ripper.

"Nope. Something came up, I guess," he said vaguely. He flapped a bandanna at the no-see-ums. "Sammie's been driving Miss Dora. But she called my dad and asked if I could take her around for a couple of days. I'd just lost my job at the ice-cream store," he said forlornly. "They closed down because of a new frozen-yogurt place."

Annie would be forlorn, too. An ice-cream store sounded idyllic. It was, she decided, a true indication of character that she didn't abandon her efforts immediately and head to the new frozen-yogurt store. She was an equal-opportunity dessert eater. Instead, she studied Reggie.

Reggie looked hot, bored, and resigned. But not the least bit worried or uneasy.

"You didn't talk to Samuel?" she persisted.

"No, ma'am." He wiped his face. "If you see him, please tell him I got tickets to a concert this weekend in Savannah and I sure hope he can take this job back."

"I'll do that." Annie thanked Reggie and turned toward the inn.

When she stepped inside, she was thrilled to escape the no-see-ums but it was still sauna-hot. The overhead fan stirred the air enough that her damp blouse clung to her. The open doors at both ends of the hall offered another bit of breeze. The mahogany serving table in the hallway was pure Hepplewhite. The huge old grandfather clock had no doubt been built in Charleston. Her glimpse of the dining room with its Sheraton table was impressive. In fact, the B&B reeked of authenticity, but Annie felt she could happily have exchanged the picturesque flavor for some good old modern-day air-conditioning. Besides, wouldn't a window unit circa 1950 qualify as an antique?

"Annie! How nice of you to come by. Won't

you join Miss Dora and me for tea?" Olivia Barclay popped to her feet. Her curly dark hair frizzed in the moist heat and her cheeks were flushed.

The parlor was stifling. But Olivia's smile was so eager that Annie managed a cheerful grin in return and forbore hauling out the fan she'd pinched from Pamela and flapping it like a shipwrecked sailor sighting rescue.

"I'd love to." It wasn't even a half-truth. "Hi, Miss Dora. How are you?"

Miss Dora's black eyes surveyed Annie sardonically. "Splendid." The old monster didn't look the least bit uncomfortable despite the terrarium environment of the parlor, her ruched collar crisp, her sallow skin untainted by perspiration.

At least Olivia's cheeks flamed like beets and globules of sweat trickled down her face.

"The Darjeeling is especially fine," the old lady rasped, pouring a steaming cup.

Annie reached out, took the delicate Spode cup, tried to ignore the steam wafting toward her. Max owed her. Big-time. A week in Seattle? A remote cold cavern in Montana? Iceland?

Olivia thrust forward a silver tray with sugar and cream. Annie looked at the cream. It would cool the tea, but Annie equated cream in tea with nouvelle cuisine. Something for other people.

With a tight smile, Annie picked up the cream pitcher and splashed a jigger's worth into the teacup. She sipped. Even lukewarm was a burden. And for once tea sandwiches had little appeal. Annie had a tantalizing vision of frozen lime-green punch, the mainstay at Texas tea parties when she was little.

"So lovely of you, Annie, to join us." Miss Dora's dark eyes crackled with amusement.

Okay, she could be a well-bred southern woman. Ten minutes later, deep into a discussion of Miss Dora's charcoal drawings, Annie blurted, "Samuel's dad is looking for him."

Olivia Barclay's eyes blinked rapidly. She was too polite to inquire bluntly who the hell was Samuel, but she looked avidly from Annie to Miss Dora.

"Least said, soonest mended," Miss Dora observed as she pondered the sandwiches, apparently torn between an anchovy atop a dollop of cream cheese and chicken salad sprinkled with sliced almonds.

"Miss Dora," Annie said firmly. She waited until the old lady met her determined gaze. "Samuel's been your driver here on the island."

Miss Dora's wrinkled face drew down into an outraged frown. "I'm perfectly capable of driving."

Annie and Olivia waited.

"An infringement of my civil rights," she continued obscurely, "but I am helpless against the weight of the law."

"They didn't renew your license," Annie said bluntly.

If malevolent scowls were deadly, Annie would have been dust. As it was, she met Miss Dora's gaze stubbornly.

Miss Dora's crackling black eyes dropped first. "As I told the patrolman, my foot slipped. I pressed the accelerator inadvertently. To have my license revoked—it was an affront."

"So Samuel's been driving you." Annie carefully placed her cup, still almost full, well out of Miss Dora's reach.

"Sometimes." Miss Dora finished off the anchovy sandwich, retrieved the chicken-salad sandwich.

"He drove you to the library yesterday afternoon," Annie continued. "You were there—you and Samuel—when the vase fell."

"A vase fell?" Olivia exclaimed.

Annie could sum up the saga of the vase in succinct sentences which would have been the envy of Dorothy Parker.

Miss Dora downed two more sandwiches.

Olivia Barclay offered the tray with tarts and meringues.

Miss Dora smiled.

Encouraged at this evidence of good humor, Annie persevered. "The general called the cops. Why did you and Samuel leave?"

Miss Dora's clawlike hand maneuvered the silver serving implement beneath a pecan tart.

"Miss Dora, the police are looking for Samuel."

Miss Dora sniffed. "That Yankee. Who would listen to him?" The tart reached the plate.

"The police," Annie said patiently. "But they'll listen to Samuel, too. If you know where he is, tell him his dad wants him to come home. He'll go with Samuel to talk to the police. And Max will help."

"In Chastain, everyone knows the Kinnon family. Luther's mother worked for my Aunt Hattie. If a Kinnon says it's so, you know it's true." The words were indistinct—pecan tarts are chewy—but the dark eyes met Annie's gaze squarely.

It was obscure, rather like trying to transliterate Nostradamus. Annie was firmly convinced those prognostications were whatever anyone wanted them to be. But she thought she got the point.

"Chief Saulter is a good man." Annie and the Broward's Rock police chief went back a long way. "Miss Dora, the chief will treat Samuel fairly."

"Even though that man claims Samuel pushed over that vase? Claims it and he hasn't a smidgeon of evidence?" Miss Dora's voice lifted with outrage.

"Is that why you and Samuel left so quickly? Did you tell Samuel to lie low?"

But Annie knew she'd gone too far when Miss Dora hunkered her head down in her ruched collar like a turtle spotting a cottonmouth.

Annie backtracked. "Miss Dora, if you should happen to talk to Samuel"—she kept her voice casual—"please tell him he'll be okay with Chief Saulter. I guarantee it."

Miss Dora put down her fork, finished the last bite of her tart, and fixed Annie with a piercing gaze. It went through to the bone, eerily reminiscent of Patricia Wentworth's redoubtable Miss Silver appraising a client. "I have your word."

It should have been absurd. It wasn't.

Annie knew she could be no more committed had she sworn a blood oath. She repressed the urge to stand at attention and said only, "Yes, you have my word."

Annie popped to her feet, in a hurry now to flee the stifling room. Max would have to reward her for this exercise. Annie felt sure it was going to pay off. "Thanks for the tea. It's been a pleasure. So-o-o delicious, Olivia." It wasn't until she stepped into the hall that another thought struck her. She turned, looked intently at Miss Dora. "Why were you there?"

"Where?" There was an innocence to the single word.

"At the library. Yesterday evening." Why, indeed? It was the dinner hour. Surely an odd time for Miss Dora to visit.

Miss Dora cleared her throat. "Oh, just a reconnaissance. Looking for places to put my drawings." But the old lady didn't meet Annie's searching gaze. Miss Dora used her cane to lever herself upright. "Ah well, time for me to get busy. Such a pleasure, Olivia."

Miss Dora might be elderly, but she was out the door and summoning Reggie and on her way by the time Annie slid behind the wheel of the Volvo.

The old coupé spewed dust.

Annie rolled up her windows, put the air-conditioning on high. Like Hercule Poirot, she was given furiously to think.

"So dear of you, Annie, to come and see me. Such a delightful surprise," Laurel trilled as

102

she busied herself in her small kitchen, filling huge frosted goblets with iced tea.

Annie refused to take a guilt trip. As far as she was concerned, she and Max spent quite enough time with his mother. Time is measured by the intensity of the moment and any moment with Laurel was fraught with intensity. And stress. And bewilderment. And....

"'These most brisk and giddy-paced times,'" Laurel intoned. *"Twelfth Night,"* she added kindly.

Annie took the goblet, welcoming the sharp damp cold of the glass and drank lustily. After all, wasn't everything prone to be lusty in Shakespeare? As the icy, delicious tea revived her, Annie said, "Indeed." And moving right along, though not with high hopes, Annie attacked. "Was Miss Dora your lookout?"

Laurel beamed at her daughter-in-law. "Dear Annie. How inventive of you. 'If this were played upon a stage now, I could condemn it as an improbable fiction.'"

"Twelfth Night?" Annie asked sourly.

"One of my favorites. Oh, how that man could write about love." A pause. "And everything else." Laurel's husky voice was soft with awe.

Annie refused to be drawn into a discussion of Shakespeare's literary accomplishments. Instead, she put down her glass, grabbed her purse and pulled out the fan she'd retrieved from Pamela. She spread it open. "You dropped this at the Whalebranch Club. How did you get into the men's locker room?"

103

"A woman must go where a woman must go." Laurel smoothed back a strand of golden hair and fixed Annie with a beguiling gaze.

Annie was not beguiled. "Not Shakespeare."

Laurel's smile was gentle. "Of course not."

"Laurel." Annie could hear the note of desperation in her voice. "Please, tell me what's going on. Why did you rifle the general's locker at the golf club? And break into his cabinet at the library?"

"A Godiva chocolate, Annie?" Laurel wafted to her feet. She was so damn graceful Annie felt like a clod even though she hadn't moved a muscle. Stars and bars undulated as Laurel sped to the refrigerator. She returned bearing a crystal platter with a magnificent assortment of truffles.

Annie knew them all, of course. She spied the dark-chocolate raspberry truffle. Was it on a level of becoming a co-conspirator to accept the candy?

Some decisions are foreordained. It had been a long day. Short in hours, perhaps, but long in duration. Mmmm. A sense of well-being spread over Annie. After all, someday— metaphorically speaking—she would be but a pile of bleached bones. She took a second truffle.

"And so," Laurel said cheerfully, "are you ready for the festival?"

Not even the magical powers of chocolate could assuage the sudden nibble of panic. Oh God, the books, not even yet packed! Boxes were haphazardly strewn around the storeroom of Death on Demand. The festival opened at noon tomorrow with a trumpet fanfare. The bagpipe society marched at one o'clock. Mariachi players were scheduled at two and an oompah band at six. Irish leprechauns and Cherokee braves would be serving as runners for the booths. It would be a very American Fourth.

Annie lunged to her feet. Okay, okay. Laurel and Miss Dora could clever themselves right into the Broward's Rock jail. Fine. Be her guest.

"The festival—Laurel, I've got to run." But at the door she looked back. Laurel regarded her warily. "Laurel, don't break into anything. The general is not a nice man."

Laurel observed her with interest, her dark blue eyes thoughtful. Then she grinned, that insouciant smile that dared the world. "'I bear a charmed life.'"

Annie felt a prickle down her back. "Oh, God, Laurel, not *Macbeth!*"

Annie's back ached. She sneezed. Used books were always dusty. She tried Max's cell number one more time. No answer. Of course she'd left a message at his office. Didn't he pick up his messages? Not, a little voice whispered, when he was on the golf course.

She wasn't resentful. Of course not. She wanted Max to enjoy life. She slammed the last box of books onto the tarp at the back of the booth. Okay. Tomorrow Max could help her arrange the books. She shoved a box with her foot and the lid flipped open. The immediate pleasure wasn't as intense as chocolate, but spotting Dorothy Cannell's *Down the Garden Path* ran a close second. And tomorrow would be buckets of fun. Mystery lovers would descend, more eager for a book to complete a collection than Pam and Jerry North for a martini. Annie's merchant instinct quivered. The mystery lovers would be great, but even greater would be the curious, attracted by the name—Death on Demand. Some of them wouldn't have read a mystery since *The Footprints under the Window* or *The Secret of the Old Clock*. Did Annie have a message for them! The world was now in the very throes of the Second Golden Age of the Mystery and Annie was just the bookseller to acquaint these novice readers with their exciting future—new books and old by present-day masters of mystery Nancy Pickard, Gar Anthony Haywood, Cynthia Harrod-Eagles, Bill Crider, Gillian Roberts, Jeffery Deaver, Pat Benhke, William Bernhardt, Barbara D'Amato, Tony Hillerman, Earlene Fowler, and so many others. Once hooked, as most would be, they would come time and again—she looked around for notepaper, instead scrawled "Reorder Finney" on her palm—to plumb the incredible variety of mysteries available at Death on Demand. Annie gave a sigh of sheer happiness.

Piccolos sounded discordantly. Angry voices rumbled like distant thunder. Annie poked her head out of her booth, shaded her eyes against the blazing sun. Suddenly, harsh as a wounded bird, a piccolo squalled—long, flat, shrill. A group of people was bunched near the area that had been marked off as a small parade ground. At the edge, bystanders began to move, stepping back, turning away. Bud Hatch walked briskly out of the center of the clump. Even at the distance of a football field, Annie saw his swagger. Good old Bud, sharing his charm and good humor, no doubt. Well, this audience of one wasn't interested. She closed the last box, then checked to be sure the tarp was securely in place, just in case an ever-possible thunderstorm ushered in the Fourth. She nodded, satisfied that everything was ready for tomorrow. She stepped out of the booth into a scene that would appear frenzied and chaotic to an observer unfamiliar with the final hours before the opening of an outdoor festival.

Dust rose in clouds as volunteers dragged wooden tables over humpy ground. Hammers resounded as the last few booths were assembled. Henny Brawley stalked toward the forest preserve, moving faster than a Virgil Tibbs's karate chop. Henny's eyes glittered, and her mouth was a thin straight line.

Annie waved hello, but Henny didn't even see her. Henny dodged around the mobile food vans—hot dogs, hamburgers, pizza, tacos, gyros and wraps as well as cotton candy, saltwater taffy and funnel cakes—and plunged into the forest preserve.

Annie was hot and tired and ready to go home and plunge into the swimming pool, after, of course, greeting exuberant Dorothy L. and assuring her she was the most beautiful cat in the world with her arctic-white fur and gentian-blue eyes. Annie could do this because Agatha, who was resident queen of the bookstore, wouldn't hear a word of it. Each cat was the center of her own universe, imperious Agatha at the store, genial Dorothy L. at home, and please God the two would never meet again. When she and Max went on vacation, cat sitters came to the store and the house.

Annie looked toward the preserve. Another figure plunged out of sight on the forest path. So Jonathan Wentworth had seen Henny's distress. Annie took a step or two toward the parking lot, feeling the familiar old Jell-O sensation as the moist air rolled over her. Their swimming pool had never seemed more appealing. But if she intended to support Henny on the library board, now was the time to stand up and be counted. Obviously, Bud was up to no good again. If she joined Henny and Jonathan, it wouldn't be a quorum but they could make some plans. At the least, Henny could vent some steam. The high red flush of anger on her face wasn't good for her.

Annie swung around, hurried past the food trailers to a weathered gray wood that proclaimed "Lucy Banister Kinkaid Forest Preserve." Majestic loblolly pines swayed almost imperceptibly in the breeze. Annie ducked beneath a low branch of a magnolia, drew a deep breath of the sweet scent, and paused until her eyes adjusted to the soft gloom beneath the forest canopy of interlocking live oaks, magnolias, and slash pines. A rustle sounded to her right. The puffy white tail of a deer disappeared behind a curtain of royal ferns.

Annie was vaguely familiar with the terrain. Several paths, a couple of them boardwalks, led to a gazebo in the center of the preserve. Far ahead Annie heard a clatter on the boardwalk.

"Henny," she called. "Jonathan?"

A mourning dove burst from a tree limb. The dove's ooh-ooh-ooh combined with the frenzied attack of a pileated woodpecker on a nearby trunk to drown out her voice. No-see-ums swirled around her like the sports media spotting Martina Hingis. If it were anybody other than Henny, Annie thought grimly, as she ran lightly along the boardwalk, she would be out of here in a South Carolina second. She didn't outdistance the gnats. In fact, they seemed to think it quite sporting of her and billowed alongside in a wavering cloud. Hitchcock was off base with birds as villains. He should have picked swarms of nasty, pervasive, blood-sucking, unshakable gnats.

Annie's jog freeze-framed into statue stillness. She was about two feet from the snout of the biggest alligator she'd ever seen. Okay, maybe not the biggest, but God knew it was the closest. She came down softly on the balls of her feet. "Just passing through," she observed chattily. The reptile's unwavering gaze was more attention than Annie wanted. "Hope you are a papa, not a mama." Mother alligators protect their young for eighteen months and alligators can outrun humans for fifty yards. A dentist would love them as patients, with a minimum of seventy cone-shaped teeth that rip their prey. Annie moved slowly, softly, quietly. She didn't start breathing again until she was around the bend.

Yes, okay, she'd admit it, she was terrified of the black swamp kings. They were not sweet little animal friends. They were cold-blooded, huge, powerful beasts. She darted uneasy glances behind her, but the boardwalk remained empty. She continued to step lightly. Drooping palmetto palm fronds hung across the path. Yaupon holly and saw palmettos fought for space. Swaths of Spanish moss hung eerily still in the forest quiet. That faint breeze never reached the interior of the forest, though high above no doubt the crowns of the pines gently swayed. Annie felt as though she were hundreds of years from the present. Only the weathered wood walk beneath her feet testified to recent human presence. She felt an intruder in a world not meant for her. She peered forward. Something moved swiftly up the trunk of a huge live oak. Annie shivered as she recognized a red rat snake. She'd once attended a lecture where a naturalist referred to the red rat snake as handsome, proving that civilized people differ markedly in their enthusiasms.

Annie moved lightly on her feet and tried to avoid touching anything in her path. She tiptoed around a clump of saw palmetto as stealthily as Raffles slipping silently through the hallways of the rich, ready to crack yet another safe. Reaching out, she carefully pulled down the sharp, serrated frond of a saw palmetto and saw Henny in the preserves gazebo. She wasn't alone.

The weathered wooden gazebo afforded a superb view of a serene lagoon rimmed by cattails. Henny stared out at the still green pond, her eyes steely, her mouth set in a hard line, her angular shoulders hunched. Jonathan Wentworth, his handsome face grave and somber, stood beside her.

"I've got to do something this time." Henny's hands balled into tight fists. "I can't let Hatch get away with this. It was barbaric."

"Let it go, Henny." Jonathan's deep voice was grim. And commanding. He looked every inch a military man, his lined face stern and determined, his posture upright.

"Not this time, Jonathan." She was breathing fast, her cheeks spotted with red. "I came out here to decide what to do. If I have to, I'll cancel the pageant. Hatch is going to apologize—"

Annie lifted her foot. She looked down and saw a garter snake. She knew this was an environmentally helpful creature. But she couldn't move.

"No. Henny, listen to me." Jonathan reached out, gripped her shoulders. "It's dangerous to cross him."

"I don't care. Sometimes you can't look the other way. Sometimes you have to face down—" She broke off.

Wentworth's face, always seamed and weathered, turned to a stony mask. His hands slipped from her shoulders, hung straight beside him.

The garter snake slithered away. Annie's right foot came down. But she didn't move. There was something going on here that she didn't understand. But she knew pain when she saw it.

And so did Henny.

"Oh God, Jonathan, I'm sorry. I'm so sorry." Henny reached for his hands. Held them tight.

It was only an instant but it seemed an age, then Jonathan turned his hands to grip hers.

"Jonathan, please forgive me." Tears brimmed in Henny's eyes.

Annie took a step backward. This wasn't the time for her to intervene. And before she said a word to Henny, she needed to know what Hatch had done.

"There's nothing to forgive. But I want you to think about Hatch, about what he will do when he's angry. Henny, I want you to be safe." Jonathan's seamed face softened. He managed a half-smile.

They looked squarely at each other.

Henny stepped back, freeing her hands. "Do you?" Her voice was sharp. "But you're leaving me." Then she shook her head impatiently. "I'm sorry. That was uncalled for. I have no claim on you, Jonathan."

Once again, his face was stern. "No claim? You know better than that. All you have is my heart."

He held out his arms.

Henny looked at him with love and despair, then stepped into his tight embrace.

Gently, Annie let go of the saw palmetto frond. She moved quietly but quickly, especially once past the somnolent alligator.

It seemed ages since she'd set out to find Henny in the forest preserve, so it was disconcerting to regain the festival grounds and hear the high sweet tone of piccolos, the bang of hammers, occasional shouts, the clatter of metal chairs being stacked. Nothing looked different, but Annie felt very different indeed. She now possessed knowledge she didn't want to have. But it was none of her business. She'd never have occasion to mention it to a soul.

She reached her car, slid behind the wheel, gasping for air in the 100-degree-plus interior. She turned on the motor and the air-conditioning. Sweat oozed down her face, her back, her legs. The swimming pool—to dive into the cool, serene water.... Annie sighed, turned off the motor, got out, slammed the door.

Back on the festival field, she shaded her eyes in the late-afternoon sun. She saw several familiar faces: the director of the Red Cross, the president of the Chamber of Commerce, the assistant manager of her favorite grocery store, an interior decorator, the president of the Arts Council, the oldest member of the bird-watching club. Annie knew them, but not well enough to march up and demand what the hell had Bud Hatch done now. Then she saw Edith Cummings slinking alongside the bandstand, clearly escaping.

Annie slogged through the moist air. She reached the side of the library. The dusty path ahead was empty. Where could Edith have gone? Not even Houdini could already be out of sight.

Annie sniffed, then turned and ducked beneath a bricked arch into the musty darkness of the original basement. "Edith, for God's sake, snakes love dark places."

"So do I," came the acid response.

A heavy waft of smoke swept over Annie. She coughed.

"Nobody invited you," Edith snapped.

Annie took a careful step sideways. Something soft and filmy brushed her face. She jerked away. "Oh God, if it's a black widow—"

"Lady black widows have the right idea," Edith said with definite satisfaction. "Eat the jerk and keep his sperm, produce babies whenever. Of course, you may have disturbed a brown recluse which—"

"Edith, dammit, stop. What happened with Hatch and that crowd by the parade ground?" Annie scarcely breathed. Her muscles ached from the rigidity of her posture. She didn't want to disturb any creature that chose this musty dark region as its habitat.

"Oh, it was pure Hatch. I'd chose a black widow or a brown recluse over him any day." Edith's cigarette lighter flickered. Her deep-set eyes looked dark as caverns, her dark hair shimmered like a witch in firelight. "You know Toby."

It wasn't a question. "Sure." Broward's Rock was a small town. Anyone who knew Ned Fisher knew Toby Maguire.

"I will have to say the old bastard's got

guts." But Edith's voice quivered with disgust. "Toby's a hell of a big guy."

Indeed Toby was. Probably six-four, maybe two hundred and thirty pounds, mostly muscle.

"Anyway," Edith sighed, "Toby plays the piccolo. And he and some kids from the band and a lady from the music club dressed up in uniforms, different kinds, a Revolutionary War uniform and the War of 1812 and a cavalry officer. They were playing 'Yankee Doodle Dandy,' practicing an intro for the band concert."

A thick wave of smoke rolled over Annie. She still didn't move. She would rather asphyxiate than encroach on a web. "Hatch doesn't like piccolos?"

"Hatch doesn't like gays." Edith's voice was flat.

"Oh." Annie had an idea what was coming, but that didn't make it any more palatable.

"Macho man marched up to the flutists, barked out, 'Heroes have worn those uniforms. Don't let me see any of you dressed like that tomorrow.' It went from bad to worse. Toby told him to get lost and wanted to know who the hell Hatch thought he was. Hatch came back that he, by God, was a patriot and a man—unlike Toby." The lighter flickered again. Edith's face puckered in weariness and distaste.

"What did Toby say?" Annie asked reluctantly.

Edith was slow in answering. She spoke jerkily. "They shouted at each other. Hatch made some crack about maybe Toby wouldn't have been such a pansy if he'd ever worn a uniform like a man."

"Oh, Edith." Annie couldn't see the librarian, but she didn't have to. She heard the sadness and the pain in her voice.

"Yeah. But that's not the worst. The worst—" Edith broke off.

Annie waited.

Edith breathed deeply. "Toby stood there and all of a sudden I know he didn't see Hatch, he didn't see any of us. His face caved in. Have you ever seen a derelict building blown up? They fix the dynamite so the bricks all fall inward." Smoke spewed. "Shit." She drew another ragged breath. "I'm going home. They can take the frigging festival and—"

Feet scuffed.

Annie plunged after Edith. Out of the basement gloom, she blinked against the glare, then followed the librarian up the dusty path toward the parking lot.

"What happened then, Edith? What did Toby do? Was Henny there?" But Annie knew the answer to her last question.

Edith stopped beside a VW with a faded orange paint job spotted with darker orange rust, a crumpled left fender, and a tilted bumper.

Annie looked at it in awe. Restored, it belonged in a museum.

The VW windows were rolled down. Edith opened the squeaky door, flung herself behind the wheel.

Annie clapped her hands on the door.

"Ouch." She yanked her hands free, bent down to yell. "What happened then?"

The motor whirred. Edith's dark eyes glittered with irritation. "Leave it alone, Annie. Go watch one of those TV let-your-guts-hang-out shows. Or get a life."

"No. I have to know." She talked fast. "Edith, somebody has to do something about Hatch."

Dark eyes blinked. "Sweetheart, you're a nice girl. But you're out of your league." A tiny smile tugged at Edith's downturned mouth. "But, hey, why not? What can Hatch do to you? And maybe you'll annoy the hell out of him." She paused, shook free another cigarette. "My mouth feels like toasted shoe leather." But she lit the cigarette and sucked hard.

Annie kept quiet.

"All of sudden, like I said, Toby's face went slack. He got this glazed look. Like a bull that's been pricked and poked and he's bloody and hurt and doesn't know where to go or what to do and the goddamn pricks keep on coming. He shook his head and said real low and harsh, 'Mike was sitting right next to me. He grinned and told me someday he'd take me to the best barbecue in Memphis, in an alley across the street from the Peabody Hotel. It was the last thing he was ever going to say. The last. They blew his head off. He was still sitting there but he didn't have a head and blood was everywhere. Blood on my fatigues. Mike's blood.' Toby took his piccolo and held it up and blew and blew and blew and then he blundered away."

Annie had heard that high, shrill scream of

117

a piccolo. She shivered despite the heat. The VW jolted forward and she stood in the dust, staring after it.

A firefly glistened near the pittosporum hedge. Annie loved fireflies. But tonight she didn't announce the cheerful glow to Max. She rested in the crook of his arm and looked up at the blaze of stars. Occasionally he pushed his foot against the flagstone and the wooden swing moved back and forth. Moonlight turned the pool water a light jade. Cicadas rasped like rusted hinges. In the thick tangle of woods near the lagoon, a great horned owl gave its mournful cry.

"Max?" She clasped his hand in hers.

"Hmm?" He rested his chin against her head.

"Don't you wish we could be like The Saint?" Leslie Charteris's gallant protagonist Simon Templar was known as The Saint.

In his years with Annie, Max had learned much about mysteries, from arch criminal Dr. Fu Manchu to gentleman adventurer Bulldog Drummond. He took The Saint in stride. But he'd also learned caution. "Well, The Saint's quite a guy."

Annie sat up very straight. "You know how he talked about 'blipping the ungodly over the beezer'? I just wish—"

"Annie"—Max pulled her back into the circle of his arm—"that's fiction. We can't go around bashing Hatch. And you wouldn't want to. Not really."

"Well," she said grudgingly, "I know. I don't even like to squash palmetto bugs." It

118

still intrigued her that South Carolinians had given roaches—huge, waddling, aggressive roaches—such an attractive name. "But Hatch is making so many people miserable."

Max didn't reply. He shifted in the swing.

"Max?" They had been married long enough that Annie picked up on nonverbal cues.

"Yeah." His voice was worried. "It's a mess. It's certainly better than when Samuel was missing. Thank God Miss Dora told him to come to me. But I didn't tell you what Samuel said after we got out of Chief Saulter's office."

"I thought that went really well?" She peered at him in the soft darkness.

"Oh, it did. It did. Samuel made a good impression on the chief. I think that's all straightened out. Of course, somebody pushed that vase over—"

Annie had a fleeting memory of Laurel in the library ladies' room.

"—but the chief has an open mind. Yeah, that went fine. I had the feeling Samuel has his own ideas about who might have done it. But he knows what it's like to be accused of something he didn't do, so he's not going to throw somebody else's name out. That's okay. And he seemed absolutely convincing when he said he didn't shove the vase. That isn't what worries me. I took Samuel home and when he got out of the car—"

Faraway lightning crackled in clouds banked up to the south. A storm was moving up the coast toward Broward's Rock.

"—he said, 'Somebody's gonna kill that man, for sure.'"

Chapter 5

Annie stood at the edge of the festival ground looking for Henny. Everyone was in motion, a swarm of purposeful, peeling faces and tanned arms and legs crisscrossing the dusty ground. Men's deep voices and women's high voices made a human counterpoint to birdsongs and the chittering of insects and the rustle of palm fronds. Occasional rat-a-tat-tats came from every direction—beneath the bandstand, behind the food trailers, near the lagoon. Lady Fingers, of course. Annie sometimes wondered if Southern children were born with a packet of the tiny firecrackers clutched firmly in one hand. Every holiday called forth the minuscule explosions. The sounds melded into a dull, cheerful roar. Certainly the library could already count this venture a success. It looked as if everybody in town plus hordes of tourists were milling happily around the festival area.

But Annie's sense of disquiet on Henny's behalf wasn't assuaged. No matter how gloriously the festival succeeded, the library board would meet next week and clearly the general intended trouble. Henny needed to know she had Annie's support. Annie shaded her eyes. Was that Henny over there by the lemonade stand?

A sticking, tearing, crunchy sound erupted behind her. Annie swung around.

Samuel Kinnon leaned close to one of the

redbud trees that lined the east side of the festival ground.

Annie moved close. "Hi, Samuel. Velcro?"

Samuel paused in his effort to loop a two-inch band of Velcro around the trunk of a redbud. "Hi, Mrs. Darling." His broad face eased into an impish smile. "I asked Miss Dora why we didn't just bang a nail and hang the drawings. She acted like I wanted to drive a stake into Bambi's heart."

At Annie's clear lack of comprehension, Samuel added, "Living things. Trees, too." He was deft, the Velcro circle quickly complete. Then a plastic-covered sketch with Velcro taped to its back was pressed in place.

"Oh, yes, of course." Annie tipped her head to one side to view the drawing. It hung with one side lower than the other. Even askew, the charcoal radiated serenity: an aristocratic woman in a silk dress perched on a wooden stool, her sketchbook in her lap.

Samuel adjusted the Velcro band, righting the picture. "The trunk's still wet from the rain."

Ah, last night's late rain. It was still humid, but the sun shone from a pastel-blue sky without a single cloud. A perfect day for a festival.

A festival, Annie realized with a grin, that was going to be treated to a superb display of Miss Dora's charcoal sketches, despite Bud Hatch's opposition. Annie was impressed with the method of display. Certainly no one could accuse Miss Dora of damaging the environment. Annie peered closely at the bottom of the painting.

A raspy voice at her elbow announced, "Miss Alice." There was reverence in Miss Dora's tone. "One of Charleston's great watercolorists, Alice Ravenel Huger Smith. Spanish moss, a rice field at sunrise, the black waters of cypress swamps—no one ever captured the shift of light and shadow with greater felicity."

"Yo," came a brusque shout, "Fisher."

Annie's head jerked. Samuel's big hands gripped the portfolio of paintings. Only Miss Dora remained oblivious, with a clawlike finger to her cheek, surveying the line of redbuds.

A temporary arbor wrapped in red-white-and-blue bunting marked the entry to the festival grounds. Bud Hatch strode out of its shadow, his head at an arrogant angle, his hands clasped behind his back.

Ned Fisher stopped on the third step of the temporary bandstand by the lagoon. From the back, he looked young and vulnerable, a swallowtail coat bunching over his narrow shoulders, garishly striped pants flapping against thin legs, a crisp Uncle Sam hat riding high on his thick hair. Slowly, he turned. His shoulder-length hair, curling under the tall hat, was touched with gold by the sunlight, an odd contrast to the arctic white of the artificial beard. But the costume had no power to re-create Uncle Sam's clear, sharp visage that beckoned generations of Americans to service. Instead, the fake beard underscored the poignant gentleness of Fisher's features—a high forehead with deep-set eyes, smooth cheeks, a pleasant mouth. A boyish face. But in the sharp July sunlight Fisher's face was pale beneath the jaunty hat, a pasty white like a time-bleached figurine unearthed in an attic corner.

Hatch lifted his arm in a peremptory gesture.

The library director remained on the third step, staring across the dusty ground. A general hubbub enveloped the festival grounds, trumpets and drums and the occasional squeal of a bagpipe, the clang of metal from food trailers, the flap of canvas awnings at the booths, shouted directions and instructions, the throaty oompah of a lone tuba, the caw of excited blackbirds hoping for crumbs, the rattle of Lady Fingers.

But Annie felt caught up in a bubble of intense silence that encircled the general and the director. It must have been only a few seconds, but the time stretched like film played out in slow motion.

Beneath the bulky coat, Fisher's chest heaved like a swimmer at the end of a race. Then he ducked his head, the tall hat wobbling, and came jerkily down the steps. He crossed the dusty ground to face the general.

Hatch spoke. Whatever he said, it was short and crisp.

His face bleak, Fisher listened, nodded once, and turned away. He walked fast, head down, the tall hat tilting.

"Somebody"—Samuel's voice was soft and deep in his throat—"is gonna kill that man."

Annie reached out, grabbed his arm. "Don't,

Samuel. Don't say that! It's"—she thought of the three witches in Macbeth—"it's bad luck."

"Bad luck!" Samuel glowered. "I'd like to bad-luck him."

Miss Dora cleared her throat. "Samuel, I believe we'll put the Nell Graydon drawing by the sign to the forest preserve. That would please my cousin. She did so love books."

Annie glanced at the sketch in Miss Dora's hands, a sweet-faced woman and a stack of books, the titles clearly legible: *Tales of Edisto, Another Jezebel, Tales of Beaufort* and *Tales of Columbia.*

"One of South Carolina's finest authors," Miss Dora said with satisfaction. "Of course, I didn't put in all of her books, simply my favorites."

That was then; this was now. Annie shook her head impatiently. "Miss Dora—"

"When there is unpleasantness," Miss Dora said firmly, "gentility will prevail."

"Miss Dora, I admire the sentiment." And she did. "But—"

"Should we permit a boorish Yankee to destroy the joy of this day?" Miss Dora's dark eyes challenged Annie and Samuel.

"No way, Miss Dora." Samuel's deep voice boomed.

Miss Dora looked at Annie.

A South Carolina woman to the core, Annie wished she had a banner to wave or a picture hat to toss. Lacking props, she simply stood straight and said firmly, "Gentility will prevail." Definitely a motto with élan.

Miss Dora's thin lips curved in an unexpectedly sweet smile. "Good girl." She looked toward her big helper, "Come, Samuel, we've work to do."

Annie watched the big young man and the diminutive elderly lady, as always attired in a voluminous black dress, cross the hummocky ground. Samuel's hand hovered protectively near Miss Dora's elbow.

Annie smiled, then glanced at her watch. The program opened at noon with a trumpet fanfare, an official welcome from Henny, a report on library programs from Ned Fisher, a concert by the high school band. Throughout the day, costumed volunteers were reenacting particular historical events in short vignettes repeated every half hour. Annie decided to open her booth after the program. Max was arriving with a calculator and change box soon.

Annie shifted a jug of iced tea from one hand to the other and headed for the food trailers, continuing to scan the crowd for Henny. It was only wise—not piggy, as some might say—to stock up for the long, hot, hungry afternoon. Much as she loved to sell books—and wouldn't that paperback of A. B. Guthrie Jr.'s *Murders at Moon Dance* thrill some Western fan—she loved to do so in air-conditioned, well-fed comfort. She couldn't do anything about the muggy heat, but she didn't have to starve. She picked up a basket of fried clams, a sack of boiled peanuts, and a chef's salad (for Max). She virtuously resisted cotton candy, but grabbed a couple of Moon Pies, purely for a late-afternoon energy kick. If Max didn't want his, well, it wouldn't do to save it because of the heat. She curved around the south end of the festival ground, admiring the Points of Patriotism and the Gallant Women of South Carolina.

The historical vignettes were presented on small stages arranged in a semicircle on the south end of the huge empty area behind the library. The booths, selling everything from books to potted plants to quilts to jams and jellies, were tucked between the backs of the stages and the parking areas. The temporary bandstand rose at the opposite end of the long field in front of the lagoon. The fireworks would be shot off after dark from a raft in the middle of the lagoon. Food stands lined the front of the forest preserve to the west. This left plenty of room between the stages to the south and the bandstand and lagoon to the north for families to spread out picnic blankets or set up folding chairs for the concert and, after dark, the pièce de résistance, the culmination, the finale: fireworks to rival the Braves winning a World Series.

Annie's mind felt like a patchwork quilt, gaily decorated with smidges of vivid history, before she had walked even halfway around the semicircle of low stages where volunteers in period dress recalled danger and combat: the Yemassee Indian uprising in 1715, the Revolutionary War, the War of 1812, the War Between the States, World War I, World War II, Vietnam. Woven through and around the battles and the marches were the stories of South Carolina women—daughters, wives, mothers, widows, teachers, authors, nurses in peace and war, doctors, abolitionists, couriers, naturalists, preservationists, artists, musicians, farmers, sculptors, athletes....

It was easy to forget that every act depicted in a history book was the result of human effort and emotion and that those long-ago men and women laughed and cried, loved and lost, and each of them once knew the feel of a hot July sun on living skin.

Annie paused at the tableau honoring Lieutenant Juanita Redmond, Army nurse on Bataan and Corregidor in World War II and later acting chief of the Air Force Nurses Corps. Lieutenant Redmond, her red hair curling from beneath her helmet, her khaki uniform stained and dirty, knelt by a wounded soldier in dusty Malinta Tunnel on Corregidor.

Annie almost stepped forward to visit with Gail Oldham, but the look of pain and despair on Gail's pale freckled face wasn't simply a festival volunteer's portrayal of Lieutenant Redmond's harrowing experiences in the Philippines.

A trumpet fanfare trilled.

Gail Oldham stared emptily at the rumpled blanket over a still form on the stretcher.

Annie looked toward the bandstand. Henny climbed the steps, moving swiftly, as always. Her crisp white blouse was a bright contrast to the red and blue stripes of her swirling cotton skirt. Her broad-brimmed straw hat sported a wide red-white-and-blue-striped band. On

127

the stage, she lifted her hat and thrust it high in a jaunty wave.

Cheers. Shouts. And, of course, the staccato of firecrackers.

It should have been a moment of triumph for a woman who'd spent countless hours creating a magnificent spectacle for her community. Henny smiled, but it wasn't her joyous, scintillant, first-jonquil-of-the-spring smile. It was a measured, on-demand, requisite smile.

Damn Hatch. Annie wished she'd found Henny before the program began. If nothing more, she could have given Henny a hug. Hugs help hearts heal. Over the sea of tiny waving flags—and plenty of Laurel's fans—Annie tried to catch Henny's eye. Their gazes connected for an instant. Annie balanced her food and the thermos of tea in the crook of her left arm. She held up her right hand, fingers clenched, thumb up. Henny's practiced smile widened for an instant, then her glance moved on.

Kids darted past, scuffing up dust. Mothers called out. Dads instructed. Teenagers sauntered. Tourists took photographs. Annie ducked a wobbling cone of cotton candy and took a step toward the small stage. Gail offered a leaflet to a harried-looking woman herding a gaggle of Brownies. Trust Henny to plan well: a moment of history onstage, a handout for anyone interested in more than a snippet.

The trumpets sounded again. Gail winced, pressing thin fingers against her temple.

Another group stopped by the stage, hiding Gail from view.

Annie turned away. This wasn't a good time. Later today she would catch Gail on a break.

Annie struggled against the flow of the crowd as people streamed toward the bandstand. Reaching the double row of booths, which faced the small stage, Annie stopped in surprise. Booth number 3. Yes, that was hers. Why were all those people thronging around the booth? Then she saw people moving away, clutching plastic bags emblazoned with the Death on Demand dagger. Why, Max must be selling books faster than the Green Hornet gas-gunning bad guys!

Annie wiggled through the crowd, ducked beneath a flap. She dropped the provisions on a flap of canvas. She slid onto the empty chair by Max and smiled up at an eager customer. "May I help you?"

Over the loudspeaker, Annie caught snatches of Henny's welcome, "...great history of the great state...malaria and yellow fever...women who vowed...fastest-growing area in the United...accord thanks to the members of the library board and to our wonderful volunteers...Points of Patriotism and the Gallant Women of South Carolina..." heard an inaudible murmur that had to be Ned Fisher's report (the Death on Demand customers really picked up then) and the high school band's grand beginning with "America, the Beautiful." Annie sold books and blinked back tears. Why did that song always make her want to cry?

Later, she snarfed down her cold but still delicious fried clams. She only vaguely heard the mariachi serenade. At one point, there was a blur of blond hair, a sweet smile, and a fan dropped onto the counter. Annie glanced at the quotation: "Fortune brings in some boats that are not steer'd." Annie frowned, decided to ponder it later. By the time she looked up, Laurel was lost in the crowd. But she couldn't get into any trouble passing out fans with quotations from Shakespeare. Could she?

The festival was a bookseller's paradise. In the past, Max had occasionally made comments about the quiet pleasure involved in selling books, how intellectually stimulating yet relaxing. Exchanging scarcely a word except for frantic inquiries about the whereabouts of titles, they sold an entire set of Harry Kemelman's Rabbi David Small books, a first edition of *Jamaica Inn* by Daphne Du Maurier, assorted titles by Mary Higgins Clark, Dick Francis, Dorothy Gilman, and Elizabeth Peters. There were the usual erudite shoppers:

"I'm shocked you haven't read Elliott Paul's *Hugger-Mugger in the Louvre!*"

"Hilda Adams certainly wasn't interested in Inspector Patton romantically."

"In New Orleans, I wouldn't bother with dinner at Antoine's but I'd definitely have my hair done by Claire Claiborne."

"Lisa Saxton's new baseball mystery series outscores all the competition."

"If I could be any woman in a mystery series, I'd pick Selwyn Jepson's Eve Gill."

130

• • •

However, not everyone belonged to the mystery freemasonry. A thin-nosed woman sniffed, "All those books about murder. Don't you have any literature?"

A Speak Your Mind begged to be said: You aren't conversant with mysteries? (Mild shock evinced at such cultural deficiency.) Then, of course, you are unaware that mysteries are the modern equivalent to the medieval morality play. (The last in a gently patronizing tone.)

However, Annie resisted, replying simply, "The jams and jellies are up that way. Right next to the Coke-bottle sculptures."

The woman moved away, her face puzzled.

Max grinned.

Annie said virtuously, "I didn't say she was an idiot, now did I?" She retrieved the Moon Pies, generously offered one to Max. "So now you see what it's like to be a bookseller."

Her handsome husband looked skeptical. "Well, of course, it is a holiday—"

Annie picked up the message immediately. "Max, since you've enjoyed this afternoon so much, I'm sure you'd like to work in the store on Saturdays in the summer."

Max was too busy eating his Moon Pie to say another word.

Annie finished her delicious concoction of peanuts, fudge and marshmallows. Of course, she'd been counting on two. Max never ate that kind of candy. She shook the iced-tea jug. "Empty! I'll go get some root beer."

Max opted for more tea. Annie hurried to the food trailers. She was stricken to find a "Sold Out" sign on the Moon Pie box.

"Annie." The voice combined steely determination with relief.

She turned.

Henny's cheeks flamed a fiery red. Not from the sun. She took off her straw, fanned herself. "I need Max. Look over there." She pointed toward the semicircle of stages.

The crowds had thinned in the late afternoon. Bud Hatch waited until his view was unobstructed, then quickly photographed the volunteers, beginning with the Yemassee Indian War.

"Oh, I guess he's going to take pictures of the—"

Henny's hat flapped. "Watch."

Hatch, finished at the first stage, moved past the tribute to Colonial women symbolized by Judith Manigault, adjusted his lens at the third display, the Revolutionary War.

Annie started to speak, then stopped. She got it. Hatch was taking photographs all right. He was making a record of the historical moments. But not the historical moments that focused on South Carolina women. Only the Points of Patriotism.

Annie forgot about Moon Pies. "What a jerk. Of course, I guess it's vintage Hatch. But I heard your speech at noon. You thanked everybody for participating, the Points of Patriotism, all that. You included everybody."

"Yes." Henny's dark hair was touched with silver and dust. She wore too much makeup for a hot July afternoon, makeup that attempted to hide the dark smudges beneath her eyes, smooth out the tight lines by her mouth. "I don't know what's going to happen." She drew in a sharp, hard breath.

For the first time in the years Annie had known Henny, there was a tone of defeat in the sharp voice.

"But"—the dark eyes glittered—"I won't have women demeaned by Hatch. Not now. Not ever. The volunteers have worked so hard. It's been the greatest celebration of women's lives in the history of Broward's Rock. Please, Annie, ask Max if he'll photograph the women's presentations. There's no one else I can ask." She thrust a camera case at Annie.

Ned Fisher walked past, going fast, his face shiny with perspiration, his long hair limp. He carried his Uncle Sam hat, now smudged and crumpled.

Henny saw the glance. She quickly shook her head. "Not Ned. I can't do anything else to jeopardize his job. Hatch has no power over Max."

Jonathan Wentworth was coming up behind Henny. He stopped to catch an errant beach ball, hold it out to a little boy. Annie didn't mention Jonathan. She doubted that she would ever mention Jonathan Wentworth to Henny.

"Sure, Henny." She grabbed the camera. She looked back once. Henny was pointing again toward the small stages, talking fast. Jonathan Wentworth stood beside her, his head bent as he listened.

Back at the booth, Max agreed almost too willingly. Maybe he wasn't cut out to be a book-seller. "We few, we happy few...." She broke off the quotation in her mind. No. Absolutely not. She was not influenced by Laurel, not one whit.

Deep shadows quickly spread across the food stands. Annie wished the Death on Demand booth were closer to the forest preserve. Absently, she picked up one of Laurel's fans and swooshed hot air over her face. Max was quickly making the circuit of stages, snapping pictures. Annie sold *Death of a Dunwoody Matron* by Patricia Houck Sprinkle to a charter-boat captain, *The Hotel Detective* by Alan Russell to a museum curator, *Murder on the Iditarod Trail* by Sue Henry to a tennis pro, *Dead in the Cellar* by Connie Fedderson to a million-dollar-club real estate agent, and *Fat-Free and Fatal* by Jacqueline Girdner to a barber. Annie stashed the money in the metal box and delighted not only in the variety of mysteries but the variety of her clientele. Oh, what a wonderful way to—

"Hi, Annie." The conventional greeting, but David Oldham pushed the words through his teeth like Sergeant Buck greeting Grace Latham. His face wasn't wooden, though. He looked like a kid who'd lost his dog, his eyes red-rimmed, his lips pressed together hard to keep from trembling. He lifted a shaking hand to push back a lock of sandy hair.

"Hi, David. How—" She couldn't ask how he was. He wasn't good. Anybody could see that. Almost never at a loss for words, she simply sat there and stared upward.

"You got any Eric Ambler books?" But he wasn't looking at the books ranged behind her. Instead, he looked toward the stages. To be precise, David Oldham looked at one particular stage, empty now except for the props: the grainy cement wall of Malinta Tunnel; the pallet for a wounded soldier; stained pieces of gauze and a dented steel helmet, the white cross painted on it so long ago barely visible.

Annie carefully did not look toward the place where Gail Oldham should be. "I think so." She busied herself checking the top of the makeshift shelving. "Yes, here we go." She faced him, held out *The Light of Day,* one of her all-time favorites, and *A Coffin for Dimitrios.*

David rubbed the side of his narrow face. Now his lips did quiver. Tortured eyes sought Annie. "This morning—when you called Gail—" He stopped, his breath coming rapidly.

Annie's eyes widened. "But David," she blurted out without thinking, "I didn't call Gail this—"

His head jerked up. His eyes flared. He whirled away, broke into a stumbling trot.

Annie still held out the Ambler novels. A shirtless, sun-burned, boisterous group of teenage boys swaggered across the ground, blocking out her view of the empty stage. When they'd moved on, she couldn't spot David Oldham.

Annie's heart thudded. Oh God. When

would she learn to think before she spoke? But how could she have known? Obviously, someone called Gail this morning and when David asked who the caller was, Gail said it was Annie. But it wasn't. Gail had lied. She lied to her husband.

Annie shoved the Ambler books back in place. Where was Max? She craned her neck. The stages were empty now, even the props cleared away. The presentations were done. Festivalgoers were appropriating the spaces, spreading blankets to enjoy picnics at a remove from the ants. She had to find Max, have him take over in the booth. But it was almost five. What did a few more minutes matter? Annie picked up the "Closed" sign, put it on the counter. She slid out of the booth, clutching the money box. She lowered the overhead awning and all the while she scanned the crowd.

She had to find Gail. Warn her that her husband knew she'd lied. It wasn't a task she relished.

Annie checked again for Max. She could give him the change box. No Max. And there was Hatch, his camera sheathed in its leather carrier. He glanced at his watch and walked briskly toward the food trailers. So even Hatch could succumb to hot dogs.

But the general didn't join any of the lines. Instead he slipped between the gyro and popcorn stands.

Annie frowned. The late-afternoon heat pulsed like layers of hot-water bottles, sticky, clammy, sweaty. Behind the food stands lay the tangled woods of the forest preserve. It wouldn't be any cooler in there, simply a quieter, heavier, danker heat. But maybe the general wasn't seeking a cool spot. If people wished to meet unobserved, the gazebo in the preserve was an obvious choice. Annie doubted the general was on a nature tour.

Whom was he meeting? And was it any of her damn business?

Across the festival ground, David Oldham, head rigid, back stiff, walked methodically from one group to another, paused, looked, walked on.

Her mind felt like leftover fried mush. Maybe she was jumping to conclusions. The general could be going into the preserve to meet anybody. Surely not Gail. But if it was, maybe Annie could intercept Gail, tell her that David, a very upset David, was looking for Gail to find out who had called her that morning.

Annie shaded her eyes, scanned the festival. She didn't spot Gail's bright red hair anywhere. All right. The only thing to do was go in the preserve. Maybe the general was in there communing with his cold-blooded brothers, the black swamp kings. Maybe he just wanted to get away from the crowds for a while.

But Annie had looked for Gail and David Oldham was looking for Gail. Where was she?

Annie started toward the forest preserve, heard the jangle of change in the metal box. She glanced up the line of booths, put on a burst of speed. Already sweating—even the slightest exertion threatened meltdown—

she skidded to a stop in front of Sharon Gibson's booth.

She'd last seen Sharon in a grocery aisle, glaring at the general. "Hey, I'm glad to see you. I thought you weren't going to set up at the festival." Oh, damn! What a thing to say. Maybe it was time for a personally directed Speak Your Mind: Shut up, stupid!

Sharon managed a weary smile. "My dad thought I should. I'd already paid for the booth. And it's been swell." She brushed back a strand of pale blond hair. The smile slipped away, leaving her finely chiseled face tense and remote.

"Sharon, could you do me—"

The loudspeaker thrummed. Edith Cummings's voice cut sharply over the festival hubbub. "Ned Fisher. Ned Fisher. Report to the bandstand." It was a quick, harsh, somehow urgent summons.

Annie wondered what catastrophe threatened. She knew Edith's voice well enough to be sure something of import was up. But, for once, it couldn't involve the general.

Sharon toyed with the top fan in a stack. "Awfully nice of your mother-in-law. She gave me a bunch for free. They've been very popular." She motioned over her shoulder with the fan. "And we've sold all of her wooden cutouts. You know, the Statue of Liberty." A faint grin. "Statues of Liberty with quotes from Shakespeare. Guaranteed unique."

"Laurel is unique." Annie was proud of her tone, pleasant, nonjudgmental, if a trifle dry. So why the sudden dimple in Sharon's cheek? "Anyway," Annie said hurriedly, "I'm glad you've had a good day. I need—" She couldn't very well announce she did not want to be burdened with a jingling change box because she intended to plunge into the recesses of the forest preserve in pursuit of a man Sharon loathed. "Could you keep my change box for me for a few minutes?"

Sharon glanced at her watch. "I've got to go pick up my mother pretty soon." A fine line creased her forehead. The hand holding the fan tightened until the knuckles were white. "She shouldn't come. She shouldn't!"

Annie looked at Gail in surprise. "Why not? Is she sick?" Emily Wentworth was always a bundle of energy and a popular worker for several island charities. Annie had also heard she was just this side of vicious at the bridge table.

"Sick?" Sharon didn't meet Annie's gaze. She stared down at the fan. Slowly she let the fan drop on the counter. "No. Oh, no. She's fine. But she's not much for Fourth of July celebrations." A quick, meaningless smile. "Anyway, as per usual when she decides to do something, one of her retainers must be on hand. And dad's busy, so I'm the lucky one. I have to pick her up in about half an hour. You won't be long?"

"Not long at all." Annie plunked down the change box and sped away. She was moving fast, but no faster than Edith Cummings and Ned Fisher as they cut through the booth area. Edith was gesturing emphatically to Ned. As they swerved toward the parking lot, too absorbed to see Annie, Ned said, "Oh, Christ, what else can happen today!" He no longer wore his Uncle Sam hat and his coat hung open over trousers rolled to mid-calf.

Annie knew her own clothes were not objects of designer envy at this stage of the festival—spatters of red sauce on her pink blouse (fried clams without sauce would be an absurdity) and a splotch of chocolate on her skirt. In fact, she felt unutterably grubby and more than a little disgruntled. She reached the entrance of the forest preserve.

No-see-ums. Alligators. Snakes. Of course, snakes. They lived in there—sluggish, fat brown cottonmouths, sleek copperheads, testy rattlesnakes (Step on me and I'll fang you quick.) That didn't even count all the dangerous spiders dangling in their webs. Dammit, if Gail was stupid enough to plan a rendezvous with the biggest bully on the island.... Annie's irritation melted like a Moon Pie left on a July picnic table.

Bully.

Gail's misery-laden face rose in Annie's mind. And another picture too: David Oldham inexorably searching, searching.

"Why did I have to be Little Miss Tell-Everything-You-Know?" Annie said aloud.

No-see-ums swirled around her.

Annie swatted at them futilely and plunged into the preserve. She walked softly, as much in fear of disturbing a poisonous creature as attempting to be stealthy. She tiptoed past the spot where she'd seen the alligator yesterday. A log moved in the dark brown water. But logs don't move. Annie held her breath, slid around the curve. It was dim in the late-afternoon forest, the sun too low to pierce the forest canopy. Spanish moss hung still and straight. A sudden flutter and patches of white marked the swoop of a mockingbird to snag a garter snake. Annie cringed, then moved ahead. Despite the windless quiet, leaves rustled on a live-oak branch. Annie looked up at a pink-nosed, dark-eyed, weasel-faced creature with an oddly misshapen furry body. Squinting, Annie distinguished tiny claws and tails, baby possums clinging to their mother's silvery back. The mother possum hissed, then moved slowly along the branch to the trunk and crawled out of sight. Annie passed the tree with a nervous glance, although Mom Possum was probably equally reluctant to further their acquaintance. A few more feet and Annie reached the clearing where the gazebo stood. She stopped behind a saw palmetto. Cautiously, she pulled down a sharp-edged frond.

Gail Oldham stood at the base of the gazebo steps, looking up, her face almost unrecognizable, her eyes bulging, her skin suffused with red, her mouth rigid.

Bud Hatch leaned against the pillar by the railing to the stairs, his arms crossed. "Don't make it worse for yourself, Gail." His voice was cool, mocking. His strong-boned face looked dispassionate. But a vein throbbed in his temple.

"I won't do it." Gail's voice was thick.

"Oh, you will. You will unless—"

A branch cracked behind Annie.

The man and woman in the clearing didn't hear it. Pulsing anger thrummed blood in their ears.

Annie jerked around.

David Oldham stood only a few feet from her. The pallor of his face was shocking. His eyes glowed with a vivid brilliance. He stumbled toward her, gripped her arm with fingers that bruised.

"—you want me to mention that birthmark to your husband. The little pink one that looks like a heart and in such a—"

David drew his breath in as if he'd been slammed in the chest. His hand fell away from Annie as if his fingers were suddenly nerveless. He wavered on his feet. He turned and moved heavily away.

Annie released the saw-palmetto frond. She didn't listen to the harsh voices in the clearing. She listened to the swish of footsteps on dried pine needles, listened until that alien rustle was gone and there were only the sounds of the evening forest, the crackle of twigs, the varied birdsongs, the faint rat-a-tat of a woodpecker.

To lie on a blanket under the summer stars with Max and listen to Sousa marches was among Annie's favorite pursuits, even though this was a blanket in a very public place which precluded their very favorite pursuit.

Max reached for her hand just as she reached for his. Nice timing. Nice life. Nice evening except not even a stirring Sousa

142

march could banish the underlying melancholy. Annie wished she could revel in the night and the stars, the music and the celebration. It was all Hatch's fault. Or, if not his fault, certainly the ugly events flowed from him, his rude summons to Ned Fisher and that dreadful encounter between Hatch and Gail Oldham in the forest preserve.

"Penny for your thoughts." There was the faintest hint of concern in Max's almost casual question.

If ever Annie counted the reasons why she loved Max, empathy might be at the very top. She'd been very quiet all evening. And, as Max and the world knew, quiet was not her natural state.

But she didn't want to tell Max about the forest preserve. He liked David and Gail Oldham. They'd played doubles together and sailed. She sighed and squeezed Max's hand. "Oh. This and that. Hatch is such a jerk."

"Out of the mouths of babes," a weary voice observed. Edith Cummings pointed at a silver thermos poking out of their picnic basket. "I don't suppose you've got martinis in there?"

"It's against the rules." Annie pointed to the back of the festival program. Red type boxed with large asterisks announced, "PROHIBITED: Smoking, Firearms, Alcohol, Dogs, Boom Boxes, Unsupervised Fireworks." The latter was apparently included more in hope than in expectation, as Lady Fingers exploded from every direction in an almost constant sputter along with occasional larger bangs.

Edith flapped her hands in dismissal. "Void. Null and void."

"Why so?" Max inquired, his voice amused.

"A regulation which overlooks an entire category of pests would obviously be ruled deficient. Prima facie," the librarian pronounced didactically. "What causes trouble? Not dogs. Not boom boxes. Not even guns, though I hate to parrot the National Rifle Association, an organization that I do not admire."

Annie got it. "People," she cried. "You want to prohibit people."

"Give the lady a silver dollar. Although if I had a silver dollar, I'd use it to buy a drink. Okay, a quarter of a drink. If Alan Greenspan wants to get serious about inflation, why doesn't he address the cost of a drink?" She peered down at them forlornly. "No whiskey? None at all? Maybe a beer tucked in your cooler, frost beading the can?"

Annie rattled the program.

"Jeez, you don't get a silver dollar. You get a merit badge. And you can wear it in your hair. Guaranteed to get attention." Edith peered through the dusk. "Those Chinese lanterns don't give a lot of light, do they? I can't see a damn thing."

Pastel-colored lanterns swayed in a faint breeze. They were strung in trees around the periphery of the festival ground. The lanterns were a lovely idea, but as Edith accurately observed, they gave very little illumination. The dusky gloom of the festival field was emphasized by two big spotlights beaming up toward the corners of the bandstand. Those brilliant swaths of light threw the bandstand into sharp relief. A bedraggled Ned Fisher stood at the top of the stage-right steps as the band thundered to a climax. Annie's foot kept time and she whistled "Stars and Stripes Forever."

"Sometimes I think Fitzgerald had the right idea. Just carry a silver flask wherever—" Edith poked her head forward to survey sprawled groups on beach blankets. "Hey, Annie, Max. Have you seen Pamela?"

Annie swatted. Damn that mosquito. And she had on so much repellent she was surprised her clothes didn't simply slide right off. "Pamela Potts?"

"You got it. Our own dear amoeba brain. Have you seen her?" Edith swiveled to look behind.

"Pamela Potts..." Max's tone was musing. He had a great memory for women. That he didn't place the name immediately should have alerted him.

Annie picked up the plastic bottle of repellent, sloshed some in her hand. "First you want gin, then you want Pamela."

"Pamela may not be my choice for amiga of the month, but she always carries a little vial of vodka in her purse." Edith had now turned 180 degrees. "She has to be here somewhere. She gave her all for the festival and Lord knows she wouldn't miss a minute."

"Pamela carries vodka in her purse?" Annie stared up at Edith in shocked surprise.

Edith snorted. "Sweet little Annie. And no doubt you believe in yellow brick roads and assorted childhood fantasies. Did you realize *The Wizard of Oz* was actually written as a sophisticated economic allegory?" She sighed. "I see that you did not. Ah, there's more to life than appears on the surface, dear Annie. Did you think that vacant glow in Pamela's baby blues was nature's—

"Mom, hey Mom." A bony twelve-year-old with a mop of black hair cut in the latest modified bowl fashion skidded to a stop beside the blanket. "Hey Mom, can I have—"

"Whoa, Ken." Edith's voice lost its sardonic curl. "Say hello to Mr. and Mrs. Darling."

"Hi, Mrs. Darling. Hi, Mr. Darling." Ken tugged impatiently on his mother's arm. "Please, Mom, they've got a place roped off for kids to do firecrackers. Please, can I have some more money?"

Edith dug a ten out of her pocket. As Ken raced off, she called after him, "Be careful."

But he was lost in the crowd milling near the bandstand.

"Come on, Edith," Annie urged. "Sit down and relax. We don't have any whiskey. How about some chocolate?"

The librarian sank onto the quilt, her hand outthrust.

Annie rustled in the picnic hamper and found a candy bar. "Here. This will give you some energy."

"I need more than energy. Not even a pound of endorphins will answer." Edith unwrapped the bar, took a big bite. "Had I but known," she intoned, "I would have called in sick today, taken a plane to Rio (God, wouldn't it be nice to be that rich!), planned a new career. Do you suppose I could color my parachute pink and become a nuclear physicist or an arctic explorer? But no, I know the answer. I am, at least until that bastard gets me fired, a librarian in this island paradise. Which could be a paradise if it didn't have any people. Which brings us right back where we started." She wrapped her arms around her knees. "And the hell of it is, I'm scared." The last sentence was hard to hear. Edith's voice was uncharacteristically subdued and altogether lacked her usual dry, wry tone.

"Scared?" Max sat up, looked at her through the gloom. "What's wrong?"

"I hate scenes. God, how I hate scenes." Her voice was deep and tight. "I grew up—well, that doesn't matter. Then I married a jerk who yelled around when anything didn't suit. So I think I've got a phobia. Some people don't like snakes; I hate scenes. This week's just been one bloody scene after another and this afternoon—God, it was awful."

Annie reached out, touched Edith's arm. Edith was trembling.

"What happened?" Annie patted her shoulder.

"Toby Maguire showed up. Ned's significant other?"

"Yes," Annie said quickly. "We know Toby."

"I don't know what would have happened"—her voice was dull—"if I hadn't seen him. He'd been drinking. He slammed into the library looking for Ned. Of course, Ned was on the festival field. Toby said he was going to find that son of a bitch—"

"Ned?" Annie asked, shocked.

"God, no. The general. Anyway, I got Toby to sit down in my office. I promised I'd bring him something to drink and I ran out to the field and called for Ned over the loudspeaker. But by the time we got back to the library, Toby was halfway to the field, yelling he was going to kill the son of a bitch. Ned had me take over the festival and he maneuvered Toby back to his car and took him home."

"Well, that's all right." Annie thought it was a hell of a lot less harrowing than the scene she'd witnessed in the forest preserve. "Tomorrow he'll be hung over but—"

"No, it's not all right. Ned sent me over to their place a little while ago. To take Toby some dinner. He wasn't there. His car wasn't there. Ned's scared to death Toby's going to show up tonight and beat the general into a pulp. Ned wants me to patrol the festival grounds, look out for Toby and come get him quick if Toby shows up."

"We'll help, Edith." Max was brisk, as if this were the way he usually spent the Fourth of July. "I'll take the area near the parking lots. Annie can keep an eye on the entry arbor. And you can wander around by the forest preserve. How does that sound?"

Edith bounced to her feet. "Max, you are a hell of a guy if nobody's told you that lately."

Annie felt fine. She told Max at least once a day.

The sound system crackled. A trumpet fanfare drowned out the static.

"Fireworks," a little girl screamed. "It's time for the fireworks!"

"Ooo-ooh." Cascading fingers of fire flared against the purple-black sky—orange and green, rose and pink, blue and white. Each display surpassed the last. Rockets blossomed like rose petals, hung like the drooping fronds of weeping willows, blazed in crimson puffs each larger than the last. Kids squealed; adults cooed. Bud Hatch kept up a running commentary, but it was easy to filter out his voice. The fireworks dominated the night. The rat-a-tat-tat of Lady Fingers was a steady staccato background to the hiss and crackle of the rockets.

Annie periodically checked the arbor and wandered a few feet either way along the line of redbuds. Toby Maguire was a very big man. He should be easy to spot. But if Toby wanted to slip in unobserved, certainly he could do so. The crowd moved and shifted restlessly. People wandered toward the food stands and the portable toilets near the parking areas. In the gloom, it was difficult to make out features. And there were always the paths that snaked through the forest preserve.

She glanced at her watch. Almost nine. The grand finale would be soon. All in all, it had been a good Fourth. Certainly the day had been a great financial success for Death on Demand. And the festival, for all the difficult moments, was a triumph. Henny could surely take pride in it. And maybe the general was enjoying emceeing the fireworks enough that it would put him in a good humor for the board meeting next week.

And Hercule Poirot would compliment Inspector Japp on his little gray cells.

But in any event, the festival was a success. Annie leaned against the bole of a redbud and knew she was eager for the grand finale. Then she and Max could go home and enjoy fireworks of their own. A high squeal brought her upright. Surely it was just a malfunction in the sound system. Once again came the piercing, harsh sound. She'd heard that sound yesterday, a piccolo blown in fury.

Annie headed across the festival ground toward the bandstand. She couldn't be sure. It was hard to pinpoint any particular sound among the pop of firecrackers, the boom of fireworks, children's excited yips, adults' exclamations, the occasional beat of a tom-tom. She threaded her way around blankets. "Sorry. Excuse me." She jolted to a stop, almost turned to go and find Max. He'd taken the job of patrolling the parking lots because it was the most likely spot to intercept Toby Maguire. But, if Annie was right, if that was Toby blowing his piccolo, spewing out anger and despair, Max hadn't spotted him.

The savage squeal came again. Now Annie was certain it came from the dark area west of the bandstand. She hurried forward. That anguished howl of music was very close to the bandstand and Bud Hatch. Ned Fisher had to be nearby. He could snare Toby. Annie wove her way among blankets like a crazed roadrunner in a video game. She was breathing hard by the time she reached the base of the stage. The wild, high cry of the piccolo pierced the night. She looked toward the forest preserve and a clump of willows perhaps fifteen to twenty feet away.

Boom. Boom. Boom.

"...dedicate this final round of fireworks to the gallant soldiers who have kept America safe from—" Hatch's words ended in a gurgle.

Annie's gaze jerked back to the bandstand. Hatch lurched to his left. He doubled up, sank slowly to the stage. Stars erupted. Gold and silver and green and orange burst in tendrils of brightness across the sky, bright and shiny and vivid. Hatch's crumpled body lay motionless.

Chapter 6

"He's down. The general's fallen." An anxious cry.

"Somebody do something." A brusque shout.

"What's happening?" A high, querulous demand.

"Down in front." A raspberry yell of irritation.

The crowd behind Annie moved like a live creature, sensing drama.

Most of the viewers, seated across the

broad grassy expanse, saw the general sprawled on the stage. They could not see, as did Annie standing only feet from the stage, the scarlet edge of blood seeping from beneath his body.

Edith Cummings jolted to a stop beside Annie. "Oh my God, that's blood! What happened?" Edith grabbed Annie's arm, clinging like a castaway to a lifeline.

Running feet rattled the stage-right steps. Chief Saulter grabbed up the microphone. "Police Chief Frank Saulter here. Remain calm." His sallow, bony face was untroubled, which Annie considered a high-class piece of acting. Saulter's tone was matter-of-fact. "General Hatch has been taken ill. Is there a physician in the audience? Please assist us. Everyone must remain in place so that emergency equipment may reach the stage without delay. Sergeant Cameron, Officers Tyndall and Pirelli report immediately."

Those three, Annie knew, comprised Chief Saulter's force. She wasn't surprised they were in attendance tonight. Chief Saulter took his duties seriously and this was a large gathering.

Fireworks spangled the sky, a flowing blue cascade simulating a waterfall, enormous white stars, a rippling American flag. Whorls of blossoming color and deep, heavy booms punctuated Saulter's calm announcement. The fireworks were launched from a floating platform in the middle of the lagoon. Those in charge couldn't see the front of the bandstand, and the display continued as scheduled. The restiveness of the crowd eased, the viewers reassured as the fireworks blossomed.

Blood spread in irregular rivulets, slowly, bright red lines on the stage. Henny Brawley rushed up the steps, her face pinched and pale. A stocky man loped past her. "Dr. Riordan." The rotund doctor, festive in a Hawaiian shirt and pink shorts, knelt by the general. A surprisingly adept pudgy hand picked up a flaccid arm, held the wrist.

Saulter thrust the microphone into Henny's hand. "Keep the audience calm." He turned away and reached the steps in two strides.

Billy Cameron met him at the base. "Ambulance en route. Lou's standing by at the exit to the parking lot. Ed's on the path by the forest preserve."

"Good work, Billy. You're in charge here. I'll take this end of the path." The chief pulled a flashlight from his belt and unsnapped his holster. He aimed the beam of the flashlight at the dusty gray path and kept one hand on the butt of his gun as he walked swiftly toward the weeping willows. The pastel lanterns cast tiny splotches of light across the path.

Edith Cummings clutched her throat. "Oh my God, where's Ken?" She whirled away, hurrying past the bandstand. "Ken? Ken?"

Facts and suppositions ricocheted in Annie's mind: The general must have been shot, the sound lost in the fireworks. Nothing else could account for his sudden lurch and the blood on the stage. The shot most likely came from the clump of willows to the west of the bandstand. That was the nearest spot offering concealment. A path ran along the edge of the forest preserve. Near the bandstand the path curved around the willows. The chief had to know that whoever shot the general was probably still armed.

Henny said harshly, "The fireworks conclude tonight's program. We have a medical emergency here. Please await instructions from the authorities."

Ned Fisher rushed up the stage steps, his tall hat wobbling, his baggy Uncle Sam trousers flapping around his ankles. He skidded to a stop, stared down at the general. Fisher began to shake, and his face turned greenish white.

Billy Cameron hustled to Henny and grabbed the microphone. "Ladies and gentlemen, remain in place until advised to depart by a police officer. Thank you for your cooperation." Ignoring the rumble of protest, Billy clicked off the sound. He looked at the doctor crouched by the general, then at the audience. He jerked his head toward Ned. "Give me a hand." He pointed at a music stand.

Billy and Ned carried a music stand to the front of the stage and placed it horizontally between the general and the audience. A second stand effectively screened the general and the doctor from view.

The doctor rose, stepped toward Billy. "He's dead, officer." Riordan's bushy black eyebrows bunched in a tight frown above narrowed eyes. "Massive hemorrhaging.

Apparent gunshot wound. Nothing I can do."

"Will you stand by, Doctor? Please keep everyone off the stage. We need to secure the area." At Riordan's nod, Billy pointed at Ned and Henny. "Round up some people quick. Get everyone's name and address and where they were in relation to the bandstand when the general was shot."

The fireworks steadily increased in intensity, rumbling from the roll of bass drums to the roar of thunder. Four enormous rosettes flowered, red, orange, green, and blue, each larger than the last. A final enormous boom and a silver-and-gold Statue of Liberty glistened in the night sky.

Lusty cheers echoed from most of the audience. Only those near the bandstand realized the general hadn't moved and that the flurry of activity on the stage presaged something more than an accident or sudden illness.

As the hurrahs subsided, Billy Cameron switched the mike on. His voice boomed. "We appreciate your patience. Please do not move from your present location. You will be permitted to leave as soon as a police representative has obtained your name and address."

Annie watched the bobbing light from the police chief's flash. Did a killer wait somewhere in the darkness of the forest preserve, gun in hand? But why would the general's killer wait to be caught? Reassured, Annie took one tentative step, then another, toward the willow trees, skirting groups of fireworks viewers.

The beam from Chief Saulter's flashlight made the shadows behind the saw palmettos even darker, threw jagged, uneven bars across the dusty gray path. Willow fronds rustled. Saulter edged around the willows, abruptly stopped, his posture rigid.

"Don't move. Drop that gun." The chief spoke calmly, but there was an underlying edge of menace.

"What's the matter?" The young voice was familiar. "Look, I found—"

"Drop it. Now." The command was harsh and swift.

Annie came close enough to look past the chief. It was the last thing she'd expected to see. Chief Saulter held his gun steady. Clearly visible in the light of the flash was Samuel Kinnon, a handgun dangling from his right hand.

Samuel let go and the gun thudded on the dusty ground. Samuel slowly held up his hands. "Chief, I found the gun. I found it just a minute ago." His broad face was strained and frightened. "I picked it up because of all the kids. Why are you pointing a gun at me? What's happened?"

Saulter called for Officer Pirelli. As he stood waiting, Samuel repeated over and over, "I just picked it up. I just picked it up."

Pirelli strode quickly up to the willows, his eyes carefully scanning the darkness. He was young, couldn't be more than in his early twenties, but his smooth round face under short black hair had the carefully blank expression of a cop at a crime scene.

Saulter pointed at the gun. "I'm going to get some deputies to assist us. Stand guard until they arrive, then take it into evidence. Photographs first, then loop a string behind the trigger, place it in a sterile container." The chief jerked his head at Samuel. "I'm taking you into custody as a material witness." Reholstering his gun, Saulter walked with Samuel toward the stage.

The onlookers were restive now, calling out, some standing, beginning to mill about.

Saulter faced the audience. "STAY PUT." The stentorian bellow brought an instant of silence. "This is an order of the law."

Annie watched Samuel carefully as he neared the stage. His steps faltered. Despite the horizontal music stands, the general's body could clearly be seen by anyone approaching the stage from the west. Samuel's face sagged in shock. "Chief, what happened to him? What happened?"

Saulter's answer was short and brutal. "Looks like he was shot."

"Not me." Samuel trembled. "Please. It wasn't me. I found—"

"That'll do, Samuel." Saulter directed him to a wooden bench east of the stage. "We'll talk later. You stay here." Saulter beckoned to Billy Cameron. "Watch him. No talking. With anybody." Samuel slumped on the bench, his eyes huge with fear.

Annie was halfway back to the stage, walking quietly behind the chief, when Max loomed up beside her. "Hey, what's happened? I heard Hatch had a heart attack."

"He was shot. He's dead." Annie pointed back at the bench and Samuel. "Samuel had a gun over there in the willows."

"Samuel?" Max's voice rose in shock.

"Yes. He—"

"Annie! Max!" Ned Fisher's voice was high and reedy.

They hurried to the stage. Henny stood with her hands clenched, scanning the restive audience. Ned and Edith waited at the bottom of the stage-right steps. Edith held several yellow legal pads. Although Ned was pale and his eyes occasionally flicked toward the stage and the general's body, he spoke calmly. "We need your help to get names and addresses and locate where everyone is sitting."

Edith handed each of them a pad and sheets of nickel-size round stickers, red, yellow and blue. "When you get the names, give each person a sticker to show the police. That way, they can get out of the lot."

Annie's section started halfway back on the west side. Annie got her spiel down pat. "There has been an apparent homicide. If you saw anything which might be helpful to the police, please contact Chief Saulter's office tomorrow."

"I don't see why I have to give you my name." A fortyish redhead glared at Annie.

"This is simply to help clear the area, ma'am. Anyone who does not wish to give their name, and receive a sticker permitting them to leave, may remain and speak personally with the police officers. However, it is estimated that it will be at least two hours before an officer—"

"Oh," the woman huffed. "All right. All right." But she leaned forward and whispered, "This won't get out, will it? I mean, my husband—" She broke off uncomfortably.

Annie was reassuring. "Oh, no, ma'am. This is confidential information."

As Annie made her way slowly up the rows, respondees fading quickly away, she stopped a couple of times to note the progress of the crime-scene investigation—photography, measuring, filming. Several sheriff's deputies arrived to assist Saulter and his officers. It was shortly after eleven when an ambulance backed up to the stage and the general's body was removed.

By the time she'd written down sixty-eight names—

"That's K-R-Y-Z-Y-N-S-K-I..."

Annie had met an engineer from Poland, a ballerina from Savannah, an interested policeman from Afghanistan, and a chef from Tahiti, as well as an entire softball team from Columbia and a convention of eye surgeons and their spouses from Indianapolis. It was almost midnight when she finished her segment and wearily walked toward the stage. Max joined her, his legal pad under one arm. "From a demographic standpoint," he said, "this was fascinating. For the progress of justice, I think it was a waste of time." The last was spoken softly as they joined Edith, Ned and Henny, a disconsolate group bunched on the stage-left steps. Annie spotted Miss Dora sitting in a camp chair, hands clasped on her cane, her wrinkled face remote and thoughtful. Samuel hunched on the bench, his arms around his knees. Billy Cameron stood guard. Samuel's parents stood a few feet away. May's round face looked stricken. She clung to Luther's arm. The festival ground was empty except for discarded cups and hot-dog wrappers and popcorn boxes.

Ned gathered up the address lists. He was walking up to the chief when Saulter beckoned to Billy Cameron. "Time to go."

Luther Kinnon bolted forward. "Where are you taking Samuel?"

"Jail. He's a material witness." Saulter's voice wasn't hostile, but it was firm and clipped.

Max gave Annie's arm a squeeze, then joined Saulter and Samuel's dad. "Chief, I'll arrange for a lawyer for Samuel. I'm advising him to defer answering questions until the lawyer arrives."

"As you say." Saulter motioned for Samuel to precede him.

May Kinnon began to sob. "Samuel. Samuel..."

He twisted to look back. "It's all right, Mom. I didn't do it, Mom."

Max used his cell phone to call a Chastain criminal lawyer, Johnny Joe Jenkins. Luther and May listened to Max's every word.

"...so that's the situation, Johnny Joe. We'll count on you." Max clicked "end."

"We'll go to the jail." Luther's voice shook.

Max reached out, caught his arm. "Jenkins will see to Samuel. We need to talk."

Miss Dora stumped wearily toward them. "Luther, May, I suggest we meet at your house."

• • •

The wood-paneled game room was crowded. May Kinnon huddled in a walnut rocking chair, fear glistening in her dark eyes. A petite woman with smooth chocolate skin and a soft voice, she twisted a handkerchief tighter and tighter until it was an ugly rope in her fingers. "Can that lawyer get Samuel out of jail tonight?"

Annie glanced at the grandfather clock. It was almost one o'clock in the morning.

Max's face furrowed. "I don't think so. The chief took Samuel in for questioning as a material witness. Tomorrow Saulter will talk to the circuit solicitor, Brice Posey, and if Posey thinks there's enough evidence, they'll charge Samuel with murder."

May Kinnon buried her face in her hands. Her husband stood by the rocking chair, his face hard and angry. "Samuel didn't do it."

Max shoved a hand through his thick blond hair. "The circuit solicitor will look at the facts: Hatch caused Samuel to lose his job. Hatch believed Samuel shoved the vase off the library. Samuel said somebody was going to kill the general. Saulter found Samuel holding a gun only a few feet from where the general was shot."

What Max didn't say, Annie knew. Ballistic tests would confirm whether the gun that Samuel had held was the murder weapon. A gunshot residue test could prove whether Samuel had recently fired a gun. If either test came back positive, Samuel could be a candidate for a first-

161

degree murder charge. Conviction could result in death by lethal injection.

"Samuel found the gun," Luther Kinnon insisted.

A brisk throat-clearing. "The situation is very clear." The raspy voice exuded confidence. "We must clear Samuel."

They all looked at Miss Dora.

She stood in the center of the Kinnons's game room, her wizened face determined. She was such an old woman. Her parchment face was pale and fatigued, her black dress dusty, but her dark eyes burned with an anger that mirrored Luther Kinnon's. "We will clear Samuel."

It was a call to arms.

Annie poked the papaya. Was it ripe enough? It was streaked with orange and yellow, so maybe.... She sliced it open, gouged out the seeds, peeled the skin. Hmm. Good. She opened a screened door to the patio. "Do you want some papaya?"

Max sat at a glass-topped table near the pool. "No, thanks. I've already fixed a bowl of strawberries. The coffee's ready. And I heated the cinnamon rolls."

Annie paused by the breakfast table to touch his cheek.

He turned his lips to kiss her hand, but he didn't look up from the yellow legal pad.

Annie slipped into her chair. Yes, no-see-ums swirled, but it was too lovely to stay inside. Meadowlarks warbled. Bobwhites sang to each other. An osprey circled over the lagoon, then, in a rush of wings, hurtled down. Annie was glad she wasn't a catfish or menhaden swimming near the surface. But everybody had to have breakfast.

She lifted her spoon, put it down slowly, papaya still intact. "What do you suppose Samuel's getting for breakfast?" She suddenly didn't have much appetite.

Max looked up swiftly. "Annie, we'll do our best. Come on and eat. We've got a lot to do. I'm working on a plan." He tapped his pen on the table.

Of course he was. That was what Miss Dora had instructed the night before. Annie remembered only too clearly the orders she had received: "Gossip, missy, get all the gossip."

The cordless phone rang. Annie scooped up the receiver.

The raspy voice was brisk. "Good morning, missy."

Why was she not surprised? "Good morning, Miss Dora." Annie sat up straight.

"Is Maxwell available?"

For an instant, Annie bristled. Then, recalling Miss Dora's purely feminist pronouncements Wednesday at Death on Demand, Annie said pleasantly, "Yes. Here he is." She thrust the receiver at her husband.

Annie noted that Max sat up very straight, too. Annie trotted into the kitchen, picked up the other cordless phone. Back on the patio, she settled into her chair, then clicked the phone on.

"...assume you have machinery in place

to obtain detailed personal information about all those involved."

Max glanced at his watch. "I'll call my secretary at nine. She knows how to conduct that kind of investigation."

"I will be happy to speak with Miss Barbara. With your authorization. I'm presently at the telephone on the boardwalk outside your office. I can get to work immediately. We have a great deal of information to collect."

Max winked at Annie. "That's great, Miss Dora. If you don't mind being in charge at the office, I'll conduct some investigations around the island today. You'll find the key to the front door under the second flowerpot."

The thump of Miss Dora's cane on the wooden walkway sounded hollowly over the phones. A rustling sound. "Ah, very good. Here it is. I'll call Miss Barbara first." A click as she hung up the receiver.

Max clicked his phone off, looked at it pensively. "I wish I could hear Miss Dora informing Barb that she needs to come to work at eight o'clock on a holiday weekend."

Annie clicked off her own cordless. "I'll bet you fifty that Barb is there in fifteen minutes."

Max laughed. "So you think Miss Dora is not to be withstood?" He nodded in agreement. "It's okay. I'll give Barb a bonus. And a week off."

The gate at the side of the house squeaked. Annie had been intending to oil it for several weeks. Footsteps clicked on the flagstones. Frank Saulter came around the pittosporum shrub. He stopped at the edge of the patio.

164

"Hi, Annie, Max. Got a minute?"

Annie squelched a Speak Your Mind: Heck no, Chief, it's Saturday morning and we have to catch the next rowboat out of the lagoon.

Max rose. The men shook hands. "Come have some coffee."

"Thanks, I'd like that." Saulter's faded-brown eyes were bloodshot and he moved tiredly, slumping into the wicker chair. He punched the cushion higher behind him, leaned back.

Annie brought a cup. Dorothy L. nosed through her cat door. Unlike Agatha, Dorothy L. adored company. She sped across the flag-stones and leaped to the chief's lap. She pushed her front paws against his chest and began to knead.

Saulter smoothed her short white fur. "Nice cat." He reached for the coffee cup, drank. "Good coffee."

Annie wanted to explode with questions, but she'd known Frank Saulter for a long time. He was the chief of police when she first came to the island. He had been a good friend of her Uncle Ambrose. Frank Saulter was not a man to be hurried.

They drank their coffee in silence for a moment, then Saulter cleared his throat. "Miss Dora's second cousin was my grand-mother's third husband."

They digested that in silence. It didn't need amplification. In the South, it doesn't matter how much money you have or what you do for a living. The first and only questions is always, "Who are your people?"

"Sharp old lady." His voice was subdued.

Annie squelched another Speak Your Mind: And she's got your number, hasn't she, old buddy?

Saulter stroked Dorothy L. and a buzz-saw purr competed with the whir of the no-see-ums. Annie absently checked to be sure her neck was still greasy with bug repellent.

The chief stared down at the plump cat and spoke as if to her. "Hard for kids to pay for college these days. A police record could queer any scholarship, maybe keep him from enrolling this fall."

Max nodded. Annie nodded.

"Of course"—and Saulter stared out at the lagoon, his eyes following a group of white ibis as they moved delicately near the shore, curved beaks flashing down for unwary crayfish and frogs—"I can't comment about an ongoing investigation."

Annie opened her mouth. Max kicked her under the table.

"Thing about it is, an officer of the law has the option of releasing a suspect into the custody of his parents. Seemed the thing to do when there was no substantial gunshot residue on his hands." He reached up, rubbed his bony nose. "A little bit. Lab said it could have come from picking the gun up, like Samuel said. Or from firecrackers. He said he'd blown off a few."

"I guess if we call the Kinnon house," Max said carefully, "Samuel will be home."

Saulter drank more coffee. Dorothy L. kneaded faster. The police chief scratched behind her ears. "Problem is, the circuit solicitor's going to want to know what evidence I have in the Hatch murder. When he hears it, he's going to press me to file a murder charge, probably first-degree. He'll pounce on the trace of explosive material on Samuel's hands, say he'd got rid of most of it by rubbing his hands on his pants. Or on the bench. Anywhere. Or Posey'll say Samuel must have worn gloves, got rid of them quick. Now, Posey's out of town. Gone fishing. Out to the Gulf Stream. He's partial to bream. Due back Monday." Saulter finished his coffee.

Annie knew Brice Willard Posey, a circuit solicitor of the great state of South Carolina. Annie and Posey were not fond of one another. Posey and Bud Hatch would have been soul mates—put women in their place, stamp out gays, bully the help, and keep kids like Samuel from being uppity.

Monday. They had until Monday to find Hatch's murderer. If not, Samuel Kinnon could find more than his chances for college ruined. Samuel Kinnon could be in jail on a charge of first-degree murder.

Saulter massaged his temples. "Tell me about Hatch. Tell me everything you know. Who hated him? Who was afraid of him or mad at him or jealous of him? Why would anybody gun him down? And it damn sure wasn't a redneck cowboy shooting off a gun to celebrate the Fourth. I talked to the autopsy doc early this morning. He said Hatch was drilled. Two bullets within an inch of each other in the aorta."

"Shot down in cold blood." Max drew a big black X on his notepad. "It's a damn shame. He could be a great guy. Wonderful golfer. Terrific military record. But—" Max broke off.

Saulter's gaze sharpened.

Max said reluctantly, "Hatch had a way of putting people's backs up."

Annie looked at him levelly. One good old boy talking about another?

But Max finally got to it. "He was on the wrong side of the women in town." He carefully didn't look toward Annie. "Hatch wanted to take over the Fourth celebration. He and Henny Brawley tangled."

Annie almost chimed in. She knew a lot more than Max. There was Sharon Gibson's angry glare Wednesday afternoon at the grocery; Edith Cummings's fear that Hatch was going to ruin the Haven for her son, and, even worse, get her fired from the library; Ned Fisher and his taut exchange with the general the morning of the festival; the screech of Toby Maguire's piccolo; Jonathan Wentworth's warning to Henny at the gazebo; Gail Oldham's violent anger as she looked up at Hatch; and David Oldham's blundering departure from the forest preserve with Hatch's too-intimate remark burning in his mind. And that didn't even address Laurel's odd behavior at the library and in the men's locker room at the Whalebranch Club. And Miss Dora's rock-hard determination to have her characoal drawings exhibited.

Annie almost spoke, then stopped. She was in a quandary. She wanted to help Samuel.

They had to help Samuel. After all, she'd given her word to Miss Dora that everything was going to be all right. And at the present, everything was about as bad as it could be.

So, Samuel was Number One.

But Annie didn't want to tell Chief Saulter about these people. Yes, if one of them was guilty, she'd be the first to bring evidence to him. But she didn't want to reveal their sad, private miseries unless it was absolutely necessary. If one of them was guilty, if she found reason to believe that, she'd go to the chief. That was fair enough, wasn't it?

"Annie, didn't you say some of the others on the board were mad at Hatch?" Max was looking at her.

So was the chief.

Annie opened her mouth, shut it, wished she'd paid attention when Laurel urged her to have a mantra. She needed a mantra right now. Or, at the least, she needed a cogent, convincing reply.

She smiled.

Saulter blinked tired eyes. Max looked suddenly alert.

"Yes, definitely." So she was on the side of the angels. And on Samuel's side. "But I'm not sure exactly why. There was going to be a board meeting next week. Let me nose around and see what I can find out."

"Posey gets back Monday," the chief said quietly. He gave Dorothy L. a final pat and stood. The cat dropped daintily down, paused, jumped on the table, floating up as easily as wind-blown thistle.

"You don't like papaya, Dorothy L.," Annie said absently, pushing her away. Annie slowly ate a slice of the succulent fruit. An odd taste but one she loved.

The hinge squeaked on the gate. The chief was gone. And so was her chance to tell him everything she knew.

Dark blue eyes regarded her sternly.

Annie pushed back her chair. "Think I'll get—"

"Annie." Sometimes Max was not to be ignored.

"I feel bad for people who have their names dragged—"

"Samuel's in trouble." Max's jaw had an unaccustomed tilt.

Annie sighed. She looked into those watchful blue eyes. She started talking.

Max listened and wrote in his precise, exceedingly legible hand. Even upside down, she could read his list:

Sharon Gibson—what's her connection to Hatch?

Edith Cummings—afraid for her job? And her son?

Ned Fisher—was he going to be booted as director?

Toby Maguire—was he really drunk?

Jonathan Wentworth—what kind of danger did he envision from Hatch?

*Gail Oldham—what did Hatch want her to do?
And why was she furious?*

*David Oldham—he was mad enough to kill.
Did he?*

Max reached for the cordless.

Annie reached across the table, caught his hand. "Wait. I'll tell the chief. But give me today. Let me see what I can find out. You know he won't have any luck with these people. He wants us to see what we can find out."

"Yeah." Max's voice was thoughtful. "He came to us because of these kinds of things that he couldn't possibly know. That's fair enough, Annie. But we'll give him a full report tonight."

Tonight. Less than twelve hours from now. "There's lots for you to find out, too. Samuel had the gun. Why was he over there by the willows?"

It always came back to Samuel and the gun.

"Right. That's important." Max drew a gun, overlaid it with a big question mark.

Annie finished the bowl of papaya and sipped her coffee. Mmm. So good. Colombian, always her favorite for breakfast.

What was Samuel having for breakfast? Kids always wanted Cokes. But did he have any appetite this morning? Annie remembered Samuel's face as Saulter and Billy escorted their prisoner to the car. Scared. Scared to death. Sick-scared, his eyes huge and wild.

171

Annie put down her coffee cup. Of course, if Samuel shot the general, that's how he would look. But if he hadn't shot the general, he was suffering the helpless agony of the wrongly accused.

It was up to her and Max to find out the truth. Even if the face of a murderer turned out to be one they knew well.

The faces flashed through her mind:

Sharon Gibson's smile was infectious. But she hadn't smiled much lately. Sharon worked hard for the community chest drive and sang in the choir at church. She'd glared at Hatch in the grocery, yet the general appeared not to know her.

Gail Oldham was bouncy and pert but sometimes recently, when she thought no one was looking, the pertness seeped out of her face and her big green eyes stared forlornly into the distance. She and Annie had met playing tennis. They often played singles. Gail had a wicked backhand. But she could be distracted if a hunk played on the next court.

She and Max often played doubles with the Oldhams. Intensely competitive, David Oldham fought for every point. David served harder to Max than he did to Annie.

Edith Cummings was a superb librarian. Ned said Broward's Rock was lucky to have her. Bigger systems often tried to hire her, but she wanted to stay on Broward's Rock because she thought it was a great place to raise a kid.

Ned Fisher had infused the Lucy Banister Kinkaid Memorial Library with enthusiasm and good humor. He got to know the patrons and was especially encouraging to the kids, all the kids, rich and poor.

Toby Maguire was reclusive. Annie had only seen him a few times and that was unusual on an island with a total population around 1,600. She knew of him, of course. He was Ned's companion and he was an artist. And—a late piece of knowledge—he played the piccolo. He was also a very big man, which was surely neither here nor there, since Hatch had been shot, not strangled. But wouldn't it take great strength to topple the vase at the library? Or merely excellent leverage?

Jonathan Wentworth was urbane and charming, and apparently knew Henny Brawley a good deal better than Annie had realized. He had warned Henny not to cross Hatch. He insisted Hatch could be dangerous. Dangerous? That seemed a strong word. And why was Wentworth so adamant with Henny? How well did he know the slain general?

Yes, Annie knew some people who didn't like Bud Hatch.

Including Henny. Last night Henny was one of the quiet onlookers who watched Saulter and Billy take their prisoner away. But Henny didn't come to the Kinnon house.

Henny, who'd always loved a mystery, Henny who'd read more mysteries than Annie and the rest of her customers combined, Henny who fancied herself the equal of Miss Marple, Miss Silver and Miss Seeton, not to mention Sherlock Holmes, Hercule Poirot, and Sam Spade—where was Henny?

"Where's Henny?" Annie had never thought she could utter her best customer's name with so much foreboding.

"Hmm." For once Max's famous empathy was on a holiday. He said absently, "Is she coming over?" He didn't even notice Annie's worried frown. He made a final notation and handed her the legal pad. "What do you think?"

The sheet was headed:

PLAN OF ATTACK

1. Obtain names of festivalgoers sitting near the bandstand.

2. Check out Ned Fisher, Toby Maguire.

3. Talk to Samuel. Where did he find the gun?

4. Check ballistics info.

Max pushed back his chair. "Why don't you talk to the Oldhams and Edith Cummings and Sharon Gibson? You know them better. I'll start with Ned Fisher. He hung around the stage most of the evening, didn't he?" Max picked up his breakfast dishes. "How about you?"

"I believe I'll drop by Henny's." Annie watched a yellow-beaked gallinule pick its way gracefully on the lily pads, intent on a floating carpet of duckweed. Direct and determined, just the way Henny used to go after clues.

"Henny." Max looked back from the kitchen

steps. "I'm surprised she hasn't called this morning." He stepped inside.

Annie didn't respond. She was too worried to answer. Why hadn't Henny called? Henny loved playing detective. She'd been known to wear tweeds and lisle stockings à la Jane Marple even in August. Wouldn't it be great if Henny was her old self, plunging into detection in a starched nurse's uniform with the verve of Mignon Eberhart's Sarah Keate or in hat and gloves with the style and manner of Louisa Revell's Miss Julia Tyler?

If wishes were horses.... Which reminded Annie: Where was Laurel last night? And why hadn't they heard anything from her?

Black clouds boiled in the southern sky. Another storm coming. Annie checked them out in the car mirror. It was a relief to turn onto the dusty gray road that wound beneath interlocking branches of live oak trees, which hid the sky. But the moisture-laden air presaging the storm was so still that the Spanish moss hung unmoving as rusted anchor chains from a long-sunk galleon.

The Volvo slowed. It wasn't far now. Around the next bend. This was a lonesome road leading to a single gray weathered house on stilts overlooking a broad sweep of marsh. Sometimes on a soft summer evening the view from Henny's porch included sleek dolphins nosing around the cordgrass stems for succulent minnows and mummichogs. Annie had been to oyster roasts at Henny's. They'd planned the annual church white-elephant sale sitting on webbed chairs on the high porch. They'd co-hosted a baby shower for Billy Cameron's wife, Mavis, and put Billy's stepson Kevin in charge of the cookies. They'd cooked a cauldron of fudge to raise money for the local hospice.

Annie and Henny went back a long way, as bookseller and prized customer, co-workers for their community and, finally, fast friends.

Annie nosed the Volvo onto a sandy patch of ground by a clump of palmettos. The slam of her car door seemed overloud in the heavy quiet. Henny's 1982 black Dodge sedan was in its parking place. Her bicycle was in its rest. The front door was closed.

Annie climbed the wooden steps. They creaked, the sound intrusive. She knocked on the door.

No answer.

But there was some sound within. The dull murmur of voices. Annie knocked again, firmly, insistently, determinedly, several raps past the norm.

She was turning, ready to return to the car and her cell phone when the door creaked open.

Henny stared combatively through the screen. Always thin, she usually looked elegant, sometimes in well-cut suits, sometimes in silk or linen dresses, depending upon the season. For casual clothes she liked bright colors—a crimson shirt with soaring swallows and sharply white slacks, Hawaiian prints, Malaysian batik. This morning a pink blouse jarred with orange slacks. Her silver-streaked dark hair was brushed, but she wore no makeup. Every line in her face was deep and harsh. Her dark eyes were cool and unreadable.

"I'm on the phone, Annie." She bristled with irritation. "The phone's rung and rung. I have to make some decisions about the festival proceeds."

Annie said, "Look, Henny—"

Henny barreled on. "Pamela Potts is proposing that we name the reading room after the general. I'm on the phone right now." She closed the door.

Annie stared at the blank panel. If Henny thought she could be brushed off like that, she hadn't read her V.I. Warshawski books very carefully. No way, José.

Annie pulled open the screen, opened the door. She did hesitate for an instant. Even for old friends, this was presuming. Then she thought of Samuel and his big scared eyes. She stepped softly down the hall.

Although the cloudy sky was somber and gray, Henny's living room still had a quality of light. The wicker furniture was snowbank white, the wooden floors golden. Windows spread across the back of the room and all along one side, so the room seemed to float above the marsh and the unending ripple of bright green cordgrass. The brightest color in the room came from the low bookshelves running beneath the windows. Every bookshelf was full. There were hundreds of books. The spines of bright jackets provided a palette of colors. A golden oak desk sat near the back windows.

Pamela Potts's voice radiated tremendous good humor. "I'm confident this is simply the least we can do. I've been on the phone with the general's friends, the men he played golf with and some of the other pilots in the Confederate Air Force, and I've already achieved pledges of more than ten thousand. Henny, don't you think that's marvelous?" The disembodied voice flowed cheerfully from the speaker phone on Henny's desk.

Henny stopped by the desk. "Yes, Pamela, it's very good of you. It's a thoughtful project. I think Annie Darling would be willing to help out. Why don't you give her a call? Thanks, Pamela." Henny was skilled in the art of dealing with motormouths. She punched the phone and the connection ended.

"Henny—" Annie began.

Henny jerked around. "I've got to rush, Annie." She bustled across the room, picked up her purse. "I've got a meeting of the volunteers at the hospital."

Annie reached out, gripped a thin arm. "Henny, listen, I need your help."

Henny was fumbling for her car keys. "I'm not taking on any projects now."

"I'm not talking about projects, Henny." Annie wanted to shake her, force Henny to meet her gaze. "Listen to me. We've got to find out who shot Hatch."

The old Henny, the true Henny would have responded like a hound to tallyho, immediately spouting theories—a conspiracy, of course, or cherchez la femme, or watch out for the least-likely suspect—while looking up at the ceiling to denote careful thought à la Elizabeth Daly's Henry Gamadge or donning a shapeless hat and an overlarge overcoat à la Edmund Crispin's Gervase Fen or worrying about big brothers à la Margaret Maron's Judge Deborah Knott.

This morning's Henny snapped shut her purse. The keys clinked in her hand. "That's for the police, Annie. Frank will take care of it."

"Henny, you saw them take Samuel off to jail last night!" Annie clutched both arms, willing Henny to listen, to respond.

Henny pulled away. "Circumstantial evidence. That's all they have." She headed for the front door.

Annie was hard on her heels. "You know Posey. You know what he's like. Henny, you have to help."

Henny opened the screen.

Annie followed her onto the porch. "Samuel could die for a crime he didn't commit."

"That won't happen. Of course it won't happen." Henny clattered down the steps. She was almost to the bottom when Annie said loudly, her voice brusque because otherwise she'd never get it out, "What did Jonathan mean when he said it was dangerous to cross Hatch?"

Henny froze, one hand gripping on the wooden railing. Her body tightened, drew in on itself. Even from the back, she looked diminished, small. There was a long, sickening silence with only the sounds of the summer marsh, the rustle of the saw grass, the whine of greenhead flies, the chirr of cicadas.

Henny turned, looked up. In the stark summer sun, her bony face was pitilessly exposed, her brown eyes stricken, her mouth slack. For the first time since Annie had known her, Henny looked old, old and defeated.

Annie put out her hand.

"Jonathan..." Henny's voice trembled. "Oh, Annie, please. Leave him alone. He has nothing to do with what happened to Hatch. I know that. I'm sure of that. Annie, he's good and decent, through and through."

Annie felt a sting of tears. "I heard Jonathan say"—she took a deep breath—"he said you have his heart."

Henny pressed her fingers against her face. For an instant, the pain fled and the fear. A joyous smile touched her lips. "Yes. Yes, he did. And he has mine. Annie, he will always have mine." She swung around, stepped onto the ground.

Annie wanted to cry out for her friend, indomitable, brave, and gallant.

Henny walked swiftly to her car. She slipped into the front seat, pulled the door shut.

Annie watched her drive away, dust roiling into a dense cloud at the car's swift acceleration.

Annie put the cash box on the coffee bar. Agatha watched with glittering green eyes as Annie opened a small can of cat food. "I know I'm late. I'm sorry."

Agatha's tail switched. Annie put down the bowl and narrowly escaped Agatha's incisors. Nobody, especially not Annie, ever claimed Agatha was a good sport. That was a human concept. If Agatha could do a Speak Your Mind (which she probably often did in sharp meows), it might go something like this: Sorry, my ass. I can't eat sorry.

Annie carried the cash box to the front, wrote a note asking Ingrid to tally the receipts. Added a P.S.: "Got to run errands. Will you see if Duane can give you a hand if it gets busy?"

Thunder rumbled. The query was nothing more than window dressing, but Ingrid was good-humored and easygoing and wouldn't hold it against Annie that the store would be wall-to-wall with disconsolate vacationers if the storm materialized.

Annie lugged in the boxes from the festival, almost all less than a third full. She flipped open the lid to the first box, picked up Janet Laurence's *Death at the Table* and was immediately hungry. And there was Camilla Crespi's *The Trouble with a Small Raise*. Annie felt an urgent pang for pasta.

She put the books back, slammed the lid shut. Okay, she was dithering. That was an interesting word. Did Mr. Dithers or the word come first? If the comic strip character, it certainly proved the power of mass entertainment on culture.

A scarlet flash of pain emanated from her ankle. She didn't even look down. "Agatha, I said I was sorry." In the bathroom, she found an old bottle of antiseptic and dribbled some on the bright red welt.

She owed Agatha. Seeing blood reminded her forcibly and unpleasantly of Hatch crumpled to the floor of the stage and the thin, straggling rivulets of bright blood. So she couldn't evade. She couldn't piddle around putting up books, thinking of word origins. But she wished for the dispassion of most fictional sleuths, the emotional detachment of a detective exploring the lives of suspects who meant nothing to them. Stuart Palmer's take-charge Hildegarde Withers treated both police and criminals like recalcitrant schoolchildren. Phoebe Atwood Taylor's Asey Mayo observed everyone with a sardonic and critical eye, including his cousin Jennie and her husband, Syl.

Maybe it was time for another self-directed Speak Your Mind: Annie, bite the bullet.

Not that she was eager to think about bullets. Bullets reminded her of the chief's chilling announcement: "And it damn sure wasn't a redneck cowboy shooting off a gun to celebrate the Fourth....Two bullets within an inch of each other in the aorta."

Annie slapped on a Band-Aid. On her way to the back door, she paused to pick up Agatha and nuzzle the back of her neck. "Henny's a hell of a shot," she told the elegant cat, who responded by writhing free.

Outside, Annie took a look at the sky and retrieved her umbrella from the backseat floor. She climbed into her car, then sat with her hands clenched on the wheel.

Could Henny have shot Hatch?

Yes. Physically, yes. Henny was more than

appeared at first glance. To many on Broward's Rock, she was a familiar presence, active in good works, intelligent, capable, and, some might say, ruthlessly determined. She was a widow, a retired schoolteacher, a connoisseur of detective fiction. Everyone knew that.

Only a few knew that in World War II, she served as a pilot in the Women's Air Force Service, ferrying bombers across the country. She was one of the first jet pilots, testing the YP59 twin turbine jet fighter at Wright Field in Dayton, Ohio. After her retirement from teaching, she spent two years in Zaire with the Peace Corps. She'd visited every continent and backpacked in the Himalayas. She was accomplished at trapshooting. She was active in the Confederate Air Force and often went to air shows to fly her restored P51 Mustang. She tossed aside queries about her age. "As long as I can pass my flight physical, I'll keep right on flying."

And if anyone had ever suggested to Annie that Henny Brawley, mystery reader extraordinaire, could be present at a murder and not plunge into the chase, Annie would have said they simply didn't know Henny.

Now she had to wonder if she knew Henny. Because the Henny she knew, the friend she treasured, would be outraged at Samuel's arrest. Or possibility of arrest.

Annie took a deep breath, bit the bullet. Okay, these were the possibilities:

1. Henny shot Hatch.
2. Henny was protecting someone.

And there was only one person that could be.

As Annie gunned the Volvo, thunder exploded like the rumble of artillery wheels on cobblestones. Rain pelted the windshield.

Chapter 7

"**I** can't remember everybody I saw." Ned Fisher's tone was just this side of petulant. His face glowed tomato red from too much sun. He pushed back his chair, clumsily rose. He turned away from Max to look out the graceful Palladian window. Rain sheathed the glass, hiding the festival field. "I've got a computer class scheduled in a few minutes."

"You were looking for Toby last night." Max said it casually, as if it didn't mean much, simply a statement.

Fisher swung around. The glow of the sunburn emphasized dark circles beneath strained blue eyes. His shave was uneven, a patch of stubble near the jawline, a red nick on his chin. Even for Saturday at the library, his dress was casual, a wrinkled pink-and-white-striped shirt and age-whitened jeans. No suspenders. The jeans sagged around his thin waist. "I don't know what the hell you're talking about. Now I've got to—"

"Edith Cummings was looking for him, too. She said you asked her to hunt for him. My wife and I offered to help. Annie heard the piccolo. I figure you did, too." Max rose. He stood in the way to the door. He didn't make a big thing of it, but he folded his arms and looked immovable.

Ned Fisher clenched his fists. But he wasn't looking at Max. He stared down at the floor as if he saw a pit ringed with fire. "God-damn. What do you want out of me? Yeah, I was looking for Toby. That bastard"—he stopped, gulped—"Hatch was a first-class bastard, man. But Toby, he wouldn't kill any-body. Not since 'Nam. He saw too much killing there. He hates killing. His best friend, he was sitting next to him and the VC blew his head off. Do you know what that does to a man?"

Max didn't have an answer. He'd never faced the draft, hadn't seen his friends die in a guerilla war no one could win. The sixties meant music to him and funny clothes to wear to costume parties.

Fisher leaned against his desk. He looked down at a picture of Toby Maguire in swim trunks—massive shoulders, a chest matted with silvered black hair, tree-trunk-thick legs, grinning as he threw a Frisbee high above golden sand. "He was supposed to play his pic-colo at the festival. Three piccoloists doing 'Yankee Doodle Dandy' to introduce the band. When they were practicing Thursday, the general came up and ordered them off, said only real soldiers could wear uniforms. Like Toby was some kind of fag scum who didn't know about war. Toby was wild."

Max looked at the picture, at a big man on a happy day. "So he got drunk and came after the general yesterday. Edith Cummings alerted you. You took him home, but later he was gone."

"I found him last night," the librarian said quickly. "Just a couple of minutes before somebody shot the general." Fisher's gaze was steady, Boy-Scout earnest. "I took Toby to my Jeep, told him to wait. I was heading back toward the bandstand when Hatch keeled over."

"Where was Toby?" Max had a clear picture of the terrain in his mind, the bandstand on the north end of the field, the forest preserve to the west, the stages and booths to the south and beyond them the parking areas, the redbud trees to the east bordering the back of the library. He glanced toward the opaque window and wondered about Miss Dora's artworks. Had anyone retrieved them?

"The sound of a piccolo carries a long way. Especially when you blow it hard." Fisher rubbed a finger along the rough streak of stubble on his jaw.

The piccolo had squealed, like a creature in pain. Max had heard it in the parking lot, though he'd not understood its significance then.

Fisher flung his left arm, pointed northwest. "Paths curl all through the preserve and around it and by the lagoon. Toby was way over on the west side of the water, sitting on the end of an old pier, blowing his heart out. He wasn't anywhere close to the bandstand when"—he stopped, added jerkily—"when I found him."

Max left it alone. If he had to place a bet, he would wager Fisher didn't find Toby Maguire until after the shooting and then hustled him to the Jeep. Max wasn't willing to grant either of them an alibi.

Instead, Max said, "Let's get back to the people close to the stage, Ned. That's what matters."

The librarian hunched his shoulders. His eyes never left Max's face.

"Please try to remember everyone you saw." Max pulled a small notebook from his pocket. "I know it was dark, but you were hunting for Toby. You must have looked hard everywhere you went."

Fisher shoved a hand through a long tangle of hair. "Christ, man, it was packed. And so what if somebody was there—"

"The shots came from behind those willows. Look, Ned, Samuel Kinnon's going to jail if we don't find something else for the police to look at." Max swiftly sketched the festival ground.

Ned Fisher pulled out his swivel chair, slumped into it. "Samuel's a good kid. He started coming here for computer lessons when he was just in ninth grade. He's damn good. Course all the kids are." A faint grin. "They could all be librarians when they grow up. Yeah." His voice was weary. "I didn't think about Samuel." His head jerked up, flouncing his hair on his shoulders. "It wasn't Toby. Okay? You got that?"

"I got that." Max finished his map, tore it out, placed it on the desk in front of Fisher.

He pointed to the clump of weeping willows. "Somebody stood there and shot Hatch. You were in that area, looking for Toby. And later, you took the names of the people who were sitting near the willows. Who did you see?"

Fisher glanced at his watch. He frowned, reached for his phone, punched in an extension. "Rosalie, take my computer class for fifteen minutes. Okay?" A pause. "Put up a sign. Say you'll be back at ten-fifteen. Thanks.

"Fifteen minutes," he said firmly. He picked up the map, stared at it, then jabbed with a stiff finger. "Okay. The shot came from there but anybody could get to the trees from right in front of the bandstand or by skirting along behind the concessions or two or three different ways through the forest preserve. So I don't know what the hell it means to say somebody was seen near the bandstand."

"It's a place to start. It would be easy to get behind that clump of trees if you were close to the stage. Somebody showed up with a gun last night. This was planned. Don't you think that person got as close to the stage as possible? And," Max repeated stubbornly, "it's a place to start."

Fisher crumpled the map, tossed it on his desk. "Hell, I don't know everybody the general knew."

"You know some of them." Max was insistent. "And you know who was crossways with him on the library board. And if we don't find out who shot the general, Samuel's going to go to jail."

Fisher rubbed his face, pulled his hand

188

quickly away from sore skin. "You're serious? You really believe Frank will arrest Samuel?"

"Samuel could be on death row." Max's face was somber.

Fisher's tone was harsh. "So you want me to finger everybody I saw who might have it in for the general?"

"Right." Max held Fisher's gaze.

The librarian shoved his chair back, popped to his feet. He glared at Max. "I don't like this."

"Ned, I'm not going to blab everything I hear to the police. But I have to know what was going on. If you tell me something and that person didn't have anything to do with Hatch's murder, no one will ever know we talked. Okay?" Max kept his eyes away from the clock. Fisher was due at his computer class in nine minutes.

The librarian opened a drawer, pulled out a jar of sunburn ointment, gingerly spread the cooling salve on painful skin. He closed the jar, dropped it in the drawer, pushed the drawer shut. The click sounded loud in the waiting silence.

The thick white paste looked like misapplied clown makeup, but there was nothing entertaining about Fisher's grim face. He took a deep breath. "Okay, I'll tell you what I know, the little I know. And none of it was big enough to cause a murder. I only knew the jerk because he was on the library board. He came on board this spring. He treated it like a fiefdom from day one. He and Henny Brawley squared off right from the first. Strong women were probably tops on the general's hate list. At first I kind of got a kick out of it, but it got old real fast. I'd always liked board meetings. We've got a great library and there's so much good to talk about"—for an instant his face lightened and eagerness glinted in his eyes, then he sighed—"but the meetings turned into verbal swordplay. Probably been fun if you were Ambrose Bierce or Alexander Woollcott. 'He damned his fellows for his own unworth, And, bad himself, thought nothing good on earth....'" A quick look at Max. "'There is less in this than meets the eye.' Anyway, it was no damn fun. But Henny Brawley wouldn't shoot a man because he was a pain in the ass on a board, would she?" He didn't wait for an answer. "There was some darker stuff, too. Gail Oldham and Hatch were crossways bigtime. It wasn't the festival. It was something personal...."

Very personal, Max thought. The kind of personal that could lead to murder.

"...and Jonathan Wentworth, he's another retired military guy. Navy, not Army. Do you know him?"

"A good guy," Max said. "He's on the board for the animal shelter."

"Wentworth is a gentleman." Fisher's voice was mocking, his smile faintly satirical. "A gentleman of the old school. Whatever the hell that means. But you know what it means." Fisher spoke as if across a divide that he could never cross. "Wentworth didn't like Hatch. Not at all. I don't know why. But when a man like Wentworth won't shake hands, that tells you something. And somehow, whenever it would have been appropriate, well, what do you know, Wentworth had something in his hands or he turned and went in the other direction or he dropped something or held the door. You get what I mean?"

Max wrote down "Wentworth," circled the name three times. "Anybody else on the board?"

"Me. Edith Cummings." His mouth closed tight.

Max was direct. "How were your relations with Hatch?"

"Rotten. He didn't like gays." Fisher looked levelly at Max. "He was going to try and get me booted as director."

"Did that bother you?"

"What the hell am I supposed to answer, man? Sure, it bothered me. We like it here. Toby's making a name for himself as an artist. And God knows there isn't a better place to live in the world—barring snakes and hurricanes. But was I going to shoot the old bastard to keep my job? I don't think so. I could get a half dozen jobs tomorrow. I'm damn good at what I do. And if I left here, I was going to sue the hell out of the old bastard and the library. Nice thing is, somebody's saved me a lot of effort. The board meeting next week was shaping up to be a shouting match. Me. And Edith. He wanted me to fire her."

"Could he have managed it?" Max wrote down "Edith" with a big question mark.

"The general was a handy, dandy guy." Fisher gave a dry snort that might have been amusement. "That's what the song said about Yankee Doodle, wasn't it? Yankee Doodle Dandy. Hatch pranced into town last March like Yankee Doodle, ready to run everything, everybody. But he ended up Yankee Doodle dead, didn't he?" The librarian swung around, moved to the window. "Right down there. Deader than hell." Fisher's voice was an odd combination of satisfaction and uneasiness.

Max joined him at the window. The rain was easing. The field was sodden now, forlorn with its aftermath of the festival, the shiny wet bandstand, shuttered booths, scattered clumps of debris.

Fisher pointed toward the forest preserve. "So you want to know who I saw near the bandstand? That's easy. All of them. Every damn one—Gail and Jonathan and Henny and Edith. Plus Samuel. And me, of course." He scooped up a folder, started for the door. As he passed Max, he added slyly, "And several hundred other people, too."

"Ned!"

The librarian paused in the doorway, jerked a sharp look at Max.

"How about David Oldham? Did you see him?"

Ned's eyes narrowed. "David? No. I don't think so. Oh, he was around in the afternoon. I saw him talking to Gail. But I didn't see him when I was hunting for Toby." Ned shrugged. "Hell, Darling, give it up. There were people everywhere. And there could have been a damn regiment in the forest preserve." He swung away.

Max listened to his footsteps clattering down the hallway. Ned was right. There were hundreds of people. People sitting, strolling, shifting from one spot to another. Fireworks. Rockets. Sousa marches.

And the fierce cry of a piccolo piercing the night, sharper than all the noises of the crowd and the firecrackers and the rockets and the band.

Despite running the Volvo's air-conditioning at top speed—it should have cooled the car to meat-locker specifications—the temperature was both tepid and soggy. And anybody who didn't think warm air could be soggy wasn't familiar with the Low Country after a July thunderstorm.

Annie braked for a doe followed by two fawns. She drove slowly. She didn't have any idea how to approach Jonathan Wentworth. She scarcely knew him. She needed the perceptiveness of Earlene Fowler's Benni Harper or the charm of Kate Morgan's Dewey James. Instead she was Annie Darling, bookshop owner and unintended observer of a friend's personal moment. Jonathan Wentworth.... Henny said he was good through and through. But did a man who was good through and through love a woman who wasn't his wife? Maybe yes, maybe no, but that shouldn't have anything to do with another man's murder. Yet Henny was refusing to help solve Hatch's murder—and there had to be a compelling reason why. Perhaps a terrible reason why.

Sandspur Lane sliced inland and three homes came into view. One was very old, perhaps built around 1815. The latecomers were re-creations of Low Country architecture and they fit smoothly into their piney environment.

Annie studied the first house with an eye honed by many house-and-garden festivals. The one-story white frame was raised on low brick pillars. A single dormer overlooked a front porch with four simple Doric columns. The house was in excellent repair and its shiny white paint had been recently applied. Its nearest neighbor was a much larger house, a two-story weathered gray wood built on sturdy concrete pilings. The planked roof was painted a bright red. The third house, although clearly new, was built in the familiar Low Country boxlike design—two floors of four rooms each, divided by a central hallway, again on a high brick foundation and with a shaded piazza on the front.

A yellow road sign warned: DEAD END. The first mailbox bore the name "Wentworth."

Annie heard a personally directed Speak Your Mind: Get your guts up.

She turned into the drive, parked, and strode briskly up the oyster-shell walk. A FOR SALE sign sat in the middle of the front yard. Shells crunched beneath her feet. A mourning dove cooed nearby. Spartina grass rustled in the gentle breeze. Her footsteps were the only human sound. She pushed the doorbell, heard chimes within. The mourning dove's plaintive cry rose and fell, rose and fell.

Annie frowned. Hers was the only car, but there was a garage. Probably she should have called, but darned if she could think of any reason why Jonathan Wentworth should be willing to see her. Her plan was to show up on his doorstep and trust to luck and instinct and Wentworth's good manners to get her inside.

The door opened.

"Are you here about—" Emily Wentworth looked at Annie with a commanding air. Her green eyes blinked. There was sudden recognition. She smiled. "I thought perhaps you were here about the house. But you're the book girl. The mystery store. Jonathan always does a good job when he picks out books for me there. Come in, come in." She held the screen door open. "Got rained off the course this morning. I have coffee on. We'll have an old-fashioned coffee klatsch."

Annie stepped into a shining foyer laid with bright black and white squares. A Chinese lacquer screen set off the dining room to the left. Emily Wentworth led the way into the small living room, filled with comfortable easy chairs and a few good pieces—an Italian fruitwood settee, a Hepplewhite shield-back chair. A Japanese silk brocade hung against one cypress-paneled wall. Two delft covered jars sat on a narrow Adam mantel over a small fireplace.

After settling Annie in a tulip-print easy chair, Emily bustled about, bringing in a

195

ceramic coffeepot and pottery cups and a plateful of brownies. "My own special recipe. Chocolate chips and macadamia nuts."

Annie's nose wrinkled appreciatively as her hostess poured a cup of rich dark coffee.

Emily Wentworth perched on the edge of a matching chair, her eyes bright. She looked trim and fresh in a white piqué blouse and crisp green cotton golf skirt. "This is so cheerful. I love having coffees and teas. I did so much of that when Jonathan was in the service. I used to have tea every Sunday afternoon in our quarters and all the wives came. It was a way to get to know them. Before things changed so much. Now so many of the wives work. It's a different world. Now how can they be good officers' wives, if they work?"

Annie had plunged into many different lifestyles in the thousands of mysteries she'd read, from Dorothy L. Sayers's England between the World Wars to Robert van Gulick's exploration of seventh-century China, from Steven Saylor's ancient Rome to Sparkle Hayter's zestfully up-to-date Big Apple, from Alistair MacLean's World War II adventures to Tony Hillerman's Navajo and Zuni reservations, but not a one had given her a pointer on the mores of being an officer's wife.

"I don't know," she said honestly. She did know she must quickly decide whether to continue her visit under the false pretense of a social call on Emily Wentworth or baldly state her hope of talking to Jonathan Wentworth about the library board and the murder of Bud Hatch.

Annie temporized. "I've been meaning to come and see you. I've worked with Sharon on some community projects."

"Sharon is so good to us. When Jonathan retired, she asked us to come and live on the island so we could be close to her and the children." She nodded briskly at the photographs atop a baby grand piano, many of two fresh-faced blond girls playing tennis or horseback riding. "But now both the girls are out of college. We're going to move to Scottsdale. I can play even more golf there. I'm thrilled. It's so wonderful of Jonathan to think of it. He knows how much my golf means to me. And Jonathan can fly as much as he wants. Much better weather. We're hoping Sharon might move her store there. Sharon and her dad are so close. It's hard when there is a divorce." Emily looked toward a wall of pictures, a young Sharon in a wedding dress. "Charles upset us so much at the time. But he seemed to love Sharon. I don't know what went wrong for them. Their marriage faded. That's what it did. It started out bright and strong and it faded."

Annie had vaguely known that Sharon Gibson was divorced and had two daughters. And she recalled Sharon's mentioning her parents' retirement on the island. It was, she had said, a very good fit because many retired military settled on Broward's Rock. But now it looked as if they were ready to move on to another retirement area.

"Sharon loves having you here." Annie was sure she did.

She and Emily Wentworth both spoke at once.

"Hope you can come—"

"You know all about mysteries—"

They stopped. "Please," Annie said.

"Oh, well, perhaps you don't want to talk about it." Emily fingered the jaunty silver pin in the shape of a golf ball on her blouse. "That shooting last night." Her bright green eyes appraised Annie. "I've never been involved— oh, I don't suppose someone like you would say simply being there was involvement—but I've never been so close to something so— oh, it's wrong to say it was exciting. But it was. The way that man fell so suddenly and then people streaming onto the stage and that brisk policeman. So intense. The sheriff? It was all so surprising. Perhaps I shouldn't be so interested." Her laugh was self-deprecating. "But I've always loved mysteries and I never expected to be this close to one. I apologize if he—the man who was shot—was a great friend of yours. But I don't suppose anyone knows as much about murder as you do and if you don't mind talking about it...."

Emily Wentworth was a mystery reader. She was ripe for the plucking. Annie repressed a jubilant Speak Your Mind: Talk about it? Hot damn, let's get to it.

And, of course, Emily Wentworth was quite right. No one in the island knew as much about murder as she did. Except, of course, Henny Brawley. But she wouldn't think about that now. And certainly she wouldn't think about it here.

"Oh, that's all right, Mrs. Wentworth." Annie perched on the edge of her chair, a just-us-girls smile on her face. "I don't mind talking about it at all. I didn't know General Hatch well at all. Probably you and your husband knew him much better."

Her hostess looked at her blankly. "We didn't know him personally at all. Of course, Jonathan is on the library board, so he must have known him. But he never mentioned him to me."

"That's how I met him," Annie said chummily. "I suppose Jonathan told you all about the troubles on the board."

For an instant, Emily Wentworth looked embarrassed. "Oh, I suppose he told me some things about the board. He'd mentioned there was some controversy, but I'm afraid I didn't pay much attention. The stock market's been just fascinating and I've spent a lot of time buying and selling. And been quite successful." A pleased smile. "But what happened? Tell me about it."

Oh, oh. Jonathan Wentworth attended that last library board meeting where Henny's troops had rallied, where Miss Dora prevailed, where Hatch made it clear there would be a reckoning next week. And if Wentworth told his wife, she hadn't listened.

Was it simply that he was a quintessential male: How was your day? Fine. Who was there? Bunch of women. What happened? Nothing special.

Or was it something else entirely?

And how could Emily Wentworth say so positively that she and her husband didn't know General Hatch at all, yet Jonathan Wentworth had warned Henny about the peril of angering Hatch? Obviously, Wentworth's wife didn't know anything about the general, and she was waiting for Annie to bring her up-to-date on the general and the library board.

It was time to be as adroit and careful as Kay Mitchell's Chief Inspector John Morrissey.

"Oh, there was a disagreement about the festival, how it should be produced. And where some artwork should be placed." Annie carefully didn't mention names. "And Hatch wasn't happy with the library director and some of the staff, things like that. Your husband hadn't mentioned it?"

Emily poured fresh coffee and gave her a rueful smile. "He may have. But Jonathan has so many activities. I don't hear everything he says."

Sunlight slanted in through old glass panes, bringing life to the muted colors of the Japanese tapestry. But the room, despite its crisp cleanliness, didn't have a lived-in look. Maybe that's why Jonathan said little to his wife. Maybe she hadn't been listening for years.

Emily offered seconds on the brownies.

Annie accepted and loved that sweet chocolate rush.

Emily sipped from her cup, leaned forward eagerly. "What do you think happened?" Her eyes glistened with avid interest.

Annie couldn't resist showing off just a

little bit. After all, she'd seen more than most who were there and quickly figured out what happened. "The person who shot him was standing in that clump of willows to the west of the bandstand."

Emily Wentworth's eyes widened. "Why, we were sitting quite near there!" She pressed her lips together. "And we left. Immediately. I told Jonathan we should stay. That's what the official asked us to do, but Jonathan said we hadn't seen anything and there was no reason to stay. And really, I know him so well after all these years. He's always so protective. I suppose he thought there might still be some danger. He insisted."

"Jonathan was with you when the shot was fired?" Annie kept her face bright and interested.

Emily Wentworth gave her a quick, surprised look.

For an instant, Annie was afraid her question was too direct.

But Emily's answer was calm. And definite. "Oh, didn't I tell you? I reached out, clutched his arm. I suppose I must have gasped. And Jonathan always takes such good care of me. He wouldn't even take time to pick up our blanket. He said it was old and didn't matter. He just wanted to get me home." She looked past Annie. "Oh, Jonathan, come in. Such a nice surprise. Look who's come to see me."

Annie's eyes jerked toward the hallway. She'd not heard a door or a footstep.

Jonathan Wentworth walked into the room and it suddenly seemed much smaller. He was a tall, thin man, a very handsome man with his short white hair and bronzed face and bright blue eyes. Annie had a sudden memory of a picture of Jimmy Stewart in his World War II pilot uniform. It was the wrinkled tan flight suit with occasional smudges of carbon and the highly polished ankle-high brown leather boots. He carried an old-fashioned brown cloth flying helmet in one hand. "Hello, Annie." His manner was impeccable, but his eyes were cool and wary.

But he'd been beside his wife when the shots rang out. Hadn't he?

The husband and wife exchanged a measured glance.

Or was mystery reader Emily Wentworth giving her husband an alibi?

That undercurrents rippled beneath the social surface was clear to Annie. But what they signified she had no idea.

Wentworth stood in the doorway, filling it. "Hate to break up a tea party. But don't you remember, Emily? You promised Sharon you'd help unpack some things in the store. I gave up on flying. It's too stormy. So I thought I'd help you."

There was an instant's silence, broken by Emily's musical laughter. "Jonathan, you treat me like a glass figurine." She stood, lithe and swift, held out a hand to Annie. "Come, my dear, we're being shushed. Nice women don't talk about murder. Maybe Sharon will indulge me. I'll have to ask what she saw."

Annie was on her feet. She wondered that

the trilling woman didn't sense her husband's tense determination. It was certainly evident to Annie as Wentworth held open the front door, took his wife's elbow.

Annie went down the steps in front of them. If it wasn't a bum's rush, it came close.

Emily was still chattering. "I can go to the shop for a little while, but I'm playing bridge at two."

Wentworth held the car door for his wife.

Annie climbed into her car.

Emily gave her a friendly wave, then looked at her husband. Her bright red lips spread in a smile. Though the car windows were closed, Annie knew she'd given a peal of laughter. But Jonathan Wentworth's face might have been chipped out of stone.

Max walked swiftly along the dusty gray path, skirting occasional marshy spots. Loblolly pines closed overhead. The thick canopy shut out the sun, but not the heat. Sweat beaded his face, rolled down his back and legs. No-see-ums swirled around him. Wet ferns seemed to reach out and grab him, and soon he was not only hot but damp. He decided that Toby Maguire was a better man than he if he marched through this muck every day to his studio. Why didn't he work on the screened-in porch behind the house he shared with Ned?

When the path plunged out of the pines, Max understood. An old, weathered shack stood on pilings and faced the ocean. A skylight had been cut into the steeply pitched roof. Max heard the boom of the surf, smelled the tangy odor of seaweed and fish, and watched the flutter of the sea oats. Someday too soon, whoever owned this patch of land would be able to sell it for a huge sum for an oceanfront home. But Broward's Rock still had beachfront views that could be enjoyed even if you weren't a millionaire. He shaded his eyes to look out at the gray-green water, stirred up from the morning storm. A tree trunk bobbed offshore. Watching the ocean was exhilarating, endlessly fascinating, always awesome, well worth being mugged by no-see-ums.

Max wished he were deep-sea fishing. He climbed rickety wooden steps that squeaked underfoot. The door was propped open.

Toby Maguire stood in front of a canvas daubed with green and blue and splashes of silver, one man's view of a white-capped ocean and Wedgwood-blue sky.

He had to have heard Max approaching. But he continued to paint. He was so big, the canvas looked small, the room cramped. Only the vast expanse of ocean was larger than the man painting it. The unscreened window was wide open, the shutters folded back. The room smelled like paint and turpentine, pungent and nose-wrinkling, overlaid with the fresh, wild, rich-with-life scent of the sea.

"Mr. Maguire." Max scanned the room. No telephone. If there was a cell phone, it wasn't in sight. Good.

The artist tilted his head, made a soft brush stroke. "Private property." His voice was hoarse and rough, like a rarely used winch on a well.

"Would you rather talk to the police?' Max stepped inside.

Maguire slowly turned. "Get out." Blood-shot brown eyes glared from beneath a shock of silver-streaked black hair drawn back into a ponytail. His face bulged like potatoes in a sack—a broad forehead, lumpy cheeks. An oddly neat flaming-red beard contrasted jar-ringly with his hair and tapered to a sharp point beneath his chin. He held a brush in one massive hand, the palette in the other. Paint stained his faded red polo shirt and ragged denim cutoffs, had spattered down on worn leather sandals.

"Will you give me two minutes?" Max's tone was quiet and pleasant.

"Why should I?" Toby's voice was as deep as the growl of a brown bear disturbed in his lair.

Max was short and crisp. "So a teenage kid won't go to jail for a murder he didn't commit."

Maguire put the palette on an upended crate, poked the brush in a jar. He pulled a pack of cigarettes from his pocket, lit one. All the while he ignored Max. He walked out onto the porch overlooking the ocean.

Max followed.

The tangy breeze rippled the sea oats, buoyed a skimming cadre of pelicans, tugged at their clothes.

Maguire didn't look at him. "How do you know he didn't kill the bastard?"

Succinct, bald and unvarnished, there was no artifice to the question.

Max answered honestly, "I don't know it.

He could have. But so could you. Or Ned. Or a bunch of other people. Only difference is, Samuel's going to jail Monday whether he did it or not."

Smoke curled from the edge of Maguire's mouth. "Ned never shot a gun in his life. City boy. Raised by a librarian mother. Nice woman. Babied him. Thinks I encourage him to do wild things. Scuba. Rock climbing." He faced Max. His red beard shone like molten lava. "But not guns. I got enough of guns a long time ago."

"So I understand." Max didn't pursue it. He waited. This man would say what he wanted to say and nothing more.

"I was a good shot. It would take a good shot. Somebody pinged the old bastard from the willows, right?" Maguire took a final drag from the cigarette, ground it underfoot. "That's what Ned told me. Said they caught the kid near there with the gun in his hand."

"That's right. Did you hear the shots? See anybody there?" Max slipped the questions in.

His lumpy face untroubled, Maguire shrugged his massive shoulders. He reached up to scratch at his beard. "Who the hell knows? I was bombed, plastered, skunked. I don't remember a damn thing till I woke up this morning with a head that felt like rats were gnawing on it. You'll have to ask Ned. He says I was blowing my piccolo like a banshee and he got me on my feet and to the car and that's when somebody took the old devil out." Those big shoulders moved again in a faintly mocking slouch. "Sorry I can't help you." He moved back into his studio, ponderously as a bear, and picked up his palette. Max was dismissed.

All the way back to the car, Max flailed at gnats. As far as he was concerned, that alibi could be filed under possible, but improbable. Or, as Annie likely would put it, more directly and less elegantly, in a pig's eye.

Annie revved up the air conditioning as high as it would go. As she drove toward town, she called Max. No answer. She picked up their messages from home:

"Annie, Miss Dora." The raspy voice was confident. "I'm certain that if we follow the great example of Eliza Lucas Pickney, we shall extract the truth just as she successfully boiled the dye from indigo. Her success was predicated upon perseverance. I trust you are persevering in your search for those subtle scraps of information obtained through personal industry. As Eliza was accustomed to enjoying intellectual discourse in Charleston, I suggest we gather for an exchange of ideas, albeit of a less illustrious nature, at six P.M. at your store. Certainly it will be an appropriate location for an exploration of our topic and the coffee area affords more space than Max's office. Miss Barbara will assist me in conveying there the information we are amassing. Max, of course, will also be in attendance. Until then."

A click.

Subtle scraps of information. Gossip, of

course. Annie knew she was failing to meet the standard expected of a South Carolina woman. So far, her gossip retrieval success was zero. And what gave the old harridan the right to take over Death on Demand for her headquarters? But Annie knew she wouldn't complain. Iced coffee at the ready. And she'd just replenished the cookie jar with peanut-butter cookies. Six o'clock. Mmm. They could order pizza. Miss Dora would not be focused on food, however. Annie wondered how many subtle scraps she could gather before six.

"Annie, dear. Such a difficult time, of course, for all the library board members." There was no mistaking Laurel's husky, effer-vescent tone. Dammit, how could she always sound like Lauren Bacall on her way to the Stork Club to meet Bogie? "We can take our counsel from dear William: 'Always the dull-ness of the fool is the whetstone of the wits.' I'm sure we will prevail over Mr. Posey." A pause, then, as if in a careless afterthought, Laurel said lightly, "Oh, I happened to have a chat with dear Frank. He seems to have an odd idea that someone we both know"—now the tone was definitely arch—"might have some knowledge about the tip-over of that vase at the library and the purported"—great emphasis—"rifling of that man's cabinet at the library and locker at that bastion of male dominance."

Yep. Someone Annie and Laurel knew very well indeed. Annie grinned, then swerved to miss a raccoon who shot her an outraged and too-intelligent frown. She focused on the road and hoped Frank Saulter had put the fear of the pokey, if not of God, into Max's free-spirited parent.

"'...O, how full of briers is this working-day world!' Au revoir, my dear."

A familiar, beloved, wonderful male voice. "Hey, Annie, let's meet for lunch at one. At Parotti's. Okay? Leave me a message."

Annie immediately felt brighter, happier, warmer, though perhaps the last wasn't a plus. It was supposed to hit ninety-six. As Henny had once remarked irritably on a steamy July afternoon, "Dear God, and to think tourists are paying for the privilege of enduring this natural sauna. Why don't they go to Maine?"

Henny. No message from Henny. Not that Annie expected one. She stopped for Broward Rock's single light. Gossip. Henny was a trove. She knew everybody, had connections that reached into every abode on the island, whether a mansion or a shack. If Henny were herself she would be the obvious source of information about everyone concerned with Bud Hatch's murder.

The light changed. Annie started forward, then unexpectedly wrenched her wheel to the right and pulled into the dusty gray entrance of the oldest cemetery on the island. A horn honked irritably.

Annie ignored the driver's rude gesture. Couldn't a woman change her mind? All right. Gossip. Ingrid? Maybe. Her husband Duane? A better possibility. Vince Ellis? Oh yeah, good idea. She glanced at the car clock. Twenty minutes to noon. Which reminded her. She called, said, "Parotti's at one and I hope he still makes the best fried-oyster sandwich on the island." But not Vince right now. As editor of the *Island Gazette,* he was right on deadline for the Sunday paper and she was sure the newsroom was taut and tense with a murder to cover. The *Gazette* didn't publish on Saturdays, which was probably breaking Vince's heart at this very moment.

Gossip. Who—

Oh, of course! The Volvo jolted out of the cemetery.

Chapter 8

Muscles bulged in Samuel Kinnon's bare, sweaty back as he heaved clippings onto the bed of the pickup. He turned, grass catcher in hand. His eyes widened, his face a mixture of hope and fear. "Have you found out anything?"

Max swiped his face with a sodden handkerchief, wished he could as easily wipe away the terror that flickered in Samuel's dark eyes. He spoke robustly, "It's coming along. I'm talking to people. Could you spare a minute?"

Samuel's big shoulders slumped. His hand tightened on the grass catcher. "Mr. Jenkins"— he swallowed tightly—"Mr. Jenkins says the circuit solicitor's going to arrest me."

"Don't borrow trouble, Samuel." Max had an uncanny echo in his mind of his mother's lilting voice through the years, "Don't borrow trouble, Max, 'nor invite an evil fate by apprehending it.'" But how difficult it was to do. Which Thoreau well knew. As for Laurel—Max focused his mind upon the moment, as it would take a lifetime to focus on his mother. "It's a long way yet until Monday." But that wasn't true and Samuel's uneasy face made that clear. What did they have? Less than forty-eight hours.

The whine of a leaf blower echoed the uneasiness in his mind, but he kept his voice calm and reassuring. "Let's go back a little bit, Samuel. Back to Wednesday. You said you didn't push the vase off the library roof. Now's the time to tell me anything you know about that." He saw a flicker in Samuel's eyes. "That was an attempt on Hatch's life. It was serious then. Now the man's dead. If you saw anything, anyone...."

Samuel held tight to the grass catcher. He didn't look at Max. "I didn't want to say anything. 'Cause I don't really know anything...."

Max waited patiently.

Samuel sighed. "Mr. Maguire. He went in the library a few minutes before it happened. Then he came out a side door and went off on his motorcycle."

Toby Maguire. Big, strong, and no fan of the general's.

"I'll ask him if he saw anything. Okay, Samuel, tell me what you did last night."

Max looked around. "Let's get out of the sun."

Samuel pointed to a bench near the lagoon. Pine needles were slick underfoot as they ducked among a clump of tall evergreens. Even though the bench was well shaded beneath the spreading limbs of a magnolia, the wood was hot to the touch. Samuel flung himself down without noticing. He clenched his big hands. "I'm scared."

"Don't borrow trouble," Max said again and perhaps something of Laurel's insouciance and confidence and tranquillity infused his voice because slowly, slowly, Samuel's big hands relaxed.

The young man took a deep breath and even managed a sheepish smile. "Yeah. I guess I got spooked. It's going to be okay, isn't it?" His dark, scared eyes clung to Max.

"Sure." A promise, Max knew, that somehow he had to keep. Had to. "Last night you found the gun. How did that happen?"

Samuel's face creased in concentration. "I kicked it with my foot. Scared the hell out of me when I looked down and saw it. I'd been looking for Mr. Maguire—"

Max looked sharply at Samuel.

"—and I kept hearing a piccolo making a funny noise. My big sister plays the piccolo. I know Mr. Maguire plays the piccolo. He gave a program once at the Haven. Then he talked to us about painting. It was cool. He's such a big guy and he looks so tough. The kids were really impressed. Anyway, I figured it had to be him with the piccolo because Mrs. Cummings—that's Ken's mom—asked me to look for Mr. Maguire, said Mr. Fisher wanted to know if he was anywhere around. So I nosed around on some of the paths in the preserve. I didn't go in very far because it was dark and I didn't have a flashlight. But that's where I thought the piccolo was coming from."

Max pulled his soppy, now grass-flecked slacks away from his legs. The piccolo. Always the piccolo. "Did you see Mr. Maguire?"

"No. But I heard something rustling in the willow trees." Samuel's eyes were huge, knowing now what that rustle portended. "I was about twenty, twenty-five feet away. The light was spotty, just those little lanterns in the trees. I saw something—somebody. But I don't know who. If I'd been a little closer—"

Not even the hot-tub heat dispelled the chill that edged through Max. If Samuel had been closer, he might have come face-to-face with a killer. "Samuel, think hard. Did you see anything, smell anything? Hear anything besides the rustle in the trees?"

Samuel's big round face squeezed tight in concentration. "There were shadows everywhere and so much noise from the fireworks and people whistling and clapping. A rocket had just gone off. But I thought somebody whispered, a deep kind of whisper. And then"—his voice was uncertain—"I think somebody laughed. Just a choked-off, short, ugly laugh." He rubbed his face. "Maybe that was somebody out in the crowd. I don't know. The more I think about it, the weirder it seems."

Max looked at the anxious, uncertain young face. "It's all right, Samuel. Try to relax. Don't think about it. Maybe something more will come to you."

Samuel's eyes lighted. "Those noises, whatever they were, I heard them when I was coming along the path, just before I kicked the gun."

Once again, Max felt cold. So near to death, so terribly near.

"My foot kind of tingled. I looked down and saw something dark. I picked it up. I couldn't believe it when I saw it was a gun." He still sounded surprised. "I knew I had to take it to somebody. I didn't know how anybody could lose a gun, and besides, you aren't supposed to bring guns to the library. I stood there a minute. I didn't know what to do. But I couldn't leave it on the path. There were so many kids running around. What if a kid found it? So I picked it up and started toward the field. That's when Chief Saulter came around the trees. He pointed his gun at me. He meant it." Samuel swallowed hard. "I've never been so scared."

Max gave him a hearty poke on the shoulder. "It's going to be okay." But, as he turned to leave, he said soberly, "Samuel, stick close to your folks. Okay?"

He knew Samuel was watching him as he walked to his car. Max slid into the driver's seat, gave a farewell wave. But the smooth rumble of his car didn't drown out the memory of Samuel's words:...a short, ugly laugh.

Who laughs after shooting a man?

. . .

As Annie pulled into a parking slot at the
Laughing Gull Condos, she wasn't altogether
persuaded cell phones were a great advance
for the happiness of mankind. If it weren't for
cell phones, she wouldn't have caught Pamela
Potts just as she was walking out the door of
her condo, en route to yet more good works.
If it were the good old pre-cellular-phone days,
Annie would simply have driven to Pamela's
and found her gone. No such luck.

Annie was sure Pamela probably knew
more gossip than anyone on the island, barring Henny. Of course, to obtain information
Annie would have to discuss the objects of her
interest without even a hint of malicious
intent. Pamela would never stoop to gossip.
But an elevated discussion of mutual acquain-
tances just might be possible.

But no matter how bright the prospect of
zeroing in on the board members, Annie
really, really, really didn't want to accompany
Pamela. But she had to. Even if it weren't her
responsibility as an aspirant to full-fledged
South Carolina womanhood, it was the kind
of invitation that could be rejected only
by a superclod or a Speak Your Mind devotee
at a level far beyond Annie's toddling at-
tempts.

It would demand a world-class Speak Your
Mind: I'd rather eat worms. Or, Pamela, why
don't you find a nice desert and wear skins?
You'll love it!

Instead, Annie crunched morosely up the

oyster-shell walk, too dispirited to combat the no-see-ums.

Pamela bustled down the steps, her white piqué dress and pristinely white sandals immaculate. Annie blinked in disbelief. Pamela was wearing hose! Why not a hair shirt? It couldn't possibly be any more uncomfortable.

Annie knew her once equally pristine apricot cotton top now clung to her like road tar to a sandal and her cotton twill skirt hung limp and wrinkled. She knew it was hopeless, but she gave it a try. "Pamela, I'm not really dressed—"

"Oh, Annie"—a sweet remonstrance—"it isn't how we're dressed that ever matters. It's what is in our hearts."

Since Annie's heart was curdling with sheer hatred, there was very little to say. And the Speak Your Mind had to be ignored: Then why the hell are you decked out all in white like a ministering angel?

"Annie, I'm so glad of your help. You are so good-hearted." A hail-sister-well-met smile exposed perfect small white teeth. "It's been such a pleasure to work with you on the festival publicity. Though, of course, it's simply tragic what happened. And so heartbreaking for the Kinnon family. To think that fine young man would commit such a violent act. Everyone is shocked."

"Samuel didn't do it." Annie spoke with authority. "He was just in the wrong place at the wrong time. He found the gun. Someone threw it on the path."

"Really!" Pamela's eyes glistened with eagerness. "Tell me all about it."

"Max is going to talk to Samuel and see if he can't remember something, anything to help the police. A sound or noise or smell." Perhaps Annie got a little carried away. "We're sure Samuel can help solve the crime. The police wouldn't let him talk to anybody last night, but if he knows anything, Max is going to get it out of him. After all, he was pretty close to those willow trees."

"Oh, that is so exciting." Pamela clapped her hands together.

Annie felt confident the phone lines would buzz all afternoon. By the time Pamela was finished, there would probably be rumors across the island of a masked band of predators secreted in the willows. At the very least, it would divert attention from Samuel. Annie felt a quiver of satisfaction at work well done. Who said gossip was always a bad thing?

"My goodness." Pamela got a grip on herself. "Who knows what will happen next? But, of course, our duties remain. I've collected all the publicity materials." She thrust an accordion folder into Annie's hands. "The program and the list of advertisers and, of course, the pre-festival publicity in the *Island Gazette*. It's simply serendipitous that you called when you did. It's saved me having to make a special trip to your house—"

God be praised for small favors.

"—and given us the opportunity to come together upon a mission of support for the bereaved family."

Annie felt lower than bubble gum on a shoe. She steeled herself. Miss Dora expected subtle scraps, subtle scraps she would be served, no matter the cost to Annie's self-esteem.

"I'll meet you at the church." Pamela handed her a note card. "Here's the address of the house."

Annie slammed into her car and threw the folder on the passenger seat. It promptly flopped wide open in good accordion fashion. Out spurted sheets of newspaper clippings neatly mounted, with time, date and publication noted in black letters. Annie stretched to retrieve the sheets, slapped them back into the folder in no particular order, several with photos of Henny in her finest club woman's apparel, three of Ned Fisher, and one of the entire board standing on the festival lot, squinting against the sun, the half-finished bandstand behind them, plus four round-up stories detailing the great pleasures awaiting the Broward's Rock public, including the tributes to the Gallant Women of South Carolina, with special reference to the contributions of Miss Dora Brevard of Chastain and reference librarian Edith Cummings. Trust Pamela Potts never to neglect her duty. Annie was sure that if a hurricane had devastated the island, Pamela would be rescued clinging to a treetop clutching her annotated, completed publicity folder.

Annie followed Pamela's car at an excruciatingly sedate pace to the church. If Annie'd felt frazzled when the trip began, she was now quivering with frustration. She didn't want to do this, but surely, if it had to be done, it could be done faster.

Pamela popped out of her car with a cheery smile. "The casseroles are in the kitchen. I was on the phone half the morning."

The gray wood church was in a grove of pines, peaceful, serene, and lovely. As they crunched up the oyster-shell walk, Annie scolded herself. Pamela meant well. Whenever there was a need she came forward to help if she could. Annie slid a quick sideways glance. Maybe it was the setting, maybe it was heightened awareness because of the raw emotion swirling around the death of the general, but Annie really looked at Pamela and saw the sad loneliness in glazed blue eyes, the fine lines at the corners of determinedly upturned lips, felt the enduring hunger for connection.

Annie reached out, squeezed Pamela's thin arm. "You're very good to do this."

As the old oak doors soughed shut behind them, Pamela's face lightened. She glowed, murmuring, "Oh, it isn't anything really. You're wonderful to come and help because after all you have things to do on the weekends." As in, a husband.

Annie felt a pang of sheer shame which made her even more voluble than usual as they transferred casseroles from the refrigerator to a serving cart. "I've never met Mrs. Hatch. I don't want to intrude. I'll just help take the food in, then slip away." Miss Dora could gouge out her own subtle scraps. There were limits and Annie had just reached one.

Pamela placed a casserole precisely on the cart, a second one exactly two inches away and centered. "The family will appreciate your coming, Annie. I've done this so often, I'm sure of that." As they moved back and forth from the counter to the cart, Pamela's brows drew down. "I'm worried about poor Mrs. Hatch. I saw her at the festival and I was so pleased and surprised because she rarely came to any functions. Then to have it end so dreadfully." Pamela paused and looked at Annie, her eyes huge with wonder. "I was actually speaking with her when the general was hurt. Oh, it was awful! Poor woman. She'll be so lonely. The general was such an exuberant man. He was everywhere. There wasn't anything on the island that he didn't attend even though they've only lived here a few months. Now that's the way to become a part of a community."

Annie stacked several loaves of french bread atop the casseroles.

Without missing a beat, Pamela rearranged them in a precise row.

Annie simply handed her the package of paper plates. "So she didn't get out much?"

Pamela studied the cart, tucked the plates between two casseroles. "Hardly at all. And she was almost unfriendly if you called her the first thing in the morning."

Annie didn't see that as a social offense. She held the kitchen door open and Pamela pushed the cart.

"We'll put half the casseroles in your car and half in mine." Pamela wheeled the cart with the precision of an admiral maneuvering a battleship. "That way we can place them flat in the trunk and nothing will tip over."

Annie wasn't about to challenge Pamela's casserole delivery expertise, though she reluctantly bid farewell to her final hope of escaping further participation. "You saw Mrs. Hatch at the festival?"

"Annie, I was standing in line behind her at the cola stand just before the general was shot. We were walking down toward the bandstand together and saw him fall. I stayed with her then, of course." Pamela tightened the foil wrap on one casserole. "There. I think you're ready to go. I'll be a few minutes later. I'm going by the grocery to pick up a sheet cake."

Annie climbed into her Volvo. A few minutes later—the island was so small—she pulled up in front of a one-story pink stucco house at the end of a cul-de-sac. The turnaround was lined with cars. Maybe she could get in and out quickly.

Miss Dora's spirit accompanied her up the well-kept walk. Subtle scraps. All right. As long as she was here, she'd make an effort.

A gardener lived at this house. Purple and gold petunias, pink and white impatiens, orange marigolds and yellow roses glowed with color and vigor.

The door stood open. Annie balanced a casserole on her hip and rang the bell.

"Come in, please." The deep voice was

subdued, but it had an innate quality of vigor. "Let me hold the door." A narrow-faced man with shiny brown eyes and short brown hair welcomed Annie. "I can take that to the kitchen."

"I have more casseroles in the car." Annie looked in the bright, cheerful game room to her left. The room seemed to be full. An older woman sat on a sunny yellow sofa with the rector from church. Father Cooley's head was bent as he listened intently. Several clusters of people dotted the long room. A teenage boy aimed a dart at the familiar red-and-white-ringed target. A teenage girl carried a tray with glasses of iced tea.

"I'll help you bring them in," her greeter said. He put the casserole on a side table. "I'm Chuck Hatch. I live in Savannah."

"Annie Darling. From the church." They shook hands. Chuck's only resemblance to his father was his trim muscular build. He followed her briskly to the car and took three casseroles. Annie picked up a fourth and balanced the bread on top. As they walked back to the house, Annie asked, "Is that why your folks came here to Broward's Rock? To be close to you?"

"Well, me and the Confederate Air Force. There's a very active chapter on the island. Mom and Dad roamed around after he retired. They went to San Diego in '93. My sister Lacey and her family were there, but Lacey and Craig moved to New York, so my folks decided to come here. There are lots of retired military here." They crowded the foods onto the kitchen table, which was covered with dishes.

If she had felt an intruder en route, she now felt like a disgusting ghoul. Out. She wanted out. Miss Dora could produce her own subtle scraps. Annie backed toward the hallway, talking fast. "The names of the cooks are on the cards taped to the casseroles. Also the kind of food, along with the contents," she chattered. "In case anyone has allergies, that sort of thing. We've all learned so much from the labeling laws. Why, it's amazing how many people have food allergies. I'll run on now—"

"Oh, please, come say hello to Mother. She'll want to thank you." He took her firmly by the elbow. Obviously, if he wasn't a chip off the macho block, he was still a take-charge guy. No doubt learned at Papa's military knee.

Chuck maneuvered Annie slickly through the assorted groups, pausing every so often to toss quick introductions: "...my son Alan, my daughter Cathy. That's my wife over there, Judy. My sister and her family. And my brother, Rip...." Faces swirled in Annie's mind.

They fetched up beside the sofa.

"Mom, this is Annie Darling. From the church. She just brought a bunch of casseroles." Chuck clapped her on the shoulder and turned away. Annie couldn't have felt lonelier if she'd been on top of the Empire State Building and the last light in New York City had twinkled out.

Father Cooley looked up, his pink-cheeked

face creased in a welcoming smile. "My child," he murmured.

Mrs. Hatch was an older replica of her son. Or, of course, it was the other way around, Annie thought confusedly—a long narrow face, elegant like a high-class horse, brown eyes but these were red-rimmed and dazed, a thatch of short curly brown hair frosted with gray, and a tremulous smile. "You are so kind." Her light, soft voice wavered. "Everyone has been so kind." She reached up, held tight to Annie's hands.

Bubble gum on a shoe didn't even come close. Lower than a snake's belly, that's what they said in Annie's native Texas. She qualified.

"Of course," the wavering voice said, "you're that young lady on the library board." An odd pause. "Bud was having some trouble there. People weren't up to snuff, he said. But I'm sure he didn't mean you. Please, come sit by me." She patted the cushion next to her. Father Cooley nodded in approval.

Annie sank onto the daffodil-yellow couch, wished she could disappear at will like the rowdy ghosts in *Topper*.

Mrs. Hatch clung to Annie's hand. Her hand was hot and dry. "We haven't been on the island long. I'm not involved the way I used to be." The widow's voice was vague.

Father Cooley patted her shoulder. "It's hard coming into a new community."

According to Mrs. Wentworth, service wives were supposed to blend smoothly into a new environment with each duty station.

"I hadn't had a chance to meet many people." Mrs. Hatch stared across the room, but her gaze was empty and unfocused. "So many people have come by and brought food. Everyone is so kind."

Annie felt an odd prickling down her back, that hot hand and that wandering gaze.

Father Cooley looked as satisfied as a well-fed pigeon. He could count on his parishioners. He cleared his throat. "Yes, Ruth. You were telling me about Bud—"

Ruth Hatch shivered. She dropped Annie's hand, pressed her hands tightly together. "Bud was strong." She spoke clearly, but tonelessly. "He always got what he wanted." Her red-rimmed eyes moved to the priest's face. "Until now. Isn't that remarkable?"

Father Cooley's plump face drooped with concern. "My dear, such a dreadful moment. But we will recall Bud as he lived. That's what matters now."

"Bud." A musing tone. "How to describe him." She looked away from the priest. Her eyes were no longer vague. They were somber and deep with remembrance. "He'd want us to say that he always did his best. And he expected everyone else to do the same."

"But what would you say?" Annie wanted to demand. Instead, she watched that narrow, contained face.

"Bud always ran a tight ship. I remember the time"—her eyes were no longer vague—"when the housing office at Leavenworth approved our moving on the post. Bud figured out we'd been slipped ahead of some officers with earlier AD dates, so he went straight to the major in charge and told him. That meant we didn't get housing on post for another six months and we were cramped in a tiny little one-room walk-up apartment with the boys and I was pregnant. But Bud followed the rules. And there was the time he found the boys smoking on a Scout camping trip—"

"Talk about a sore butt!" came the call from across the room. Chuck stepped close and picked up the story. "Dad was frosted. I'm surprised Rip and I lived through that one. Not only demerits but six weeks under house arrest. Dad put—"

Annie scarcely listened to the rest of the story, she was looking over a wall of photographs: Bud and a young bride ducking beneath the upheld swords of other fresh-faced young officers, Bud straight and handsome in his dress blues, Bud in the cockpit of a single-engine plane, Bud and his wife with the children between them, Bud in a major's uniform in an alien street with pedicabs and VW taxis and "Saigon" written across one corner, Bud standing tall while his wife pinned on his general's insignia, Bud deep-sea fishing. But not only Bud, of course. There were many pictures of the kids—growing up, dances and ball games, awards assemblies and camping trips, high school and college graduations, then weddings and babies. Pictures, pictures, pictures.

A dainty Dresden clock on the mantel chimed the quarter hour. Annie looked at the hands and bolted to her feet. "Oh, gosh,

I'm late. I have to meet my husba—" She clapped a hand to her mouth. Lower than a stalagmite in the world's deepest cave.

Bud Hatch's widow looked at the wall of pictures, her eyes held by that long-ago wedding day. Tears brimmed. She looked up forlornly at Annie. "Your voice! You love him very much, don't you? Yes, of course. Hurry to him."

Annie was two blocks from the end of the island and the ferry dock and Parotti's, the combination bait shop, bar and grill and ferry headquarters, when she saw the Island Bakery, one of her favorite destinations. But it wasn't a sudden desire for raspberry brownies that caused her to yank the wheel right. An irate honk behind her made Annie wonder if maybe the island population was growing too fast. Why were people always honking at her? She swerved off the paved road onto the dirt lane, dust pluming behind her. So, yes, maybe she had neglected to signal, but was that a capital crime? She gave a regretful glance at the bakery, but she wasn't a pig like Joyce Porter's Wilfred Dover, so she resisted temptation. She drove a block and a half, passing small homes on huge secluded lots dotted with towering pines and blossom-laden magnolias. This was the town side of the island. These houses, mostly modest white frames interspersed among larger tabby homes, had been here years longer than the new and elegant houses on the recently developed end of the island which was reached through a gated entry. This end of the island was the site of the small shops, the grocery store, car repair, the schools, the hospital, the athletic fields. The most recent coffee for the Women's Tennis Association had been held at 19 Bay Street, the residence of Gail and David Oldham.

The cottage was a story and a half on raised brick pillars with a covered front porch supported by slender, unadorned pillars. Huge live oaks rose on either side. The shaded front yard was almost bare of grass, but clumps of ferns flourished.

Annie parked at the end of the unpaved drive, beside Gail's black Jeep. David drove a tan coupé. Annie felt a rush of relief. She needed to talk to David Oldham, but she didn't want to do it in front of Gail, not with a searing memory of David's stricken face as he turned and moved heavily away through the forest preserve.

If, at that moment, David had crashed through the brush to attack Bud Hatch, Annie wouldn't have been surprised. She didn't know that she'd ever been that near raw pain.

The quiet morning held no echo of that anguish, only the squawk of blackbirds, the high chut of cardinals, the constant zzz of no-see-ums. But Annie hesitated at the foot of the steps. What kind of misery was she going to encounter? The ultimate confrontation between Gail and David last night must have been fraught with bitterness.

Annie took a deep breath, forced herself to climb to the porch. If ever two people had reason to hate a man recently dead, it was Gail and David Oldham. Where were they when the shots rang out?

Annie stepped to the door, lifted her hand and rang the bell. The door was ajar. Though no lights were on, she could see a portion of the hallway and a cheerful yellow-and-green braided rug.

No answer.

Annie knocked again, called out. "Gail?" She was sure she must have been heard. The house was small, a living room and bedroom on one side of the hall, dining room and kitchen on the other, a stairway to a loft which had been finished into a second bedroom. David kept his computer there.

She rattled the door, went down the front steps and around the back to the kitchen steps. She peered through a window.

No lights. No answer. No movement.

Annie felt a clutch of uneasiness in her chest. That open door. Gail's car. And no response.

She came again to the front door, hesitantly opened the screen, pushed the door wide. That's when she saw the note, a sheet from a square pink pad with "Gail's Kitchen" in the upper right corner.

Annie bent down. It was hard to read because the hallway was dusky in the morning gloom.

"David—Please, wait for me. Please. We have to talk. Gail."

On the side table, a delicate china clock tinged the hour. Annie looked to the right. The small living room was empty. She stepped inside. A bedroom pillow was rumpled on the couch. A small plate with a half-eaten sandwich, the bread now dry and stiff, sat on the coffee table. A glass held a dark liquid. Lipstick stains marked the rim of the glass. Annie walked around the room, she peered behind the couch. Then she crossed the hall to the dining room. Nothing was out of place.

In the kitchen, a single bowl sat on the wooden table, half-filled with milk and sodden cornflakes. A cup of coffee was beside it.

Even Watson or Hastings could figure this out. Breakfast for one, no effort made to clean up.

Gail was a fanatically neat housekeeper.

Outside, a car door slammed.

Annie's heart thudded. Her hands were suddenly sweaty. She darted to the dining room window, drew back a curtain.

No tan coupé. A green sedan was newly parked across the street.

Okay, she was scared, scared of the ominous quiet and the anger this home must have seen. She couldn't leave until she was sure the house was truly empty. Darting an occasional glance over her shoulder, she stepped to the end of the hall. Using all of her willpower, she opened the bedroom door.

A pillow was gone, the bedspread was rumpled, but the bed hadn't been slept in. She poked her head into the tiny bathroom. The closet door was closed. Annie felt more secure now. The closet smelled faintly of potpourri. Dresses and suits. Shoes. Nothing unexpected.

Annie left the bedroom, hurried up the half-flight of stairs. The office was neat and tidy and empty. It wasn't until she heard her own huge sigh of relief that Annie realized how tense she had been. It was all right. Everything was all right. Or, if not all right, not dreadful. The unused bed, the pillow in the living room, the dirty dishes for one might argue distress. But not murder.

She trotted downstairs, passed the note lying forlornly on the wooden floor. She didn't touch it. It wasn't her business. And she'd better get the heck out of the front hallway before either Oldham returned.

As she pulled away from the curb, she twisted her head for a final look at the silent house.

Was it simply that she knew there must have been an ugly and angry confrontation between Gail and David that she found the house so disquieting? Or was her intuition signaling hard that she pay attention here?

Parotti's was an island institution, situated right at the ferry landing. The ferry, under the autocratic command of Captain Ben Parotti, followed a schedule of sorts, but anyone who offended him could face an all-day wait. Annie and Max had always found Parotti's a perfect spot for a delicious lunch in comparative solitude. Heaviest patronage was just before charter fishing boats cast off in the mornings or in the evenings, especially game nights. The menu featured Southern delights—fried oysters, barbecued-pork sandwiches, ribs, fried catfish, hush puppies, french fries, and beer.

Annie pushed open the heavy wooden door and plunged into the welcome dimness. The cool air smelled horrendously fishy with an underlying scent of old, often-fried grease. Max was already there, at one of the round wooden tables close to the 1940s jukebox. As soon as he saw her, he stood and smiled.

Dear Max. He never cared if she was late. His smile, so full of love and eagerness, his admiring, welcoming, God-I'm-glad-you're-here smile, come-let-me-touch-you smile. The emotional buffets of the morning coalesced. She felt the hot burn of tears. By the time she was halfway to the table, he was across the sloping wooden floor, his arms open, his smile replaced by a searching look of concern. She stepped into his embrace, clung to him, buried her face against him.

"It's okay, honey. It's okay. I'm here." His arms tightened around her. "Tell me."

She pulled back a little, tried to brush away the tears. "It's so awful. Mrs. Hatch and Bud. And Gail and David. And Emily and Jonathan. Oh, Max, it's so awful. Promises, and nobody kept them. Max, I hate it."

With one firm hand he guided her to their table, with the other he fished out a soft handkerchief.

Annie mopped at her face. "'Til death do us part.' That's the way it's supposed to be." Her voice quivered. "Not 'til I meet somebody new.'" Raggedly, with occasional sniffs, she

232

described her morning. When she had finished, she looked at him forlornly.

Ben Parotti approached gingerly, a careful eye on Annie. "The missus got a cold?" he asked Max.

"A little under the weather," Max said vaguely, then he ordered for them.

Annie almost managed a smile. A fried-oyster sandwich for her. And lemonade, a new addition to Parotti's menu. Max definitely was trying to make her feel good. He always looked askance when she ordered a fried-oyster sandwich, murmuring things like "Cholesterol on a bun" or "Why not go whole-hog, you unreconstructed Texan, see if he's got lamb fries?"

When Ben departed for the kitchen, Max leaned forward in his chair. "Okay, Annie. Take it easy. You know what's wrong?"

She took a gulp of water, icy and fresh, shook her head.

"You've never come face-to-face, up close, to infidelity. And it scares you." He reached across the table, gripped her hands in his. "It scares you because you think if it can happen to someone we know—like Gail and David—and you never had any idea this was so, then you think it could happen to you."

She stared into dark blue eyes, eyes as serious as she'd ever seen them, compelling, intelligent, loving eyes. "No, Annie. It can't happen to you. It won't happen to you. You remember when we first met—"

That long-ago evening at a rehearsal in a dingy cramped theater for an off-Broadway play. The handsomest, funniest, sexiest man she'd ever met introduced himself as Max Darling and he was never more than a foot away from her for all that evening and so many evenings to come.

"—I told you we were meant for each other. You didn't take me seriously."

She gave a small grin. "You acted like you were in a Cole Porter musical. How could I take you seriously?"

Max squeezed her hands. "I know. You said we didn't have anything in common. You were poor. I was rich. You'd always had to work hard for spending money and to make it through college and I never held a job and went to Princeton. You were from Texas and I was from Connecticut. You were serious and I refused to be serious. And so you ran away."

Annie nodded. It was a familiar story that Max loved to tell. How he, Galahad indeed, had pursued his lady love from the cool climes of the north to the muggy swampland of the Palmetto State and it was a good thing he had because shortly after he arrived in Broward's Rock Annie was suspected of murder and it was only his clever sleuthing that saved her from a murder charge.

Annie was always quick to interpose that in the denouement, she saved his life, not vice versa.

They could then beam at each other fondly.

"The thing to remember"—Max was emphatic—"is that no matter how different we are, it's the two of us together against the world. Annie and Max. Together. Gail and

David, Jonathan and his wife, Bud and his wife—they moved apart, somehow, someway. And if you asked them and they told the truth, they know that. As long as it's the two of us together, Annie, nobody can come between us."

Annie took a gulp of lemonade. A sense of peace flowed over her, soothing as a serene moon-dappled sea. Together. Yes. That's what they had, what they had to keep, no matter how much effort it took. Yes. She was full of nervous energy, driven to do and be and achieve. Max was amused, an onlooker, untroubled by society's expectations, content to be himself without undue effort or toil. But as long as they accepted their differences, took pleasure in them, saw them as a comple-ment, they would be okay. "Yes." She said it aloud, loud enough to turn Parotti's head from the bar. "Yes."

Annie flashed the tavern owner a bright, happy smile.

Startled, Parotti hesitated, then gave a thumb's-up.

Annie relaxed in her seat, listened attentively to Max's report of his interviews with Ned Fisher, Toby Maguire, and Samuel Kinnon. She eagerly grabbed her sandwich when Parotti brought their meals.

Parotti bent close to Max, whispered, "Women," gave Max a wink.

When Annie asked about the addition of lemonade to the menu, Parotti's beak-nosed face turned a rusty orange and he muttered, "My new missus. Thought we needed some pumping up." Other changes included quiche, she-crab soup, Key West lime pie, chintz curtains at the windows, and wildflowers in slender vases. Annie yearned to ask Parotti how the new look appealed to the regulars who dropped by either for beer and heated sports discussions or to fill their bait boxes from Parotti's coolers chock-full of chicken necks, squid and chunks of black bass, grouper and snapper. The rank odors from that end of the room indicated the bait business still thrived. Probably Parotti had drawn a line in the sawdust: thus far and no farther. And Annie was wise enough not to comment on his spiffed-up appearance, a natty navy polo shirt and baggy white pants. He'd always looked a bit like a raffish leprechaun, favoring tops reminiscent of long underwear and stained corduroy trousers. Now he had the air of a leprechaun fresh from the men's-wear department at Belk's.

When Max finished, Annie said tensely, "I don't know what worries me the most, what happened when the Oldhams got together last night or the way Henny's acting. Max, Henny has to be afraid for Jonathan Wentworth. Why else won't she help investigate?"

"But she said Jonathan was good 'through and through,'" Max quoted Annie.

Annie lifted her hands in bewilderment. "I know. None of it makes sense. But she's scared. I know she is. And Jonathan was furious that I came to his house." Annie peered through the gloom at her watch. "It's after two. I think I'll try to catch him. I want to know why he warned Henny, why he said Hatch was dangerous. I'll try Sharon's shop."

Max spread dill sauce on his flounder. "If he was mad that you came to the house, he's probably not going to talk to you, Annie."

"He'll talk to me." She pulled her cell phone from her purse, called information, punched in the number of Sharon's store. "If he's not there, I'll try—"

"Gifts for Everyone." Jonathan Wentworth's voice was immediately recognizable, crisp, pleasant, with a cadence that reminded Annie of a college roommate from Southern California.

"Jonathan, Annie Darling."

The slightest hesitation. "Yes, Annie. What can I do for you?"

The cell phone crackled. Another storm must be coming. Annie spoke loudly, clearly, distinctly. "Help me solve Bud Hatch's murder."

Was there a quick breath? Almost immediately, he said firmly, "That's a matter for the proper authorities. If that's all—"

Annie held tight to the phone. Henny had been so angry. Jonathan said he wanted to protect her. "Why did you warn Henny that Hatch was dangerous, tell her she mustn't cross him?"

Nothing. Not a breath. Only the crackle of static.

Henny and Jonathan. Gail and Bud. But it should have been Emily and Jonathan, Ruth and Bud.

It was Annie who drew her breath in sharply. "Did Hatch threaten to tell Emily about you and Henny? Is that why you warned Henny? Did you shoot Hatch to keep him—"

A click. No static. No connection.

Annie pushed "end," looked across the table.

Max sipped his beer and nodded. "It could be, Annie. It could well be."

"Poor Henny." Annie pushed away her plate. If that was the solution, the heartbreak for Henny— "But she's going to be all alone anyway," Annie said obscurely. "The Wentworths are moving. Maybe that's why. Maybe Wentworth was going to try and get his wife away before she found out about Henny. Oh, Max, I'll have to ask Henny. Love—it can mess everything up. And sometimes I don't think I know who loves who. When I talked to Ruth Hatch, she went on and on about how demanding Bud was. But right at the last, she looked at their wedding picture and there were tears in her eyes. Do you get it?"

Max traced a circle on his frosted beer mug. "Their marriage could have started off great. But maybe they didn't turn out to be the people they thought they were."

"She seemed like a nice lady. And maybe she really loved him. But anyway, she has an alibi."

Max quirked an eyebrow.

"Pamela Potts. Than which none could be more certain." Annie shook her head. "Dammit, I'm going to be nice about Pamela. I really, truly am. Anyway, Mrs. Hatch is in the clear. But I'm confused." Annie splayed her fingers through her mop of curly blond hair. "She said he would want to be remembered as a guy who always did his best. But I remember him as a first-class jerk, brusque and rude and generally a pompous ass and a bully who thought women were second-class citizens. That was his best?"

"Bud could be a great guy." Max crunched into his dill pickle. "Clever. And he was a hell of a golfer." A tone of awe. "He birdied the thirteenth hole three times and he only lived here a couple of months."

Max was also an excellent golfer. Except for number 13 at the Broward's Rock Golf and Country Club. His best recent round was a bogey on the par-five hole.

"You have to remember who Bud was, Annie." Max's tone was thoughtful, considering, not judgmental. "He was a military man and he never saw a shade of gray that he liked. That doesn't mean he was a bad guy or always wrong, but he saw the world a certain way. If you were a regular guy, if you agreed with him, lived like he lived, believed like he did, you were great. No problem. But if you didn't buy his program, watch out."

Parotti stumped to the table. "Missus wanted me to ask if everything was all right?"

Annie's eyes snapped wide. Who said people never changed! To see I-am-Ben-your-waiter materialize right here in beer and barbecue land was astonishing. "Fine. Wonderful. Please give her our compliments."

Parotti's face turned another peculiar shade and Annie realized he was blushing. He ducked his shaggy gray head and headed for the kitchen.

239

Max grinned. "Sex," he said softly, "is a wonderful thing."

Annie grinned in return. "Agreed." Then she sighed. But not always, not when it hurt other people. There was still much to find out about Gail and David Oldham. And Henny Brawley and Jonathan Wentworth.

Parotti sloshed her glass full of lemonade. Annie quailed. Another whole glass of lemonade and her stomach would be a permanent pucker.

"Another beer, Max?" He picked up their empty dishes.

"No, thanks," Max said regretfully. He looked at his watch. "Coffee?"

"Sure." Parotti beamed with pride. "Yeah. We got the regular." He blinked, obviously concentrating. "That's the house blend. And we got cappuccino, caffé latte, and espresso."

When he brought their orders, Parotti looked a little puzzled at the thimble-sized espresso for Max but admiringly at Annie's caffé latte, which was topped with a mound of steamed milk sprinkled with chocolate. Annie suspected beer had been his usual breakfast. No doubt he was acquiring a number of new tastes from his bride.

"Edith Cummings. Let's not forget her." Max sipped his espresso. "She asked us to help her look for Toby. And we did. But then she asked Samuel to look, too."

The spoon ladling steamed milk stopped halfway to Annie's mouth. "Max!" Shock lifted her voice.

"Yeah." His tone wasn't happy. "Edith may

have played us like a drum. Look at it. Only she and Ned knew Toby might show up drunk and maybe dangerous. But just before somebody shoots Hatch, you and Samuel and I are all looking for him—and absolutely sure to tell this later to the cops."

Annie liked the sharp-tongued librarian with her irreverent wit and cocky manner. But Max could be right.

"That's important, Max." She put down her spoon, pulled a small notebook from her purse. She tapped her cheek with the capped pen. "Okay. Let's figure out where we go from here."

They finished up the list as they downed the last of the coffee, Annie writing swiftly:

1. Where are the Oldhams? Did David come back to the festival after dark?

2. When did the Wentworth house go up for sale?

Annie held up her hand, retrieved her cell phone, called a good friend who was a realtor. In a moment she put down the phone. "The house went up for sale in May. Sherry said she's got a couple of solid prospects, that this is the time of year houses sell. As long as we don't have a hurricane. I guess Hatch had been on the library board for a couple of months. He could have figured out that Henny and Jonathan were involved."

"Why would he threaten to tell Mrs. Wentworth?" Max sounded dubious.

"Maybe he hadn't. But maybe Jonathan figured it would happen if Henny gave Hatch any more trouble. Or maybe Hatch had hinted at something like that. I mean, he really was a rat, Max."

"Hmm. Do you think it made him that mad that Henny wouldn't let him run things?" Max looked skeptical.

Annie remembered Hatch's flaming face at the library board meeting. "Yes." She underlined number 2 and set back to work.

3. Did Samuel hear two people in the willows?

4. Did the ballistics report reveal anything important about the gun?

5. Why did Edith Cummings spread the word that Toby Maguire was mad, drunk, and after Hatch?

6. Did Toby Maguire shove the vase off the library?

7. If there were two people in the clump of willows, who could they be?

Annie mentally appended:

a. Ned and Toby

b. Henny and Jonathan

c. Gail and David.

For good measure, Annie added:

8. Where was Sharon Gibson when the shot was fired?

Without looking toward Max, Annie wrote down:

9. Where was Laurel?

"Laurel?" Max's dark blue eyes were intent.

"Why did she burgle Hatch's locker at the Whalebranch Club? And his drawer at the library? It has to mean something." Annie said the last with more confidence than she felt. Perhaps Laurel was engaged in a peculiar treasure hunt. Or Hatch possessed a Shakespeare folio. With Laurel, anything was not only possible but likely. Shakespeare.... Neurons tried to connect in Annie's mind....

"I'll talk to her." Max put the list in his pocket.

Max's comment blew the connection, but Annie clung firmly to a tantalizing wisp. Shakespeare.... "That's okay," she said firmly. "I'll do the honors. Your mother and I"—she paused, juggled her words—"have so much rapport."

"Well." Her handsome husband was clearly reluctant. Didn't he think Annie had Laurel's best interests at heart? "If you think that's best." He checked the bill in Parotti's huge scrawl and put down a sum that included a hefty tip.

Max held the door for Annie. They stepped out into sultry air. Dark thunderclouds obscured the sky, hid the mainland from view. Whitecaps tipped the waves.

She smiled up at him. "I'll be happy to take care of it, Max." Magnanimity was an important quality in a successful marriage. Besides, Laurel could always fox Max. And Laurel's place was on the way to Edith Cummings's house. Yes, she'd have a little talk with Laurel. But first, there was a tough visit to make. She glanced at the lowering sky, pushed down the accelerator. She'd have to hurry to get there before the second storm broke.

Chapter 9

Max waved good-bye to Annie. As her Volvo sped away, he picked up his cell phone. Damn near burned his fingers. He balanced it near the air conditioning, waited a minute, tried the number. He knew it by heart now. For the first time that day, a live voice answered.

"Johnny Joe here." The voice was thick as honey but loud enough to be heard—always—on the very last row.

Max held the phone a little farther from his ear. "Johnny Joe, this is Max Darling. We met at the Chastain Guest Day Tournament last—"

"Sure. You referred Samuel Kinnon to me. Appreciate that. Got him released to his parents. I—"

Voices in the background. The receiver

was muffled. Then: "Sorry. Got to pick up my daughter at softball practice."

Max spoke fast. "A couple of points I want to check with you. Do you have any time this afternoon we could visit? I'm looking around over here for Samuel's family. I know it's Saturday but—"

A crashing noise. Jenkins boomed, "Ted, take that hockey stick out on the driveway."

Max held the phone even a little farther away.

"Max? Yeah. I've got some stuff that might help. Talked to a—"

More booming noises drowned out Jenkins's words.

"—on the gun. Good cooperation from Saulter. Okay. I pick Susie up at three. How about meeting me in my office at four?"

Max thought fast. The ferry left at three. Get to Chastain. Catch the five-o'clock ferry back. Plenty of time to get to Death on Demand as per Miss Dora's instructions.

"I'll be there. Thanks, Johnny Joe."

And plenty of time to make another stop before the ferry left. Max glanced out at the bay. Choppy. Ben Parotti loved taking the ferry across in rough weather.

Annie parked beside Henny's old Dodge. She forced herself to jump out immediately and walk fast to the stairs. If she paused, she wouldn't have the courage to continue, just as she'd forced herself to call and confront Jonathan Wentworth. He'd hung up on her. But she was going to talk to Henny face-to-face.

She knocked, called out. But she didn't find Henny until she walked around the porch to the back.

Henny stood with her hands on the worn railing, staring at water and sky that merged in tones of gray. Even the rippling cordgrass had lost its bright sheen, looked dull in the leaden air. She'd changed clothes. A faded denim shirt hung loose over white jeans. The freshening breeze stirred her silver-streaked dark hair. She half-turned, her bony face empty of expression.

Annie looked into bleak brown eyes. "Henny, it's no use fighting me. I know you. If I didn't know you so well, maybe I'd never have figured out you were protecting Jonathan."

"Protecting him, yes. And myself." Her words were sharp. "But only from Emily learning about us. Can't you see that, Annie? Jonathan's no killer. My God"—her voice broke—"he's so decent. Look at me, Annie. I promise you, Jonathan did not kill Bud. So leave us alone. Leave him alone." She reached out, gripped Annie's arm, her fingers tight. "When Bud Hatch fell, when someone shot him, I looked out—I was standing near the stage—and I saw Jonathan in the crowd, watching the fireworks. I saw him, I tell you! Now leave him alone. Leave me alone."

Max reached the Island Bakery, then, without warning, swung onto Bay Street. The car behind him blared its outrage. Max gave a jaunty wave. But he didn't feel jaunty. He didn't want to worry Annie. She was already upset enough. But her search of the Oldhams's house concerned him. He often teased Annie about her tendency to jump to conclusions based on her feelings, but he knew from experience that Annie's intuition was usually on target. As she'd often told him, she didn't like raw apples but she and Ariadne Oliver, Agatha Christie's scatty sleuth, had a great deal in common: a woman's intuition.

He pulled into the drive, behind the black Jeep. It took only a moment to knock, then duck inside and confirm Annie's report. The house was empty and it did have an air of hurried departure, of lives askew.

In his car, Max picked up his cell phone.

Frank Saulter answered. "Saulter here."

"Frank, Annie and I will have more for you tonight. But I suggest you talk to Gail and David Oldham. Here's the deal...."

Laurel's jaunty silver convertible was in its accustomed spot. The top was in place. And there was no equally jaunty Model A Ford next to it. That beautifully maintained old car belonged to Laurel's beau, Howard Cahill. Cahill had once been a neighbor to Annie and Max, but had moved after the murder of his wife in the Cahill summerhouse. Howard and Laurel were close. Annie wondered why they didn't marry, but some questions she couldn't ask. Besides, wasn't Howard gone this month, to Tahiti on a vacation with his son? Annie never dropped in on Laurel unannounced when Howard's car was in the drive.

Annie enjoyed Laurel's house, which was new but had the flavor of the Low Country, built high on stuccoed arches with Palladian windows and a screened-in porch. Everything about the pink stucco house exuded light and space and exuberant vitality.

Annie ran lightly up the broad steps and rang the bell. Thunder rumbled to the south.

She didn't exactly hear anything, but she sensed movement within. To say she was immediately wary and suspicious would be absolutely accurate. Years of dealing with Laurel had honed Annie's intuitive abilities.

She knocked sharply. Oh, how tempting was a Speak Your Mind: I know you're in there. Come out with your ill-gotten booty.

Ill-gotten booty. So, okay, Laurel was no thief. But she'd been into the general's locker at the Whalebranch Club and his drawer at the library. Annie wasn't going to leave until she knew why.

The door opened. Laurel beamed. In her soft pink linen camp shirt and ice white linen slacks, she epitomized the charm of summer. She didn't look the least bit hot.

Annie surreptitiously plucked at her blouse, the better to separate the damp cloth from her skin.

"Annie, my sweet. How good of you to breeze by, if only for a moment. I know your time is of the essence"—a tinkling laugh—"and certainly my rediscovery of dear William brings home to me most strongly the importance of love in our lives, and you and dear Maxwell epitomize in my mind that exquisite

248

phrase, 'Sweet lovers love the spring,' so I am glad you came by. Although I know it isn't spring, but the full-fruited season of summer— ah, the Boys of Summer. Indeed, that phrase has always delighted me."

Annie was sure Laurel had always enjoyed the Boys of Summer, though she wouldn't put it quite so baldly to Max.

The husky voice resonated with philosophical import. "Such ramifications, if you will."

Annie wouldn't.

"But I know you must rush"—the door began to close—"you must fly home to celebrate love."

Annie thrust out her foot, blocked the door. She beamed in return, though Laurel's smile now had a slightly set expression. Annie wanted to pronounce in an equally husky voice this Speak Your Mind: Put a sock in it, Laurel. Instead, she murmured a tad throatily— she was dying of thirst—"I know you want to be up-to-date on the search for the general's murderer."

Annie maintained her bright, eager smile though her eyes were gauging Laurel's internal struggle. A billboard announcing "Get Rid of Annie" versus "Find Out What She Knows" couldn't have made Laurel's quandary clearer.

The door swung open.

Annie skipped inside, smiling sweetly. She glanced into the living room, shadowy and untenanted.

Laurel was right behind her. She gripped Annie's elbow, maneuvering her toward the sunroom. "Let's have some iced tea, Annie. With fresh mint from the garden. It will do us both good."

It was almost like dusk outside, presaging the storm, leaching the soft honey color from the sanded hemlock walls and shiny pecan floor. When they were settled at the lace-white wooden table, frosted glasses in hand, they eyed each other with knowledge like two aged chess masters.

Annie made the opening gambit. "Love," she proclaimed airily, "ah, how love can motivate us. In fact, I suppose Bill said it best, 'We that are true lovers run into strange capers.'"

Laurel placed her hand atop Annie's. "Annie, dear Annie. And it is in that same scene that he writes so cogently, cutting ever to the heart of truth, 'If you remember'st not the slightest folly that ever love did make thee run into, thou hast not lov'd.'"

There was a tender silence. On Laurel's part.

Annie felt the first twinge of panic. Surely Laurel hadn't been involved with Bud Hatch!

Annie forgot all her fine resolutions about tact, circumspection, and indirection, blurting, "Oh, God, Laurel, what the hell did you steal from Hatch? Love letters? Photographs?" A bright red stained her cheeks. Could she actually have asked Max's mother that question?

"'The wounds invisible that love's keen arrows make,'" Laurel intoned softly.

Annie took a huge gulp of the tea, welcoming the infusion of caffeine, and desperately tried to think. "Look, Laurel, you simply have to tell me all about it. I don't care what happened. I mean, I understand that—" She faltered, regrouped. "Sometimes things happen," she continued lamely, "but whatever happened, tell me. I won't tell Max. The thing about it is, all hell's going to break loose Monday. The circuit solicitor will either charge Samuel with the murder or start looking at everything about Bud Hatch. And there's a police report about the break-in at the library, so Saulter's going to come after you."

Laurel folded her arms, a vision of angelic determination. "I have nothing to say. One can't be jailed simply because one was there!" But there was the beginning of worry in her Alpine-lake-blue eyes.

Halting steps came from the hallway to the bedrooms.

Annie jerked around.

Gail Oldham held out a trembling hand toward Laurel. "I can't let them put you in jail." Her red hair was tangled and dull, her freckled face splotchy and puffy. She still wore the too-large worn khakis from last night's festival.

Laurel surged to her feet. "Oh my dear, I'd hoped you were resting. Don't worry. It will all come right."

The neurons connected: Laurel. Shakespeare. Love. Lovelorn, i.e., Gail.

Annie looked from one to the other. "What did Hatch have?"

Laurel spread her hand toward a chair. "Please, Gail. Come join us." She looked at

Annie. "Poor dear. She rode her bicycle here, seeking my help." Laurel made it sound like crossing the Pyrenees barefoot in a blizzard. "As you know, I always try to help those in love, though love can often take us down dark and dangerous paths. 'The web of our life is of a mingled yarn, good and ill together.'"

Gail clung to the back of a chair. "I'll tell the police I took the letters. It won't matter now, will it? Since he's dead? And they were my letters. He had no right to threaten me with them."

Annie felt a double-dip chill. Gail was wholly focused on her own misery. Hatch's crumpled body was nothing more than a convenience to her. And she was setting herself up as a prize suspect.

"You and Bud Hatch." Annie's tone was bemused.

Gail's face turned an ugly shade of red. "I didn't mean anything. I really didn't. It's just—Bud could be so charming. And he was so nice to me. At first, I ran into him by accident. Then I realized he was making an effort to meet me. We had coffee. And we walked on the beach. And we started meeting sometimes in the evening. We walked on the beach in the moonlight."

"I thought you and David—" Annie broke off. She didn't know what to say or how to say it.

Gail's hands fell to the table. They lay limp and upturned, defenseless, defeated. "David travels so much." Her voice was dull. "I was lonely. Sometimes he's gone for two or three weeks at a time." She stared at the shiny white tabletop. "And things went"—the ugly red stained her face again—"farther than I intended. Then I realized I didn't want to go on. I hated myself. I told Bud I wouldn't see him again." She lifted a hand to claw at her throat as if breath were hard to find. "He was angry. He insisted I was going to meet him. He said"—the sheen of tears glistened in her eyes—"I had to meet him as long as he wanted me to. If I didn't, he would send David some notes I'd written." Her face puckered like a child too tired to cry. "Those notes—I couldn't explain them to David. I had to get them back. But I didn't know how." Her eyes flickered toward Annie. "I came to your house. I thought maybe Max—but I wasn't thinking straight. I couldn't tell Max about the letters either. I couldn't do that. I was so upset and I came to your house and you weren't there. And I just broke down."

"I found the poor child sobbing her heart out." Laurel smoothed back a golden curl. "Of course I offered to help." A pert smile. "'Flat burglary as ever was committed.'"

Annie kept a straight and unapproving face, though she would have loved to reply, "'A good heart's worth gold,'" but Laurel definitely did not need encouragement.

"And," Laurel said firmly, "All's Well That Ends Well. Although we don't want to be too specific, the letters were in the drawer at the library. They were retrieved and no longer exist. So, you see, dear Gail is rid of the worry of David ever learning of this sad episode and, fortunately, Gail disposed of the letters before the general was shot, so she clearly had no motive."

Annie applauded Laurel's kind heart. But, at some point, she would have to explain to her mother-in-law that breaking into private property wasn't permissible, no matter how well-intentioned. Furthermore, Laurel might believe the matter of the letters was settled and perhaps it was, but Hatch's threat to inform David about his affair with Gail was definitely still on the table.

Gail had a motive despite regaining the letters.

Laurel didn't know that.

And Gail didn't know Annie had overseen the encounter between Gail and Bud in the forest preserve.

Laurel popped to her feet, brought back a glass for Gail. Laurel's insouciant smile was in full force. "Now that we have that situation"—it made the theft of the letters sound like an unimportant, almost forgotten episode in a distant past—"clarified, dear Gail can relax. Gail had arrived just a moment before you did, Annie." Laurel looked expectantly at her newly revealed guest.

"David's not home." Three bleak words. Frightened eyes widened. "He wasn't there when I got home last night. I fell asleep on the couch. But he never came. This morning I rode my bike all over the island. I went to all his favorite places, the old lighthouse, the Abney Gardens, Trent Beach. I can't find him." Gail's hands clenched. "I shouldn't have come here. But you'd been so kind. I thought maybe you could help."

"When did you last see David?" Annie tried to keep her voice casual. She felt about as casual as Bulldog Drummond noting a damsel in distress.

Gail spread fingers against her cheeks. "Yesterday afternoon." She spoke dully. An eyelid flickered with a tic.

Annie scarcely breathed. Yes, it was in the afternoon that Gail and Bud quarreled. And David watched.

"I don't know what got into him." Gail's face creased in pain. "I'd just gotten back on stage." She spread a hand to indicate the khakis. "And he came up to me and said we were leaving. Right that minute. I told him I couldn't. I had to play my role. And I was going to—oh, it doesn't matter now."

Annie thought that it mattered. Gail was going to stay and talk to Bud Hatch, plead with him one more time not to destroy her marriage. Did he turn her down? But where could she have found a gun? Nowhere. That would mean she had brought a gun with her. Then why didn't she shoot him when they were in the forest preserve?

"I had to stay," she mumbled. "I thought David would understand. My role in the festival and everything...." Her voice trailed off. "I'd never seen him so angry. His face was a gray white, like he was dead. He said if I didn't come then, I never needed to come. And he turned and walked away. I called after him. But he kept on going." Tears rolled down her cheeks. "I went in the library several times and called home. He never answered. Then it was time for the fireworks." She looked at Laurel. "I almost asked you for a ride then. David and I came together and I didn't have a way home."

Why hadn't she? Hatch was emceeing the program. He wouldn't be available until it ended. Why had she stayed? Because she had a gun and was prepared to use it?

"Then someone shot Bud. I couldn't believe it. And it took so long before they let us leave. It was awful." She slumped in her chair.

Annie agreed. Damned inconvenient. Especially for Bud Hatch.

Laurel's dark blue eyes glowed with empathy. "My dear, I feel simply dreadful. I had no idea David wasn't there when I took you home. And you didn't seem to want me to stay...." Laurel's voice was full of regret.

"So you took Gail home. Were you together when Bud was shot?" But Annie watched Gail, not Laurel.

"I wasn't with anybody." Gail's voice was dull. "I wasn't paying any attention to anything. The fireworks were so loud. I'd taken my blanket over by the trees behind the library. I just wanted it all to end."

David Oldham left the festival in mid-afternoon, but Gail was still there when Hatch died. Of course, David could have returned.

"Well"—Laurel was brisk—"we'll simply have to find David." She popped up, picked up the phone from the shining oak counter.

Gail looked hopeful.

Annie was following her own train of thought. "Do you and David have any guns?"

"Guns?" Gail spoke as if in an unknown language.

Laurel held the telephone, looked at Annie in surprise.

"Guns." Annie's gaze was direct and somber.

"No." Gail's voice was sharp. "Why do you ask?" Her face flattened with shock. She shoved back her chair, jumped to her feet. "Are you talking about the gun used to shoot Bud? That's crazy. They found that boy with the gun. They arrested him. That doesn't have anything to do with me and David."

"Samuel found the gun. He heard someone in the willows. A whisper. And after Bud fell, a laugh." Annie was on her feet, too. She felt the same uneasy prickle down her spine that chilled her when Max repeated Samuel's words.

"But they arrested Samuel." Gail talked so fast the words ran together. "He's the one who was causing trouble at that place where the kids meet. Bud said he was obnoxious. He shot Bud because he lost his job."

"The police don't think so." Annie took great satisfaction in that statement. And it was true. Gail, whom she'd thought she liked, was so caught up in her own unhappiness—unhappiness she'd brought about—that she hadn't spared any thought about Bud Hatch's murder.

"What do they think?" Gail's gaze was wild and frightened.

"They're looking at everything, everybody." Annie willed it to be true. If she and Max could manage it, that's exactly what would happen.

"Not David." It was a strangled cry. "He didn't come home because he's mad at me. Not because—oh God, not because of Bud. David left hours before that happened."

Laurel came around the table. "Don't be upset, Gail. You mustn't worry. David didn't know about you and Bud."

Annie hoped it wasn't cruel, but it was time to speak. She took no pleasure in the words. "He knew, Gail. David knew."

Max pressed the doorbell. No answer.

"Stay!" The crisp call came from the other side of a huge, sweet-smelling pittosporum hedge.

Max walked toward the gate.

"Stay." A command with an edge of irritation.

Max knocked on the wooden gate.

In a moment, it swung in. Anthea Kerry was as tall as Max, lean, rawboned with sharp cheeks, a pointed chin, and, at the moment, a disgruntled expression. Her ragged work shirt hung loose over khaki shorts. She stood with her faded red sneakers wide apart, a confident, no-nonsense stance.

A blond cocker wriggled his rump and lunged for Max.

"Down!"

The cocker's big brown eyes slid away from his mistress. His head hunkered, then he flopped on his back, tangling his leash and quivering with excitement.

"Max, you're hopeless. Get up." She jerked the leash.

Max could have sworn the dog hid his eyes behind a shaggy paw before rolling to his feet. Then he stood stiff and straight, as gorgeous a stay as Susan Conant's Holly Winter might achieve with one of her magnificent malamutes. Max was not a mystery reader on Annie's level, but he collected mysteries with dogs.

"Yes, what can I do for you? More, I hope, that I'm doing for this cretinous animal." Anthea Kerry's tone was sharp, but she patted Max's head (the dog's) as she unsnapped the leash. "You're Annie Darling's husband, aren't you? A better-trained Max than this one, I hope."

Max grinned. "Very well trained, ma'am. And you can be very helpful to me. I want to find out all I can about Samuel Kinnon and General Hatch. And General Hatch and anybody else you know about."

A floppy green canvas sunhat shadowed her bony face. "I won't be quoted?"

"Not publicly." Max stood as straight and tall as his canine counterpart.

"My, my. Butter wouldn't melt, would it? You are a bonny lad, as my old Scot grandmother used to say. Hell, come on in. This Max"—she pointed toward the prancing, eager dog—"isn't any fun at all. Maybe you'll be better."

She squinted at the sky. "Going to rain again. But it may not come for while. I like that smell, fresh and dusky. Let's stay in the

259

yard, if you don't mind." She put the cocker in his run, then insisted on bringing huge goblets of iced tea with slices of lemon and lime. They sat in weathered gray wooden chairs beneath the spreading limbs of a magnolia. Sweet white blossoms nestled among the huge glossy green leaves. A male cardinal, a shiny crimson, lighted on a birdbath and cocked his head toward them. The backyard was overgrown—tall swatches of cane, untrimmed jasmine, pines crowded close together. The dog run was well-kept.

She followed his gaze. "Pretty much a mess. I don't have a lot of time, and gardening is work." She glanced at his hands. "You don't garden."

"No. Actually, the Kinnons take care of our place." Max welcomed the refreshing tea. Annie was right. Beer on a hot day just made you hotter. "You fired Samuel."

Her slate-blue eyes met his directly. "You got that one right. Look, it wasn't a moment I recall with pleasure, but I learned a long time ago you can't buck the system." A sardonic shrug. "Or yes, you can if you don't mind losing your job. Nobody likes whistle-blowers. And actually I didn't have a whistle to blow. Samuel smarted off to the general. The general was on the board and he was getting to know everybody on the island with deep pockets. Yes, I could have nobly told the general I wouldn't fire Samuel. The result: Samuel and I would both have lost our jobs. I didn't think a summer job for Samuel was quite that big a deal. I make a difference on this island for some kids who don't have any place to go and nobody at home to give a damn. I learned how to handle people like General Hatch a long time ago when I was an NCO. I'd just gotten the general to agree to a fund-raiser so we can offer breakfast and lunch at the Haven. Ended up thinking it was his idea. Of course he did. I planned it that way." She picked out the lime, sucked it, made a face. "Hatch was okay. Full of himself, but that comes with the territory. Now"—she took a deep drink of the tea, leaned back in the chair—"do I think Samuel shot the man? No. Samuel's got a temper, but I've watched him over the years. You know what he does when he gets mad?"

Max relaxed, too. The chirr of locusts, the beer at lunch, the sodden air combined to make him sleepy despite the shot of espresso and the icy tea. He blinked and tried to listen hard.

"Plays basketball. Gets a bunch of boys and they roughhouse and gibe each other and sweat like pigs, and when they're done he's got a smile on his face again. You don't need to worry about Samuel. Whatever happens to him he can handle." Anthea pulled off her hat, used it as a fan.

Max's sense of comfort fled. "Going to prison for a murder he didn't commit?"

She dropped the hat in her lap and sat up, placing her broad hands on her weathered knees. She frowned. "I heard Samuel was at home."

Max was once again astounded at the incredible underground dissemination of

261

news in a small community. The story of Hatch's murder wouldn't hit the newspaper until tomorrow. But Anthea Kerry knew all about it. She didn't know everything.

"He's home now. But the circuit solicitor will look at the evidence Monday." Max held her gaze. "I've dealt with Brice Posey before. There's nothing he likes better than an easy case. Man gets kid fired. Man shot. Kid found holding the gun. Set it for trial."

Anthea's bony face set in a harsh mask. She stared down at the scuffed tips of her faded sneakers. "Shit."

Max felt as if he'd been jolted by a double espresso. Anthea Kerry knew something. Or thought she did. But she didn't want to tell him.

Cicadas whirred like bass fiddles warming up. Distant thunder rumbled like a beer keg rolling down steps.

"Help one kid, hurt another." She pleated the brim of her hat. She looked at Max, her cold eyes intent. "You understand I don't know a damn thing. But you want to know who hated Hatch? Edith Cummings. She'd have shoved him under a train without blinking an eye, been sure she deserved a medal. I heard about that vase falling at the library. Funny thing it happened the day after Hatch announced the new program for the Haven, basic training that would include drill teams, weekend map expeditions, maybe even rappelling eventually. Lots of the kids were excited. I think it would have been real popular."

"Would have been?" Max finished his tea.

"I can do a new program if someone else provides the money and the manpower. Without that—" She turned her hands palms-up.

"What was Edith's objection to the program?" Max quickly figured the librarian's age. Late thirties, maybe. Why was she antimilitary? A big brother who went to Vietnam?

"Her son's really come into his own the last couple of years. He's super at Ping-Pong. That's been a pretty cool game since it got into the Olympics. And he's pretty good at baseball. He manages that even though he's diabetic. Insulin-dependent." Anthea unrolled the brim of the hat, plopped it on her head. "But I don't think"—her tone was considering—"that he could hang in for a real tough, boot-camp-type program. And you know how kids are. If the new program really caught on, all the cool guys would be in it. Everybody except Ken. That's what Edith was afraid of."

A coach glanced toward the building thunderclouds. Lightning rippled down through the dark layers, flashing like strobe lights at a celestial rock concert. A bat connected with a ball and the clear, tinny sound mingled with cheers and moans.

"There you are," Annie said brightly.

Edith Cummings leaned against the jagged bark of a palmetto. She looked at Annie without enthusiasm. "Yeah, here I am. On my own time, so to speak. Watching my kid play ball. Not doing reference questions at the present moment."

That made Annie mad. "Really? I've got a pretty good one. What kind of person stands by and watches an innocent person go to jail?"

"They caught him red-handed, didn't they? Oh, no blood dripping, but the closest thing to a smoking gun you'll ever see. Almost trite, wasn't it?" She leaned forward to watch an out at first, yelled, "Way to go, Rafael."

"Samuel found the gun. And the only reason he was even near the willows is because you asked him to hunt for Toby. He was coming along the path and he stumbled into the gun. Then he heard somebody in the willows."

"Voilà!" Edith spread her hands. "Our stalwart youth can save the day, announce to the police the identity of the culprit and all will be well."

"Dammit, Edith, he didn't see anybody, he heard them."

"Them?" Her glance was sharp.

"He heard somebody whisper. Then a laugh."

Edith slapped a hand to her brow. "I've got it. Eureka! Assemble the suspects and ask everybody to whisper, then laugh. The murderer will be undone."

"You're being a bitch."

"I didn't show up twenty feet from a dead man with a gun in my hand."

How would Miriam Ann Moore's Marti Hirsch approach Edith? With panache. Annie settled for a blunt "How many résumés did you have out, Edith?"

Edith pushed away from the palm, placed her hands on her hips. "So what the hell are you talking about?"

Annie didn't mince words. "Hatch was going to get you fired."

Edith glared. "Listen, sweetheart, I could get another job in a flash. Who's been spreading these glad tidings about me?"

Annie didn't answer.

"My esteemed boss, Director Fisher? Well, let me tell you a little secret, my dear. Hatch was going to get Ned canned. And you can put that in the bank."

Cheers rose from the stands. Edith's head jerked toward the field. She pumped her hand in the air. "Did you see that? Ken caught the ball."

The scoreboard flashed: "Visitors 2 outs." The pitcher went into his windup.

The palmetto fronds rattled in the freshening wind. Annie raised her voice. "Ned says he could get another job in a flash, too."

"Sure he could." Edith's eyes glittered. "Only one little, tiny drawback. He'd have to sling his rucksack over his shoulder and march off into the distance alone. No way will anybody ever get Toby off this island."

Max leaned on the horn. His crimson Ferrari roared toward the ferry landing like a stealth bomber through a mountain pass. Often Ben Parotti ignored the frantic beep of a horn and the ferry moved away into the sound, leaving a motorist trapped until the ferry returned. Today Parotti waited. Max didn't know whether to thank his lucky stars or the good tip he'd left at lunch. The red car rumbled over the planks, the last one aboard.

Parotti waggled his cap. The ferry moved heavily away from the dock and immediately began to rock.

Max waved back and relaxed in his seat. Be interesting to know what Johnny Joe Jenkins had—Max peered up at the wheelhouse.

Parotti was waving his cap vigorously.

Max craned his head. Damn, was Parotti paying any attention to the crossing? Certainly the ferry ride from the island to the mainland wasn't on a par with crossing the Bosporus, but it did take some attention.

Now Parotti's bony arm pumped like a windmill in a gale.

Max waved.

Parotti took his other hand off the wheel, lifted both hands to the heavens, then, as the ferry lurched, grabbed the wheel with one, thrust the other, still holding the cap, straight at Max.

"Oh." Max pointed at himself.

Parotti nodded vigorously.

The deck was slippery. Max skidded to the ladder leading up to the wheelhouse and climbed up.

Parotti looked at him skeptically. "Some detective you are!"

Max wished he had a fedora. Without props, he leaned close, said from the corner of his mouth. "Sorry. I was pondering a clue."

Parotti might not have been absolutely clear on the meaning of pondering, but he got the clue part. "Oh, sure. Yeah. Way to go." His bristly eyebrows practically stood at attention. "I heard you and your missus at lunch. You're working on the Hatch kill."

Max refrained from asking whether Parotti's favorite cop show was "NYPD Blue" or "Law and Order."

Parotti's eyes glistened. "And you were talking about that washed-out-lookin' redhead, Mrs. Oldham?"

"That's right." The deck whooshed up. Max clutched the metal railing.

Parotti adjusted the wheel, but he was looking at Max. "I rented her husband a motorboat this morning. Early. Around seven. And he ain't brought it back yet." The ferry captain frowned as he peered out at the white-capped sound. "Damn fool should have come back by now."

"Where did he go?" Max had to raise his voice above the whine of the wind.

"How the hell should I know?" Parotti demanded. A big wave slapped the side of the ferry and it heeled to port. Parotti grinned like a climber planting a flag on Everest. "Man, did you feel that one?"

Max was holding on to the railing with both hands. "Yeah. Kind of rough. Listen, Ben, let me know when Oldham gets back."

Max slid like a six-year-old in the fun house as he made his way back to his car. He tried three times to call Saulter on his cell phone, but all he heard was static and squeals.

Purple-black clouds hung so low Annie felt that she could reach up and grab a handful like black cotton candy. The air was as full of moisture as a soaked sponge. She almost drove past the entrance to the library, but at the last moment yanked the wheel and turned in. The library closed at noon on summer Saturdays, so she had the road to herself. In the darkening air, the pink tabby had a purple tinge. Annie glanced up. There was still an empty pedestal where the blue vase had sat.

No cars were parked in front. She drove to the back of the library and her car was the only one in the lot. Annie hurried toward the festival field. Thunder rumbled nearby. She almost turned back to fish out an umbrella. She checked the sky again. Black, black, black. But the lightning was still to the south. She wouldn't take long.

The temporary arbor, made with red-white-and-blue crepe paper strung through the latticework, was a soggy mess, the colors dripping onto the ground. But the coming storm would wash away the puddles of dye left from the morning shower.

Annie walked around the arbor and surveyed the field. It was an even bigger mess. No one had picked up the debris. Annie headed for the bandstand, taking care not to step on the paper cups and plates, candy wrappers and popcorn boxes, along with the occasional odd flotsam—one navy sneaker, a Frisbee, a lidless Styrofoam cooler, plastic bottles of sunburn lotion, several broken fans (Laurel would have to do a quality check before she bought her next batch), red firecracker wrappers, a calico bandanna.

When she reached the bandstand, she climbed the stage-right steps, walked a few paces. No crime-scene tape barred the way. Chief Saulter must have returned early this morning before the first rain and made his final photographs and sketches. There was nothing to indicate a man had died inches from where she stood. The bloodstain was now a darkish, irregular splotch, the wet wood still glistening from the rain.

Annie turned, looked toward the willows and at the paths, clearly visible in daylight, and the sweep of the field.

She tried to place everyone at the moment Hatch was shot.

Edith Cummings and Samuel Kinnon were in the forest preserve, hunting for Toby Maguire.

Ned Fisher claimed he was taking Toby to his car. But Annie had heard the piccolo only a moment before Hatch fell.

Gail Oldham was sitting by herself near the redbuds. David Oldham? No one knew.

Ruth Hatch and Pamela Potts were walking back from the soft-drink stand.

Henny Brawley was near the stage. She claimed to have seen Jonathan Wentworth in the audience when Hatch fell.

Sharon Gibson? Apparently she wasn't with her parents. Neither had mentioned her. Emily Wentworth said she and her husband were sitting on their blanket and they'd left it behind.

Annie looked straight down and to her right at a sodden blue comforter. She trotted down the steps, walked across the squishy ground. The comforter was good quality. Perched at the back was a cardboard holder with two tall red-striped Coke cups covered with plastic tops. Dark liquid showed through the plastic. The cups were full to the brim. A couple of Laurel's fans lay in the center on top of some festival programs, now soggy and limp.

The wind rattled the palmettos, fluttered the live-oak leaves, swayed the tall pines. Annie glanced again at the sky. The storm could not be far away. She moved swiftly toward the willows and the forest preserve. She followed the curving path, glancing back often. Ten feet. Fifteen. Any farther and the willows were lost from view around the curve. Samuel must have found the gun near here.

Annie found nothing to mark where the gun might have landed in the path. That was no surprise. Too many people had walked here since that moment. But she wasn't looking for that kind of evidence. Instead, she picked up a stick, pulled aside ferns and dangling vines on either side of the path, all the way to the willows. She ducked beneath the dangling fronds of the nearest willow. It was gloomy and quiet in this secluded lair.

She didn't look for shell casings or footprints. After all, Frank Saulter had already been here. Instead, she once again poked with her stick, hoping she wasn't going to disturb a rattlesnake or cottonmouth. Then she stopped, shook her head, dissatisfied.

The murder happened quickly. Quickly!

Hatch was shot. Someone whispered. Someone laughed. Samuel was coming along the path. The gun was thrown. A rustle.

Thunder boomed, close now.

Samuel bent down, picked up the gun. The person in the willows slipped away, moved through the darkness back into the crowd.

Annie peered up into the willow branches, then she darted out on the path. Now she scanned the ground on both sides all the way to the field.

No gloves.

That's what they needed to prove Samuel's innocence. Gloves. Work gloves, gardening gloves, summer white gloves from another era, some kind of gloves.

Annie stood in the middle of the field. All right. Perhaps the murderer had simply stuffed the gloves in a pocket, taken them home, destroyed them later. Or perhaps dropped them into a washing machine, erasing all traces of gunpowder residue.

Lightning blazed above her. Thunder followed almost immediately. Annie turned and ran toward the parking lot. Raindrops big as jelly beans pelted her.

Chapter 10

Rain turned the windows of the lawyer's office as milky and impenetrable as a conch shell, made the glittering prisms of the modest chandelier even brighter in contrast. The walnut desk and furniture had a rich sheen in the light and the shelves of law books were stolidly reassuring.

Despite his informal garb, a white polo shirt and faded jeans, Johnny Joe Jenkins was an impressive man, a little under six feet, stocky and athletic with a lean hawk face and curiously metallic-blue eyes. He pushed a flimsy fax sheet toward Max. "I've got a good friend in the state investigator's office. They're already cracking on this case. The Broward's Rock town fathers don't want big-deal retirees gunned down. They think it's bad publicity for the island. They don't want anything to discourage golden oldsters from settling in. Plus Frank Saulter's got friends and he put out a call for information PDQ."

Max scanned the fax. The gun was a Colt .45-caliber semiautomatic revolver. The serial numbers placed it as having been manufactured in 1942 and included in arms distributed to officers en route to England. The gun was free of fingerprints except for those of Samuel Charles Kinnon. A detailed list of the portions of Kinnon's prints followed, pinpointing where each was found. Deciphering the cumbersome language, Max realized the prints were exactly where they should be if Samuel reached down and picked the gun up from the ground, grasping it from the top.

Max quickly wrote on his legal pad: Jonathan Wentworth in England WWII?

His bright blue eyes glistening with eagerness, Johnny Joe peered intently at Max. "Hell of a thing about those prints." He had the full, rich voice of a courtroom lawyer.

Max matched Johnny Joe's volume to be heard over the crackle of palmetto fronds and the rattle of rain against the windows. "But we all knew Samuel's prints would be on the gun. He picked it up on the path."

Johnny Joe grinned like a kid first in line for the roller-coaster ride. He quoted in clarion tones, the kind lawyers reserve for opening statements or closing arguments: "'The gun was free of fingerprints except for those of Samuel Charles Kinnon.'" He cocked his head, eyed Max like a killdeer spotting a luscious grasshopper. "Tell me what that reports says," he said cheerfully.

Max wasn't in the mood to play games, but some of the lawyer's evident excitement touched him. Slowly, Max repeated, "'The gun was free of fingerprints—'" He broke off, stared at Johnny Joe. "Literally?" His voice rose eagerly.

"Literally. Look, I've worked with the state office lots of times. The lab is careful. No high jinks like the FBI. And this report was made by J. T. Buckingham. I know Buck and he's so damn literal you'd never want to tell him to go jump in the lake because he would. I called him at home, caught him watching the Braves. He talks like molasses in January, but when he finished I had the picture." The lawyer spoke slowly, clearly. "Not a single other print on that gun. Not anywhere. Not outside. Not inside. Not on the butt or the magazine or the casings, not a smudge. That .45 was polished like the entrance hall at the Supreme Court. And the trigger was clean as a whistle."

It might be a little hard for a jury to understand and Max hoped like hell Jenkins never had to face a jury on Samuel's behalf, but Max knew this was an ace in the hole. Somebody had cleaned up the .45, polished it so painstakingly and so carefully that it was like a mint-new gun without a trace of any fingerprints other than Samuel's. Zip. Zero. Even a slow jury might wonder why a killer would take all that trouble, then not bother to wear gloves. Even Circuit Solicitor Brice Posey might see a hole the size of a bomb crater in his easy little case.

"Wow!" Max exclaimed.

Johnny Joe turned two thumbs up.

Max and Johnny Joe grinned at each other like fraternity brothers whose blind dates turn out to be babes.

Water sloshed ankle-high over Annie's feet, submerging her once brightly colored woven leather flats. They'd been such a cheerful shade of apricot, perfect with her blouse. Right now they looked like basted eggplant.

A swirl of wind turned her umbrella inside out. An upended bucket of cold water couldn't have made her any wetter. Annie plunged through the sheeting rain. For the first time in days she wasn't hot, but she was equally miserable. She thudded up the wooden steps to the boardwalk. Perforce, she slowed. The wet wood was as slick as a water slide. She didn't need to hurry. Miss Dora had set the meeting for six and it was only half past five, though it could easily have passed for seven, the sky was so dark from the storm.

The covered walkway protected her from the downpour. Annie squelched down the boardwalk. Hadn't she'd left her gym bag at the store earlier in the week? There should at least be shorts and a top. And there was a stack of clean dish towels at the coffee bar. She'd prefer a bath towel, but she'd settle for paper towels if necessary. Oh, to be warm and dry. Annie stopped in front of Sharon Gibson's gift shop. Towels. And a chance to talk to Sharon.

Annie grabbed the door handle and stepped inside. She squished toward the cash desk. She scanned the store. Only two other customers, one studying the card section, the second balancing a dried decorated coconut in one hand and a necklace of bleached sand dollars in the other.

Sharon Gibson swung around, the shopkeeper pirouette Annie recognized immediately. She also recognized the practiced smile intended for customers. It left Sharon's face faster than Amanda Cross's Kate Fansler tossing off a bon mot. The fluorescent light slanting down from almost directly above was unflattering, marking deep lines in Sharon's thin face. Her faded brown eyes looked anxious and wary.

Annie wished she had the chutzpah of Selma Eichler's full-figured PI, Desiree Shapiro. Drawing on that inspiration, she smiled cheerily at Sharon. "You're a lifesaver. I want to buy a beach towel. We're having a meeting at Death on Demand and I'm wetter than an otter." Annie picked up a huge shocking-pink towel with a fearsome black shark snout. "This one's perfect." She placed it on the counter. "It's a pretty important meeting. We're gathering a lot of information for the police about Bud Hatch and the people who were mad at him." Was this chutzpah or what? Annie steeled herself to ignore the quick flash of panic in Sharon's eyes. "If we don't come up with some good leads by Monday, the police are going to arrest Samuel Kinnon."

Sharon fingered the bar-code tag on the towel, but her eyes never left Annie's face.

Annie opened her purse, found her credit card.

Sharon made out the ticket. "I thought Samuel was arrested Friday night." Her voice was sharp.

Annie fingered a miniature plastic lighthouse key chain. "The chief released him to his parents. He has to stay at their house, not leave the island. Samuel's trying to remember every little thing about the shooting. He heard someone in the willows laugh. And he thinks there was a second person there, someone who whispered."

Sharon swiped the credit card through the machine. "But they found him with the gun, didn't they?"

Was there anyone on the island who didn't know that? Annie explained patiently, "He was coming down the path. Someone threw the gun right in front of him."

Sharon handed Annie the sales slip to sign. "I suppose he had to say something. Why are you so sure he's innocent?" She put the towel in a sack.

Annie wasn't sure. But she wasn't sure of Samuel's guilt either. She didn't answer directly. "Do you know Miss Dora?"

"Yes, I do." Sharon pointed to three water-colors mounted at the end of the ceramics aisle.

Of course, of course. How had Annie imagined Miss Dora would miss this shop as a likely spot for her art?

"Miss Dora's known the Kinnons a long time. And their family. Samuel was driving Miss Dora around the island. Miss Dora says no way did he do it." That was putting the old lady's certainty in the vernacular, but she didn't think Miss Dora would mind. "Anyway, she's set up a meeting at Death on Demand. With me and Max. And Max's secretary. We'll work all night if we have to," she said grandly. "Max and I have been talking to people, picking up lots of interesting stuff. Miss Dora's putting together personal information about everyone involved." Annie dropped her copy of the sales slip in her purse.

Sharon closed the register. "And who is involved?" She made an effort to speak casually, but her tone was tight, the words carefully formed.

Annie skirted the question. "We're checking out the members of the library board."

"The library board. Why, that seems silly to me. None of that would matter enough to cause someone to shoot him." Sharon's tone was derisive, but one hand clenched into a fist.

Annie shivered and pulled the towel out of the sack and wrapped the soft terry cloth around her shoulders. "Has Miss Dora talked to you?"

"No." Sharon's tone was crisp. "I'm not involved with the library. Or the festival. I simply had a booth there."

Annie looked at her curiously. Touchy, touchy. "But your family's known the Hatches for a long time, haven't they?"

Sharon moved out from the counter, looked toward the card section. "Are you finding everything you need?"

The plump woman with a sun-burned nose and rain-damp sun dress nodded.

"Your family—" Annie began.

Sharon faced her. "My family and Bud Hatch? No longer than anyone on the island has known him."

Annie looked puzzled. "Someone told me they went back a long way."

"Someone's wrong. My dad's probably known him for a couple of months. Whenever Hatch joined the library board. And my mother never met the man." The answer was smooth and quick, glib. So why were Sharon's eyes intense and worried?

"Oh. Well. " Annie reached the front door.

Sharon stood in the aisle, watching her leave. Willing her to leave?

Annie stepped onto the boardwalk. But she knew Desiree wouldn't give up. She looked back. "Then it must be you who knew him well."

"Wrong again, Annie." Sharon sounded utterly confident. "He came in the shop once to buy a birthday present for his wife. Picked out a silver charm. A butterfly. Said his wife was crazy about monarchs."

Annie waved good night, but as she walked toward her store she wondered about Sharon Gibson. Why, if she didn't know Bud Hatch, did Sharon remember that single encounter with him so clearly? How many silver charms had she sold this year?

Annie pushed a damp sprig of hair under her bandanna and finished her third piece of barbecued-chicken pizza, which sounded heavy but was on a delectable light crust with a piquant Chinese sauce. Water chestnuts, too. Mmm. And even though her shirt and shorts were crumpled from the gym bag, they were a great change from her sodden blouse and skirt. She'd turned down the air-conditioning when she arrived. The dry clothes and food plus a steaming cup of caffé latte and Ingrid's note about the day's fabulous receipts (oh, how merchants in resorts love rain) combined to lift her spirits, but she was still a little miffed.

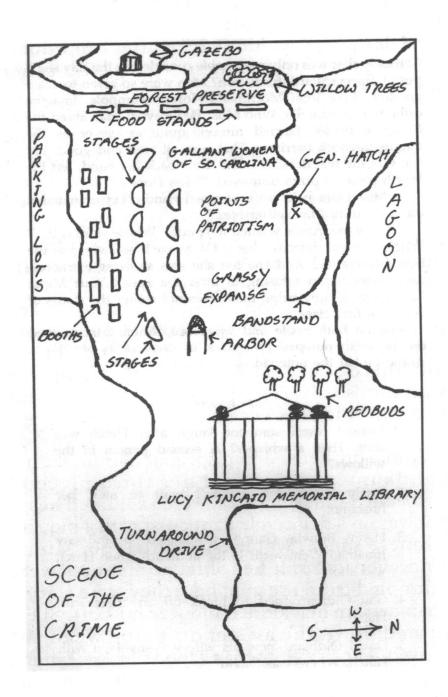

GAZEBO

FOREST PRESERVE

WILLOW TREES

FOOD STANDS

STAGES

GALLANT WOMEN
OF SO. CAROLINA

GEN. HATCH

X

PARKING LOTS

POINTS
OF
PATRIOTISM

LAGOON

GRASSY
EXPANSE

BANDSTAND

BOOTHS

STAGES

ARBOR

REDBUDS

LUCY KINCAID MEMORIAL LIBRARY

TURNAROUND
DRIVE

SCENE
OF THE
CRIME

W
S — N
E

After all, Death on Demand was her mystery bookstore. She looked up at the great watercolors for reaffirmation. And at the nifty dump near the coffee bar, featuring detectives with unusual occupations, Lou Jane Temple's restaurant owner Heaven Lee, David Leitz's fly fisherman Max Addams, Deborah Valentine's sculptress Katharine Craig, Norman Partridge's boxer Jack "Battleaxe" Baddalach and Valerie Wolzien's contractor Josie Pigeon. It was just a little odd to find her coffee area transformed to a command post with several computer terminals and a printer in place, plus a blackboard with the Scene of the Crime neatly delineated in pink chalk.

It might be her bookstore, but she was apparently invisible. Nobody said a word to her after murmuring abstracted hellos. Even Agatha, after a surreptitious effort to snag some pizza, had retired to the top of the coffee bar, eyes glittering, tail switching. Max's secretary Barb was keying rapidly on her computer with occasional dashes to the printer, and Miss Dora was making notes, pince-nez firmly in place. According to Barb, Max was still en route and would arrive with spectacular information.

Annie's hand wavered over the pizza box. Four pieces? Certainly that was only reasonable considering the day she'd put in. Spectacular information? Men were so given to exaggeration. Like John Mortimer's Horace Rumpole. Imagine calling your wife She Who

Must Be Obeyed! Max loved the Rumpole books, fancied himself quite as clever as the tongue-in-cheek barrister. That was all well and good, but she was the real detective. She drew back her hand, left the fourth piece of pizza unmoved. "Miss Dora—"

Miss Dora held up a wizened hand. "Let us marshal our facts until Maxwell arrives."

Excuse me, Annie wanted to sputter. Whose store is this? Who's the real detective here? Okay, we'll see who has the best information. And she felt she was showing extraordinary character in refusing to utter the Speak Your Mind: Miss Dora, simply being male does not confer the status of detective first class.

Feeling both noble and squelched, Annie concentrated on the fresh notepad and stack of dossiers at her place. Annie pulled the notepad close, wrote down:

KEY POINTS

1. Samuel heard someone laugh after Hatch was shot. Then a whisper? A second person in the willows?

2. Emily Wentworth couldn't wait to alibi her husband.

3. Henny Brawley claimed she looked out and saw Jonathan Wentworth in the audience when Hatch was shot.

4. Gail Oldham tried to break off an affair with Hatch.

5. David Oldham knew his wife was involved with Hatch. Where was David?

6. Toby Maguire would never leave the island, according to Edith Cummings.

7. Hatch was going to get Ned Fisher and Edith Cummings fired.

The phone rang. Barb answered. "Confidential Commissions—"

Annie bristled.

"—at Death on Demand. I appreciate your returning my call. We are seeking information...."

Annie relaxed and tuned Barb out and refused to be jealous when Agatha pointedly (and anyone who thinks cats can't make points hasn't lived with one) jumped in Barb's lap and purred. Loudly.

Chalk screeched.

Annie winced.

Miss Dora stood on a book ladder, modifying the Crime Scene. Screech. Screech. Annie steeled herself. After all, you could get used to anything. And where the hell was Max so this meeting could come to order? And why, continuing sore point, did they have to wait for him? Annie almost spoke, but one look at Miss Dora's militant carriage and she forbore. Instead, she snatched up a thick folder. Maybe Barb and Miss Dora had winnowed out some fact that would make a difference.

She riffed through the dossiers, put them in alphabetical order. Henny's she didn't need to read. Henny she knew all about. Like the fact that she could shoot off a bottle cap at fifty yards. Not a thought Annie wanted to concentrate on. She put Henny's dossier down, picked up the next.

Maybe she didn't have karma, but could this be an occult hint, right on a par with the jerky revelations of a Ouija board? After all, in a murder case one of the first questions to be considered was that of opportunity. There had to be a reason why Hatch was gunned down at the Fourth of July fireworks display behind the library. Why that night? Why that place? Could the choice of that location have the simplest answer of all, familiarity? No one would be more familiar with the field behind the library than a librarian or the library director. (Except Henny, the co-chair of the festival. Why did every road lead back to Henny?)

The dossiers contained bare-bones biographical facts and quotes from friends or former associates.

EDITH BELL CUMMINGS: Thirty-seven. Divorced. Born Columbia, South Carolina. Parents Grace McCoy Bell and John Mark Bell, still living in Columbia. Father assistant manager local department store. Salutatorian high school class. Editor school newspaper. BA, MLS University of South Carolina. Librarian Huntington Beach, California; Fort Worth, Texas; and Boise, Idaho, before accepting post as research librarian Lucy Kinkaid Memorial Library 1992. Married Gerald Cummings, health club aerobics instructor 1983, divorced 1986; one son, Kenneth Bell, born 1985. Enjoys performing in community theater. Collects thimbles. Active in son's school activities.

Mae Lou Windom, high school journalism teacher: "Smart as a whip. But with a deep streak of anger. Not a happy home life. Her parents don't get along, never had much time for her. John drinks too much and Grace whines. Edith makes a lot of jokes to hide what she's feeling."

Gerry Cummings, ex-husband: "Bitch, bitch, bitch. I didn't work hard enough. I wasn't serious. I didn't come home on time. And always digging at me, then laughing—like that made it all right. I went on a road trip on my bike and the bitch put sand in the gas tank. I lost power going around a hairpin curve near Big Bear. I could've been killed. That's a joke?"

George Nunley, previous boss: "We hated to lose Edith. Always lightening up the place—and energy? She's one in a thousand."

Christy Porter, Ken's home-room teacher: "If all the mothers made the effort Edith does, we'd have a happier world. He's a great kid. Some of it is him. A lot of it is coming to school wrapped in love."

Edith Cummings was fun, if you liked pointed remarks and acerbic comments. Annie usually did. But maybe her ex-husband knew her best and maybe the real Edith could be ugly when angered. Sand in a gas tank. How about loosening a vase to topple from a roof? Annie scrawled VASE in all caps by Edith's name.

NED HARRIS FISHER: Forty. Bachelor. Born Wichita, Kansas. Mother Janine Phillips Fisher, librarian; father Michael Theodore Fisher, oil and gas landman, killed in a car wreck when Ned was five. BA University of Kansas; MLS University of Chicago. Librarian Champaign, Illinois; Albuquerque, New Mexico; New Orleans, Louisiana. Grows roses. Gourmet cook specializing in Pacific Rim cuisine. Shares home with local artist Toby Maguire.

Mother: "Ned works so hard and he's always tried to make a difference for students from disadvantaged backgrounds. He knows what it's like to grow up without a father. How would I sum up Ned? Oh, that's easy. He's a mother's dream, honest and kind and good. Truly good."

Jack Macklin, co-worker in New Orleans: "Not my kind of guy. Prissy. Don't suppose he's ever been to a ball game. Shoot a gun? Hell, he'd probably faint."

William McKinney, previous boss: "Faults? It's hard to come up with any. I suppose his greatest weakness is that he isn't tough enough. Sometimes an administrator has to fire people, make decisions that will irritate people. That's hard for Ned. He always wants to please."

Jessica Tucker, chief nurse Broward's Rock Rehabilitation Clinic: "I see it all.

People who don't give a damn if their husband or brother or mother lives. Or dies. But when Toby Maguire was seriously injured in a motorcycle crash, Ned was there for him. He helped him recuperate. He helped him learn to walk again. That's the kind of devotion we'd all like to have from a loved one."

Agatha jumped up on the table, green eyes glowing. Annie reached out, stroked the silky fur. Everybody needs love, including cats. A powerful, urgent, consuming need. What would Ned do to stay on Broward's Rock with Toby?

SHARON WENTWORTH GIBSON: Forty-six. Divorced. Born Honolulu, Hawaii. Father Captain (ret.) Jonathan Edward Wentworth; mother Emily Elizabeth Anderson Wentworth. Attended University of Southern California. Dropped out in 1969 to marry Charles William Gibson, an anti-war leader who later completed his degrees and taught American Colonial history at the University of Tennessee. Two children: Stacey and Julia. Divorced 1986. Spotty employment as a florist, office temp, assistant boutique manager. Used divorce settlement to purchase shop on Broward's Rock in 1986. Opened Gifts for Everyone September 1986. Capt. Wentworth and his wife moved to Broward's Rock December 1986.

Charles Gibson: "We never agreed on

anything. I can scarcely blame Sharon for her background. Looking back, I can see how a military family put duty first, even when a war was unconscionable. Or unconscionable to many of us. And when her brother Jimmy was killed, she lost confidence in life. Like Kennedy said, 'Life isn't fair.' But she grew up thinking it should be. Jimmy's death underscored how puny we all are in trying to control our lives. He was three weeks short of completing his year. Three weeks, the difference between life and death. If you think about it, you can go mad."

Marian Kellogg, former boss: "By the book, that's Sharon. Everything done in order, on time, right. Incredible memory for detail. I've never had another employee her equal."

Heidi Bristow, next-door neighbor: "Sharon's so pleasant. I've encouraged her to come to the church singles group, but she always begs off. I know she's lonely. I see her out in her garden on weekends and there's something so defeated in the set of her shoulders."

There hadn't been a lot of sunshine in Sharon's life. But she was close to her parents, especially her dad. Why did she almost drop out of the festival?

SAMUEL JACOB KINNON: Eighteen. Single. Parents Luther Kinnon, landscape gardener and May Kinnon, day-care instructor. Youngest of four children. All-around athlete—football, basketball, baseball, golf. A-minus average. Accepted at Armstrong State College. President "O" Club. Worked part-time all the way through school. Interested in computers. Last job student instructor at the Haven, dismissed according to director because of fund squeeze.

Maureen Howard, high school counselor: "Everyone loves Samuel. He's got a grin bigger than a Jurassic dinosaur. He's nice, really nice. But, of course, nobody's perfect and Samuel's had some ups and downs. He can get mad pretty quick. Coach Silvester suspended him from the basketball team for a month because he and Ricky Daniels got into a fight. I've worked with Samuel. Maybe part of it is being the youngest in a family and having to tussle to get attention. Maybe it's just Samuel's weak link. I know he's trying."

Harry Wileman, best friend: "Man, he's a cool dude. I'd rather party with Samuel than anybody on the island. And he's solid, man. If he makes a promise, he'll do it. Or be there. Whatever it takes."

Anthea Kerry, director of the Haven: "I hated to lose Samuel, a really willing worker, and bright, very bright. He's going to be a big success."

Annie tapped her pen on the table. Agatha was delighted. In a moment, the pen was on the floor, Agatha batting it toward the coffee bar, and Annie was sucking on a bright red scratch on her thumb. Interesting. The Haven director knew how to keep her mouth shut. But it was too late to help Samuel, wasn't it?

TOBIAS HENRY MAGUIRE: Fifty-one. Single. Born in Pontiac, Michigan. Father assembly-line worker, mother homemaker. Five brothers. Outstanding high school athlete; lettering in football, basketball and track (decathlon). Enlisted in Marine Corps 1963. Vietnam 1964. Honorable discharge 1965. Erratic job history: house painter in Oregon, truck driver in California, river-rafting guide in Wyoming, bartender in Georgia, beach rentals South Carolina. Long-time history of alcohol abuse, periodic binges. While in a public treatment program became interested in painting. Primarily self-taught but a voracious reader of art manuals and art history. Has gradually become known as an exceptional Low Country artist, primarily of wildlife. None of his paintings include people. Some of his paintings are carried by one of the prestigious galleries on Hilton Head Island.

Charlie Maguire, brother: "With Toby, it's B.V. and A.V., Before Vietnam, After Vietnam. A hard-charging kid, always grinning, you couldn't put him down, never heard a discouraging word. When he came home from Vietnam, he was like Scarecrow, the stuffing seeping out. He won't talk about it, gets drunk if you bring it up. I was lucky, missed the draft. To squelch a kid like Toby, man, it had to be bad. He bummed around after he got out of the Marines, couldn't seem to stay put. But about fifteen years ago, he ended up in South Carolina. I guess it's got a call on his soul. He's been close to happy there, as close as he'll ever get. And he's got Ned. His painting and Ned, that's all he cares about. I guess it's enough."

Forbes McCail, gallery owner: "I feel like an old miner who stumbles onto El Dorado. Toby Maguire's going to be classified as one of the great American impressionists, right up there with William Merritt Chase and Childe Hassam. He won't exhibit much of his work, only enough to keep going. A remarkable talent. There's a haunting quality to his work, a sense of sadness and pain and yet a touch of the ineffable. His love for the Low Country shines out of his paintings."

Jessica Tucker, chief nurse Broward's Rock Rehabilitation Clinic: "Toby was a mess when they brought him in. A tourist didn't see him on his cycle. And Toby's one of those idiots who wouldn't wear a helmet. He was in a coma for a couple of weeks. I'll always think it was Ned Fisher who brought him out of it. Ned was here every minute he could, talking, coaxing, bullying. I saw Toby on his motorcycle the other day. I guess even an old rebel like Toby can learn a lesson. Had on a shiny helmet. I gave him a thumb's-up. Toby's always kind of morose, but I think he grinned at me."

The day of the library board meeting, when Henny rallied her troops and vanquished

Bud Hatch, Toby Maguire sat in the audience and glowered. That was before his encounter with the general at the festival practice. Was he frowning because he knew Ned's job was in jeopardy? Toby Maguire wasn't a man to be trifled with. Maybe Bud Hatch leaned on the wrong guy.

DAVID EUGENE OLDHAM: Twenty-nine. Born in Pensacola, Florida. Father Eugene Willard Oldham, career Coast Guard; mother Teresa Michaels Oldham, retail sales. BBA University of Florida. One younger sister, Judy. Judy injured in a gymnastics accident in elementary school. Parents spent every possible moment trying to help her walk again, had little time for David. Always vying for his parents' attention. Straight-A student. Went to work for a national accounting firm as a bank auditor, a job requiring long periods of absence from home. Met Gail Jackson in 1994 at a Club Med resort, married her two months later. Settled on Broward's Rock because of Gail's teaching job.

Mother: "Oh, we haven't talked to David in a while. We're just back from visiting Judy and her family in Seattle. Our grandson Kevin is four now and we were so excited to see him. Visit David? Oh, we might. But David's so busy, you know, with all his travels. Gail's a nice little thing, but she never has much to say."

Joe Colt, best friend in high school: "David's a nice guy. Too much into 'Star

Trek,' but I guess it took the place of having a family. I mean, sometimes it was like he was invisible. He spent a lot of time at my house."

Frances Jorski, boss: "David works exceedingly hard. He's always ahead of schedule and his work is impeccable. I see a very bright future for him. Weaknesses? Hmm, he has some difficulty relating to people. He's great with numbers. We have some employee-interaction weekends scheduled. I hope he'll do well there."

A lonely kid. An isolated adult. How much did marriage mean to a man who rarely achieved rapport with others?

GAIL JACKSON OLDHAM: Twenty-seven. Born in Beaufort, South Carolina. BEd University of South Carolina. Father Curt Jackson, high school principal; mother Rebecca Simms Jackson, elementary school teacher. Middle child. Mediocre student. Enjoyed sports, especially tennis, though she didn't make the high school team. Initial teaching job in Columbia. Accepted lower-paying job on Broward's Rock because of the beach. Married David Oldham 1994.

Cookie Calloway, best friend in high school: "Oh, we were the nerds, the kids on the outside looking in. Kind of the story of Gail's life. Her big sister Sandra was a National Merit Scholar, went to Yale, works on Wall Street. Her younger brother Tom is in Paris on a Fulbright. Kind of like being a wren in a cage full of macaws. And we were always looking for dates. But maybe Gail had the last laugh. Neither her brother nor sister are married. If that's a big deal...."

Margaret Heaston, principal at Gail's school: "Not an inspired teacher. A good deal more interested in the beach than in the kids. I'd put her on a B level. I've had worse."

Mickey Smith, bartender at High Jazz, the largest nightclub on Broward's Rock: "Lonely eyes. She's got 'em. Lot of women who come here do. Used to come in with a couple of other teachers on Friday nights. The other two are single. She isn't. But I'd say they were all looking."

Gail didn't want to lose her husband. She'd gotten in too deep with Bud Hatch, tried to break free of him. How far was she willing to go to try and save her marriage?

EMILY ANDERSON WENTWORTH: Seventy-four. Born Fort Benning, Columbus, Georgia. Father Colonel Cameron Field Anderson, Regular Army; mother Louise Crowell Anderson, Army wife. Lived various Army posts. Married Ensign (j.g.) Jonathan Wentworth 1943, Annapolis, Maryland. Two children: James Cameron (dec. 1967), Sharon Wentworth Gibson.

Marianne Porter, a longtime friend: "Such a devoted couple. We knew them years ago in the Philippines, then came together again when they ended up in Thousand Oaks. Jonathan worked long hours. But Emily never seemed to mind. Busy, busy, busy. It always made me tired to even think of her schedule. And sometimes I thought she loved golf more than Jonathan. But he's always so sweet to her. And you have to admire them both. It's hard to lose a child. I remember when the kids were little, we'd have so much fun, especially since Jimmy's birthday was July 4. He always thought the fireworks were for him. When you look back, it all seems so insane, Vietnam, and those thousands and thousands of troops. And Emily was hurt by all the wars, her dad died on Omaha Beach, her brother in Korea. My husband came home from Vietnam, but he's never forgotten. Never. Anyway, Emily's a trooper. She's one of those outgoing athletic women, good at everything from river rafting to mountain climbing. And she has a treasure in Jonathan. He waits on her hand and foot. It would never occur to Emily to get her own glass of water or wine or whatever. Now my Sam expects me to fetch and carry like a Roman slave. I remember one time...."

Rear Adm. (ret.) Bradley (Buzz) Price: "No woman ever served a man better in his career than Emily. Always there, always strong. Would've made a first-rate officer herself. Her dad taught the kids to camp and hunt and she could swim a river, climb a mountain. No stopping Emily."

Forrest McKinney, golf pro: "Always in

the Championship flight, shoots in the mid-seventies. Very competitive, a golfer who thinks her way around a course."

Emily Wentworth had welcomed Annie and she was eager to learn what Annie knew of the shooting. But she claimed not to know about dissension on the library board. Was that to protect Jonathan? She'd instantly claimed that her husband was with her when Hatch was shot.

CAPT. (RET.) JONATHAN EDWARD WENT-WORTH: Seventy-five. Born in Long Beach, California. Father Dr. Theodore Wentworth, general surgeon; mother Jeanne Baker Wentworth, homemaker. Senior Class president, quarterback football team. Graduated U.S. Naval Academy 1943; completed flight training and received his Naval Aviator "Wings of Gold" at Pensacola, Florida, 1943–44; combat pilot in a Hellcat Squadron with VADM Mitscher's Task Force 38 within Admiral Halsey's Third Fleet, taking part in the final phase of the Pacific War with the assault on Okinawa and later the battles of Formosa, Luzon, and Leyte Gulf, remained with the squadron 1944–47; Air Forces Pacific Staff Honolulu, Hawaii, 1948–50; pilot jet squadron flying F9F's on board the USS *Princeton* 1951–52; naval aviation training squadron, Beeville, Texas, 1953; assistant navigator on board USS *Roosevelt* 1954–56; operations and executive officer East Coast, then air group commander's staff, Naval Air Station Miramar 1957–59; attended Naval War College 1960; assumed command of a jet squadron Naval Air Station Miramar; operation officer, then executive officer on board USS *Constellation* 1962; staff of the Commander and Chief of Atlantic Fleet 1963–64; commanding officer of the USS *Princeton* 1965–66; Navy Bureau of Personnel in Washington, D.C., 1967–1973, retiring as a captain in 1973. Military decorations include Bronze Star, Silver Star, Distinguished Flying Cross. Served as a consultant with aircraft companies in southern California, living in Thousand Oaks, California, from 1974 to 1985. Married June 12, 1943, Annapolis, Maryland, to Emily Anderson, daughter of Colonel Cameron and Louise Anderson. Two children: James Anderson, born Pensacola, Florida, July 4, 1944, died November 13, 1967; and Sharon, born October 19, 1949, Honolulu, Hawaii.

Cmdr. (ret.) Burton McRae: "I never served under a better officer. Always set an outstanding example for his men. He was personally courageous, absolutely honorable, totally in control."

Mitchell Mackey, CEO Whitestar Aeronautics: "Jonathan Wentworth was the most level-headed man I've ever dealt with. He had an uncanny ability to spot possible problems before anyone else tumbled to them. I'd say he saved my company in excess of two million dollars through his suggestions."

Julius Richards, next-door neighbor: "We couldn't ask for better neighbors than the Wentworths. She's a bundle of energy and Jonathan works hard for the community. We sometimes play bridge with them, though she takes her cards a bit too seriously for me. But a charming woman."

Annie scrabbled in her purse for another pen. So Jonathan Wentworth was a straight arrow, from start to finish. Was that the kind of man to shoot a man he didn't like? And she couldn't even find a reason for that dislike. Okay, Sharon said the families weren't acquainted. Maybe Hatch's dossier would suggest a lead. She looked around the table, then called out, "Barb, where's the stuff on Bud Hatch?"

Barb picked up a folder next to her computer. "Here it is. I was just adding some final stuff." She brought the file to Annie, reached down, plucked up a piece of pizza.

BRIGADIER GENERAL (RET.) CHARLTON (BUD) HATCH: Sixty-three. Born in Syracuse, New York. Top senior scholastically. Graduated U.S. Military Academy 1955. Lieutenant, U.S. Army Infantry Center, then 75th Ranger Regiment, Airborne and Ranger training/qualification, Fort Benning, 1955–58; Captain, 1st Cavalry Division, battalion intelligence officer (S-2), Fort Hood, 1959–62; Captain, battalion operations officer (S-3), then company commander, Vietnam, 1963–64; Captain, U.S. Army

Command and General Staff College, Fort Leavenworth, 1965–1966; Major, brigade intelligence officer (S-2), Vietnam, 1967–68; Major, instructor military history and tactics, West Point, 1969–73; Lieutenant Colonel, 25th Infantry Division, brigade executive officer, then battalion commander, Schofield Barracks, 1974–77; Colonel, U.S. Army War College, Carlisle Barracks, 1977–78; Colonel, U.S. Army Intelligence Center, Fort Huachuca, 1978–81; Colonel, U.S. Army Infantry Center, Fort Benning, 1982–85; Brigadier General, Assistant Deputy Chief of Staff for Intelligence, Pentagon, 1986–88. Military decorations include Bronze Star and Silver Star. Trapshooting champion Fort Hood, Fort Benning. Retired 1988. He and his wife sailed a sloop from Long Beach, California, to Tahiti. Lived Tahiti 1989–92; San Diego, California, 1993–96; Broward's Rock, South Carolina, 1997. Married Ruth Margolis, Fort Benning, Georgia, May 17, 1958. Three children: Charlton, Jr., born September 6, 1960, Fort Hood, Texas; Roger Margolis, born November 3, 1961, Fort Hood; and Lacey Elaine, born January 23, 1966, Fort Leavenworth, Kansas. Hatch's wife and children all have alibis for the time of the murder. However, personal information is included.

Annie ignored the reports on the children, but she scanned the bio of Ruth Hatch, noting the personal information, especially from one source who had known her well for years.

MARGUERITE POWELL, LONGTIME FRIEND: "I was her maid of honor. She was crazy about Bud, absolutely adored him. She didn't find out about his girlfriends until they were in their forties. The change in Ruth was shocking. She lost her sparkle, like a bright blouse dropped into bleach. But she stayed with him. She always said it was because of the kids but the truth was she still loved him and he wasn't exactly a rat. He cared for Ruth. She was His Wife. The others, well, he was quite a man, you know, and that was part of the credo for him. Shoot him? Well, it would be about twenty years late, wouldn't it?"

Screech. Snap. Miss Dora stared down at the floor in disgust.

Annie popped to her feet. If the old bat wanted fresh chalk, she could have it. No one could ever say the amenities weren't observed at Death on Demand.

This piece was orange.

"Thank you, missy." Miss Dora returned to her efforts.

The pink and orange offered an interesting contrast. Annie squinted. What was that X near the top of the chalkboard? "Miss Dora?" She pointed.

Miss Dora shot her a reptilian look, erased the X and drew a quite beautifully executed revolver.

Annie retreated to the table and retrieved the dossiers on Jonathan Wentworth.

The phone rang. Annie didn't even bother to look up. But of course she listened to Barb's end of the conversation. "...Mr. Darling is not here. May I have him return your call?.... Oh, sure, Ben"—her voice relaxed—"I'll have him call you as soon as he gets here." She hung up and wrote a message. She looked over at Annie. "Ben Parotti. Says he needs to talk to Max. Something about a boat."

A huge crack of thunder and the lights flickered, blinked off, came back on.

Barb stared at her computer like a shaman studying entrails. Her sigh of relief provoked Agatha into hissing and jumping down.

Annie peered toward the front windows, awash with rain. Where was Max? She checked her watch. Even though it was storm-dark outside, it was only ten past six. Surely he'd be here soon. She picked up the Hatch and Wentworth dossiers. Carefully, she listed the chronology of their careers. Okay, one up to Sharon Gibson. There was no overlap. Not only had they been in different branches of the service, Hatch the U.S. Army and Wentworth the U.S. Navy, they were twelve years apart in age and they'd never served at the same place at the same time. So much for a connection between the Hatch and Wentworth families. Different ages, different careers, and far different men. "She was His Wife." "Such a devoted couple."

Annie flipped to a fresh page. After all,

everything in life came down to character, didn't it? That's what she needed to know. Who were these people? Not where they went to school or where they'd lived. She riffled through the dossiers, making notes as she went:

BUD HATCH: Great friend, vicious enemy. Never saw the other side to any question. Black or white.

RUTH HATCH: The family came first. Her house was immaculate, her interests predictable, her eyes sad.

SAMUEL KINNON: Bright, smart, energetic, but too quick to get fighting mad.

NED FISHER: Top student through school, picked to head Broward's Rock Library from a final field of eight. Worked long hours, spent free time puttering around the home he shared with Toby Maguire.

TOBY MAGUIRE: Reclusive, a blue-ribbon artist of the Low Country, once said he'd come to Broward's Rock to live and to die.

JONATHAN WENTWORTH: Honorable, a straight arrow. Outstanding as a leader, forceful but empathetic. Could always be counted on.

EMILY WENTWORTH: A perfect military wife. She had great charm, but there was a hardness to her glitter.

SHARON GIBSON: A woman who felt pressed upon by life, encroached, surrounded. Worked long hours to keep her shop going. A considerate employer and a willing volunteer for island charities.

DAVID OLDHAM: A hard worker, adept at his job. Gone from home for long periods. Fair at tennis. Liked boating. No close friends. A solitary man. Never formed any close friendships in high school or college.

Annie doodled on the last sheet, drawing a gazebo by Gail's name. And that reminded her. There was one more name. But she didn't need to see a dossier.

HENNY BRAWLEY: Devoted to her community. Quick-tempered. Loyal to a fault.

Annie underlined the last sentence and sighed.

Screech. Screech.

Annie watched Miss Dora at the blackboard, fascinated by the elaborate spidery writing.

SIGNIFICANT FACTS

Accomplished marksmen: Jonathan Wentworth, Emily Wentworth, Henrietta Brawley, Tobias Maguire, Edith Cummings, Samuel Kinnon.

No history of firearms use: Gail Oldham, Ned Fisher.

Annie was just about to point out to Miss Dora that she'd not included several of the suspects when the front door banged open. Max surged down the center aisle. Everyone greeted him at once.

Miss Dora brushed chalk dust from her bodice. "Maxwell, the dossiers await you."

Barb picked up her message pad. "Ben Parotti wants you to call him immediately. He says"—she glanced down at the pad—"that the boat's still missing."

Annie clutched her list of key points and her character sketches. "Max, where in the world have you been?" After all, sometimes she couldn't help sounding like a wife.

"Clearing Samuel!" He threw off his raincoat, spattering the floor with water. They gathered around him as he triumphantly announced Johnny Joe Jenkins's information from the state crime lab. "So," he concluded, "the circuit solicitor will be an idiot if he arrests Samuel."

"He is an idiot," Annie murmured, but in the general aura of celebration no one heard.

Barb reached across the table for a piece of pizza, her good-humored face wreathed with an admiring smile. "Gee, that's good news, Max. We've been on the phone and the net all day and I don't think we've come up with anything to help Samuel. And you went out and got what we needed."

Annie folded her arms across her chest. Good. Fine. Of course Barb admired her boss. That was first on the employee smart list. But all Max did was go to Samuel's lawyer's office and get a state lab report while she,

Annie, had trudged around the island butting heads with people who damn sure didn't want to talk to her. And she had solved the mystery of the rifled locker at the Whale-branch Club and the broken cabinet at the library and nobody'd even asked her what she'd done all day!

Max turned first to Barb. "What was that phone message?" He listened, then reached for the phone. "Ben, Max here. Oldham hasn't brought that boat back?"

Annie sat bolt upright.

Max frowned. "Yeah, I tried to call the chief earlier to tell him Oldham had rented the boat from you. I'll track Frank down. If the boat's not back now—"

Lightning erupted and the pale flash reached even to the coffee area. The rattle of the thunder drowned out Max's words. "—God help him. I'll call." He hung up, then quickly punched the numbers.

Thunder exploded again, like boulders bounding down a mountainside. Annie looked toward the rain-lashed windows. To be in the open water in a storm like this....

Chapter 11

Chief Saulter's yellow poncho glistened greasily in the rain-shrouded lights of the marina. He looked out at the choppy water. Sea and sky merged into a moving mass of dark gray. "I've contacted the Coast Guard. They'll be out at first light. But if the rain doesn't ease up...."

He didn't finish. They all understood. It was hard enough to spot a small boat in the great expanse of the ocean on a clear fine day when the sea was calm. In a steady rain, the chances dwindled to almost nothing.

"Damn fool," Ben Parotti observed.

Not a fool, Annie thought. An angry, brokenhearted man.

"If I'd caught you earlier...." Max began.

Saulter shrugged. "I tried to find him to talk to him. But I figured he'd turn up. Not your fault, Max."

The rain abruptly intensified. Annie tried to imagine being out on that white-capped ocean in a boat. She scarcely heard Saulter conclude, "He ran away because he killed a man."

Case closed. A happy ending for Samuel Kinnon. Heartbreak for Gail Oldham.

Annie slept restlessly. She was tired, so tired. Too many people, too many places, too much emotion. Phantasms drifted through her dreams:

David Oldham, looking at her with hope and fear in his eyes.

Gail Oldham, her neck distended, her mouth stretched in fury.

Bud Hatch, bullish and yet stricken.

Edith Cummings, sly and defiant.

Henny Brawley, turning away from Annie, desperately pretending it was life as usual.

Samuel Kinnon, scared to death.

Ned Fisher, self-contained and worried.

Toby Maguire, blowing a piccolo.

Jonathan Wentworth, courtly and handsome. But in that last glimpse Annie had, his face was taut and strained while his wife was amused.

Emily Wentworth, drawing on a social manner that had seen her through good times and bad.

Sharon Gibson, confident yet tense.

Ruth Hatch, eyes shiny with tears.

And a motorboat bucking huge waves, lightning streaking across the sky, an anguished cry—

Annie flailed up out of bed, but Max had already grabbed the phone. His voice was groggy, "Hello...."

The luminous dial of the bedside clock read twenty past eleven. Exhausted and drained, they'd gone to bed early, just after ten.

"Shot?" Max was on his feet, clutching the receiver. "My God, we'll be right there."

May Kinnon held up a splotched bath towel, once a pale blue, now streaked with blood. "Samuel—" Her face screwed up like a baby's and tears rolled down her cheeks. She struggled to breathe.

"It's all right, Mama. It's all right." Luther Kinnon pulled May close, held her tight. "Our boy's all right, Mama." He looked over her head at Annie and Max. "The doctor said he'll be fine." Luther's voice was loud and deep. "They're going to fix him up just fine."

Annie knew Luther was reassuring himself.

"Luther, when—"

The curtain to the emergency cubicle parted. Luther's head jerked toward it.

The doctor—Cary Martin, a golfing buddy of Max's—stooped a little to come under the bar. He was six feet seven with a mop of curly brown hair and bright brown eyes. His easy smile pricked the tension in the room like scissors in a balloon.

Luther and May Kinnon waited, the beginnings of relief on their strained faces.

"Samuel's fine." Cary's soft-as-silk accent was pure Broad Street. "All stitched up. He's had a shot for pain and another for infection. He won't need surgery. He's very lucky. The bullet just clipped his upper arm, but no muscle damage."

May Kinnon held up the towel. "So much blood!"

"Flesh wounds bleed a lot. Same thing with ears." Cary patted Luther on the shoulder. "He's real drowsy now. But you can come in and see him if you like. We're going to keep him overnight."

Max looked at the doctor sharply.

"Hi, Max, Annie. It's okay," Cary said. "Chief Saulter thinks he'll be safer here. There will be a policeman outside Samuel's door."

Despite the full effort of the windshield wipers, Max peered uncertainly ahead. "I know this road." He was exasperated. "We should have—oh, here we are." The car slowed to a crawl. Max nosed his car onto the road leading to the Kinnon house. Around the second curve, a patrol car blocked the way, its headlight beams a bright swath against the forest darkness.

Max stopped the car. A slicker-clad policeman approached, his hooded brown poncho shiny with rain.

Max punched the window button. Rain spattered inside the car. "Officer—hey, Billy, it's us. The Kinnons asked us to come out and check with the chief."

Billy squinted through the rain. "I don't know, Max. It's a crime scene. I'll see what the chief says. We've got the road blocked."

Annie, bouncy with the sheer relief of Samuel's narrow escape, resisted the impulse to offer a Speak your Mind: Oh, gee, Billy, it's so clever of you to tell us since we might otherwise never have noticed the patrol car parked across the road.

Billy trotted to the car, slid into the front seat. In a minute, he returned. "Chief said no cars, but if you want to walk the rest of the way, it's okay. He said to keep to the middle of the road."

Annie and Max walked swiftly. Even though each carried a flashlight, it was several shades darker than hell once out of sight of Billy Cameron's patrol car. Their feet squelched in the mud. Tall pines crowded the edge of the road. Ferns reached out to flick beads of cold water at them. The rain was steady, although no longer a downpour. This time, however, Annie was dressed for the elements with a slicker and rain hat to keep her warm and dry. The wind soughed in the pines, but the trees no longer bent and cracked.

In the wavering beam of her flashlight, Annie saw two possums, a raccoon and five deer before they reached the end of the road. It was well past midnight and obviously party time for the forest denizens.

The Kinnons's two-story wooden house was built up on stilts. Lights blazed from every window. A flashlight beam bounced along the east edge of the yard. The front of the house faced south.

Max cupped his hands and shouted. "Frank?"

The bobbing flashlight continued its steady survey. The front door opened and Frank Saulter rattled down the steps, pulling up the hood of his yellow slicker. Saulter strode toward them. When he reached them his tired face was irritated. "Tell Luther everything's under control. And we don't know who the hell shot Samuel. Whoever it was got out, quick. There's nobody out here now but cops and owls and damn wet raccoons. Just ran off a couple of 'em trying to open the garbage."

Raccoons are as adept as Houdini in opening containers others wish to keep shut.

"So I can tell Luther and May it's okay to come home?" Max managed to sound as if he were part of an official delegation.

"Sure, sure. But we won't be done for a couple of hours yet." Saulter's voice was edgy. "And we'll have to come back when it's light to get shots outdoors."

"That's fine. Luther wants to cooperate to the fullest. Listen, Frank, we don't want to get in the way. Maybe you could fill us in on the investigation and we'll report back to the hospital."

Annie watched admiringly. Was it Max's lawyer background that gave him an unassailable air of officialdom or was it simply that he was a white male?

"Samuel okay?" Saulter still stood in their way.

"He's fine. The bullet grazed his upper right arm. No serious damage." Max looked past Saulter. "Where did it happen?"

A whistle blew shrilly.

Saulter blew out his breath in an irritated spurt. "I don't have time to baby-sit. Don't touch anything. Don't walk anywhere you see crime tape. And keep quiet." He turned away, breaking into a heavy lope toward the side yard, where the flashlight beam pointed into a thicket of bamboo. Annie and Max followed at a discreet distance.

"What've you found, Lou?" Saulter squatted beside the stocky, smaller officer holding the flashlight.

Annie recognized Officer Pirelli's round face under the brim of his hat.

"There's where he waited, Chief." Pirelli had a high, musical voice. "Look how the bamboo's crushed down." The light zoomed along a trough in the center of the bamboo thicket. Broken yellow stalks formed a springy platform.

Saulter swiveled to look toward the house.

"Good view," he muttered. "Easy to see people moving around in the house. Let's say the guy waited here. Maybe for a couple of hours from the looks of that bamboo. But why the hell?"

"Figuring out where everybody was, Chief. He waited until Samuel was settled." Pirelli pointed toward a window on the east side of the house. "He wanted a clear shot."

Saulter reached for the big flash, then stood. He moved the beam inch by inch over the glistening strands of broken bamboo to the knee-high clumps of ferns. "Look, those are broken." The light followed a trail of bruised and drooping ferns to an old live oak with low spreading branches. "Tomorrow we'll get pictures of the bamboo and the ferns, then we'll check out the tree. We might find snagged cloth, something. And maybe some footprints." He didn't sound hopeful. This was rough ground with matted vegetation.

Max gently poked Annie, nodded toward the house. They slipped away, leaving Saulter and Pirelli by the bamboo. Max led her on a roundabout route, avoiding any ground between the sniper's lair and the house. Instead, they walked up the oyster-shell front path. "You can bet the guy didn't come up the path. Before or after."

"Where are we going?" Annie whispered.

Max kept his voice low. "Let's take a look at the room where Samuel was shot." He walked swiftly and she hurried to keep up.

"But how will we know—"

312

Max gestured at the live oak tree. "Has to be a room on that side of the house. If Saulter yells at us, we'll say May asked us to bring her a sweater. Then we'll get out before Saulter throws us out."

The steps creaked. They wiped their shoes on a mat. The front door was open. Max pulled open the screen door and they stepped into the central hallway. A dining room opened to the left, a living room to the right. There was no sound except the gentle splash of rain. The house had the unmistakable silence of space empty of humankind, but there was evidence of habitation everywhere—a pair of glasses on a sideboard, a partially open umbrella tucked in a corner. In the living room, a half-full coffee mug sat on a side table, a tipped-over basket spilled out bright yarns, a magazine lay crumpled beside a sofa.

Bright yellow crime-scene tape was strung across the second doorway on the right. As they walked down the hall, Annie noted spatters from wet rain gear and the occasional smudge of mud on May Kinnon's spotless floor.

Crime tape barred them from the game room where they had gathered Friday night after the general's murder. The grandfather clock ticked slowly, steadily. Family pictures were tucked on tables, atop the piano, on the television set. There was the rocking chair where May Kinnon had sat and the small Windsor chair that Miss Dora had selected. Annie and Max had shared the green-and-beige-plaid sofa. Luther had paced the floor.

Tonight they looked at an overstuffed easy chair, beige checks on a light green background. A paperback book lay on the floor in front of the chair, its cover spattered with blood. Blood had stained the chair, dripped onto the wooden floor. The chair faced the doorway with its back to the windows. The upper pane of the south window was shattered. Pieces of glass glistened on the floor.

Annie felt suddenly queasy. "Max, Samuel's head—"

She didn't need to finish. It was easy to picture Samuel relaxed in the comfortable green chair, reading. He must have been leaning on the armrest, the back of his head and a portion of his shoulder and arm visible.

Samuel reading and out in the rainy darkness, someone climbed a live oak tree and waited and watched and finally, resting the gun on a branch to steady it, squeezed the trigger.

Annie leaned inside the doorway, careful not to touch anything, and craned to see the pine wall. Splinters fanned out from a pocked spot about four feet from the floor. It looked as though the slug was still embedded in the wood. She scanned the rest of the wall. Only the one mark. And the floor was untouched. Samuel must have jolted out of the chair and dropped to the floor, out of sight.

Annie wondered if the crack of the shot had been loud, startling. Or had it merged into the noises of the storm and Samuel's first warning had been pain and the shower of his blood?

Coffee. Hot, strong, energizing. Annie's eyes burned with fatigue. They'd caught a little sleep but not much. She'd tossed and turned and finally wakened with an uneasy sense of some fact that she knew but hadn't understood, something terribly important. And sad. Upon awakening the sense of urgency fled, leaving weariness in its place.

Annie sat at the kitchen table and sipped coffee and looked at the blank sheet of her notebook, waiting for some thought, any thought worthy of being recorded. Through the archway, she could see Max at his desk in the study. Funny to see him there so intent in wrinkled blue pajamas. Papers littered the desk.

The clock said seven but rain still drizzled down and the morning was as gray and indistinct as an old lithograph. The phone was ringing off the hook, but Max ignored it, letting the machine pick up:

Ring. Luther Kinnon's voice swelled with relief and gratitude. "Max, Samuel's fine, just fine. Says it isn't nearly as bad as the time he cut his leg open with a fish knife. Chief Saulter just left. He wanted to know about the sounds Samuel heard from the willow trees. Apparently the word's out all over the island about Samuel talking to you. The chief figures that's why someone came after him...."

Annie scrunched down in her chair. Nobody, she thought defensively, had told her not to tell anyone. And so yes, okay, she'd happened to mention the bit about the willows to Laurel and to Pamela Potts and to Gail Oldham and to Edith Cummings and to

315

Sharon Gibson. Yes, the island grapevine could well have spread the word from house to house. Everyone could have heard. There was only one exception: David Oldham, who'd headed out into the sound early Saturday morning and not been seen since.

"...Now, listen, Max." Luther's tired voice was insistent. "Tell everybody you see. Samuel doesn't know a thing he hasn't told the police. He's told Chief Saulter every scrap he can remember about that night. Got that? He didn't see anybody. He heard a kind of laugh—ugly, Samuel said—and maybe a whisper, and he doesn't know if it was a man or woman or maybe it had nothing to do with the shooting. Get the word out, Max."

Annie doubted that Samuel Kinnon would go home anytime soon. Luther and May would be sure of that. Not until the murderer was found. But surely the murderer would relax. After all, if Samuel knew anything he would have told the police. Samuel should be safe enough now.

Ring. Ned Fisher said stiffly, "Is the visit from the constabulary courtesy of you, Max? I want to go on record that Toby and I were home all evening. And yeah, I had some wet stuff in the washroom. I had to go out and break up a cat fight. Stan's getting old but he's pretty definite about his territory and that damn Manx next door doesn't get the message. And yeah, the phone rang a couple of times but we chose not to pick it up. It's still a free country, isn't it? And I don't work for the library twenty-four goddamn hours a day. And I don't care what people are saying, Toby wasn't anywhere near those willows. Samuel sure as hell didn't see him."

Annie scrawled in her notebook: Ned pissed. And worried. And it sounds like what Samuel heard in the willows got better and better as the story made the rounds.

Ring. Laurel's husky voice was crepe-edged. "'We are in God's hand.'" A pause. "Certainly the news that David is now free of suspicion was very welcome. I've been to Gail's house this morning. Poor child had almost no sleep last night. I brought her home with me and I've tucked her in bed. I've promised to wake her if there's any word about David. Do please let me know, Annie."

Annie looked toward the windows and the gray day. How well would a search-plane pilot be able to see? And how seaworthy was the little motorboat in last night's storm? Could David Oldham have slipped back onto the island to shoot Samuel? It was conceivable but unlikely. Where would he get a second gun? Where, as far as that went, would he have obtained the first gun? Why would he go back out on the water in a storm? And how would he have heard about Samuel's talk with Max?

Ring. Chief Saulter was brisk. "Max, when you pick up this message, see if you can figure out how many people you—or Annie—told about Samuel and the willow trees. If we can trace the stories, we might be able to eliminate some suspects."

Had the chief ever tried to catch confetti

in a wind tunnel? Annie ranged the suspects in her mind: Ned Fisher, Toby Maguire, Edith Cummings, Jonathan and Emily Wentworth, Sharon Gibson, Henny Brawley, Gail Oldham. Annie was willing to wager the bookstore that every one of them had heard of Samuel's comments. The chief was searching out a dead end.

Ring. Edith Cummings sounded serious and not the least bit sardonic. "My God, Annie, I just heard about Samuel Kinnon being shot. What's going on? I'm getting scared." Or was she hoping for a return call and a low-down on the status of the investigation?

Ring. Miss Dora's raspy voice was thoughtful. "I knew Samuel was innocent. It's unfortunate that it took a shooting to prove me correct. I am glad Frank is such a thorough officer. He carefully searched the Kinnon house. There was no trace of wet clothing or wet footprints, which would have been unavoidable had either May or Luther fired the shot, but they were both, as Frank put it, bone-dry. There are some puzzling aspects to the assault. May and Luther live on a dead-end road. They didn't hear a car all evening. Of course, a car could have been parked far up the lane. But Frank believes the assailant spent quite a bit of time in a lair, watching the house—"

Annie recalled the crushed bamboo.

"—which would have left the car vulnerable to observation. Frank believes this is a gamble the assailant would be unlikely to take. Therefore, another mode of transportation must have been used. And although rental bicycles are often stolen during holiday weekends, last night was an unlikely time for a bicycle to be stolen for a joy ride, as Frank put it—"

Annie agreed. For an instant, she envisioned a dark figure riding through the night, cold rain pelting down, the sky split by jagged lightning. Not, definitely, a joyous ride, pedaling fast and hard with murder in mind.

"—however, Island Rentals reported a bicycle missing this morning. The chain looped through a stand of twenty bicycles was cut through and a road bike taken. It has not yet been recovered. A search is underway."

If it were Annie, she'd have worn gloves and now the bike would be resting at the bottom of a lagoon.

Lots of calls with plenty of food for thought. Speaking of food—Annie's stomach rumbled. But no call from Henny, and certainly if anyone was ever in the center of information dissemination and reception on the island, it was Henny. She definitely must know about last night's shooting. But no call.

Annie looked glumly at breakfast, courtesy of Max. Papaya. That was nice. A bowl of oatmeal. Healthy, to be sure. But providing energy? Annie shot a quick glance through the archway at Max as he paced back and forth in the study. Moving with the grace and stealth of Evelyn E. Smith's Miss Melville on a job, she eased across the kitchen to the refrigerator, fished out the pizza left over from last night and popped it in the microwave. It came out bubbly and delicious.

Dorothy L. appeared from nowhere. "You pizza hog." Annie broke off a cheesy piece. Dorothy L. purred, ate, looked expectant.

"You don't like barbecued chicken." She found another morsel of soft cheese.

Dorothy L. finished first.

"Serve you right if I gave you oatmeal."

The cat hopped down from the table, strolled toward her cat door.

Annie ate the oatmeal, too, and felt exceedingly virtuous as she rinsed her dishes and put them in the dishwasher. Thus fortified, she carried a cup of coffee into the study, exuding, undoubtedly, a positively overwhelming aura of hearty vigor.

Max leaned over the desk, felt-tipped pen in hand. He made a series of jabs with the black tip, then tilted his head to study the result. Annie studied him, loving the tousled blond hair and stubbled chin and rumpled pajamas. She put her coffee on a side table, then came up behind Max and slipped her arms around him, peering around his right shoulder.

Max made a nicely appreciative, interested noise, then shook his head. Annie knew him well enough to be sure the head shake was directed at his drawing and not at her. It would be an icicle day in Fiji when Max lost interest in personal—very personal—contact.

Annie gave him a later-dear squeeze and stepped closer to the desk. She took it in at a glance, a map of the island and neat notations pinpointing the homes of Gail and David Oldham, Sharon Gibson, Ned Fisher

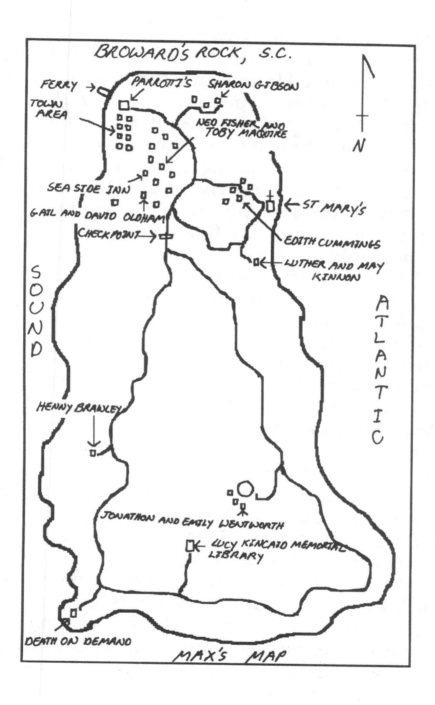

and Toby Maguire, Edith Cummings, Luther and May Kinnon, Henny Brawley, and Jonathan and Emily Wentworth.

Everyone lived on the town side of the island except Henny and the Wentworths. Did that matter? Annie pointed at the Wentworth house. "He"—they both knew she meant Jonathan Wentworth—"would have to drive through the checkpoint." A manned gate separated the private development of homes from the little town. The cars of residents had an identification decal on the windshield.

"July. Tourists," Max said briefly.

"But it was a stormy night." Annie pulled up a straight chair.

"Hmm." Max picked up the phone. It took three calls before he found Ray Kienzle, who'd been on duty at the development gate.

"Between ten and midnight, probably." Max listened. "Sure, I understand. Thanks, Ray."

"No soap?" Annie asked.

"Ray says there was a bunch of cars in and out until midnight, but it was raining hard and he just flashed his light on the cars to be sure they had a decal. He didn't pay any attention to the make of cars or who was driving." Max scooted the blunt end of the pen along the island road, through the checkpoint and to the bike shop. "And where would Wentworth leave his car?"

Annie tapped Saint Mary's. "Behind the church. That lot's hidden from the road."

Max squinted at the map. "That works.

He could take the bike, put it in his trunk, then drive to the church. Same for Henny. If it was one of the others, they all live close enough to the shop to walk over there, steal the bike, ride out to the Kinnons, ride back."

"The bike's still missing." Annie picked up her coffee, welcomed a deep dark jolt of pure pleasure. Annie poked at the problem of the missing bike like Agatha would pounce on a mouse unfortunate enough to wander into Death on Demand. If the bike was spotted not far from one of the suspect's houses.... But who would be stupid enough to leave it near home? Okay, why not drop it off in an alley in the little town? That couldn't be tied to anyone. But if you parked behind Saint Mary's, then where would be a good place to dump the bike? Only Jonathan or Emily Wentworth or Henny would need to park at Saint Mary's. Annie knew if she were setting out to shoot someone, she'd be exceptionally careful not to be seen. Wouldn't everyone claim to have stayed snug at home? And why steal a bike anyway? To avoid leaving a car near the Kinnons's, a car that might be noted. The bike could be abandoned and the assailant could flee on foot into the woods, if necessary. And the bike was faster than walking or running. What if Luther had grabbed a gun and set out to find the assailant? But Luther, understandably, was much more concerned with getting Samuel to the hospital.

Max grabbed the phone, punched the numbers. "Luther, have the police finished their search out there?" He listened. "No trace of a bike?" He frowned at the drawing. "Okay, thanks." He rubbed his bristly chin. "Annie, I feel like I'm being stupid. Where did that bike go?"

Annie made a commiserating sound, but she had her own vagrant thought that she couldn't pin down. Something about Samuel and the shooting. Something odd. Something wrong.

"Okay." Max's tone was one of intense concentration. "We've got to find that bike. Come on, Annie, let's get dressed and go hunt. We've got time before the eleven-o'clock."

Annie preferred the eight o'clock service, but their schedule was all askew this Sunday morning. They could skip the nine o'clock service and go to the eleven o'clock service.

Max was halfway across the room, when Annie looked vaguely after him. She waved her hands. "You go on, Max. I want to study the dossiers. I'll meet you at church." She found the reports on his desk, now heavily underlined, the pages rumpled.

The dossiers. And her notes. And her recollections of everything she'd learned. Somewhere in that mass of material some fact troubled her, edged into her dreams. And she had to figure out what puzzled her about the attack on Samuel.

Annie moved in slow motion, her eyes abstracted. She showered, brushed her hair, already trying to frizz from the humidity, slipped into a rose linen dress and matching rose sandals. She thought regretfully of her once equally pretty apricot sandals.

She gathered up the dossiers and her notes

and settled at the kitchen table. She loved her kitchen, white, white everywhere—walls, cabinets and appliances—a vivid contrast to the impressionist view of their terrace and the sloping lawn to the lagoon. Through the French windows, the shrubs and trees were smudges of green, the bougainvillea muted scarlet.

Annie found her list of Key Points, wrote quickly:

8. Henny claims she saw Jonathan just before Hatch was shot. Was this a lie?

9. The attack on Samuel cleared David Oldham.

Annie felt a tingle of excitement. Wasn't that the only thing accomplished by that attack? Because Samuel was still alive. If the objective was to silence him, then the attack was a failure. But what if the attack was to protect David Oldham?

Annie picked up the phone, punched a familiar number.

"Dear Annie." Laurel's husky voice rose in delight. "It's always such a pleasure to hear your charming voice. 'O, wonderful, wonderful, and most wonderful wonderful! and yet again wonderful, and after that out of all whooping.'"

Annie resisted responding with, "'Well said: that was laid on with a trowel.'" In fact her tone was rather dry. "Thank you, Laurel. I'm sure the feeling is mutual."

In a short silence, each considered where the honors lay.

They both began at once.

"Annie, have you heard—"

"Laurel, last night were—"

A shorter silence. Annie struck first. "Laurel, you are always so attuned to your surroundings."

"It's so important," Laurel trilled, "to be at one with the world."

"Very important," Annie agreed heartily, not having any idea what her esteemed mother-in-law meant. It was often helpful when dealing with Laurel to be totally focused on an objective. "Gail came to you for help yesterday—"

"'A wretched soul, bruised with adversity.'" Laurel's voice was gentle.

For an instant, Annie saw Gail's face, pale, drawn, laden with misery, her eyes aching with tears. "I know," she said quietly. "I'm sorry. And it was very good of you to help her, Laurel."

"She is so alone, Annie. No one to help. Yesterday afternoon, she insisted on going home. I went with her, of course. I fixed us a light dinner. But she couldn't relax. She called everyone she knew. But no one had seen David. Then, without warning, like a thunderbolt, Frank came. I was so glad I was with her. Frank was kind but it was clear he was sure David killed the general. After he left, she was hysterical. David accused. And worse than that, David out in the ocean in that storm in a motorboat. I finally calmed her down and put her to bed about nine."

"Did you stay all night?" On her pad, Annie wrote: Laurel at Gail's house.

"No. I thought she was all right for the night." A soft sigh. "I should have been more perceptive."

Annie waited.

"She was so upset. It's understandable, certainly. As she told me this morning, she simply couldn't sleep. And so she got up and drove to all his favorite places. Isn't that absurd? In that storm? But she didn't find him and she came home, oh, she said it must have been two or three o'clock and then she waited by the phone. I found her huddled there when I went over early this morning. I do feel that I was remiss. I should have realized how distraught the dear child was."

Distraught. Yes, that was quite likely. But she had a convincing answer for an excursion into the storm and rain. Perhaps she'd shot at Samuel to save David. But perhaps she shot at him to save herself.

"But," Laurel concluded, "she's quite safe now. And perhaps they will soon find David."

Annie put down the receiver. She frowned and added:

10. Gail out in the storm.

11. Samuel still alive. Is he in danger?

That depended, didn't it, on why he was shot? To silence him? Or to divert suspicion?

Annie sighed and put the list aside. She

thumbed through her notes, picked up her summation of character.

Bud Hatch. Everyone agreed that if Bud liked you, he was your friend for life. But equally important was the obverse. Bud Hatch was a bad enemy. And he didn't mind making enemies.

What of the character of his murderer? What, actually, did they know about Bud Hatch's murderer? Okay, it all began with the levering of the vase from the roof of the library. That was on Wednesday. The general was shot Friday evening.

Annie wrote:

1. The murderer was a good shot. What was it the chief said? "Hatch was drilled."

2. The murderer planned ahead coldly and carefully, the gun wiped clean of all prints, shiny as if new

Cool calculation, a well-thought-out plan. But the vase? That couldn't have been planned. The general wasn't expected at the library. Someone took advantage of his presence to push the vase from its parapet. The vase missed him, shattering into huge pieces, chunks of earth and pottery. It was quite a mess. The shooting was obviously a different matter entirely, with plenty of forethought and premeditation. A murderer who acted on impulse one day, followed out a careful plan two days later?

"No." Annie spoke aloud.

Dorothy L. looked at her with piercing blue eyes.

"Not you," Annie said absently. "The murderer. The vase was stupid if he—or she—had murder in mind. The vase was malicious. Who among the suspects was quick to anger and impulsive?"

Annie found the phone book, picked up the cordless phone and called.

"Hello." Edith Cummings sounded not so much sardonic as surly.

"Edith, there's an eyewitness who saw you shove the vase from the roof." Wasn't Annie seeing it so clearly in her mind's eye the equivalent?

Was there a snicker of amusement quickly controlled? "Annie, dear"—the drawl wasn't friendly—"why don't you get back to your bookstore. Fiction sells well there."

Click.

Annie punched the "off" button. Okay, she couldn't take it to court, but she felt confident she'd figured out the truth. And that truth cleared the ground. She needed to focus on Friday night and the careful, thoughtful, cold acts of a murderer. This was a person who planned ahead, so—

3. Why was Hatch killed on a public stage in front of hundreds of spectators?

Annie considered the third point. Why, indeed, did Bud Hatch die at the Fourth of July festival? Wasn't it an odd and very public place for murder? It argued urgency or fury unable to be tamped. Or perhaps there was a practical reason.

Annie listed the possibilities:

a. Because fireworks would mask the sound of the shots.

b. To prevent Hatch from causing the dismissals of Ned Fisher and Edith Cummings at next week's library board meeting.

c. To keep Hatch from revealing his affair with Gail to her husband.

d. Because he had enraged Toby Maguire.

e. To keep him from informing Emily Wentworth about her husband's liaison with Henny Brawley.

None of them satisfied her. She was left with an uneasy feeling that the time and place of the murder mattered and that if she knew the answer to that, she would know the killer.

All right, back to character. She'd tagged Edith as the vase pusher. Maybe she could tag the murderer, too. She scrabbled through the stack of papers, found her notations on the suspects:

Ned Fisher, a man happy in his work and his home life. Capable at work but perhaps too unwilling to face dissension. Patient. Sensitive.

Toby Maguire, a vet who would never

forget. He'd once been an unsquashable kid. Now he was a loner, except for Ned.

Edith Cummings, smart and clever, but her quick tongue and caustic laugh hid a wide streak of anger.

Jonathan Wentworth, an outstanding military man, which meant great organizational ability. Calm, cool, confident.

Emily Wentworth, always busy, quick to talk, but uninterested in listening.

Sharon Gibson, a hardworking shopkeeper, meticulous and humorless.

Gail Oldham, an unfaithful wife, an unwilling mistress. She was concerned first about herself, then David.

Henny Brawley, a closer friend to Jonathan Wentworth than the world knew. Henny was a great detective. But not this time.

Annie poured a fresh cup of coffee, taking the last in the thermos. She riffled through the papers, noted Miss Dora's careful list of those familiar with firearms. She read the dossiers, placed the sheets for the general and the captain side by side.

A sharp age difference. No correlation between their duty assignments. Different services.

She read the dossiers one more time, drew her breath in sharply. There was one possible point of contact. And if that was so—

Max stood at the far end of the parking lot behind Saint Mary's. He ignored the half dozen or so cars still in the lot after the eight o'clock service. Cars were streaming in for the nine-o'clock. Steamy air pressed against him.

No-see-ums swarmed around him. He stood still, ignoring the heat and the humidity and the insects, and pretended it was dark with rain pelting down and his heart thudding from a careening ride away from the Kinnon house, a revolver heavy in his jacket pocket, running on adrenaline, glancing warily toward the road, the bicycle propped against the car. What the hell to do with the bicycle? Leave it in the church lot? No, that would link the stolen bike far too directly to the Kinnon house. As long as the bike wasn't found, investigators could guess it was used but never prove it.

Max climbed in his car, drove slowly out of the lot, turned toward town. Last night, in the dark, the murderer had been in a hurry, desperate to be rid of the bicycle, hearing the cry of sirens en route to the Kinnon house.

Max drove the most direct route to the sound. There were no convenient lagoons. Then he branched out, making short forays. There was a good-sized lagoon near the softball fields, but you had to know it was there. Edith Cummings would know, but Edith wouldn't discard the bicycle anywhere with a link to her. The lagoon near the hospital was ringed by pines. Again, you had to know it was there. Henny Brawley would know and again probably Edith Cummings. The others? Quite possibly not. The fleeing attacker was in no position to hunt for lagoons.

Max turned the car and headed back to the cluster of houses. Then he swerved to the side of the road, stopped, and looked back.

Sea Side Inn. Weathered gray wood, chintz curtains at the windows, masses of camellias. A "No Vacancy" placard hung beneath the sign. An arrow at the front of the drive pointed toward the back: "Parking."

In the sleepy Sunday morning quiet, Max made a U-turn. He drove up the gravel road. Almost every spot behind the inn was taken, but there were a few empty spaces. Those same places were likely to have been empty last night also unless a guest was out early to attend church or go for a damp walk on the beach.

Nothing could be more anonymous than a car parked in the lot of a fully occupied hotel. Max felt a glow of excitement and satisfaction. No, the assailant hadn't used the lot at Saint Mary's church. That had always seemed risky. Although no one was likely to come to a secluded church parking lot late on a Saturday night, it could happen—a courting couple, a drug deal. But the inn parking lot was perfect. No one would pay any attention to cars going in and out, even quite late. Moreover, the island bike-rental shop was no more than two blocks away.

Okay, okay. Max mapped it out in his mind. Drive to the inn. Leave the car. Walk to the bike shop. Steal the bike. Ride to the Kinnon house. Reconnoiter. Shoot. Run like hell to the bike. Pedal fast. And then? Ride straight to the harbor, shove the bike off the end of the ferry dock, walk to the inn. Done. Safe. Home free.

Maybe, maybe not.

Max checked out the three empty spots

and chose the most secluded, an angled slot on the back row of cars at the deep end of the lot next to the garbage dumpster.

Who could see this spot? Anybody?

The two-story inn was L-shaped, the base of the L fronting on the street. Pittosporum shrubs hid the angled slot from view on the ground floor. Max climbed the steps, walked along the balcony. A row of pines down the center of the lot screened the empty spot from view until he reached the top of the L.

Rooms 36 and 38 had a clear view.

Max slipped off his shoes and socks, tucked them around the corner of the building. Then, rumpling his hair and donning an expression compounded of sleepiness, sheepishness, and good humor, he knocked on the door of Room 36.

Water glistened on the plastic-sheathed Sunday-morning paper on the front porch. The white wooden house was modest, a single-story ranch-style with a gray shingle roof and jaunty red shutters. Bright floral curtains were drawn in the front windows. Annie's car was the only one in the drive. There was no garage, simply a carport on the east side. Wood was stacked neatly near a garden shed. Rosebushes flourished in a front flower bed, yellow and pink and darkest red blossoms, lush and full. Their sweet scent mingled with the smell of damp earth and salt marsh.

Annie knocked sharply on the door.

No answer.

She tried again. And again. She circled

the house, knocked at the back door, peered inside, tried the kitchen window.

There was no light, no movement. Sharon Gibson was not at home. She could, of course, be at church. But the unopened Sunday paper argued against a quiet, usual Sunday morning. No, Sharon was likely at her parents' house. Annie had every intention of going to the Wentworth house.

But not yet. First she had to have information. She knew where to go to get it. But these answers wouldn't come easy.

If they came at all.

Chapter 12

As Annie came around the last curve, sunlight spilled down from the thinning clouds in great shafts, touching the bright green cordgrass with gold. A great blue heron stood on a hummock. The tide was in and water covered the mudflats, but there was, as always, the rich, dank smell of the salt marsh, an island elixir to those who loved it, repulsive to those who didn't.

Annie parked the Volvo next to Henny's old Dodge. The bicycle was in its wooden stand, just as it had been yesterday. Annie moved fast, gray dirt scuffing beneath her shoes. She ran up the steps, knocked sharply on the door. Henny was her friend, no matter what. But would Henny ever forgive her for what she was about to do?

There was no answer. Annie cocked her head. Was that a voice? She knocked again, harshly. Footsteps sounded. The door opened a scant few inches. "Annie." Dark eyes looked out warily. "Whatever it is, I'm pressed for time. I'm leaving for church in a minute and I have some things to attend to." Henny's silver-streaked hair was swept back in a smooth chignon. Her makeup was carefully applied but the hint of blush did little to dispel the grayish whiteness of her face. Her eyes lacked their usual gleam. Her aquamarine silk dress was lovely for summer but the garnet necklace was a hasty, unconsidered choice. "As I've told you, I don't have any interest in the investigation—"

Annie's hands clenched. This was hard. So hard. "You lied to me." There was wonder and dismay in her voice, though it was just another indication of how much Jonathan Wentworth mattered to Henny. "Oh, yes, you wouldn't want Emily Wentworth to know that you and Jonathan care for each other. But that couldn't account for your terror. I should have known that. No, you were frightened because you knew Jonathan had every reason to kill Bud Hatch. The strongest reason a man can have. Bud Hatch caused the death of Jonathan's son."

Henny's eyes flared. Her sharp-featured face froze.

"I'm sorry, Henny." Annie gently pushed on the door. "But I know." That was a lie. She had no proof, but she did at long last have a link between Hatch and the Wentworths.

There was one point of correlation between the dossiers of Jonathan Wentworth and Bud Hatch. They were 12 years apart in age. They never served at the same post. But Jimmy Wentworth died in Vietnam when Bud Hatch was stationed there. A link.

Annie saw it as a deadly link. Henny's response proved her right.

Henny spun away. She fled, her shoes striking sharply against the parquet flooring.

Annie called out, "Henny!"

Henny didn't stop, didn't respond.

Annie plunged into the house.

The floppy white pajamas sported cerise polka dots. Huge bushy white eyebrows angled up in a belligerent V. "Do you know what time—"

"Sir" Max spread his hands in appeal. "I'm so sorry to bother you." An engaging smile. "I'm on my honeymoon. Just got married last night. And somebody's played a joke on us—"

"Roger, who is it?" A shrill voice angled high. "Roger, is everything all right with Wes and Katie? Roger—"

"Shush, Velma. Young fellow here. Nothing to do with the kids." The eyebrows had relaxed. A pudgy hand reached out to poke Max. "Hell of a thing, weddings. Got our oldest boy married off last night. Danced till three o'clock in the morning. Remember that song?" In a reedy baritone, the father of the groom launched into the first verse. Another comradely poke. "Course you don't.

You're too young. So what's the problem?"

"Our car!" Max's voice was plaintive. "We parked right down there." Turning, he pointed toward the empty slot by the dumpster. "Somebody told me it was gone at eleven. But I guess if you didn't get in until late, you wouldn't have noticed."

"Eleven?" The man in the doorway turned. "Velma, didn't you bring Sissy back about eleven?"

"Yes, I did." The tone was just this side of grim. Velma flounced to the doorway, holding her seersucker robe at the neck. She'd made an effort to brush her tangled blond hair. Without makeup, her face was as white and puckered as a new golf ball. "Since you'd drunk enough champagne to set you off on a search for a bridesmaid's garter—and I told Wes he should tell Katie not to include that Morrison girl in the wedding party—"

Shaggy eyebrows beetled.

"—I had to bring Sissy back. *Your* sister. Of course, she was having palpitations! No one paying any attention to *her*. So I had to bring her. All by myself. In that terrible storm." Velma's tone put the journey on a level with backpacking up Mount Everest. She edged out onto the balcony. "Was it a dark car? A BMW?"

Max tried hard to keep a slightly vacant, sheepish look on his face. "Yes, ma'am. I know they didn't mean any harm. But I'm trying to figure out who took it so I can track it down. My wife has her heart set on a drive into Savannah."

"Oh, well, I saw the car leave. We'd just driven in. And there was the biggest crack of lightning and it lit up the whole parking lot, light as day." Velma had a good eye. She described the driver in minute detail. "Do you know who that was?"

"Yes, ma'am." With an effort, he kept his tone light. "Yes, I do. I know where to find him. Thanks for helping me."

Max hurried down the wooden steps, broke into a run as soon as he reached the parking lot.

Henny's living room ran the length of the house. A wide window at the back overlooked the marsh. The Sunday paper, still in a tight roll, lay atop a rattan table. Henny walked all the way to her desk, gripped the curved back of the swivel chair, stared out into the marsh. On the desktop beyond Henny, the computer screen glowed. Annie glimpsed papers, folders, a speaker phone, a small CD player.

Henny's shoulders bowed. "So you've found out about Jimmy Wentworth." Her voice was harsh, overly loud in the quiet room. She pulled herself to her full height and turned to face Annie.

Annie had always thought of Henny as vivacious, in a hurry, full of fun. Yes, she'd seen her in more serious moments, her face grave, her eyes full of wisdom and understanding. But she'd never seen her as she did that morning, her dark eyes calculating, her sharp-featured face combative. "Who did you talk to?"

"Max got on the net," Annie said carefully. This was the tricky part. This required skillful lies, carefully presented, just so much and no more, enough to garner the response she needed.

"So you got the whole ugly story." Henny's eyes glinted with disgust. "What a bastard Hatch was. But slick. Nobody could prove it was deliberate. All it took was asking a friend at battalion level to issue new orders."

"Everyone said it didn't do to make an enemy of Hatch." Annie hadn't realized how much that meant.

"He was ambitious. And he wasn't going to be thwarted by a lowly second lieutenant. Hatch intended to create the body counts his commanding officer wanted and everybody had to cooperate." Henny folded her arms across her chest. "He even told Jimmy about it, said see if you like being a forward observer better than being in an office in Saigon. Jimmy'd been out in the field a week when he was killed. But"—Henny took a deep breath—"it's okay that you know. The truth of it is, that was a long time ago. Life goes on. Sometimes"—she looked toward a small silver frame on her mantel—"whether we want it to or not, you survive. The Wentworths survived."

Henny's husband was lost in a bombing raid over Germany. More than a half century had passed, years of a beloved voice stilled, a smile not seen, love unshared.

"The Wentworths hated Bud Hatch." Annie knew this was true. She didn't have to have proof.

"It was a long time ago." Henny's tone was reasonable. "They've known what Hatch did since shortly after Jimmy died. If Jonathan wanted revenge, he would have shot Hatch long ago."

"Except Hatch only moved to the island a few months ago." Came marching into town to die.

"So Jonathan brooded and decided to kill him? After all these years? Don't be absurd." Henny's hands clenched. "When Bud moved here, Jonathan put their house up for sale. They're going to move to Scottsdale. That's the right way to respond. Get away from it. Surely you aren't going to Frank with this absurd tale."

"Murder, Henny. Murder!" Annie's tone was explosive. Her eyes burned with disappointment.

Henny's gaze was defiant. "Frank won't believe you. Yes, you have a motive for Jonathan. But that's all you have. A motive for him and motives for all the others. This is a crime that won't be solved, Annie, ever. There's no proof. There never will be." It was a plea. She reached out, a thin hand that trembled. "Annie, leave it alone. Jonathan's a good man, a kind man, a decent man. Leave it alone."

"I know he's a good man." Annie's voice shook. She hated this. Hated it. "A good man who was a top marksman. He was clay-shot champion at Schofield. Wasn't he?" Annie knew Miss Dora's list by heart. "Frank said Hatch was drilled. You and Jonathan and Emily Wentworth and Toby Maguire and Samuel Kinnon are excellent shots."

Henny's eyes watched her intently.

Annie ticked them off on her hand. "You didn't do it. Toby Maguire is a great shot, but he was drunk at the festival so he couldn't have killed Hatch. As for Samuel, he didn't climb up in a tree and shoot himself. That leaves Jonathan and Emily, doesn't it? And I don't think it was Emily."

Henny's eyes were dark pools of misery.

Annie met that gaze without flinching though she could feel tears behind her eyes. "Do you know why I'm sure it was Jonathan and no one else?"

Henny clutched at the string of garnet beads, held tight to them.

"Because he is a good man."

Henny sighed and turned away.

Annie spoke quietly, sadly. "I knew there was something wrong with the shooting of Samuel. But I didn't put it all together. Until now. An excellent marksman killed Hatch. So why was Samuel only wounded? Very slightly wounded. A great deal of blood and dramatic effect, but no danger at all."

Henny moved around her desk, leaned her head against the glass.

"I figured it out. A good shot one night doesn't miss the next night. Oh, sure, the weather was bad. But the marksman after Samuel took his time, waited until his quarry was settled, a perfect target. So what went wrong?"

Henny said nothing, just leaned against

the glass. Beyond her, out on the marsh, the cordgrass wavered in the breeze. An egret spread glistening white wings and soared on the warm air. The water surged and eddied. The blue sky arched clear and clean, the clouds gone, yesterday's storm only a memory.

"Nothing went wrong." Annie's voice was gentle. "That's how I knew. The man who killed Hatch wouldn't have missed. If he missed, then he intended to miss. And why, for pity's sake, would he do that?"

Henny's silence was painful.

Annie repeated the words soberly. "For pity's sake." She wanted to step forward, slip an arm around those thin, rigid shoulders. "Because Jonathan Wentworth is a good man. And he knew Samuel was going to be charged with murder. You know why I'm sure it was Jonathan, not his wife? She'd never go to the trouble for someone like Samuel. She's a spoiled, self-centered woman. But Jonathan's not like that. Jonathan couldn't permit Samuel to be arrested, his life ruined, perhaps his life put in jeopardy. Jonathan saw only one way to keep that from happening. He waited until it was dark, then he drove to the village. He stole a bike, rode to the Kinnon house. Jonathan's a very careful man, isn't he? He reconnoitered. He didn't hurry. He was very, very careful. Samuel was wounded. What are the police to think? Exactly what they did, what we all thought. Samuel had heard something, seen something that endangered the murderer. But it wasn't that way at all. Samuel didn't know any more than he had already told.

343

But Samuel was at risk and Jonathan Wentworth wasn't the kind of man to let someone else suffer for his crime."

Annie didn't mention David Oldham. She would never speak of him to Henny. She hoped no one else ever did. Since Henny hadn't been involved in the investigation, she didn't know that David Oldham had taken a motorboat and disappeared and that Frank Saulter had already decided Oldham was the murderer. Samuel Kinnon was no longer at risk when Jonathan Wentworth rode through the stormy night with a .45-revolver in his pocket and a careful plan in his mind.

If Jonathan Wentworth hadn't been a good and decent man—but Annie didn't want to think about that.

Henny swung around. The bones in her face jutted against skin drawn tight with pain. "There's no proof. No proof!"

"They can always find proof when they know. Someone will have seen Jonathan last night. Or at the festival; the police can talk to everyone who sat near the Wentworths. Someone will have noticed that he was gone from the blanket. Someone will know that he and Emily weren't together when Hatch was shot." Annie heard the sadness in her voice. But that was wrong. Bud Hatch was dead and whether he was a good man or bad, it wasn't Jonathan Wentworth's right to determine the span of Bud's life.

"Sometimes when you roll the dice, they come up snake eyes." Jonathan Wentworth's deep voice filled the room.

Annie jerked around, looked behind her. She'd not heard a door. She swung toward Henny's bedroom. That door was closed.

Jonathan spoke pleasantly, but there was a quality of finality. "You're right, Annie. So here it is officially. You and Henny can testify to it. I, Jonathan Wentworth, do hereby confess to the murder of Bud Hatch and to the shooting of Samuel Kinnon. That's—"

Henny whirled from the window. She leaned against her desk. "Jonathan!" The cry was wrung from Henny's heart. "No, don't. They don't have any proof." Henny was bending toward her speakerphone. The tiny red light glowed on the upper-right-hand side. All this time, the phone had been on and Jonathan had heard them talk. That's why Henny had led Annie close to the desk. That's why Henny had spoken up so sharply, so loudly at the first.

"It's all right, my dear. This is the way it must be. The only possible way." A pause. "Henny"— for the first time his voice wavered—"someday, someday—in the wild blue yonder."

Click.

The sound was loud and clear. Jonathan Wentworth had hung up. The conversation was over.

With a cry, Henny ran across the room, gathering up her purse and keys. She flung open the door, clattered down the front steps.

Annie raced after her.

Max slammed out of his car, swatted at no-see-ums. "Frank, Frank!"

Frank Saulter stood midway between the

345

live oak tree and the still-shattered window of the Kinnon house. His khaki trousers were spattered from the wet vines and ferns, and mud clung to his shoes.

Max skidded to a stop, poured out his story.

Saulter shrugged. "Next time I need a deputy, I'll call on you. A good piece of work. But it's not proof of anything. Maybe he's got a girlfriend at the inn." Saulter held up a thumb, sighted to the window and began to walk toward the house.

Max kept step. "Okay, Frank, tell me one thing. Was the gun used to shoot at Samuel a .45 like the one that killed Hatch?"

"Don't suppose that's a state secret. Yeah. A pal in ballistics took a look early this morning. A .45 slug. So?" He looked back toward the live oak, shook his head a little in disbelief. "Hell of a long way to shoot. No wonder the killer didn't get Samuel."

Max stepped in his way. "Frank, stop for a minute. Listen to me. That shot"—Max swung his arm from the tree to the window—"that shot proves just what I'm thinking. Only a super shot would even try it. Or somebody really stupid. But we're not dealing with a stupid murderer. We're dealing with a crafty, careful, methodical murderer who's a very, very good shot. And who's a top shot? Who has medals for shooting?" He answered his own question. "Captain Wentworth, that's who. And Frank, I'll tell you something else. I read a bunch of stuff about everybody involved in the case this morning, finished it just before I started out hunting for the bike.

And you know who among all those people could easily have .45 revolvers lying around? Right the first time, Captain Wentworth. His wife's dad died in the invasion of France. Don't you know his effects came home? There could easily be a .45 in them, maybe a couple of them. Or how about Emily Wentworth's brother, another career officer. She'd be sure to have his gun. I tell you, Frank—"

Frank's cell phone squawked. He listened and abruptly his body tensed, he leaned forward like a man ready to race. "For Christ's sake! Where are you?" Saulter wheeled, broke into a run. "Yeah. I'm on my way." He windmilled his arm. "It's Annie. Come on!"

The front and back cockpits were open, the sliding canopy pulled back. The propeller blades whirred, slowly at first, each blade distinct in the sunlight, then blurring as the engine picked up speed. The sea-blue Grumman TBF Avenger taxied up the runway, leaving behind two other World War II vintage airplanes, a red-and-yellow-nosed P51 Mustang and a white-tailed Bell P-39D.

Annie slowed her car to a stop, flung open the door and ran to the wire-mesh fence. Henny clung to the railing next to a white sign with bright red letters: "Confederate Air Force, Broward's Rock, S.C."

The roar of the engine was so loud Annie had to shout. "Henny, where are they going? They can't get away!"

Both the pilot and his passenger wore flying helmets and goggles.

Cars squealed into the lot behind them. Footsteps pounded. Max thudded to a stop beside Annie. Frank yanked open a gate, ran out onto the runway, waving his arms.

The Avenger rattled down the runway, faster, faster, the roar of the engine like the rumble of an avalanche, inhuman, unstoppable.

At the last minute, Saulter flung himself out of the way.

The heavy blue plane lifted up, and then it was aloft, curving away to the east. A hand waved farewell from the forward cockpit.

Annie slipped an arm around Henny's shoulders. The engine's roar dulled, fading finally to silence, broken only by the sound of Henny's quiet sobs.

"Paper's here!" Ingrid came down the center aisle, waving the folded *Island Gazette*.

Annie snatched it from her, spread it open on the coffee bar. Ingrid pressed close, reading over her shoulder.

The top headlines in the Monday afternoon issue of the *Island Gazette* trumpeted the news:

LOST BOATER FOUND ADRIFT AT SEA
PLANE CRASH KILLS ISLAND COUPLE

The ocean off Broward's Rock was the scene of both life-and-death dramas Sunday as Coast Guard planes rescued islander David Oldham from his drifting speedboat and watched in helpless horror as islanders Jonathan and Emily Wentworth crashed in

348

Wentworth's World War II Grumman TBF Avenger.

Coast Guard Lt. Milton Farriday said Oldham was boating Saturday when he was caught by a storm and swept far out to sea. Farriday said Oldham reported the motorboat ran out of fuel but stayed afloat despite waves cresting at nine to twelve feet. Oldham was suffering from sunburn and dehydration but was resting comfortably at Municipal Hospital Sunday evening, according to his wife Gail. "He's going to be fine," Mrs. Oldham told the Gazette. "We are so lucky."

Wentworth, a retired Navy captain, was a longtime member and pilot in the Confederate Air Force. He and his wife Emily left the island about ten o'clock Sunday morning. Search planes seeking Oldham witnessed the unexplained crash of the blue torpedo bomber about twenty minutes after takeoff. Lt. Farriday said the Avenger began to climb and was lost to view for several moments until it plummeted straight down into the sea.

Joshua Marshall, a resident of Broward's Rock who flies a P51 Mustang in the Confederate Air Force, expressed surprise. Marshall said, "The Avenger's oxygen tank wasn't pressurized. Jonathan was an exceptionally able pilot. I have to believe there was some kind of malfunction or perhaps he was taken ill. Of course, when the plane went over twelve thousand feet both the pilot and passenger would suffer from oxygen deprivation." Marshall explained that a pilot suffering from asphyxia loses consciousness. "Or at the very least becomes disoriented and is unable to control the plane."

The Coast Guard said only broken remnants of the warplane survived and there was no trace of either Wentworth or his wife.

Capt. (ret.) Wentworth retired to Broward's Rock after a distinguished career in the....

Annie didn't bother to follow the story to an inside page. Instead, she read a small notice at the bottom of the page:

CASE CLOSED

Police Chief Frank Saulter announced Sunday the close of his investigation into the July 4 shooting death of Brig. Gen. (ret.) Charlton (Bud) Hatch and the July 5 assault on recent high school graduate and well-known island athlete Samuel Kinnon. Saulter explained that information received indicated the guilt of island resident Capt. (ret.) Jonathan Wentworth. Wentworth and his wife Emily died in a plane crash Sunday. Saulter declined further comment

Annie stared at the paper. Images whirled in her mind—David Oldham battling to live, a pilot and his passenger, Henny clinging to the fence, Saulter's laconic face. She wanted to say, "Hey, wait a minute. Hey...."

Two weeks passed. The recently delayed

meeting of the library board was rescheduled. There were two new members, Pamela Potts and Laurel Roethke. Annie couldn't decide whether Henny had lost her mind or was seeking unusual input into the board proceedings. But the new duo had added cheer to the gathering. Gail Oldham beamed at Laurel when she came in. Laurel, of course, had the bon mot. She whispered to Gail (but loud enough for Annie to hear), "'I am sure care's an enemy to life.'"

Henny was pale and wore perhaps a bit more blush than usual. Her brown eyes were somber, but the board's business was pleasantly, efficiently conducted. There was no mention of the July 4 festival, other than an accounting by the treasurer of sums dispersed, profit made.

When the meeting ended, Annie waited out in the hall for Henny.

Gail and Laurel walked past her, Gail chattering, "I'm so excited. David's found a new job, right here on the island...."

Miss Dora's cane thumped loudly. "Ah, missy. The library is planning some new exhibits, so I must move my drawings. I'll come by the store later this afternoon."

Annie wished for the courage to bellow a Speak Your Mind: Why don't you take up hang gliding, Miss Dora? Over the Grand Canyon?

Instead, she sorted through the space in the store. Okay, okay. She could take down the end cap on the classic mystery display, put up at least two of Miss Dora's charcoal drawings.

Henny stepped out into the hall. Through the open door, Annie could see Ned Fisher and Edith Cummings in a deep discussion.

Henny's cream linen blazer was set off by a crimson scarf that matched her skirt. She ducked her head, tried to step around Annie.

Annie blocked the way. "Henny, I'm about to go crazy. I've got to talk to you. About Jonathan."

Henny's head jerked up. Her dark eyes were intent. "About Jonathan?"

"Yes." Annie was exasperated. At the same time, she was reluctant to cause pain. But, dammit, it just wasn't right. "It's not right! And you know it's not."

"It's too late for justice, Annie. And it's what Jonathan wanted." Henny's eyes glistened with tears.

"That's why Jonathan took her with him, isn't it? She's the one who shot Hatch. You looked out at the audience just before Hatch was shot and you did see Jonathan. But you didn't see her. And that's why it happened at the festival. It was Jimmy's birthday. Besides, she knew there were problems with the library board. I'm sure Jonathan hadn't told her who Hatch was, but he talked about a new board member who was causing trouble. Jonathan doubted that she'd ever make the connection, she was so absorbed in golf and bridge. Even so, he planned for them to move to Scottsdale. But she must have seen Hatch's name and picture in the *Island Gazette*. She planned the murder to occur where a lot of suspects would be present. The festival was a perfect opportunity. The fireworks would hide the sound of the gunshot. Saulter said he was drilled. She took the .45 and stood in the willows and shot him. She'd sent Jonathan to get colas. He waited on her, always. She would never have been the one to go to the refreshment stand. The next day I found their blanket where they'd left it and the cardboard carrier with two full drinks, still capped. Full drinks, never touched. He came back to the blanket with the drinks and she was gone. When Hatch fell, Jonathan must have known and he hurried to the trees and found her. And she laughed. Then Samuel was under suspicion. So Jonathan set out to wound him to divert the attention of the police."

"It's an interesting theory," Henny said quietly. "But Jonathan confessed. The case is closed, Annie."

She pushed past Annie, walked away, her carriage straight, her head high.

Annie almost called after her, then stood silent. Henny was right. A good man died to protect his wife. Case closed.

She was still standing there when Ned and Edith came out the door. Edith caroled, "Annie, I'm going to drop by Death on Demand this afternoon. Has anyone named the mysteries portrayed in the watercolors? If not, I want my free book."

Before Annie could answer, Ned rattled off the titles, "*The Dutchman* by Maan Meyers, *Hearts and Bones* by Margaret Lawrence, *Seneca Falls Inheritance* by Miriam Grace

Monfredo, *The Strange Files of Fremont Jones* by Dianne Day, and *Blood and Thunder* by Max Allan Collins." He bowed, grinned at them both. "I'll be by after work, Annie." He squinted in thought. "I'll take a free copy of *Eater of Souls* by Lynda S. Robinson." With an easy wave, he trotted down the hall toward his office.

For once, Edith Cummings was speechless.

About the Author

CAROLYN HART is the author of nine other best-selling Death on Demand mysteries featuring Annie Laurance and Max Darling, the third of which, *Something Wicked*, was an Agatha winner. She is also the author of four Henrie O mysteries, including *Dead Man's Island*, which received the Agatha for Best Mystery of the Year and was made into a movie for television. Carolyn Hart lives in Oklahoma City with her husband Phil.